BYZANTIUM
ENDURES

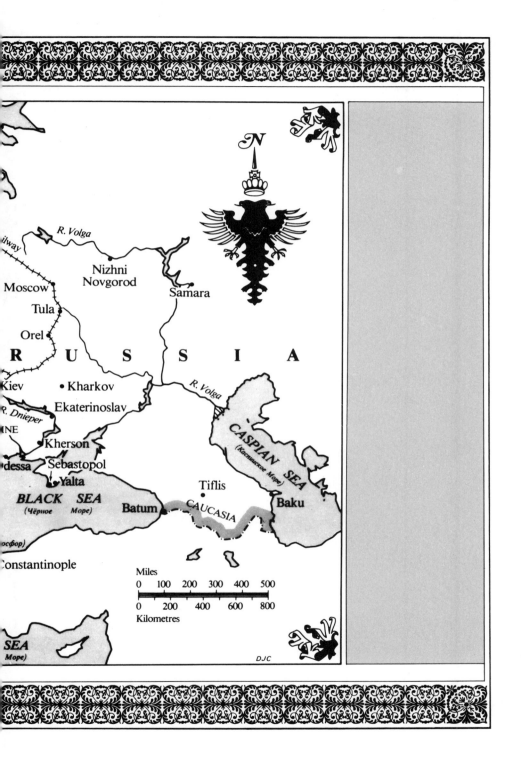

N

R. Volga

ilway

Moscow

Tula

Orel

R U S S I A

Kiev

• Kharkov

Ekaterinoslav

R. Dnieper

INE

Kherson

dessa

Sebastopol

Yalta

BLACK SEA
(Чёрное Море)

Batum

Nizhni Novgorod

Samara

R. Volga

CAUCASIA

Tiflis

CASPIAN SEA
(Каспийское Море)

Baku

осфор)

Constantinople

Miles

| 0 | 100 | 200 | 300 | 400 | 500 |

| 0 | 200 | 400 | 600 | 800 |

Kilometres

SEA
Море)

DJC

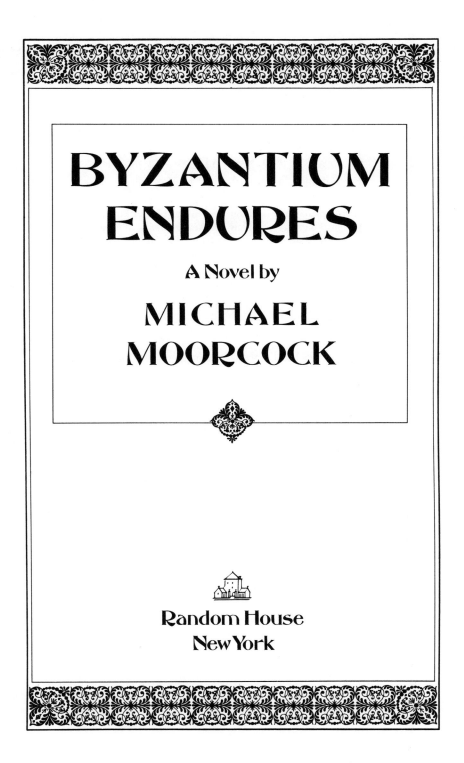

BYZANTIUM ENDURES

A Novel by

MICHAEL MOORCOCK

Random House
New York

Library of Congress Cataloging in Publication Data
Moorcock, Michael, 1939–
Byzantium endures.
I. Title.
PR6063.O59B9 1981   823'.914   81–40210
ISBN 0-394-51972-8   AACR2

BYZANTIUM
ENDURES

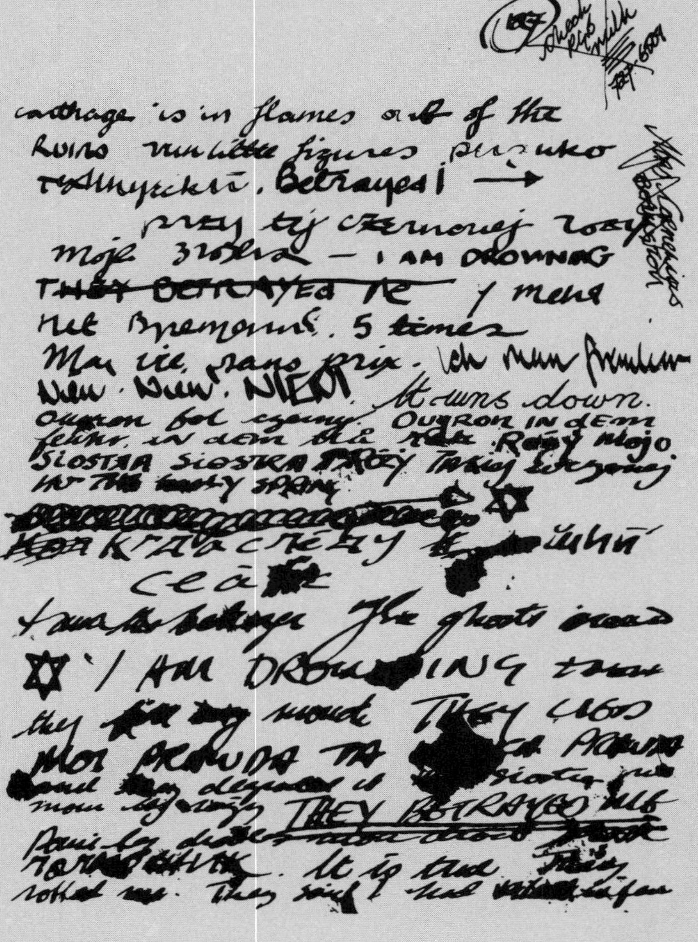

A facsimile page from Pyat's manuscript

INTRODUCTION

The man who was known for years in the Portobello Road area as "Colonel Pyat" or sometimes simply as "the old Pole," and who, in the sixties and seventies, was Mrs. Cornelius' regular evening consort at the Blenheim Arms, the Portobello Castle and the Elgin (her favorite public houses), collapsed during the August 1977 Notting Hill Carnival when a group of black boys and girls collecting for "Help the Aged" in Caribbean fancy dress entered his shop (one of the few open) and demanded a contribution. His heart had failed him. He died at St. Charles Hospital some hours later. He had no next of kin. Eventually, after a great deal of unpleasant publicity, I inherited his papers.

In the previous two years I had grown to know him well. He had found out that I was a professional writer, and had, in fact, become hard to avoid. He pursued me. He insisted we could turn to a profit his reminiscences of Mrs. Cornelius, who had died in 1975. He knew that I had already, in his terms, "exploited" her in some books and he had recognized my deep interest in local history when he had seen me, some years earlier, photographing the old Convent of the Poor Clares as it was being pulled down. Much later he had come upon me filming the slum terraces of Blenheim Crescent and Westbourne Park Road before they, too, were destroyed. That was when he first approached me. I had tried to ignore him but when he began to talk familiarly about Mrs. Cornelius, referring to her as "a famous British personality," I became curious. (I had my own interest in that extraordinary woman, of course.) Pyat became persuasive: The world would be eager to read what he had written about her. She was probably as famous as Queen Elizabeth. Amiably, I pointed out that she was merely a local figure in a tiny area of North Kensington. My own accounts of her were considerably fictionalized. Nobody thought of her as a "personality." But he insisted there must still be money to be made from what he believed to be a massive public eager to read "the true accounts of Mrs. Cornelius' life." He had approached the *Daily Mirror* and the *Sun* newspapers in an attempt to sell them his story (a terrifying collection of manuscript, handwritten in six languages on almost every possible size and color of paper, collected in eleven shoe boxes) but became suspicious of their suggestion that he submit it by post rather than in person to the editor. He trusted me, I was told, as he had trusted nobody but Mrs. Cornelius herself. I reminded him, apparently, of Michael VIII, "the last great savior of Constantinople," and it was even possible that I was a reincarnation of that Byzantine emperor. He showed me a black-and-white reproduction of an icon. Like most icons the figures depicted could have been anyone. They all wore beards. His main reason for trusting me, I suspect, was because I humored him. I did this from genuine curiosity about his own career as well as Mrs. Cornelius' (she had always been hazy concerning her past). Here, of course, I was moved by self-interest. Colonel Pyat's was not a pleasant personality, and I found his intolerance and passionately held right-wing views rather hard to take. I bought him drinks in the same pubs he had attended with Mrs. Cornelius. I hoped to gain raw material for new stories; but he had different plans. Without reference to me he decided I should be his literary adviser for 10 percent of his advance. Together, he told me, we should prepare a manuscript. I would then submit it to my usual publisher; my name and influence (as well as the fame of Mrs. Cornelius) would enable us to sell the book for "at least fifty thousand pounds."

I soon stopped trying to convince him that advances for first books rarely reached five hundred pounds and that I had no special influence with anyone. Instead, when I had the time, I visited his flat and began to help him assemble his papers. I found a translator* pre-

---

* My old friend and sometime collaborator M. G. Lobkowitz.

pared to handle the considerable quantities of manuscript written in Russian, bad German, Polish and Czech, though the majority was in bad English with, amusingly, most references to sex in French, and let Pyat talk to me as I tried to fill in the gaps in his story.

I am not sure what would have happened to the project if he had lived. My own work certainly began to suffer. My wife tells me I became half mad, completely obsessed with Pyat. I could not stay away from him. He had met a good many of the leading political and cultural figures of the interwar years (often without realizing their importance) and, although his instinct for obfuscation was highly developed, he would frequently—it seemed unwittingly—reveal quite astonishing details. At first, because of his violent anti-Semitism, his hatred of the local people, his vicious and reactionary opinions of modern life, I found it difficult to respect his age and his sufferings or to keep my temper with him. It was Lobkowitz, who had seen much of what Pyat had seen, who helped me deal with him. "The great tragedies of history," he said, "are the sum of all the individual tragedies. It takes several million Pyats at least to conspire in the fate of the twelve million who died in the camps. His is a ruined soul." I thought this view overly charitable, even sentimental, at first; but I came to respect it as time went on. Moreover, my fascination always overcame my distaste. I would visit him on Sunday afternoons to tape-record his monologues, some of which I found repeated almost verbatim in his manuscripts. I have not made much use of the obscure, polylingual material he left, but the facsimile on p. 2 may offer the reader a clue as to the difficulties involved in translating, ordering and interpreting the papers. It is one of the more readily legible pages.

Pyat was not in the usual sense a fool. Many of his remarks were astonishingly perceptive. It was his inconsistency in almost everything which made me decide not to attempt to overformalize his material. Therefore, the reader will find few literary ironies here and the use of devices common to modern fiction have, of course, been sparing: this narrative has not been shaped according to normal narrative expectations. It would be better to regard it not as the biography Pyat offered (Mrs. Cornelius appears only infrequently in this volume) but as autobiography. It is the story of an extraordinary life and, as such, it contains extraordinary coincidences, paradoxes and occasional *non sequiturs*. For the first volume, which takes us up to the end of the First World War and the last stages of the Russian Civil War, I have selected material which deals pretty directly with this period in Pyat's life. The completely discursive material I have left out altogether or set aside for later volumes where it will be more appropriate. On certain matters he remained vague—the period of his life as a prisoner in Kiev is a good example—but the reader might discover clues, at least as to why he avoids mentioning these experiences in any detail, in other parts of the narrative. I have tried not to speculate while putting the story together and prefer to leave it to the reader to decide what is relevant; for the reader's guess here is quite as good as mine.

Lobkowitz's problems of translation have been enormous. Pyat wrote in colloquial Russian for the most part and, according to Lobkowitz, his prose often resembles the conscious artifice of Bely, Pilnyak and the later *skaaz* writers from whom, Lobkowitz claims, Nabokov borrowed heavily. I am, I must admit, unfamiliar with modern Russian fiction, so have relied very heavily on Lobkowitz's interpretations and reference. Naturally, I have considerable respect for my friend. No one else could have coped so well with the problems. If Colonel Pyat possessed a "style" in the literary sense, it altered its tone quite frequently. Editing and omission have resulted in the loss of a certain amount of the original's inconsistent flavor, though I think this "stream of consciousness" writing offers at least an insight into his poor, baffled, terror-ridden mind. Lobkowitz was unable to translate in one or two places where the language used has so far been impossible to identify. A "secret" or made-up language is sometimes a device employed by people with paranoid tendencies. I suppose it is fair to make it clear that in later years Pyat had a history of mental trouble and was occasionally institutionalized.

Events in the Ukraine prefigured events through the rest of the world and that is one of the reasons I became so fascinated by Pyat's account. It was why I thought it was worth trying to make some sort of linear story out of material which was in its original state almost entirely associative and nonlinear.

I had no interest at all in the Ukraine or its troubles until I met Colonel Pyat and I must admit that many of my ideas about the Russian Empire, developed from information he gave me, have since proved at very least inadequate. His view of events in Russia between

1900 and 1920 is as biased as any other view he held and Lobkowitz suggests that I make it clear to the reader that Pyat's accounts are not always to be taken as accurate impressions of what was happening during that period, although, apparently, many of his claims, where simple fact is involved, have been adequately verified.

He was a difficult and exhausting man to interview and working with him took more than two years out of my life. (Editing the rest of his manuscript, which will tell his story up to the concentration camps and 1940, will take much longer.) Yet I look back almost with nostalgia to those Sunday afternoon sessions when my wife and I would visit his untidy two-story flat and listen to his frequently harsh, sometimes sardonic, sometimes rolling, tones as he pontificated against this race and that, against this political party and the other, against everyone who, in his view, had conspired to cheat him of his just rewards on earth.

The flat was over his shop. It had originally been an ordinary secondhand clothes shop where, as a boy, I had often bought pieces of worn-out Edwardian finery. I think it had been one of Mrs. Cornelius' sons—almost certainly Frank—who, in the 1960s, had suggested renaming it The Spirit of St. Petersburg Used Fur Boutique, to exploit the boom in tourism and fashion, which was to me a most unwelcome development. The premises are now run by a Hindu family which sells the clothes manufactured in the new sweatshops of the East End.

Colonel Pyat's place smelled of the former owners of his stock: of mothballs, stale perfumes and sour old age; of borscht and a brand of Polish vodka he favored called Starka, a matured, mellow vodka with the color of Irish whiskey. The vodka was his single extravagance and I believe he drank it because it was a private link with the Russia of his boyhood. It is for some reason cheaper than brands like Stolichnaya, which are more familiar to Westerners, but it is almost impossible to buy in England. He obtained his supply, I believe, through Russian seamen spending their shore leave in London and Tilbury. It had a more pungent odor than most vodka and was also a stronger proof. He only once offered us a glass, and that in return for some papyrussa cigarettes I had been able to obtain for him during my own travels.

Although disturbingly ignorant of much English culture (he had remained close to Mrs. Cornelius and the poorer parts of Notting Hill since, claiming Polish nationality, he had arrived there in 1940), he was neither illiterate nor a stupid man. His contemporary cultural references were peculiar—to TV programs and films in the main—yet he despised the English for their lack of "refined sensitivity." He despised us also for our lack of idealism, for our pragmatism and for our hypocrisy, yet blamed almost every problem not attributable to Jews or Bolsheviks on our "weakness" in relinquishing the Empire. Thanks to Lobkowitz's insights, I realized life had wounded Pyat so deeply that he sought refuge in fantasy and bigotry; but it could sometimes be very hard to listen to the vile and all too familiar racism with which he so frequently regaled us, particularly since by now he had come to regard me, at any rate, as a fellow spirit, "one of the few real intellectuals I have met in this country of yours." He would insist that there was virtually no cultural life left in England. What there was, he said, betrayed our appalling decadence. His day-to-day experience was that of many other bourgeois European refugees who, speaking no English and having little money and few friends, arrived in England and America before the War. They had had to settle in the working-class districts of our big cities and encountered insular people ignorant of most of the political issues and cultural background they themselves considered essential. The nuances and humor of working-class Londoners were therefore beyond him and the genial tolerance of the majority seemed to him to support the view that the English were careless and lazy, and had somehow betrayed his trust in them. He had possessed a romantic attachment to this country, as you will see.

It was this limited experience, of course, which led him to suppose that Mrs. Cornelius was as famous as the Queen. All the people he met in the area seemed to possess greater interest in Mrs. Cornelius (and more familiarity with her name) than they showed in, say, Adolf Hitler or Margaret Thatcher. This was why Pyat honestly believed the present generation would pay him more for his memoirs of a somewhat extraordinary but largely unknown Cockney lady than they would for his personal anecdotes of the great dictators. (I must admit that my own imagination was fired more by Mrs. C. than by Mussolini, but I realized that there were few who shared my enthusiasm. It could also be argued that I had a vested interest in her fame, as well as the colonel's, for I had also made fictional use of him in one or two books, even before I had come to know him personally.)

By the time I met him, his appearance had become fairly nondescript. He was an old Central European, swarthy, hunched, ill-tempered, slightly grubby, with a seamed face, large lips and a big nose. His skin was unhealthy. He wore out-of-date, musty suits or sports clothes and his dress was distinguished only by the white golfing cap he wore winter and summer. He collected junk (the upper rooms of the flat were full of it) and owned a quantity of useless bicycle parts, petrol engines, old spark plugs, electrical bric-à-brac, and so on: the place often smelled strongly of ancient engine oil. His collection of photographs and greasy news clippings were the only evidence of his claims to have been handsome and agreeable. My wife thought he looked "lovable," but all I saw was a fairly good-looking man with eyes which never seemed to focus on anything in particular. There were pictures of him standing by the gondolas of airships, sitting in the cockpits of seaplanes, taking part in the ceremonious opening of dams and bridges, the launching of ships. He had certainly traveled and been in the company of many well-known people. Mrs. Cornelius appeared in only a few of the news clippings, but most of his snapshots were of her, taken at different times in various countries, verifying her own claims to me to have "got about a bit when younger." He put all this material, together with his manuscripts, into my safekeeping. There was no question that he regarded me as heir to the memoirs and as his literary executor. The astonishing claims of Mr. Frank Cornelius, against which I successfully defended myself in Court, have long since been shown to be groundless and I now possess legal title to the manuscript, if not the pictures. It is true that I did not know Colonel Pyat well for very long, but I did come, I think, to be his only friend. He often told me that this was the case and that I would "inherit the papers" if anything should happen to him. I have been able to produce witnesses to support the fact that he often referred to me in public as "the son I never knew" and the one who would vindicate his many claims to former glory. I was to keep his memory alive. I hold his manuscript in trust. I hope I am doing what he wanted me to do.

As I have said, in editing these memoirs I was faced with a whole variety of technical and moral problems. The colonel left it to me to reproduce Mrs. Cornelius' characteristic speech, for instance, but insisted I retain his "philosophy." The vitriolic asides (on matters of sex, race and culture) were nearly always in a language other than English, so they could be isolated. To leave them out completely would be to destroy some of the reader's perspective on the material and on Pyat himself. There is no doubt, of course, that the colonel was a poseur, a liar, a charlatan, a drug addict, a criminal, but that he had once possessed great charm is evident from his successes. People felt protective toward him. People fell over themselves to help him, often at great inconvenience. It is from this evidence, rather than his own statements, that I became convinced he had not always been so obviously the ruined personality I knew. Moreover, he was not uncultured. He had a grasp of engineering principles quite unusual for a man of his time and background. He was familiar with art and literature (even if, as you will see, his taste was sometimes questionable), yet he remained, in a peculiar way, innocent.

I would prefer to let the reader judge what are lies and what is truth. That is why I have tampered as little as possible with the material, merely providing concentrated narrative links wherever necessary. I believe that M. G. Lobkowitz's translations are excellent and very true to the spirit of the original. I have rephrased and reworked many sentences to improve their readability, but I have had to allow a certain crudeness here and there in case the reader should begin to doubt the genuineness of the memoirs. The problem of length was also daunting and I have condensed some episodes (though not, as might appear, the prison scenes, which are very sparse and vague). Usually I have resorted to literary methods (to paraphrase, for instance), producing an intensified version of the original text. The alternative, to present a précis of certain sections, would have been less appealing. I have been anxious to preserve as much as I could of the original because I believe Colonel Pyat's story to be unique. He traveled widely and was involved, between 1920 and 1940, with some of the key engineering experiments of those years—years characterized by a euphoric, optimistic attitude toward technology which we have never quite recaptured (but which our hero fully exploited). I believe he possessed an insight into character rarely shared by more sophisticated professional commentators. These insights might be reduced to an observation that he was merely able to recognize his own kind, but I think he was, as he says himself, a survivor: his survival instinct, if not his moral instinct, was extremely highly developed. It enabled him to recognize those he could use and those who would think they could use him. Certainly he does not come to us, even by his own account, as a noble person. He was either malicious toward the weak or else utterly oblivious of them; he was placatory and almost nauseatingly agreeable to the strong. Yet he reflects the spirit of his age. Some might argue he reflects it far too emphatically, but the same could be said of many of us to this day.

I have left in the majority of his exceptionally grandiose claims for his genius, as well as a number of his naïvetés, examples of his unconscious humor, and I have made no attempt to correct flaws in his scientific theories or alter the dates and places he gives for events. Again, I would prefer it if the reader were to decide on the authenticity or otherwise of Colonel Pyat's often incredible accounts of an era which had so many similarities with, and such a particular influence on, our own. As Lobkowitz said to me: "Pyat's story is unusual, but his wounds are common enough."

I have, incidentally, checked with both the local Serbian Church and the Russian Church in Bayswater, and nobody there remembers Pyat. His description, I was told, fits many of those who "drift in."

Once again I should like to acknowledge the great debt I have to Prince Lobkowitz, to Leah Feldmann, who was able to confirm some of Pyat's reminiscences of Makhno (she was a seamstress on his education train), to Stuart Christie and Albert Meltzer, to Charles Platt, to Maxim and Dolores Jakubowski, to Georges and Boris Hoffman, to the Harvard Ukrainian Research Institute, to John Clute, Hilary Bailey and Giles Gordon, who helped me to organize the final manuscript: to my ex-wife, Jill Riches, who had to live with Pyat for so long and then had to live, as it were, with his ghost for much longer, to Simon King and Tim Shackleton, the editors who decided that Pyat's memoirs would be worth publishing, and finally to Rob Cowley who helped prepare this text for the American edition, which differs somewhat from the text of the British and French editions.

MICHAEL MOORCOCK
Ladbrook Grove
May 1979

Yorkshire
March 1981

ONE

I am a child of my century and as old as the century. I was born in 1900, on 1 January, in South Russia: the ancient true Russia from which the whole of our great Slavic culture sprang. Of course it is no longer called Russia, just as the calendar itself has been altered to comply with Anglo-Saxon notions. By modern reckoning I was therefore born in the Ukrainian Soviet Socialist Republic on 14 January. We live in a world where many kinds of regression dignify themselves with the mantle of progress.

I am not, as is frequently suggested by the illiterates amongst whom I am forced to live, Jewish. The great Cossack hawk's beak is frequently mistaken in the West for the carrion bill of the vulture.

I am not a fool. I know my own Slavic blood. It roars in my veins; it pounds as the elemental rivers of my fatherland pound, forever longing to be reconciled with our holy and mysterious soil. My blood belongs to Russia as much as the Don, the Volga, and the Dnieper belong. My blood still hears the call of our vast, timeless steppe under whose solitudinous skies aristocrat and peasant, merchant and worker, were dwarfed and understood how little material prosperity mattered; that they were united by God and were part of His inevitable pattern. Alien Western ideas came to threaten this understanding. It was in the factory towns, where chimneys crowded to shut out our incomparable Russian light, where people were denied the shelter and confirmation of God's wide roof, God's cool and merciful eye, where the synagogues sprouted, that Russians began to elevate themselves and challenge God's will, as even the Czar would not dare; as even Rasputin, playing Baptist to Lenin's Antichrist and spreading rot from within, would not dare. Influenced by Jewish socialists in Kharkov, Nikolaev, Odessa and Kiev, these stokers and these riveters first denied the Lord Himself. Then they denied their blood. And then they denied their souls: their Russian souls. And if I cannot deny my soul after fifty years of exile, how then can I be Jewish? Some Peter? Some Judas? I think not.

Admittedly, I was not always religious. I have come to the Greek Orthodox religion relatively late and perhaps that is why I value it so, as those persecuted millions in the so-called Soviet Union value it, worshiping with a fervor unknown anywhere else in the Christian world. I have suffered racial insinuations all my life and for these I blame my father, who deserted his faith as casually as he deserted his family. Since I was a child in Tsaritsyn I have known this suffering and it became worse when my mother (by then probably a widow) moved us back to Kiev after the pogrom. My mother was Polish, but from a family long settled in Ukraine. She told me that my father had been a descendant of the Zaporozhian Cossacks who had for centuries defended the Slavic people against the Orient and who had resisted foreign imperialism from the West. My father had picked up radical ideas first as a clerk in Kharkov, later during his military service. When he left the army he remained in St. Petersburg for two years before getting into trouble with the authorities and being deported to Tsaritsyn. Many of these names are probably unfamiliar to the modern reader. St. Petersburg was renamed into Russian *Pyotrgrad* (Petrograd) in 1914, when we wanted no echoes of Germany in our capital. Now it is called Leningrad. Doubtless they intend to change it with every fresh political fad. Tsaritsyn became Stalingrad and then Volgograd as the past was revised for the umpteenth time, and the inevitable future and the impermanent present reproclaimed in fresher slogans, sufficient to make schizophrenics of the sanest citizens. Tsaritsyn is probably called something else by now. Nobody knows: least of all those émigré Ukrainian nationalists whom I sometimes speak to after Church services. They have become as ignorant as everyone else living here.

It is hard for me to find equals. I am a well-educated man who received Higher Education in St. Petersburg. Yet what good is education in this country, unless you are part of the Old Boy Network, or a homosexual in the Central Office of Information or the BBC, or Princess Margaret's lover, like so many self-styled intellectuals who come over here and betray themselves for the peasants which, in reality, they probably are? It is incredible how easily these Czechs, Poles, Bulgarians and Yugoslavs manage to pass themselves off as academics and artists. I see their names all the time: on books in the library, in the title credits of sex films. I would not lower myself. And as for the girls, they are all whores who have found richer prey in the West. I see two of them almost every day when I buy my bread in the Lithuanian's shop. They flaunt their long blond hair, their wide, painted mouths, their flashy clothes. Their skins are thick with make-up and they stink of perfume. They are always gabbling away in Czech. They come into my premises for fur capes and silk petticoats and I refuse to serve them. They laugh at me. "The old Jew thinks we're Russians," they say. Ah, if they were. Good Russians would have a discount. The girls speak Russian, of course, but they are obviously Czechs. Believe me, I know I bring these suspicions on myself, because I cannot give anyone, not even the British authorities, my real name. My father changed his name a dozen times during his revolutionary days. For different reasons, I also had to take other names. I still have relatives in Russia and it would not be fair to them to use their title since we had very strong aristocratic connections on both sides of the family. We all know what the Bolsheviks think of aristocrats.

My mother, although of Polish extraction, was attracted more to the Greek than the Roman in her religious preferences, though I never knew her to attend formal services. She observed all the Orthodox holidays. I do not remember icons (though she doubtless possessed them). She always had a picture of my father (in his uniform) in an alcove, with candles burning. It was here that my mother prayed. She never criticized my father, but she was anxious to remind me of how he had gone astray. He had denied God. An atheist, he had been involved in the uprisings of 1905. During this period he had almost certainly been killed, though the circumstances were never entirely clear. My mother herself would become vague when the subject was raised. My own memory is a confused one. I recall a sense of terror, of hiding, I think, under some stairs. On the other hand the equation itself was clear enough: God had withdrawn his grace and his protection from my father as a direct punishment. Aside from the fact that my father had been an officer in a Cossack regiment and had thrown away his career, that his family had been well-to-do but had disowned him, I knew very little about him. Out of tact, our relatives never mentioned him. Only Uncle Semyon in Odessa ever made any reference to him and that was always to curse him as "A fool, but a fool with a brain. The worst kind." At any rate I have no memories of him, for he was rarely at home, even in the Tsaritsyn days, and my memories of Tsaritsyn itself are confined to a few narrow, dusty, nondescript alleys, for we moved in 1907 to Kiev again, where my mother had a sister. Here they both worked as seamstresses. This was a terrible descent for a woman like my mother, who possessed a refined sensibility, spoke several languages, and was conversant in all forms of literature and learning. Later she became the manageress of a steam laundry and after her sister remarried we moved into the two-room flat near Mother's job. This was in a part of town with many old trees, little copses, parks and some fields, even, very close to the Babi ravine (the "Old Woman" ravine) which, with its grass, rocks and stream, became my main playground.

Here I would defend Kipling's Khyber Pass and, as Karl May's "Old Shatterhand," explore the Rocky Mountains. I would fight the Battle of Borodino. I would defend Byzantium against the Turks. On rarer occasions I would go to the Dnieper's beaches and be Huckleberry Finn, Ahab, Captain Nemo. Even then Kiev had its share of revolutionary troubles. The agitation came mainly from the workers in the industrial suburbs beyond the Botanical Gardens: blocks of flats as featureless and smoky as any you can find today. The authorities had had to clamp down quite heavily, but all I knew of this was when my mother kept me inside or stopped me going to school. On the whole, however, I experienced little of the unpleasant side of life in Kiev. It was a wonderful city in which to grow up. Near us was a road which ran through the gorges. This area was known as the Switzerland of Kiev. Thus I had the best of both worlds—country and city—though we were not rich. Kiev, and the Ukraine in general, inspired art and intellectual activity of every kind. Half Russia's greatest writers produced their best work there. All Russia's best engineers came from there. Even the Jews excelled themselves. But they, of course, were never content.

Built on hills above the river; full of cathedrals and monasteries with glittering onion domes, green copper, gold and lapis lazuli; full of great public buildings in the soft yellow brick for which Kiev was famous; of carved wooden houses, crowded street markets, statues, monuments, the large stores and theaters of the Kreshchatik, our main street, the University and various institutes, the Botanical Gardens, the Zoo, modern tramways; its squares crammed with electric signs, advertisement hoardings, kiosks, theater advertisements; its thoroughfares crowded with motor vehicles and horse-drawn carriages, carts, omnibuses; with trees, parks and green places everywhere, with the great commercial river full of steamers, yachts, barges and rafts (she was founded by the Scandinavian Rus to protect their most important trade route), Kiev was no provincial city, but the capital of ancient Russia, and well aware of the fact. Once, centuries before, she had been a walled garrison city of grim stone and unpainted wood: "Mother City of all the Russias. The Rome of Russia." And the infidel had come and the infidel had been forced back, or converted, or accommodated, perhaps temporarily, and Kiev and what she protected had always survived. Now she was Yellow Kiev, warm and hospitable to all. In the summer sunlight it would seem she was made entirely of gold, for her brick glowed while her mosaics and posters, flowers and trees shone like jewels. In the winter, she was a white fairy tale. In the spring the groaning and cracking of the Dnieper's ice could be heard throughout the city. In the autumn Kiev's mellow light and fading leaves blended so that she was a thousand shades of warm brown. By the early twentieth century she had reached the height of her beauty. Now, thanks to the Bolsheviks, she has become a lusterless shell, just another beehive with a few nondescript concrete monuments to pacify tourists. The Germans were blamed for destroying Kiev, but it is well known that the Chekists blew most of it up in their 1941 retreat. Even the existing statues are copies. Kiev had a history older than most European cities: from her came the culture which civilized the Slavs. From her came our greatest epics. Who has not, for instance, marveled at the film version of Ilya Moremyetz and the Heroes of Kiev, defenders of Christendom against the Tartar Horde, *Bogatyr and the Beast*? Ironically, what the Tartar failed to accomplish, the armies of the Bolsheviks and the Nazis succeeded in doing with relentless and unimaginative thoroughness.

We were poor, but there was wealth and beauty all around us. Our suburb, the Kurenvskaya, was rather run-down, though picturesquely countrified, with many wooden buildings and little gardens among the newer apartment houses (which were built around courtyards after the French model). If I wished I could walk down to the main city, or I could take the Number 10 tram past St. Kyril's Church to Podol and, if I failed to be seduced by the sights and smells of the Jewish Quarter, could walk up St. Andrew's Hill to that great church, all blue-and-white mosaic on the outside and rich gold on the inside, to stare at the distant Dnieper, at Trukhanov Island where the yacht club was. On a misty autumn evening I would enjoy walking along the wide Kreshchatik boulevard, with its chestnut trees and bright shops and restaurants. But Kreshchatik was best at Christmas, when the lamps were lit and the snow was piled against walls and gutters to make magical pathways from door to door. I remember the smell of pine and ice, of pastries and coffee and that special smell, rather like newly cut wood with a hint of fresh paint, of Christmas toys. Cabs and troikas rolled through the golden darkness; the breath of horses was whiter than the snow itself; warm, rattling trams radiated orange electric light. It is a ghost in my mind. It no longer exists. The Bolsheviks blew it to pieces as they retreated from the Nazis who had helped them, only a few months earlier, loot Poland.

As a boy I was generally more interested in doing than seeing. I am by reputation an intellectual, but my chief instincts are those of a man of action. I owe my scholarship almost entirely to my mother. She insisted on my receiving an education far better than most of the other children in the neighborhood. Fortunately she had a number of friends who, I suppose, were chiefly would-be candidates for her hand (she was a beautiful and vivacious woman) and they were helpful with advice about the best schools and what special subjects I should pursue. Our apartment was never without at least one visitor. Often there were many more, and they were by no means all Russians. In particular there was Captain Brown, the Scottish engineer, a gentleman living in reduced circumstances. He had a room off the same staircase as ours. He was rumored to be a deserter from the Indian army. Certainly he knew a great deal about the Northwest Frontier, Afghanistan and also the Caucasus, where he had spent several years (giving credence to the notion that he might be a deserter). I hardly heard him repeat a single story, he had so many: about Kazaks, Turks, Tajiks and Kirghiz brigands, about Kabul and Samarkand, or the problems of building railways in Georgia. He was a small, dark man, always genial yet giving off a sense of restrained aggression, though he was very gentle with my mother in that careful, masculine, delicate way of someone almost afraid of their own strength. He not only taught me my first English words but he gave me the set of *Pearson's Magazine* which was to supply so much of the reading of my boyhood and youth, make a crucial impression on my imagination and, subsequently, my ambition. I liked him the best, I think, because my mother found him such good company. She went with him to the opera and to the theater far more often than she went with other admirers.

Kurenvskaya was one of the most cosmopolitan suburbs. My mother was popular with her customers, who were chiefly unmarried men or the servants of well-to-do people. Some of them, doubtless from boredom or loneliness, would prolong their visits to the laundry. A few old regulars would be invited into her private office, a tiny room off the main floor of the laundry, where she would offer a glass of tea or perhaps some seedcake. Captain Brown could sometimes be found there but more frequently the chief visitors were minor officials, including Gleb Alfredovitch Koryalenko. Tall, thin, lugubrious, with the appearance of a dissolute stork, he was the local postman. Previously he had been a sailor with our Black Sea Fleet until invalided home after the disaster at the hands of the wily Japanese in 1904. Gleb Alfredovitch was full of gossip and my mother and her little circle of women friends were willing listeners, though I suspect the postman and a few others were favored chiefly because they could be of use in my education. Sometimes I would be allowed to listen while Koryalenko retailed his stories of well-to-do locals. I would sit in a corner with a piece of cake in one hand, a glass of tea in the other, learning of worlds almost as romantic as those described by Captain Brown. I have a recollection of the smell of tea, of lemon, of cake, and the heavy mixture of soap and lye, starch and dye, the hot dampness of the steam which covered everything, so that newspapers and magazines were always curling and chairs and tablecloths and rugs were always just a little moist to the touch.

The postman would occasionally come to the flat, along with one or two women and perhaps Captain Brown. They would bring a bottle of vodka and discuss the gossip from Moscow and St. Petersburg and any scandal (with appropriate expressions of piety) concerning Rasputin and the Czarina. Rasputin was well known in his day—a wandering monk with a mesmeric personality and an adroit way of palming drugs into drinks, who wheedled himself into St. Petersburg society where he led a life of total debauchery, seducing even the youngest of the Czar's little daughters. After a glass or two of vodka Koryalenko was inclined to begin a tirade against the Court for its degeneracy. He believed that stronger men were needed to control the women, that Czar Nicholas was too lenient. But my mother would hush him up. She would not accept any hint of political talk. She became highly nervous, for obvious reasons, at such references. Probably that was why I have always hated the tension engendered by political argument, which is always pointless. I have never judged anyone by the way he votes, so long as he does not try to get me to agree with him. And only a fool, of course, will vote himself into the slavery of socialism. In my life I have met all sorts of people. Their political beliefs rarely had much to do with their actions.

During this period, I knew the company of adults far more than the friendship of children. I always had a certain amount of trouble in relating to other children. I suppose that once the adult world had been opened up for me the world of children seemed dull. I was not much liked, either, because I was party to grown-up intercourse and must have seemed precocious to envious would-be comrades.

There was one little girl who admired me. Esmé was the daughter of a neighbor, a gentleman who had once, I suspect, been amongst Mother's suitors. Mother was convinced that he was an anarchist living under an assumed name because he had escaped from Siberia. She had therefore discouraged him. There was no evidence, but my mother had learned to be more than cautious. No one could blame her for this. The name the gentleman gave was Loukianoff. He had been in the cavalry (he had a horseman's way of walking) and lived, apparently, on a pension. Koryalenko told us that Loukianoff's wife had deserted him in Odessa for an English sea captain, leaving their daughter when she was less than a year old. Loukianoff went out rarely. The most we usually saw of him was his washing, brought to the laundry by Esmé. I was flattered by Esmé's admiration. Our friendship was discouraged by my mother who saw an *agent provocateur* in a horse with a red ribbon in its tail. Esmé was a beautiful, blond-haired little creature, always dressed very neatly, who acted as her father's housekeeper and shared, therefore, something of my own adult ways. We must have been a comical sight, two eight-year-olds discussing the cares of the world as I sometimes escorted her home from the laundry.

I enjoyed Esmé's company as an equal but felt nothing romantic toward her. My own heart was the sole property of a dark-eyed girl who hawked secondhand tin toys from a tray on a corner near the tram stop. Sometimes she carried a cage in which sat a trained canary which would peck at letters and symbols in order to tell a person's fortune. She was a genuine gypsy, I heard, from a camp in one of the gorges. I dared to go close to the camp on an overcast autumn afternoon. It was not what I had expected. There were no carved and painted caravans, just a collection of shanties and carts, of fires which sent dark smoke to the upper air. It was not the Heaven I had imagined. It was more a scene of Hell. To some extent this vision cooled my ardor and I no longer planned immediately to marry my sweetheart according to the customs of her own people (with the King of the Gypsies, of course, presiding), but I bought as many toys from her tray as I could afford, always got an excellent fortune told by her canary, and discovered that her name was Zoyea. She had red lips and curly black hair and a manner about her, even then, which was totally entrancing. I think her parents had been Rumanians. She had none of the passive femininity of my friend Esmé. She was neither modest nor quietly spoken. She spoke a patois similar to the rolling Southern Ukrainian dialect, full of words I could not understand and in which a's and o's were all mixed up. She carried herself with the swagger of a boy. Yet I believed she thought me attractive. Perhaps it was those eyes, which seemed to look with sexual calculation upon every living creature. My mother found her even more alarming an acquaintance than Esmé and, when I suggested inviting Zoyea home for tea, had one of her most elaborate attacks of hysteria. Thereafter, Esmé was never quite the *persona non grata* of former times.

One day Zoyea was absent from her usual corner and I went to the shantytown to look for her. The camp had gone. All that remained was the sort of rubble gypsies leave the world over. I learned from a passer-by that the authorities had closed them down and moved them on. The tinkers had set out along the Fastov road, he thought, perhaps heading for the coast or the Crimea. He was pleased to see them go. He had lost more than one chicken since they had set up their ramshackle village. I felt I had lost much more than a cheap supply of German toys.

Hope took me to Bessarabskaya, as if I would find her amongst the organ-grinders, beggars and sellers of exotic pets, the noise and the color of the market. I half expected to see their carts, bearing their clay ovens and drainpipe samovar chimneys intact. There were several toy sellers with their trays. They were all old men with long beards and insincere grins. There were tinkers, too, offering to mend pots and shoes, but my gypsy had left before the first snows and was on her way to the sun. I bought myself a twist of balabhuka, the famous Kiev confection, as consolation, and went home. I think that I was to see Zoyea again.

During the following spring and summer Esmé and I would go for walks together in the nearby Kirillov woods. I remember most strongly the ravines and the smell of the massed lilacs in the summer rain as we sheltered at the top of a gorge looking down on another gypsy camp. It continued to rain. Gypsy fires sent orange flame and black smoke into the semidarkness. We became wet enough to gain courage to ask for shelter. I led Esmé down the slippery slopes, getting nearer and nearer to a colorful rabble of wretches who at first ignored us and then greeted us with greedy caution, asking if we wished to buy a toy or a lucky charm. As these grimy bargains were displayed to us on grimier hands we dumbly shook our heads and, as the rain stopped, stumbled back up to the top of the ravine. We returned the next morning, still fascinated by our discovery, until Esmé became obsessed with the idea of our abduction and fled, leaving me once again to deal with the offerings, their sly grins and their soft voices. This particular band was moved on by the police a few days later and I believe it was my mother's complaint which was the chief cause of this official action. I was forbidden ever to visit such a camp again.

A little after this incident, both Esmé and I were enrolled in an excellent local school run by a dedicated German couple called Lustgarten. The fact that we were enrolled at the same time was, I learned from my disapproving mother, merely an unfortunate coincidence. I understood that a relative was helping pay for my studies, but I was never sure who this relative might be. Perhaps it was my Uncle Semyon—Semya, as we called him.

He was strict and very generous with his malacca, but our lantern-jawed, grey-eyed Herr Lustgarten was an enthusiastic teacher. His greatest joy came from finding pupils in whom burned a genuine relish for knowledge. A very tall man, with loose limbs, he wore a formal frock coat and high collar. His black boots were always polished to mirrors. I see him now, his arms and legs flowing like scarves in a wind, his stick waving over his head, as he demonstrated some point in algebra. I was the kind of pupil he liked best. It became evident that I had a natural capacity for languages and mathematics. I gained a working knowledge of German and French, a little Czech, which the Lustgartens spoke excellently, having spent several years in Prague, and I already had Polish from Mother. English came chiefly from Captain Brown (who continued to encourage me in all my studies). Like so many others I had only a few words of Ukrainian. My first language was Russian. The mania for nationalism had not yet taken hold of Ukraine. Someone remarked to me not long ago that, deprived of their pogroms by the Reds, Ukrainians had turned to nationalism as a poor substitute. Well, I am no Jew lover, but I am no nationalist, either. Herr Lustgarten, in common with many Germans of his generation, was somewhat philo-Semitic. My mother would have been horrified if she had heard his discourses on the Russian character. I recall a favorite topic almost word for word: "The Russian people," he would say, "are like the Americans. They have no sense of ethics, only of piety. Their Church, supported by the bureaucracy and the military, supplies them with a formula for living. It is why they look to novelists for ethical models; why such importance and respect is attached to the novelist. Why young men and women ape characters in Tolstoi and Dostoieffski. These novelists are not merely writers of fiction, they are teachers, ascetics taking the place, for instance, of the Moravian Brothers in Germany and Bohemia, of Luther or John Wesley, of the Quakers. By and large Russians are a people without a moral creed, lest it be the simplest one of all: To serve God and the Czar."

I have remembered Herr Lustgarten's words because in some respects they were prophetic. The Russian people are again beginning to realize, I gather, the menace of the Zionist-Masonic conspiracy. I hear that the military is issuing instruction pamphlets warning soldiers of the dangers of international Zionism. As for the Yellow Peril, most Slavs are already only too well aware of that particular threat. The great creed Professor Lustgarten could never understand was the creed of Pan-Slavism, which flourished in Ukraine, heartland and birthplace of the greatest Slav state in the world. Potentially, it is the core of a single Slav state embracing Poland, Lithuania, Czechoslovakia, Bulgaria, Yugoslavia, even parts of Greece. It could form a bastion of its own intense brand of Western culture against the decadence represented by America or the barbarism represented by the new Tartar Empire under Mao. The hair-splitting obsessions of Germanic theology are not for us. We are concerned with our destiny. Ukrainian nationalism is at odds with Pan-Slavism. That is why I was never a nationalist. I was born into the Russian Empire and it is my greatest wish to die there, too, though I fear it will be a little longer before the Russian people return wholeheartedly to their ancient heritage.

Herr Lustgarten's historical views did not always accord with my own but I found myself responding excellently to his tuition. He was delighted and gave me extra lessons in the evenings. He assured me that if I pursued my studies diligently I would be sure of academic honors. My mother was ecstatic and it was satisfying to me that I was able to repay her for the sacrifices she had made. I had, she said, my father's intellect, but I possessed her sense of values. I determined not to waste my brain as my father had wasted his. Mother accepted sewing work to pay for the extra courses and from the age of eleven (the year Stolypin was assassinated in Kiev) I received Mathematics and Science from Herr Lustgarten and Languages and Literature from Frau Lustgarten. This wonderful lady, as quiet and impassive and short and fat as her husband was volatile and lean, introduced me to the books which were to leave such a deep impression on me. Grimmelshausen, Dickens, Goethe, Hugo and Verne were all firm favorites by the time I was thirteen. I would also read the *Pearson's* volumes which Captain Brown had given me. There were twenty-eight in all. I wish I owned them still. They would cost a fortune to buy, even if they existed. These were lost, with so much else, during the Civil War following Lenin's usurping power. They had identical bindings of gold, blue and dark green on buff. I think I read every word in them at least twice. Here were the tales of H. G. Wells, Cutcliffe Hyne and Max Pemberton. Guy Boothby, Conan Doyle, H. Rider Haggard, Rafael Sabatini and Robert Barr are other names you rarely hear these days. Films, radio and television have completely destroyed literacy. The socialists have achieved their end: everyone is reduced to the level of the muzhik. In my day we strove to improve ourselves. Today the common aim, even amongst the so-called educated classes, is to appear as stupid and as illiterate as possible.

By 1913, then, my waking life consisted almost entirely of work and reading. I saw Esmé only on the way to school (girls were segregated from boys) and we rarely spoke of anything but our education. Her father was very ill and she abandoned lessons increasingly to look after him. She was an angel. Save for my lasting friendship with her, I was essentially a solitary child and had few acquaintances. This and my penchant for scholarship earned me the jealousy of most other boys and I suffered the most horrible insults, usually without demur. I had a friend for a little while. His name was Yuri and he was about my own age, though much poorer than us. He used to come and sit by our stove while I studied in the evenings. I would help him with his lessons. My mother was delighted that I had a new playmate. But then a few ornaments were missing and only Yuri could have taken them. Next day I taxed him with the theft. He was frank in admitting it. I asked him why he had stolen from us, who had shown him kindness, and received the most shocking reply.

"Because you are Jews," he said. "Jews are fair game. Everyone says so." Sickened by this slur, I complained to Herr Lustgarten who seemed unsympathetic in a way I still cannot quite define. "I am the son of a Cossack," I told him and his wife. "Come home with me and I'll prove it to you."

Herr Lustgarten brought Yuri home in order, he said, to make the thief return personally the things he had stolen. They were not all there, but what had been recovered was put back into my mother's hands. Under the threat of Herr Lustgarten's cane Yuri apologized, although it was evident that he felt victimized. I took down the hand-colored photograph of my father in his shapka, his Cossack uniform. Proof, if ever it was needed, of his blood. I showed it to Yuri. His reply brought my mother to tears:

"It's just a picture. Everyone knows you're a Jew's bastard. What does a picture prove?"

I attacked him, wrenching my schoolmaster's cane from his thin hand and bringing it down over Yuri's head. I have never experienced such fury. And this time, again unexpectedly, Herr Lustgarten was on my side. Yuri made threats involving the Black Hundreds (patriots who sought to control the insidious spread of Jewish power) and became contrite when Herr Lustgarten said he would dismiss him from the school and tell his parents the reason. That was the end of my friendship. Yuri later drew a band of fellow-spirits about him—not all, by any means, from the poorest class—and began to make a misery of my life. This gang would pursue me home from school. It would offer me a "fair fight" and, when I refused, chase behind me screaming names like "Little Rabbi" and "Jerusalem Colonel"—epithets which, in Kiev at that time, were not merely obnoxious slander; they could be, under specific conditions, the next thing to a death sentence. Accusations like that, though, were fairly common in my childhood and often carried no weight at all. No more, say, than calling a mean man a Jew, even if it is obvious he has no semitic blood. Nonetheless, it was these insults more than the others—"Teacher's Pet," "Toady," "Sneak" or even "Blockhead"— which would make me lose my temper and become involved in stupid stone-throwing bouts and fistfights.

These city riffraff, many of whom were of foreign origin, were probably jealous of my ancient Cossack birthright. My atheist father with his ridiculous progressive ideas had not only succeeded in dragging my mother into impoverished, shameful widowhood, he had also taken personal liberties with my little body for, my mother explained, hygienic reasons. Thus I was of entirely Gentile blood but branded with the mark of the Jew. I did not know then how close, in later years, my father's action would bring me to death. He might as well have tried to cut my throat at birth. It is not uncommon these days to have the operation, but in Ukraine in the 1900s it was as good as a conversion to Judaism. Jews profess to be mystified by Ukrainian resentments. There is little mystery. Jews, renting lands from absentee Polish landlords, drained our farmers and serfs in previous centuries. When the Cossacks drove back the Poles they also took revenge on their usurer-servants. And the Jews defended the Poles with muskets and swords. I make no excuses for cruel savagery. But the Jew is not quite the blameless fellow he these days makes himself out to be. If I were Jewish I would admit the causes of Ukrainian enmity. It might have a placatory effect. But the Jews are too proud for that.

What a great deal my mother might have blamed my father for. And how little she did blame him. She spoke of him only with wistful respect (save in the matter of his atheism) and frequently told me to honor his name. This is something I was never able to do, even for her sake. As I have shown, he set me on the road of life with so many disadvantages I wonder that I am here today. All that I inherited was his mind, which has saved me more than once from death or torture; but my imagination and sensitivity could have come only from my mother, as she said. His rebellion against his great Cossack heritage, his Russian religion and culture, brought him fear and annihilation. To those he left it brought only sorrow. And what did his revolution achieve when it was successful? More death; more humiliation. As we used to say: "Better a Jew in Czarist Minsk than a Gentile in Soviet Moscow." Is that progress?

Possibly I inherited one other trait from my father—that same faith in the future which was in him a perversion of reality, a substitute for religion, was in me a belief in purely scientific progress. Verne and Wells, and also the many articles and stories in *Pearson's*, were to fire me with a sense of wonder at the marvels of science and technology. Even before reading these authors I had determined to become an engineer. In this I was motivated by a noble love of the discipline itself. I did not corrupt it with mock-humanitarian rationalizations, like some nervous monk of the Middle Ages excusing his interest in alchemy by saying it was "God's work." I maintained a loathing for all political pieties. I saw myself as one of those who would give a whole Slavic character to science and put it at the service of the Slavic soul. By introducing extraneous themes into their tales, Verne, the anarchist, and Wells, the socialist, did themselves and their readers great harm, warping their visions to fit completely unscientific themes, just as Rasputin warped religion to make it speak for every sexual perversion. We lived in an age when a pure heart and a truthful tongue were great liabilities. Even Jack London, who wrote so feelingly of nature and the nobility of the untamed North, came to betray his gift with tales of pessimism and polemics: because it was demanded of him that he did so, otherwise nobody would have taken him seriously. He would have lost prestige amongst those so-called liberals who have brought our world to its present sorry state. Everyone cares for the good opinion of his neighbors, but sometimes the price we pay for that opinion is far too high.

Ironically, I was fired in my ambition to become an engineer before I was well-versed enough in English to read the stories in *Pearson's*. Esmé and I had been walking somewhere in the center of Kiev, perhaps in Kreshchatik itself, when we had come upon a large general store on the corner of a street near a theater. I remember, too, one of those old kiosks with the domed roof copied from the French, and a public urinal, also on French lines. Most engineers I knew later had been infected by their first ride on a train, or their first contact with an automobile or monoplane. With me it was the sight of a simple English bicycle. Typical of many Kievan stores of the time, the windows were not exactly used for display, but one could look through into the interior and see the bicycle on its special stand. Esmé had seemed to share my enthusiasm for the machine (though perhaps she had merely wished to please me). She had considered how we might buy it or how the owner of the store might be induced to give it to us for some great service we did him. It was a bright spring morning. The chestnut trees had their first buds. Behind us passed horse-cabs and handcarts, wagons and cars, to and fro on the wide, cobbled street. It was not merely a dawning year. It was a dawning era. The shop also sold gramophones, pianolas, mechanical organs, guitars and balalaikas, but the bicycle was the aristocrat of the place. A handsome black beast (a Raleigh "Royal Albert Gent's Roadster," now long-since extinct), it was bright with red-and-gold transfers and polished steel accessories. It was completely beyond my pocket. It was more expensive, even, than the imported German and French bicycles available. I do not remember having any expectation that it might be mine. I did not even think of entering the shop to pretend to be a purchaser, to inspect or touch the machine, for I had no particular desire to ride it. Esmé had tried to get me to go and then had offered to go for me, but I had refused. I was not greatly impressed by the machine's function so much as what it stood for. It represented all the great inventions of the nineteenth and twentieth centuries. It stood for the airship and the aeroplane; the electric carriage, the steam-turbine, the motorbus, the tram, the telephone, wireless radio transmission; it was steel bridges and skyscrapers and mechanical harvesters. It was abstract mathematics become practicality. I studied its brakes, its chain, its spokes, its nuts and its tubular steel struts. I was impressed there and then by the divine simplicity of the mechanical system which, by producing pressure on the pedals to turn the chain wheel, which then turned the back wheel, could, with the minimum of effort, help Man travel as fast and as far as any living beast. Beyond this conception—revelation if you like—I had no special interest. Certainly almost all the scientific inventions of those times had proved themselves of benefit to mankind, but for me their beauty rested in the simple fact of their existence. They functioned. They were solved problems. Krupp cannon and Nobel dynamite were to arouse in me the same aesthetic feelings as hydraulic dams or Mercedes ambulances. I was to be inspired by the machinery, not its social uses. Pistons and cylinders, circuits and gauges would satisfy me so long as they performed their appropriate task: driving a ship, taking an aeroplane aloft, sending a message. It would have seemed improper to me even then to indulge in metaphysical or sociological speculation as to their uses. When, later, the War came and we heard about the British tanks, you did not find me tut-tutting. I had anticipated them already. They had become a vision turned into the reality of plate steel, rubber and the internal combustion engine. I was similarly impressed by Sikorsky bombers, Big Bertha and the great Zeppelins which attacked Paris and London, and I had already begun to formulate ideas of my own which, had I been born a year or two earlier, might have changed the course of the War, altering the whole development of world history. But I must try not to sound too grandiose. After all, I am a victim of history, not one of her conquerors, and to make it seem otherwise would be to show myself as a silly old man. I do not intend to confirm the view of those louts who already see me as no more than a ludicrous Russian ancient running a secondhand clothes shop in the Portobello Road.

Well, it suits me to let people think what they like. They will be all the more astonished when they read this and see what I achieved. This is my private glee: to know how the peasants and loafers, the scum of three continents, see me, but to be aware of what I really am. There are a few who respect me and to these I tell my secrets. But I do not want fame now. And honor I shall have in plenty when I am dead. I have had enough of politicians to last several lifetimes. My heart could probably not stand any publicity I might now achieve. Admittedly, a small pension, an O.B.E. or perhaps a knighthood, would help me in my old age, since I am now entirely without regular companionship. Mrs. Cornelius was the only one to offer me that. It was to be near her that I moved into this area. I could have gone to Earl's Court. I could have had a job with the government. But I will not talk about Mrs. Cornelius for the moment. It will be best to come to her when you know the kind of person who is writing about that remarkable personality who is justly famous, as are her talented children. Here I will say only one thing: she never betrayed me.

I returned again and again to the shop with its solitary English bicycle, until inevitably it was sold. I saw it once, being ridden over the bridge near the Zoological Gardens, and that was that. But I did not care. The symbol remained. Many years later I read the whole of H. G. Wells' *Wheels of Chance*, but was disappointed. It contained the seeds of his later literary decline. It was altogether too flippant and held none of the visionary wonderment I had found in *The War of the Worlds*, which I read in *Pearson's*. His *Sea Lady*, also published in *Pearson's*, was equally worthless. The desire to be fashionably amusing can infect the best of us. How is it that a writer can be so full of optimism and faith in one book and so foolish and cynical in another? My studies of Freud—who, as I was to discover, was a bad-tempered, misanthropic Viennese Jew willing to snub anyone he considered his social inferior—have yet to supply me with an answer to this mystery. Not that I have respect for the so-called psychologists, especially those of that same sordid Viennese school. You can take it from me that most of them were on the edge of absolute madness for the best part of their lives. At my single meeting with H. G. Wells I was able to ask why he had wasted so much time on his nonscientific novels and he answered that he had once thought he could "achieve the same sort of thing through comedy." He baffled me by this. I must assume he was making fun of me or that he was drunk or experiencing, as so many artists do, a form of temporary dementia. It is just possible that he could have misheard me for though my English is excellent, as this narrative testifies, I had at first some difficulty in making myself properly understood. I learned colloquial English almost entirely from Mrs. Cornelius. My attempts to apply it so as to put others at ease were not always successful. During my first year as a permanent English resident it was not unusual for me to be left in the basket quite innocently by my friend. I could actually communicate better (as I had done in the twenties) by using *Pearson's* English which was at least readily interpreted by all. My affectionate and admiring "How are you, you old bugger?" to Mr. (later Lord) Winston Churchill, at a function for celebrated Polish émigrés, was not as well received as I had expected and I was never able to thank him, thereafter, for the hearty support he had given to the cause of Russia's rightful rulers.

My sense of tact comes naturally to me. I have had it since I was a child. This virtue was encouraged by my mother in her permanent anxiety over the stigma attached to my father's activities. More than once, when there was some kind of trouble in Kiev, she would be visited by the police. In the main these men were kindly, cheerful officers, merely doing their duty. Even when investigating some major crime, they did not have the pinch-faced fanaticism of Lenin's "leather-coat" Chekists. Indeed, they were true representatives of the Czar; kindly, avuncular, a little distant in some ways. They believed that our young men were being led astray by romantic notions primarily of French, German and American origin. I recall hearing that when the Czar met Kerenski, after the first Revolution, he remarked warmly that "He is a man who loves Russia, and I wish I could have known him earlier, for he could have been useful to me." Such generosity (more than I might have felt in the circumstances) was typical of the man and typical of the system which received criticism from so many different quarters. When it did take firm action it took it thoroughly and without malice. For every Cossack charge there were a thousand incidents preceding it. Young men of good family were rarely shot for misdemeanors but sent into exile, often to stay with relatives, until their hot blood cooled a little. Only the most persistent or vicious of working-class revolutionaries received long prison sentences or capital punishment. This my mother understood, as she understood that the police had their duty to do. When they called they were always cheerfully received and invited to eat a little cake and take tea from our samovar. I remember the bulky blue-and-gold greatcoats sitting steaming by the stove. My impression of these men was not at all frightening. I admired their splendid uniforms, their well-kept beards and mustaches. I remember delighting at least one set of these visitors when I informed them, without irony, that if I were not destined to become a great engineer I would wish to become a policeman or a soldier in the service of the Czar.

As it happened, both my desires were to be granted in a modified way in the future, though even here I was dogged by bad luck and misunderstanding. My mother was extremely proud of my attitude and she was complimented by the officers. One of them, who had presumably known him, remarked that I was considerably more sensible than my father. My mother had smiled, but I could easily tell she was offended by their denigration of my father's memory. She could accept no criticism of him, even when that criticism reflected well on herself and her only son. The policemen left in good spirits (I think they had had some vodka with their tea) and I remember how my mother drew a deep breath and looked at me oddly before telling me to resume my supper, which had been interrupted by the visit. She leaned against the shelf over the stove, where I normally slept in winter. She was gasping, almost as if a bucket of cold water had been thrown over her. Being the woman she was, she soon recovered, but she was inattentive for the rest of the evening. It emerged later that my father had not been the only Red in the family. Mother's brother had been another. He had never, I gathered, been brought to justice. There was a rumor he was in Geneva. Mother received no letters from him.

No paper or pamphlet even remotely radical was allowed in the house. The mildest nationalist periodicals were banned. She was so careful she would inspect the wrappings of meat or fish for seditious propaganda. She had been known to unravel a parcel in order to throw away a sheet from *The Thought of Kiev* rather than take it home. She suffered dreadfully from her nerves and for this, too, I blame her husband.

She had nightmares, the woman I must call Yelisaveta Filipovna (a name I have borrowed from one of the neighbors who showed kindness to us; but her real name she shared with a prominent princess). Frequently I was awakened in the middle of the night, hearing her mumbling feverishly on her couch. I would peer over the edge of my shelf and see her rise like a corpse at the Last Judgment. Then she would scream: a long, piteous sound. And she would sometimes cry out: "Forgive me!" Then she would pray in her sleep, or wring her hands and weep silent tears, her unbound black hair standing around her pale head like a demon's halo. I know that I should have shown more sympathy, but I was always terrified. It seemed she felt guilty (perhaps because she was not at her father's bedside when he died), but whether that guilt had any real foundation I do not know. She would return to sleep often without realizing what had happened, but sometimes I would wake her if she seemed in danger. In time I became used to these nightmares and, as I studied harder, could often sleep through them. An ability to sleep through the wildest disturbances has been both an advantage and a disadvantage to me. My mother's nightmares came more frequently in the autumn and winter. It was because of them that I ceased to invite Esmé to stay with us when her father was sometimes taken to the hospital; my mother refused to let me go to "the revolutionary's house," but Captain Brown would look after Esmé when he could. Captain Brown began to drink more frequently and it was occasionally my mother's sad duty to ask him to leave our apartment because of his inebriation. He never, however, made any improper advances.

Mother had further cause for concern from the Odessa branch of the family. Many of the more distant relatives were in trouble with the law over purely petty matters. This was the "black-sheep" side. With the exception of my Great-Uncle Semyon, they were all cousins or second cousins of my mother's. Sometimes they would come to Kiev and very rarely one of them would stay overnight at our flat, much to my mother's dismay. We would always receive some luxury by way of payment for our hospitality: scented soap, or canned food of foreign origin, or a bottle of French wine. Mother would sell the stuff whenever possible, even give it away rather than keep it in the house. I think the young men from Odessa were smugglers of some kind. They were certainly well-to-do compared to their poor Kiev relatives. Uncle Semya was a successful shipping agent, far more respectable and wealthy than the shady "spivs" who made such cynical use of their blood ties, but he claimed to be unable to control them. It was to Uncle Semya that I think my mother chiefly appealed for help with Herr Lustgarten's fees.

As well as studying literature, languages and mathematics, I learned geography and basic scientific principles. A true scientific education was beyond the kindly German's range. I read a good deal and was particularly impressed by an American book, obtained from one of my Odessa cousins, describing current methods of building flying machines. Those were the days when one could not only learn to fly without need of special instructors or licenses, but one began by constructing one's own aircraft. The book was full of carefully made line drawings, complete with hand-lettered captions which would be mysterious to anyone not *au fait* with the modern flying machine: *Optimum Angle of Incidence—Center of Gravity—Center of Drift —Wash-In to Offset Propeller Torque*—and so on. That book was also a victim of Revolution and Civil War. From it I could have built an entire aeroplane (with the exception of the engine), from frame to the treatment of the canvas.

By the time I was thirteen and a half Herr Lustgarten was beginning, he said, to despair of teaching me more. I suppose I had exhausted his learning. In the years just prior to the Great War the Kiev Technical Institute (where logically I should go to continue my studies) was a hotbed of radicalism. My mother was reluctant to send me there, in spite of my assurances that I wished only to learn. I could never have been infected by the nihilistic emotionalism of those young men who, rather than gain knowledge of the world, would change it to make it accept their ignorance. The institute's "quota system" was altogether too liberal. There was also the question of identity papers. My dead father's hand continued to hamper my career. I believed the application board to be fair-minded, but Mother thought I should be prepared for certain specialized oral entrance examinations before contemplating application. This decision was reached after her final conversation with Herr Lustgarten. Possibly he warned her the board would find me "too clever by half." It is certainly no advantage to have more than an average share of brains in this world. To temporize, it was at last agreed I should "cram" in the evenings, with the special object of preparing for entrance to the

Institute, and that during the day I should get what Herr Lustgarten called "practical experience." I was to go to work for Sarkis Mihailovitch Kouyoumdjian.

This was the name of a well-known local mechanic whom at first I greatly despised. He was a Russianized Armenian, originally from Batoum, and a Christian. He had been a ship's engineer. He had met a Ukrainian girl in Odessa and eventually settled in Kiev, working first for the riverboat company, later for the tram company, and finally for himself. He could deal with almost every kind of machinery, from electrical generators, steam engines, compressors, internal combustion engines, to factory equipment owned by the many small industrial concerns which flourished in Kiev. Most of his clients were Podol Jews, with their horrible, grimy little factories. He was cheap and he was optimistic. I suppose he was what the English would call a bodger. He was not paid to service new machinery. He was paid to keep old machinery running at the lowest possible cost. He lived in his own ramshackle house a couple of streets to the east of ours, off Kirillovskaya. It was a wooden house full of bits of discarded machinery and various "inventions" which he had begun but failed to complete. He never listened to my suggestions, which were even then eminently sensible. He did not really possess the imagination of a great engineer. He was the last of his family, he told me. The rest of his relatives, men, women and children, had been amongst the hundred-and-fifty-thousand Armenians whom the Turks had marched into the desert to die at the beginning of the century. It is fashionable these days to treat the Nazis as the originators of modern genocide, but they could have learned a great deal from the Turks, who rid themselves of their Armenian problem with far less fuss and at far less expense. We of the Ukraine learned to fear the menace from the East long before we found ourselves at war with the West.

"Turk" was the strongest curse I ever heard Sarkis Mihailovitch utter, but the word sent a chill through me more than any other oath.

It did not suit me to become an apprentice to an Armenian jobbing mechanic but my mother insisted I learned the trade. Thus, in June 1913, I became Sarkis Mihailovitch Kouyoumdjians' "mate," going with him on almost every assignment, even doing small, simple tasks on my own, and getting my first familiarity with the nuts and bolts of engineering. My mother had been right. I began to enjoy my job. It was a beautiful summer. Even the Podol ghetto was alive with greenery and blossoms.

In one respect however it was difficult to learn from my first boss. He never gave praise and he never offered blame. His small, dark face was always set in a slight smile, his black eyes bore an expression of private amusement, no matter what the situation, as if he lived permanently in the back of his head. He was neat, swift and skillful; he was economical in everything. He rarely spoke to a customer, but would listen carefully to the problem and then purposefully set to, there and then, to tackle it if he could. In a struggle with a machine he never refused a challenge and he usually emerged the victor (even if some of those victories were only temporary). No matter how hard the job or how easy, he would devote the same grave, smiling attention to it. His expression and his manner could be irritating. People thought he displayed contempt, or at least irony. Frequently he would be shouted at by irate owners telling him not to take a job if he didn't want it. He would ignore them, set to with his spanners, screwdrivers and more specialized tools, and sooner or later they would be rewarded. Then Sarkis Mihailovitch Kouyoumdjian would wipe his hands, still smiling, indicate that I should pack the tools, work out his charges in his head and laconically name a price. Very rarely did even the most argumentative customer quarrel over that price. Sarkis Mihailovitch knew he was cheap and, unlike any Armenian I have known, he hated to haggle.

Through him I became familiar with all Kiev's industrial districts, although Podol was chiefly where we worked. Ukraine at that time was "booming." As well as being the richest-developed part of the Empire in terms of agriculture, it was also the most heavily industrialized, with coal and iron mines feeding the factories of Yuzovka, Kharkov (where the great locomotive works was based) and Katerynoslav, as well as many other towns which had grown around the new mines and engineering plants. I should make it clear that I was not alone amongst young Ukrainians in being inspired by the wonders of modern technology. Sikorsky, inventor of the helicopter, was born in Kiev and conducted his early experiments a year or two before my own. I did not, like him, have the benefit of a wealthy and influential family. Thousands of us were the first generation to see and understand the Future and in the years to come were to supply the rest of Russia and the world with many of her greatest engineers. We Ukrainian Cossacks have been described somewhere as "Russia's Scots," and in this respect, as in others, the comparison is fairly made. Kiev, however, was by no means one of the most heavily industrialized cities. It was still mainly involved in trade and banking.

At this time in my life I never got to see any of the larger factories. Most of my experience was confined to light-engineering works, textile plants and so on, usually consisting of no more than one or two sheds. But in no other city would I have had the opportunity of working for a man like Sarkis Mihailovitch, who specialized in no particular field. Thus, I became familiar with auto engines, steam pumps, dynamos and mechanical looms. This broad education was to stand me in good stead in later years, though again there was to be a disadvantage, for some would think me a jack-of-all-trades-master-of-none.

Working for the Armenian brought out all my imaginative and inventive gifts. In his employ I began properly to develop my own ideas, based on things I had read in *Pearson's* and similar journals. It seemed to me that I could develop a one-man flying machine which dispensed with the conventional fuselage and used the human body itself in this function. The Center of Gravity would be determined by the position of the engine, rather than the position of the pilot. While Sikorsky aimed at larger and larger planes such as the *Ilya Mouro-metz*, I dreamed of a kind of "flying infantry." Each man would be equipped with his own wings and engine. Wings would be fitted to his arms, a motor on a frame would be strapped to his back, to allow clearance for the propeller. Tailplane and rudder would be attached to his feet.

I described my design to Esmé, who by now was looking after her ailing father full-time, and she was greatly impressed. She wanted to know when the first men would be seen flying over the domes of St. Sophia's Cathedral. I promised her that it would be soon; that it would be me; and that she should witness my very first flight.

Having made the boast, I became determined to fulfill it. I could not bear to make a fool of myself in Esmé's eyes. She was by now a most beautiful young woman, with long, fine golden hair and huge blue eyes. She had pale skin, and that strong, full body typical of Ukrainian women. Yet I still did not see her as anything but an old and trusted friend, though I was by no means free of sexual desire. My main excitement lay in ambling along Kreshchatik at night and ogling the expensive whores who strolled up and down the boulevards. Alternatively I could go in the afternoons to Kircheim's Café, a famous emporium of coffee and cream cakes, and look at the young beauties who came there for treats with their mothers. There was more than one dark-eyed beauty who returned my impassioned glances, yet there was none to compare with my wonderful lost Zoyea. A yearning for her still took me to the gorges where the gypsies had once camped; but they camped there no more.

Since I first conceived the idea of a flying man, similar projects have been successful, but in those days the principles of power-weight ratio were not fully understood. Moreover the engine I was to use was not properly suited to the task. I had promised Esmé that I would make my flight by the next Sunday. I did not tell my boss, who had laughed at me when I had proposed the invention, but the only engine available at this time had to come from his workshop. It was part of a repair: a small petrol engine normally used to drive a motor tricycle belonging to one of Podol's largest bakery concerns. The motor was in excellent working order and had only been removed while Kouyoumdjian made some adjustments to the chain and rear wheel. A minor job. I now realize that it was completely wrong of me to borrow the engine, particularly one belonging to so important a customer, but my promise to Esmé was paramount in my mind.

When Sarkis Mihailovitch left me to lock up, as he often did, on the Saturday night, I took a small trolley and went to fetch the rest of my equipment. I had prepared the frame which would strap onto my back and give proper clearance for the air screw. This propeller was fitted over the existing driving cog on the motor. My greatest aesthetic thrill had come after I had finished carving it. I had built the frame of wood, covered in treated canvas, for wings and for the double tailplane section which would fit on my feet. By keeping my ankles together I believed I could perform the function of a conventional tailplane. I tested the engine and had the satisfaction of seeing the screw spin properly. It was gone midnight, so I left everything ready for the morning and returned home. My mother was in a state of great excitement. She had become convinced I had been murdered. She worried so much about me because there had, in fact, been a child murdered quite close to us. It had been a ritual murder performed by a band of fanatical Zionists and I do not believe they ever caught the Jews responsible. The body had been hidden in a cave in a gorge and its discovery, as I recall, had resulted in a particularly rigorous pogrom. I very much regret the grief I caused my poor mother with my escapades, but she never could understand that certain sacrifices are required not only of those who themselves advance the cause of science, but of those who share our lives.

Early on Sunday morning I met Esmé and took her to the workshop. There she helped me load all my equipment onto the handcart and we trundled it to the Babi ravine, which, being wide, was the most suitable for my experiment. I had to reassure Esmé several times that the flight would be quite safe. There was a certain amount of danger, of course, because this would be the first test, but I expected no real problems. With her help I struggled into the frame and strapped on the wings. I stood at the top of the cliffs, on a path which led to a small ledge and a bench where courting couples would often stop. I planned to run along the path until I came to the ledge and thus give myself a good launch over the gorge (which had a small river going through it). It was a wonderful morning. Esmé wore a white dress and a red pinafore. I wore my oldest clothes. There was mist coming up from the ravine and the sun shone through it. Above us the sky was a perfect, pale blue, and in the distance the smoke from Podol's tireless factories drifted across the glinting domes and spires of the churches. The morning was very still. As I instructed Esmé how to throw the propeller into motion, the Sunday bells of all our places of worship began to ring at once. I made my first flight to the sound of a hundred pealing tunes!

I remember the way the motor's shriek drowned the bells. Then I was moving. I ran in long strides down the path. Esmé kept pace with me for part of the way, but fell back. Then I had reached the ledge and had spread my arms, brought up my feet—and began to fall . . .

The fall lasted only a few seconds. A movement of my hands and I was gaining height again. I rose higher and higher above the gorge until I could see the whole of Kiev before me, could see the Dnieper stretching back into the steppe, could see it rushing down toward the Zaporozhian rapids on its way to the ocean. I could see forests, villages and hills. And, as I floated downward again, I saw Esmé, red and white, looking at me in wonderment and admiration. It was Esmé's face which distracted me. Somehow I lost control. The motor stopped. There was the noise of rushing air. There was the sound of a scream. Then the bells began to toll again and I was dropping helplessly toward the river at the bottom of the gorge. My thought before my body struck the water was that at least I was to die a noble death. A second Icarus!

TWO

The news of my flight appeared in all the Kiev papers. I had soared over the city for several minutes. This flight was witnessed by many people on their way to Church that Sunday morning. Until the Bolsheviks conquered Ukraine my achievement was a matter of record: I had dived and pirouetted in the clear sky; I had been seen over St. Andrew's, St. Sophia's and St. Michael's. I remember a drawing of me in one of the papers, in which I was shown as perching on the green central dome of the Church of the Three Saints. These records were destroyed by the Cheka in their mad desire to simplify the past. Perhaps they hoped that this would, accordingly, simplify the present which so bewildered them and was so much at odds with their overrationalized creed. If I had been a Communist or a member of their revolutionary youth or some such thing, the story would be quite different. As it was there was more than one worm in my apple. I was pulled out of the river by soldiers who had seen me fall. I awoke briefly (the propeller had dropped forward and stunned me as I landed in the water) to hear one of them laugh and say: "The little Jew was trying to fly!"

My last words before returning to oblivion were: "I am not a Jew. And I did fly." Of course it was a strange coincidence, I suppose, that so many Jewish souls were to fly to Heaven from this very gorge where the Germans set up their notorious death camp during the

Second World War. It is worth noting here that it was by no means only Jews who died in Babi Yar: Slav soldiers and civilians were killed in their thousands, as well. As usual, of course, the Jews receive the full credit for martyrdom while the others are forgotten. They are masters at publicizing their miseries.

Esmé, sliding down the gorge and tearing her dress in an effort to save me, found the soldiers lifting me from the water. It was she who told them where I lived and they carried me back to my mother who immediately fainted and had to be revived by an already somewhat intoxicated Captain Brown, who, a few moments before, had been enlisted to search for me.

One piece of good luck was that the motor was undamaged and was recovered an hour or two later by Sarkis Mihailovitch. I had sustained a broken head, a broken arm and a broken ankle. But I was elated. I had flown! I had proven myself. I would try the experiment again as soon as possible, though next time I decided to employ a smaller child—who would be lighter than myself—and train him to attempt the flight. In that way I could observe what happened if anything went wrong.

During the first days of my confinement to hospital I was visited by Esmé and, anxious to be reassured, asked her to confirm that I had indeed flown. I was delirious and could not trust my own memory. Esmé passionately affirmed the fact that I had achieved the first powered flight without use of an airframe. I stand by her word and the news in the papers which appeared again many years later in a British magazine, *Reveille,* and an American newspaper called *The National Inquirer.* I wish I had the original Russian reports, but they were lost with so much else. Not everyone had faith in me, even then. I was to learn only after some weeks that Sarkis Mihailovitch, alarmed by my borrowing the motor, had decided to dispense with me—partly, I gather, to placate the bakery. My mother said nothing during my period of recuperation. Herr Lustgarten was called in on occasion to keep me in touch with my studies and my mother spent most of her "leisure" time writing long letters to relatives, no matter how distant, concerning my further education. She was selfless beyond common sense where her own good was concerned, and when it came to my well-being, there was nothing she would not try.

Esmé was allowed to visit me and it was to her that I described my plans for a modified "birdman" machine. Speaking to her of those who remained skeptical of my achievement, I mentioned the soldiers' claim that I had merely tumbled down the gorge. She was indignant.

"Of course you flew. Of course you did. You flew for miles and miles. All over Kiev!" This was an exaggeration, naturally, from loyalty, but Esmé was well known for speaking the truth and was called "the little saint" in our neighborhood, for the way she looked after her father.

When Esmé was not there (as all too often she could not be) I contented myself with reading in various languages and drawing up improved plans for my "flying infantry." I wrote letters to our War Office, describing my success, but received no reply. It is quite possible that some jealous bureaucrat, perhaps Sikorsky himself, made sure they never reached the proper hands. I also designed a wrist-teleprinter and worked out a means of bridging the Sea of Azov between Berdyansk and Yeysk, using semibuoyant pontoons. These were just two of many designs which I was to lose during the Civil War, but they were far ahead of their time. I deeply regret not patenting any of my inventions. I was too trusting. The "word of mouth" and "shake of hands" which was good enough for honest people in my boyhood was merely, by the time I reached maturity, the mark of a thorough scoundrel. Had I been less gullible, I would be a millionaire by now. I would have been a millionaire, in fact, many times over, if only on the strength of my Ultra-Violet Light Projector.

Also while in the hospital I evolved my lifeplan, after the German fashion. I drew up a chart of the next few years, with all my various goals carefully listed. There was my education, my government work, my employment of agents to seek out Zoyea for me, the house I intended to buy for my mother where she could be looked after by Esmé and Captain Brown, whom I would employ at good wages. There was no reason to consider this plan unrealistic at the time.

Revolutionists and fanatics again conspired to thwart my destiny, however, when, in August 1914, I was healed enough to consider taking the entrance exams at the Technical School. This time an assassination at Sarajevo—"the shot which rang round the world"—led to that monstrous Armageddon, the First Great War, and my mother told me the disappointing news that Herr and Frau Lustgarten, those gentle scholars, had fled the country, apparently for Bohemia, fearing an expression of anti-German feeling already experienced by a number of people with German-sounding names, particularly those running shops in Kiev's suburbs. So, between the Armenians and the Germans, I was suddenly without tutor or employer!

It was left to my relatives to rescue me. Some of those to whom my mother had written had, by autumn, responded, including my paternal grandparents, whom I never knew, and Uncle Semya. Certainly there was now talk of my going to be educated in St. Petersburg (this delighted me for the best technical schools were there), but first Uncle Semya wanted me to go on holiday, to visit him in Odessa, all expenses paid. He never really explained why he wished to see me. I assumed he wanted to look over his "investment." My mother found Uncle Semya's interest in me rather suspicious. She did not care for him much. It seems to me now that he had come to pin most of his hopes on me, having failed to have sons who cared a lot for education. None of my cousins was particularly literate. I think this was a disappointment to him. He need not have worried. They were prepared for Russia's future. Two of them at least became powerful Commissars during the terrible famines of the twenties and thirties. The Bolsheviks considered brute strength, cunning and blind obedience far more valuable than learning. It did not greatly matter to me why Uncle Semya agreed with my mother, as he agreed on no other subject, in the matter of my improvement. That he was prepared to give me both an education and a holiday was enough. The next few months looked exciting indeed. If I had already astounded Kiev, how might I astound the lazy natives of our Southern and most cosmopolitan metropolis, or the world-weary citizens of the capital itself?

During the three weeks before I left, my mother was in tears. She packed and repacked my few clothes. She made me swear not to fall in with radicals. Not to imitate flashy Odessa ways or speech. She made me promise to have nothing to do with "those crooks of Moldovanka" (readers of the Commissar-journalist Babel will know what I mean). She wept as she reminded me of her husband's guessed-at fate. She wept as she reminded me to change my underwear. She was the most wonderful, caring mother a boy could wish for. I regret, now, that I did not humor her as much as I should have done. My patched-up skull was full of dreams about my future exploits. The night before I was to leave Kiev, Esmé came to our door with a St. Christopher medal which her father had brought back from some foreign land. This she hung, with all proper gravity, around my neck. Then she hugged me. She kissed my cheeks. And she wept. When she had gone, my mother inspected the medal, suspicious that it might be associated in some way with sedition. It was only with reluctance, and some weeping, that she returned it to my neck. I found the medal extremely reassuring and wore it for a long time afterward, to remind me that I had at least one loyal friend in Esmé.

Soon after Esmé had gone, my cousin Alexander arrived. He was called by himself and everyone else "Shura." He was a weasel-faced and cocky youth with the cropped hair and red-and-white checkered neck scarf fashionable amongst his kind at the time. He left his small bag with us, refused my mother's offer of food, condescendingly took half a glass of tea from our old samovar, and went into the city to accomplish some piece of slouching business. He returned with a tin of chocolate and something in a sack which he put immediately into his luggage, to my mother's great anxiety. He had had more than a little vodka (few paid attention to our prohibition laws) and stood at the stove rubbing his hands together and winking at me.

My poor mother came close to fainting and hurried him into our other room where he was to sleep. He did not go to sleep at once. In the darkness, where I lay on my shelf for the last time, I heard him singing some mysteriously lewd song in his soft, trilling Odessa accent, while my mother sniffled complicated counterpoint on her couch. I have every sympathy with her: Shura was not the most reassuring of escorts for a son who was to leave the city for the first time alone.

She accompanied us to the station. Even by September 1914 the train service had begun to be disrupted (though there were extra trains to important places like Odessa) and tickets were becoming hard to acquire. Nonetheless Shura spirited us through all the formalities, through all the early-morning crowds of uniformed police and soldiers and sailors—a sea of multicolored cloth and gold braid—through the sweetmeat sellers, the drinks vendors, the sellers of charts and lurid magazines or newspapers. How Russia was full of men, women and children with trays around their necks in those days.

In his knowledge of the station, its peculiar customs and denizens, Shura at least was able to comfort my mother. "I suppose if you must go into the world, it is better to go with a worldly guide," she said, when he had vanished for a moment to engage some pinch-faced maiden in furious conversation before returning with a swagger and a handful of long-stemmed cigarettes, one of which he offered to me. I refused, of course. My mother told Shura of the dangers of smoking and warned him how upset his Uncle Semya would be if he learned that the "little scholar" had been corrupted. Shura took all this with a kind of pitying tolerance for both of us and then announced that the train was in and that we should board it.

My mother came with us. She followed us along the gangway of our coach, distracting me from my admiration of its wonders: its galley, its stove. This was one of the finest expresses of the South Western Railway: She was a real beauty of a locomotive (probably a 4-6-4, though I cannot now recall the exact type) whose livery of dark green, gold and cream was matched in all the coaches. It was a very long train, comprised entirely of first- and second-class carriages. There was no third-class accommodation on this Kiev–Odessa Express, which could normally do the journey in under fourteen hours. Even the steam from the loco seemed whiter and cleaner and more impressive than the steam from other trains. In some of the further platforms I saw troop transports with heavy artillery on flat-cars and these, together with the large number of armed servicemen in the station itself, were a clear reminder that we were a nation at war. Once again I felt the old urge to don a uniform. I remarked to Shura that he must be looking forward to the moment when he was called to the service of his country. His only response was to puff on his papyrussa cigarette and offer me another of his winks. My mother burst into tears at the thought of my joining the army and she was comforted by the easygoing Shura in that same spirit of tolerant contempt. Through some trick he found us both places in a compartment and let me bid farewell to my mother while he kept the seats for us.

The collar of my new coat was damp with her tears before the guard told her kindly that she must leave. Shura shouted that she should fear nothing, that if the driver lost his way Shura would be able to put him on the right track. This raised a laugh from the other occupants of the carriage and drew a last snuffle or two from my mother, who kissed me and went to stand on the platform, dabbing at her eyes and producing, every so often, a kind of agitated grin. I took my seat. Shura and I stood out from most of the other passengers in that we were younger and did not wear uniform. Most of the people in our carriage were soldiers, sailors and nurses, all of whom were smiling at us with that peculiar complacency those who wear uniform often reserve for those who do not.

I was prepared to sit in my place the whole way, but Shura had me up almost as soon as the train left the station, and my mother's limp and glistening handkerchief, behind. He wanted to show me the first-class carriages. So we made a tour of the train, playing the innocent whenever an official asked us what we were about, telling him that we had lost our carriage.

I was astonished at the luxury of the first class, at the deep-green plush, the polished brass and oak. Shura told me that he had traveled first class more than once, but I did not believe him. He knew, he said, how to act like a gentleman: "It will be my job someday."

I could not imagine what business he planned for himself. What could elevate him permanently to this world of plush and glitter? I did not, however, disapprove of his ambition. Those wonderful carriages looked like the abode of angels and smelled like a well-groomed beast. And the people who inhabited them were demigods. I loved them. I longed to share their life, to be accepted by them.

I was to retain my enjoyment of luxurious travel no matter how frequently I came to experience it. It raised me from the deepest gloom to the highest imaginable sense of well-being. Some years would pass before I was to familiarize myself thoroughly with that most delicious form of transport. It has now all but disappeared from the world. Today it is replaced by the ultilitarianism of plastic and nylon; the bleak, characterless, "efficient" State-operated railways and airlines. And not only the trains have steamed their way into oblivion. The great ships, the monarchs of the Cunard and P&O lines, have gone completely. What do we have instead? Car ferries. No wonder all the transport systems are losing money. What human being really wishes to travel in something resembling a less-than-clean hospital ward? As one who has used every form of modern transport, from the great prewar liners to the sadly missed and much-maligned Zeppelin passenger ships, I can honestly say that democratization has worked entirely against everyone's interest, including the public's. Save for a few pathetic cruise vessels, there is nothing left of the flying boats and luxury steamers which so frequently confirmed the maxim that to travel was better than to arrive.

When I speak nostalgically in the pub about the C-class Imperial Airways planes, I am laughed at openly. Those ignorant polyhybrids occupying their featureless housing estates resent anyone who remembers days when "civilization" was something more than a word for labor exchanges and municipal art galleries. Romance has vanished from their lives.

The sense of comfort and security was everywhere in the train. And it was obvious that many of our fellow passengers shared this mood. Every place in the compartment was, of course, taken. There were uniformed people filling the corridors. It was almost impossible to see past them to the mellow wheatlands of the Ukrainian steppe, now churned with chaff and scattered with sheaves and haystacks, for the harvest had been gathered. The sky had that wonderful pale-gold and silver-blue quality which comes at about nine o'clock in the morning, promising a warm autumn day. The two Catholic nursing nuns, one in her twenties and the other apparently not yet reached maturity, asked if the window could be opened and we all agreed that it would be good to have some fresh air. I offered to open it for them, but failed to understand the sash-cord method. To my great embarrassment Shura had to help me. The wind blew the smell of the countryside, sweet and rich, into my face, and my spirits rose still higher. As well as the nuns, who had the window seats, we shared space with two youngish naval lieutenants; a Cossack captain in grey shapka and caftan, with bullet pouches and a wide belt, into which was stuck a dagger and from which hung a typical Cossack sword; a gentleman in a dark homburg and a coat with an astrakhan collar; and a Greek priest who spoke little Russian but who smiled at us a great deal, as if in blessing. The Cossack captain sat next to Shura and more or less opposite me. He had a clean-shaven jaw but a huge, curling grey mustache with waxed ends. He sat with his saber between his knees, his back stiff and unsupported by the seat behind him, as if he rode an invisible horse. He had that manner Cossacks often have, of his horse never being very far away, and I imagined (though in all likelihood I was wrong) that a box at the end of the train bore a chestnut stallion.

Having asked for the window to be opened, the nuns faced one another, apparently in telepathic communication. They spoke not a word for the whole journey, making it embarrassing when we needed to approach the window to buy something from a platform vendor if the train stopped at a station. These vendors lacked the smoothness of the Kiev hawkers, but they were just as noisy. Barefooted peasant women offered us cakes or fresh milk, and their grandfathers brought up samovars on trolleys and described in husky bellows the refreshing properties of their tea. Children were there in plenty, rarely selling anything, merely begging us for a few kopecks. The nuns would sit with their feet just above the floor of the train, their skirts arranged to cover their toes, while we did everything in our power to avoid contact with them (all, that is, save Shura). It was Shura, half in the carriage after some panting expedition along the platform, who found his hand placed firmly in one's lap and apologized. Later, in the corridor, he murmured some crude speculation when they did not appear to be listening, wondering at their "impossible capacity." I scarcely understood him, but the naval officers, who had overheard, enjoyed the joke. I blushed. The Greek priest laughed uncomprehendingly along with the sailors, while the man in the astrakhan collar grumbled into his copy of *Neeva (The Cornfield)* magazine.

Shura got into conversation with the Cossack, who seemed to like him. The captain said he was a supply officer going to Odessa to arrange for certain provisions and equipment for his unit. He could not, of course, tell us anything more. He was amused when I mentioned that my father had also been a Cossack. Shura laughed, too, telling me to be quiet. Claims of that sort, he said with a look at the captain, could get me into trouble. The navy men were all the way from Moscow, where they had been on leave, and were full of tales about the delights of Russia's second great city. These delights were hinted at with looks and whispers to Shura. He was only a little older than me but seemed far more worldly, understanding the full meaning of their innuendos, made so as not to shock the nuns who, Shura swore, were nonetheless listening avidly.

The good-natured Cossack was soon offering vodka which was accepted by the priest, refused by the gentleman in the hat, ignored by the nuns. He pushed his woolly shapka on the back of his grey head and unbuttoned his caftan to reveal a shirt embroidered in black and red. He had blue breeches and soft leather boots and seemed at once more free and more of a soldier than any others on the train. At our request he showed us his long saber, his shorter dagger and his pistol, but allowed us to handle none of them. Of the saber he said, "It must never be drawn, save to be blooded," though he displayed an inch or two so that we could see the engraving (in Georgian by the look of it) on the hilt. "These blades," he said, "are so sharp that a moth settling on them would find itself cut in half before it realized anything had happened. It would only find out when it tried to fly away again!"

I was considerably impressed. I said that my father must have had a similar sword. He asked me jovially to which *sech* my father had belonged. I said the Zaporozhskaya. He asked me how old my father was. I said I did not know. He asked me if I was sure Father had not been an *inogorodi*. I did not understand him. This was a Cossack word, he explained, for Great Russians living amongst them. The word meant, more or less, outsider. I assured him that my father had never been an outsider. He had served with a Cossack regiment at St. Petersburg. He asked which one. I told him that I did not know.

Again he laughed, evidently pleased that anyone should claim Cossack blood, even if they did not, as he believed, possess it.

I became agitated and insisted that I told the truth. I recall Shura saying flatly: "His dad's dead, see." At which the Cossack softened and patted me on the knee, holding his scabbarded saber out toward me and smiling. "Don't worry, little one. I believe you. We'll soon be riding side by side, you and me. Killing Jews and Germans willy-nilly, eh?" The naval officers (and the echoing priest) joined in his laughter, as did my cousin, and I felt a happy warmth. The train journey remains in my mind as one of the most comradely times of my life. The Cossack's name was Captain Bikadorov.

Shura asked the naval officers how they thought the War was going. What was the atmosphere in Moscow? They said everyone was confident, from the Czar downward. Our allies were predicting that "the Russian steamroller will crush the Germans in weeks." Tannenberg had been an untypical setback due to our overconfidence. We had learned our lesson over Japan and were now the strongest we had ever been. We would play the game of war more cautiously but more effectually. "Particularly," one of them pointed out, "now that Japan is our ally!" This created further trumpetings from the gentleman in the homburg.

"And the Turks?" I said. "When shall they be beaten and the Czar attend Mass in the Hagia Sophia in Constantinople?"

"Just let them start something now and they're as good as finished," said Captain Bikadorov. "Though there isn't a better enemy than your Turk." It would be good to free "Czsargrad" (Constantinople) but it was the French he was unsure about. They had gone soft, since Napoleon. They had already been beaten over and over again by the Germans. Moreover he was not sure that the English were reliable allies, "since they're almost Germans themselves." But the French were the real weak link. The naval officers agreed that in their experience of the French they had met in Odessa, "the frog-eater is as effete as he is grandiose." It was impossible, the older one added, for a Frenchman to think of himself as mortal. The moment the conception impinged (usually when the real fighting started) he became outraged. "They are not cowards. They are merely possessed of a divine pomposity!"

The gentleman behind *Neeva* rose, bowed to the naval officer, and said that he was a native of Odessa and that he had the honor of bearing a French name. His grandfather had been French. He sat down again, raised his *Neeva*, then, as if upon reflection, lowered it again to add: "Napoleon was defeated not by our soldiers, my friends, but by our snow. And for our snow we have only God to thank."

"And I say thank God for our soldiers as well," said Shura.

At this second mention of the divinity the Greek priest clapped his hands together while the nuns turned their heads with one accord toward the windows.

Asking the nuns to speak up if they objected to his smoking, Captain Bikadorov took out a large pipe and began to fill it, while Shura, encouraged by his example, offered some of his papyrussa round the carriage. The naval lieutenants accepted, the old gentleman of French origin refused with a snort (but drew out a cigar as soon as everyone else was smoking) and soon the carriage was full of tobacco fumes. Happily, the window was open, which meant that neither the nuns nor myself were greatly inconvenienced. Now I associate the smell with the pleasantness of the occasion. So euphoric did I feel that later, after we had enjoyed a shared picnic in which all but the nuns and the old gentleman joined, I took my first puff at Shura's cigarette. I regretted the sausage, bread, pieces of crumbed veal and chicken, and even the tea we had bought at the station. My discomfort was mingled with a rather pleasant, dizzy sensation. I disembarked at the next station. I think it was Kazatin, a very pleasant place with willow trees and carved gables and pillars. I took another cigarette at Shura's insistence. Always get back on the horse as soon as you've fallen off, he said. Under his charming influence (and he had a very persuasive manner) I began to experience, for the first time in my life, a sense of the joys of sin. We rushed back, with everyone else, as the train began to move. We flung ourselves past the knees of the nuns. Reseated, Shura offered me a sip of Bikadorov's vodka. I winked back and accepted.

I think I was a little drunk by the evening. I watched the red-and-black clouds roll by on a wide horizon silhouetted with the occasional steeple or dome, the outline of an entire whitewashed village, the slender poplars and cypresses on the estates of kindly landowners who might have been those described by Tolstoi before he went mad. As the sun set, the Cossack captain began to sing a melancholy song about a girl, a horse, a river and a shroud. He tried to get us to join the chorus, but only Shura seemed able to learn it:

Dead eyes gleam from below the water,
The white mane waves in the wind,
Good-by, little Katya, the snow is coming.

And so on. It is the other side of the Cossack temperament. If he is
not riding his horse into battle and slicing off heads, he loves to sing
about the sadness of death and the loss of loved ones. In his deep,
almost superstitious, respect for religion and his relish for mournful
songs, he has something in common with the American Negro. I
make this observation, one familiar to those who know me, to show
I have no racial prejudice. Acceptance of a race's characteristics
leads to an understanding, not a hatred, of that race. I am the first
to say how much I respect the Jew's brain. Nobody can doubt his
cleverness or his ability to tell a good joke on himself.

It seemed a little chilly to me when we eventually arrived at Glav-
naya Station, the main terminal of Odessa, situated in the heart of the
city. Yellow gas- and oil lamps, as well as the glare of electrical
bulbs, illuminated the massive enclave. It might have been a Michel-
angelo cathedral, with such a wealth of sights and smells I immediately felt twice as drunk as I had been. Shura showed his usual
alacrity in getting us off the train. He waved a friendly farewell to
Bikadorov and the lieutenants, made a deep, grave bow to the nuns,
a sardonic genuflection to the old gentleman, then ushered me with
astonishing speed through the crowd, through officials, ticket col-
lectors, soldiers, sailors, hucksters, painted ladies, family groups,
Greeks, Hasidim, stiff-backed khaki Englishmen and out into a street
full of gaslight and shadow.

"Shouldn't we get a cab here, Shura?" I remembered my mother's
instructions.

"If you want to pay fifty kopecks for nothing," he said. "Anyway,
they'll be gone. Come on."

Behind all the other smells of spice and perfume I could detect
another scent which seemed borne on a Southern wind. It was salt. It
was sweet ozone. I realized with heady enthusiasm that it was the
sea.

Out of the night, like a beast from the ocean depths, came a two-
car Odessa tram: cream and brass, with lights blazing. And then we
were aboard it, our fares paid by Shura, sitting on the big wooden
seats and peering through the windows. "You'll see little but shit

tonight," said Shura. "I'll take you to some real sights tomorrow." He had asked for "the Goods Station." Were we going to catch another train? "Just to the corner of Sirotskaya and Khutorskaya," he said. These were obviously thoroughfares. I did not want him to explain any more. I was enjoying the magic of a strange city and would have resented any description of its limits. I have always hated to be given a map to a new city, unless it is absolutely necessary.

Disembarking from the tram, we carried our bags across a cobbled street and along beside a park full of big trees. We crossed another street and entered a well-lit square consisting of large residential houses, flats and shops. At the steps of one of the houses we stopped. Next to the house was a set of offices bearing the surname of my great uncle. We had arrived.

Shura led the way up the steps and pulled the bell. We were admitted by a dumpy maid who showed a friendly disrespect for my cousin. We entered a well-furnished parlor. Almost immediately a large, dark-eyed woman in a green silk dress billowed in on us. "You were to telephone, Shura? We'd have sent a cab or the carriage. How did you get here?"

"Tram," was Shura's laconic answer.

She was distressed, but smiled at him. "You should have waited for your Uncle Semya to order . . ."

"We'd be waiting still in that mob," Shura told her. "Have you seen it recently? It's madness with the War on. Cabs? You'd be lucky."

She patted his crew cut. "Semya still has some business. He would have liked . . . Ah, well . . ."

I lowered my bags to the carpet. She spread her arms. "Maxim!" A sigh. "I am your Aunt Genia."

We embraced.

"We are so pleased, you know. And how is your dear mother?"

"She is well, thank you, Aunt Genia."

"Such a burden. And such a brave woman. But so proud. Well, there is pride and pride."

I accepted the praise, detecting no criticism of my mother. I was to guess, when I reviewed the past, that there had been rivalry between the women. Perhaps my Aunt Evgenia, my mother's sister-in-law, had offered charity which had been refused. Perhaps they had even loved the same man, my father. Families are full of such ordinary jealousies. They are not even worth puzzling over. How some people will alter the past. I have seen mature men and women become utter fools in their attempts to pretend things happened in ways other than in actuality. We all like to see ourselves in a good light, of course, but the lengths to which some go are quite astonishing.

We sat for about twenty minutes in the parlor while Aunt Genia warbled on like a restful canary. I realized that my eyelids were beginning to droop just as she became a macaw:

"*Food!*"

I grew alert. We entered another room. The place was a castle. Here were red-and-white German soup plates and a tureen of borscht decorated with scenes of Danzig or Munich. There were two different kinds of bread, already sliced, and butter. I sat down at once, but Shura shook his head and said he had to leave.

I had learned never to refuse food. Also I was becoming so unable to distinguish reality from imagination by that time that I thought a meal would help bring me down to earth. It was wonderful borscht. It was an Odessa borscht, like drinking rubies. It was spicy and filling. While Aunt Genia continued to talk, I ate steadily. I was swollen by the time the macaw squawked again:

"*Bed!*"

The dumpy girl with ginger hair and a good-humored face reappeared. She was some sort of poor relation working as a servant. "Wanda. Take Maxim Arturovitch to his room."

My case was picked up in one wet, red hand, while the other gestured to the door. I followed. Aunt Genia chirruped a goodnight and kissed me. I should ask Wanda for anything I required. Off we went, up flights of dark, heavily carpeted stairs, with each landing smelling a little differently, until we were at the top of the house and Wanda opened a door. "I'm next to you," she said. She entered ahead of me into bronze half-light and reached to turn a tap to make the gas glow a little brighter. "Here we are."

I had not realized I was to have an entire room to myself. A real bed, dressing table, chest of drawers, blinds I could open or shut at will, a window: I went to my window. It looked out onto the square —a haze of yellow lamps and dark shadows. From one of the distant, mysterious houses came a high-pitched laugh, something of a wail, which echoed in the square, for it was late and even Odessa was half-asleep. Wanda's warm, smelly body came up behind me. She showed me how to work the blinds. "Best keep 'em shut if you've got the gas going," she said. "Moths." Her voice was lazy, soft and friendly. I was to discover later that this was a typical Southern voice, but I thought then that she was being especially pleasant. Even this heavy-featured creature rolled her r's with an emphasis which must surely be sexual. I had not heard her properly. "What?"

"Moths."

"Aha." I was reminded of the moth on the Cossack saber. I recalled the wonder of my trip, the swooning pleasure of my first impressions. I almost wept as I thanked Wanda and watched her leave. I had a bolt on my door. I had water in a jug on a washstand. I had a chamber pot and a rug, and clean, white sheets and a patchwork quilt and two pillows in embroidered cases. What generous relatives. And how rich. I had had no conception of their wealth. Mother had told me they were well off but she had never mentioned that they owned an entire building, possibly two (for there were the offices next door). Again I went to the window. The heavy scent of stocks and dying lilac ascended from the square. I felt a breath or two of the southern wind, of the warm night sea. Then I went to bed. Determined to enjoy my freedom to the full, I masturbated for a short while, thinking of Wanda and her large, passive body, then of Zoyea and finally, when it was over, of "the little angel," Esmé. How she would be impressed by my stories of Odessa. I lay on my back in the darkness looking out at the open window, enjoying the disquieting thrill of being in a room alone at night for the first time. I put my hands behind my head. I smiled with delight at the luxury. I addressed imaginary friends and told them of my luck. I realized as I went to sleep that in my half-dream I had been copying Shura's confident gestures. I was already half in his power. And I was glad of it.

THREE

I awoke in the warmth of the sun's rays, blinking. I listened for a moment and heard all kinds of alien sounds: the clanking of trams, the shunting of goods trains, horses' hooves and cart wheels on cobbles; shouts, laughter. And there was an astonishing smell: a mixture of the ocean and of deliciously rotting fruit and flowers, as if all the foliage of the Eastern seas had come in on the morning tide. I went slowly to my window. Many of the stately houses of the square were still shut up, for it was only a little past dawn. And Odessa had her autumn aurora. Each roof, railing, brick, tree, bush and wall gave off luminescence. The mellow colors shimmered almost imperceptibly in the city's glowing air.

Kiev had its beauty, but it was a prosaic beauty compared to this glorious enchantment. Every outline, whether it be animal, vegetable, stone or wood, was surrounded by a faint radiance. A red-and-gold automobile crossed the square to stop outside a newly opened grocery shop. It was like a car from fairyland. The men and women in it wore white suits, peacock feathers, Japanese silks, patent leather, and seemed to have come from a splendid performance of *The Merry Widow*.

I expected to hear music at any moment, but this was the only sensation lacking. I craned over the small, wrought-iron railing and peered in what I hoped was the direction of the sea. All I saw was pavements, trees, possibly a park. I smelled coffee. I saw girls in black-and-white uniforms come out into the street bringing jugs to be filled from a milkman's cart. I smelled fresh bread and identified the source, a baker's shop at the far corner of the square. A postman went slowly along the street, delivering his letters. Women called to one another from house to house. This was how I had imagined a city like Paris, but never our own Odessa. It was possible to understand why many Russians found the town vulgar, and why so many writers and painters loved it. Pushkin had chosen to live here, for instance.

I was at once stimulated and relaxed. I was on holiday. The conception had not dawned until that moment. A holiday, for instance from school, was when one worked at home. But here, as far as I knew, I had no work to do. I was a guest. I was to be entertained. I began to feel hungry.

Wanda was knocking on my door and calling to me. I realized I was naked and felt ashamed of my body perhaps for the only time (though I remained ashamed, all my life, of my father's mark on my penis). Possibly I remembered my dream of Wanda. I called out to her to wait and I pulled on my trousers and shirt. I unbolted the door and she entered, laughing. "Modest little boy!" She was only a year older, but all Odessans are far older, it seems, than Kievans. They give the impression of being possessed by some ancient, sardonic wickedness. Perhaps it is the admixture of blood. There are strains of every country in the world in the Odessan blood. But most typically from the Near East. Odessa itself is named after the Greek hero Odysseus and about half its population at that time was Jewish or foreign. It is probably why the pogroms were so severe there in the early years of the century. People were jealous of the power of the interlopers, though I would be the first to admit Odessa owed its atmosphere to its exotic population. By no means only Jews and criminals lived in the Moldovanka. Fiction has colored the area, particularly in the work of Isaak Babel, who lived there for no more than a week and was driven out by angry residents resenting his prying and his distortions. They say someone was murdered as a result of a lie he had written. My Uncle Semyon was a respectable merchant, for instance, trading with dozens of foreign countries through his shipping office. He undertook the import or export of goods of every sort. He had twenty or thirty clerks working full time in his office next door and never once was there a hint of scandal about his activities. Neither, I should add, did anyone ever attempt to raid him and steal the wage money in his safe.

They say the Russian disease is a poor sense of what is real and what is not, that we think we can talk anything into reality. This may be so. I personally can distinguish readily enough between truth and fiction.

Wanda had brought me a "small breakfast," some coffee and a roll, on a tray. The luxuries were continuing. She seemed brighter this morning and her words had less sexual significance. Perhaps her voice had been tired the night before and I had mistaken weariness for mystery. I was able to greet her quite normally and accept the tray. "What am I supposed to do after I've eaten this?"

"I'll go and find out." She twisted ginger hair at her neck. "Madame's in a good mood. M'sieu, too."

I was to become used to the frequent use of French in Odessa. The city thought of itself as half-French already, though in fact the greatest number of foreigners had been German, publishing their own newspaper, *Odessaer-Zeitung*. Many of the books I read while there were German.

Eventually it was my cousin Shura, not Wanda, who came for me. He looked rather more respectable this morning, in a shirt, a bow tie, a grey three-piece suit. He carried a straw boater in his hand. He was a kindhearted youth and had realized I would feel strange in the new city. He entered without knocking, leaning against the doorframe and winking as usual. Then he closed the door and asked if the clothes I wore (a perfectly good dark jacket and pair of knickerbockers) were what I actually preferred. I pointed out that I had little else. He said "something would be done," then advised me to part my hair with an English parting, in the middle, and offered me his comb, which smelled of brilliantine. I accepted and made a poor attempt at the parting. He sat me down in front of my little dressing table and, tongue between his teeth, produced a precise line. Then he ran the comb thoughtfully through his own cropped locks and nodded his satisfaction. I put on pullover and jacket. "I suppose it's fair enough," said Shura. "They expect you to look like a schoolboy."

"I am a schoolboy," I pointed out. "It's why Uncle Semya sent for me. To see who he's sending to school."

Shura grinned cynically. "Of course he is, the old philanthropist."

I became angry. "He is very kind. He has done a great deal for my mother and myself. He has faith in me. More real faith than my own father had!"

Shura softened. "You're right. Come on, then."

We passed a blushing Wanda on the stairs. She seemed as fascinated by Shura as I was. He pinched her cheek and whispered something in her ear. She groaned cheerfully and continued on her way.

We descended. We descended farther. There were smells of food. We reached the tiled main floor of the house. Sunlight came through stained glass. It shone on hangings, on paintings, on hat stands and mirrors. We moved toward the back of the house, past the parlor where I had met Aunt Genia, past the dining room where I had eaten my first meal, and came to a mahogany door on which Shura, suddenly grave, knocked.

"Come in." The voice was open, welcoming. We entered. "Maxim Arturovitch, your great-uncle, Semyon Josefovitch."

I had expected a burly patriarch, a bogatyr with a long grey beard, wearing a business suit. I encountered a small man with pointed features, a pointed beard, a linen jacket and trousers, a glossy collar under which was a neatly knotted old-fashioned black string-tie against a starched shirt front. His hands had silver rings on them and a dab or two of ink. He seemed shy. He removed his glasses, which he flourished in his left hand as, with his right, he reached toward me across the room. He grasped my arm at the elbow, then found my hand, which he pressed and shook. He was only a few inches taller than I. "My boy. My nephew. My niece's only child. What a pleasure. Is your mother as proud of you as she should be? As proud as I am of her. I am your Great-Uncle Semya. Shura has told you. He has looked after you. He is a good boy. But you must teach him your learning. You are to become the wise man of the family, eh?" He stroked his pointed beard with his spectacles, as if in delight at the idea. "You will go to Peter and be Jesus in the Synagogue, eh?" Peter was what many people called St. Petersburg. Great-Uncle Semya had a way of speaking which was more precise than most Odessan speech, but from time to time he would drop into an Odessan accent, as if for emphasis. "You will come back to us and be our voice. You have no vocation for law?"

"I fear not, Semyon Josefovitch . . . Science is—"

"Quite so. A lawyer in the family is not to be. Not yet. But a scientist mixes well, of course. A professor comes into social contact with lawyers—and there you have what is almost as good as a lawyer in the family. Advocates in Odessa, little Max, are all scoundrels. It can be said, I suppose, of most professions. But once you are part of the intelligentsia, then you have access to the best scoundrels, eh? They admit you to their secrets. They treat you as one of their own.

You are the only intellectual we have. You are precious to us. You are to be our family's pride. Do you like Shakespeare? Puccini? So do I. We'll go to the opera and the theater together."

I began to understand why Uncle Semya wished so much for me to do well at St. Petersburg. All his other relatives were succeeding in various mercantile lines. I was the member of the family destined to pursue more abstract affairs.

"Has Shura offered to show you the city?" Uncle Semya asked. "He must. I would do so myself, but there is the office. Ships and tides wait for nobody. Soap must go to Sevastopol. Coffee must come from Rio. Even though the German mines threaten peaceful vessels. Not that the War is bad for business. Indeed, it is very good for business. If business can be allowed to carry on. Let Shura show you our Odessa. You will love it." He opened his jacket and found his wallet. He gave Shura a ten-ruble note. "Have a nice lunch somewhere at my expense. I shall see you this evening at dinner. Farewell. And do not overtax the brains while you are here. Save them for St. Petersburg." He rolled the *r* in each syllable with relish, as if he described some edible delicacy. And we were dismissed.

Outside my great-uncle's study we found Aunt Genia. She had a pile of pale clothing in her arms. "You can't go out in all that stuff. It's too warm even now. Here are Vanya's things. They'll fit you. And he has his uniform." Her son was already in the army. She was a good deal younger than Uncle Semya. Wisely he had waited until his business was well established before deciding to marry. I thought I would follow his example. My father, after all, had married young and no good had come of that.

With Vany's old summer clothes we climbed the stairs again. Under Shura's eye I donned a chocolate-brown suit, a silky shirt with a soft collar, a panama hat. They seemed ineffably loud and tasteless garments to my Northern eye, but Shura sighed with pleasure. "Quite the dandy," he said. "Vanya used to cut a dash around here before they caught him."

"Caught him?"

"For the army."

Vanya was to be killed six months later. I was never able to thank him for his part in helping me fit into the life of the "Russian Riviera."

I left my knickerbockers hanging over the rail of my bed. Arm in arm with Shura I returned downstairs, sang out a farewell to Aunt Genia and Wanda, who were up to something domestic in the parlor, and sallied into the square.

From high above, the square had seemed like a fantasy land, a set for a musical comedy. Seen close up it was even more magical. It had filled up since the early morning. Now there were stalls erected around the little central park where men in peaked caps and dark aprons strolled, chatting to one another. Fat women in red or blue headscarves piled bottles and boxes in intricate, vulnerable displays. Fruit and vegetables, some of them strange to my eye, and flowers and cloth added further color. Large trees shaded green canvas awnings. There was a smell of horses, of sweetstuffs, of blood (as butchers spread wares on wooden slabs and waved away flies). Yet still the dominant smell was of ozone and flowers. Dogs barked at small boys with parcels who ran about apparently at random. A hurdy-gurdy man began to strap on his instrument. He was shouted at by a huge, round-faced woman in a Ukrainian blouse and went off without playing a note.

From far away I heard long moaning sounds and short hootings which could be the sirens of ships. Shura asked me if I wished to take the tram to the harbor or if I would rather walk. I told him I wanted to walk, even though I was anxious to reach the sea. "Right," he said, "then we'll go through the old cemetery. It's quickest from here." We turned a corner into a street. Though it was full of people complaining about the water cart coming past and soaking their boots, it seemed almost hushed. Dazed, I turned next into a main street in time to see a squadron of cavalry, its lances decorated with little pennants, its red-and-blue hussars' uniforms looking rather ordinary in that multicolored scene (I think they were part of a recruiting parade). We went through a gate into the stillness of the old cemetery: grandiose monuments of black marble, granite and limestone, huge mausoleums, ancient willows. As we got to the other side, Shura said it was possible to climb through a gap in the wall. But he did not want to spoil either his suit or mine. "I don't very often come here, these days," he said, wishing to make it clear he had put away childish things.

Another big street, more like Kreshchatik it seemed to me. It was very wide and lined with trees (elms, I think). Luxurious shops, shaded by blue-and-white blinds; kiosks like miniature Gothic cathedrals; little wooden stands where veterans sold newspapers to fashionable ladies carrying sunshades of white brocade or Japanese silk. Horse cabs—the open four-wheelers with smartly uniformed drivers (*izvoshchiks*, we called them)—in which you could recline, if you wished, like an Oriental prince, stood at curbs waiting for customers to come from hotels, restaurants, shops and offices. In those days there were almost always more cabs than customers. These days there are more cabs, but almost anyone thinks they can use them. I have seen working-class women with four or five children hailing London taxis.

The streets of Odessa went on forever. By the time we caught a glimpse of the sea, between two tall buildings, I was almost exhausted. Then we climbed iron steps and stood on a railway bridge looking out toward the harbor and saw green water and all the ships, and I became incapable of speech.

Shura was certain I was disappointed. "Wait until you see it farther up. That's where the pleasure boats are. Look back."

I turned to stare at the curving expanse of the great stone mole which stretched, it seemed to me, for miles out to sea. I looked beyond the mole to the horizon. It went on and on, as wide, as holy, as the steppe. The rest of the world became suddenly far away and at the same time more real to me. Beyond that horizon lay China and America and England and the ships I saw (some were warships coaling up) had been there, could take me to them. I saw little tugs chugging about the harbor, turning the green water white; the indolent smoke of the big liners; the red hulls of the tramp steamers; all through a luminous network of cranes and derricks.

"I'll admit," said Shura, "that it's probably just what I'm used to. I grew up with it. That's why I love it." He began to move across the bridge. "We'll go to the steps. You'll be impressed with those. And we could take a tram down to Fountain or go to the limans. Have you heard of the limans?" I knew of Odessa's salty inland lagoons where the well-to-do went for their health. But I had no wish to see them. I wanted only to stand on that bridge, while trains grunted back and forth below my feet between the main railway station and the harbor station, and dream of Shanghai and San Francisco and Liverpool as I had never dreamed. I was reluctant to take even one more step forward until pulled by Shura. "Listen, there's lots more. Better." I did not, at that moment, have the will to speak and reassure him, but I let him drag me along, down to the harbor, past sheds and warehouses and the noble funnels of the great ships, past another mole and an entirely different harbor (Odessa had many), past all the fascinating machinery of loading and unloading, of coaling and repairing, past stores which sold tackle and provisions, until later the road alongside the sea became a promenade, with trees and green-painted wrought iron instead of cranes, and it was possible to make out another harbor, where little yachts and paddle steamers sailed rapidly about. Shura brought me to the bottom of the famous granite staircase, scene of the distasteful "Odessa Steps" episode in a Bolshevik film called *Potemkin*.

To me it looked like the stairway to heaven. Behind us was the Nicholas Church, with its golden dome. I wanted to carry on along the harbor, but Shura insisted we cross to the right-hand side of the steps. Here a ticket officer accepted four kopecks for us both and admitted us into a little funicular carriage. As soon as the guard thought there were enough passengers to justify the ascent, we began to move up the cliff. I watched the sea become greener and the horizon grow wider as we climbed to the top and emerged into the warmth and privilege of the Nicholas Boulevard. Here, Shura said, the fashionable people of Odessa were always to be seen during the summer. Here were restaurants and hotels looking out to sea. Immediately below was the Coaling Harbor where two frigates and a gunboat of the Imperial Fleet flew an impressive number of colors. On one side of us were neoclassical buildings and on the other were the trees of the pleasure gardens. We heard sounds of a band. Private carriages came and went. Elegant ladies and gentlemen strolled the promenade. The noises of the harbor were muted, almost courteous.

I was very glad now that I wore Vanya's suit, for here everything was light: white silks and ostrich feathers and pale frock coats and cream-colored uniforms. The steps actually did lead to heaven.

"Now we go down again." Shura took my arm. Slowly we descended past souvenir sellers, newspaper vendors, hawkers of toys and photographs. Shura bought us ice creams and pointed far away to the right. There was Fountain, with its summer dachas and its parks. You could look in one direction at the sea and back in the other at the steppe. But the "really rich pickings" were on our left, the limans and health resorts. "There are lots of silly old ladies who have nothing to do but cash checks all day, or get someone to cash them for them. There are casinos, too. I have friends in the casinos. We'll go there one evening." In the distance were more fine buildings, churches and monuments (Odessa was full of them) and more green spaces. "A lot of really rich people live up there. They live in impregnable fortresses. They're only vulnerable when they go strolling on the Nickita, or go shopping in Wagner's."

I could not quite come to understand what Shura meant. Was he envious of the rich? Did he have revolutionary sympathies? He never displayed them openly. Perhaps it was the way all Odessans thought and spoke?

Shura led me back into the city. I had hoped to eat lunch in one of the small cafés overlooking the harbor. He told me that they were too expensive. The food was poor. "We'll go to one of my regular places. You'll meet my friends." This prospect alarmed me. I had never been able to mix very well with other people. But my mood was far more relaxed than usual. I walked with Shura through pink sunlight admiring all the advertisements, even those which suggested I join the army. Most of the foreign signs were in languages I could read, though some were in Greek or in Asian script which was meaningless to me, in spite of my Podol-learned smattering of Hebrew. Odessa seemed at once the oldest and most modern of cities. Like New York she combined all nations in one. The streets were crowded with soldiers and sailors from the harbor. There were French, Italians, Greeks and Japanese. There were also some Turkish sailors, mainly from merchant ships, together with Englishmen of all ranks. The Turks and Japanese stuck together in larger numbers. They were regarded as the next best thing to German belligerents in a town so closely involved with the War. We were not so far from the Galician front and since our initial successes in East Prussia we had had some setbacks.

The city was, in Shura's words, "a bit too full," but it meant good business for the natives. The black market was booming; the whores were "having to take on three customers at a time. They'd take on four if they had bigger bellybuttons." So innocent was I that I had absolutely no idea, then, what he meant.

We dashed through crowds of Frenchmen who were far more bewildered than I. Because of Shura I had begun to feel as if I had always lived in Odessa. We jumped for our lives in front of screaming two-car trams, caused Steiger horses to rear, made old ladies shout after us, and we laughed at all of them. We ogled the crowded windows of the Magasin Wagner (Odessa's Harrods) and flirted with the flower girls there, then we left the more fashionable streets and entered a labyrinth of smaller alleys. This was a ghetto. Tiny shops sold secondhand boots and tools; Jewish butchers and bakers advertised in Yiddish; tailors and funeral parlors and circumcision salons (as we called Jewish grog shops) were side by side. There were washing lines and yelling children and garrulous old women and bargaining, black-clad Hasidic men, and rabbis and beggars and a richer mixture of junk, canned goods, peasant carvings, German toys, ready-made clothing, hardware goods, poultry, live birds, fishing gear, musical instruments, cooked food than I have seen before or since. Like the Jews themselves, the district repulsed and attracted, was frightening and romantic, comforting and disturbing, and if I had been alone I would never have dared enter it.

Shura ducked with me into one of those dingy little Slobodka basements, and through a battered door we entered the noisy, smoky gloom of a tavern. There were old travel posters decorating the walls, all of which had been scribbled on with sardonic comments. On the floor were the remains of fancy tiles. At the far end was a tiled counter with a monstrous samovar and two jugs for dispensing vodka or grenadine. Behind this sat an ancient, bearded Jew with his hand on an iron cashbox and a permanent expression of mixed ferocity and benevolence. He was dressed almost entirely in black, save for a collarless grey shirt, his waistcoat buttoned in spite of the smoke and heat. Shura greeted the Jew in tones of bantering familiarity and got no response save a slight inclination of the head. There were women and girls here, as well as youths and men, all dressed in the flashy Odessa styles, eating exactly the same dishes—a thick borscht, *kleftikon* (lamb's knuckle), a *shashlik* (shish kebab) in tasty, greasy sauce, with macaroni and black bread. There was also a plate of peppers, pickled cucumbers and tomatoes, known as a salad. There might have been other kinds of food sold in "Esau the Hairy's," as the place was known, but I never saw it eaten and never had the nerve to order it. A thin-faced, haughty black-eyed Jewess brought Shura and me bowls of borscht and some bread almost as soon as we had found a place to sit. I was a little nervous; my mother had never liked me to associate with Jews, but they seemed to accept me quite readily and I was prepared to live and let live. Indeed, I must say I felt almost at home amongst Odessa's Jews, who are really a different race.

Near the counter, one booted foot on a bench, an accordionist played topical songs about well-known actors and actresses, about Rasputin, about our defeats and victories in the War, about local celebrities (these were the most popular, but obscure to me). I was more disturbed by the songs than the company. Some of the songs seemed dangerously radical. I whispered to Shura that the tavern was likely to be raided by the police. This made Shura laugh. "It's protected by Misha," he told me. "And Misha rules Slobodka district.

Nobody—the army, the police, the Czar himself—would dare raid Esau's. Only Misha would dare, and why should he? It's one of his investments." I asked who Misha was and several of the other customers overheard me and clapped me on the shoulder. "Ask who or what God is!" said one. They were referring, I discovered, to a notorious local gangster, the Al Capone of Odessa, known as Misha the Jap. He was supposed to have five thousand men at his command and the authorities were inclined to parley with him rather than threaten him. Almost everyone in Odessa had a nickname. I was to find myself introduced by Shura as "Max the Hetman" because of my reference on the train to my Cossack blood. "He's Hetman of Kiev," said Shura.

Although his friends took this as a joke, they also looked at me with respect. I began to realize I had been accepted. A day before, I should have been horrified at finding myself in the company of these bohemians, but now I had learned Odessan tolerance. I determined not to judge them by their appearance, just as they did not judge me. Shura had a knack for making the most of himself and those he knew. He was at once admired and admiring of all. He was a great favorite in Esau's with the older men and women. He had dozens of friends of his own age. He would boast of each of them: "This is Victor the Fiddler, he'll be a great musician one day. This is Isaac Jacobovitch, the smoothest spieler in the market. This is Little Grania, you should see her dance. Meet Boris—he may not look much, but figures are magic to him, everyone wants him to do their accounts. Lyova here is a better painter than Manet, ask him to invite you to his room. Buy a picture while you can—the canvases. A new Chagall!"

Everyone was a hero or heroine in Shura's words and, although he spoke lightly and was never taken very seriously, he could somehow dignify the meanest person and bring them to life. Before lunch was over, I myself has become the great inventor of my age, with patents pending on a dozen different machines, with ten gold medals from the Academy, with a career in Petersburg already guaranteed. I began to believe it. At least, I believed in Shura's optimism. He was to remain an optimist all his days.

I was intoxicated on vodka and grenadine and on the company of young girls in petticoats and bright blouses, with their thick, dark hair, kindly, Oriental eyes, brilliant laughter and rapid, trilling, almost incomprehensible, patios. The world had ceased to consist entirely of duty and education. It could be amusing, pleasurable. I began to laugh. I tried to join in a song, my arm around a fat matron smelling of cologne and Georgian wine who tried to help me with the words.

While I sang I saw someone point in our direction. A man in a pin-striped suit, with a yellow waistcoat, yellow bow tie, yellow-and-white two-toned shoes, stood in the doorway fingering his mustache. He seemed uncertain of himself and yet supremely arrogant. He was like a king mingling with commoners whose activities were not entirely clear to him. He pushed between the tables and came over to Shura. He spoke politely in perfect Russian. I turned my head and said he must be French. He smiled faintly and said he was. We conversed for a few sentences. Then he gave his whole attention to Shura, whom he knew. "I'm still interested in the dental supplies. They're hard to get in Paris now."

"The War's creating all sorts of shortages, M'sieu Savitsky." Shura was amused. "Last year you were in the export business. Now you're in the import business. You'll find the Dutchman easy to deal with. He has something of a habit himself and his connections are astonishing."

"Where shall we find him?" Savitsky wished to know.

"You'd better let me arrange the meeting. He doesn't like callers at his surgery. Got some paper?"

Savitsky produced a silver-covered notepad. Shura took a pencil and wrote a few words. "See you there at about six. I won't let you down."

Savitsky squeezed Shura's shoulder. "I know. I hear he's almost one of the firm."

I had been feeling twinges of toothache since my accident, perhaps a loose molar. When Savitsky had left, I asked about the dentist.

Shura smiled. "All the family goes to him. If you've got toothache, he's the one to see. He's posh, but we have mutual investments, so it's cheaper using him. And you're guaranteed the best job in Odessa. You can come some time when I go. Perfect excuse."

I said if the toothache got worse I would take Shura up on his offer. My family's connections seemed to cut across all normal social barriers. This might not appear unusual in England or America, but in Russia in 1914 there was an almost infinite number of castes. Only in bohemian or intellectual circles could there be any mixture, and even here it was often strained. That was why I think Esau's in Slobodka so impressed me. I was never to recapture that particular experience of comradeship. Doubtless I felt it as I did because I had no knowledge of any underlying tensions in the relationships there. I was, in a word, innocent. Nonetheless I lost preconceptions and prejudices overnight. I was not to learn common sense for a few months, at least. I would grow up in Odessa.

"He's a Dutchman," Shura added, "though I'll swear he's a Hun in disguise. I hope no one finds out."

"You mean a spy?" I asked. I had read the newspapers.

"That's a thought." Shura grinned. "It's not exactly what I meant. Come on. We've time to go to Fountain. You ought to see a bit of country. And I could do with the fresh air."

"I'd rather stay here," I said.

He was pleased with this. "You can come back again as often as you like, now that you're known as a friend of mine."

As we left, everyone was singing an ironic song about a Chinaman who had fallen in love with a Russian girl and, thwarted in his passion, had burned down her entire apartment building. This had actually happened a short while ago in Sevastopol. The Chinese have always been mistrusted in Russia. The irony was, of course, that they would be seen working hand-in-glove with the Jews during the Revolution: the Jews with their brains, the Chinese with their cruelty. We Slavs can be excused for our wariness of the Oriental, whatever his guise, for he has sought to encroach on our territory for hundreds, if not thousands, of years.

Shura took us to the tram stop in a quiet, wide street. Eventually we boarded a Number 16 for Little Fountain. From a seat near the front Shura pointed out various places of interest, none of which I remembered. I have a memory for tram numbers and people's names, but I can never remember much about cathedrals or museums. We left the long, straight streets behind us and entered more open country. Beyond it was the broad emerald sea. Shura said we should not have time to stay. We took the open-sided tram for Arcadia and went straight back on it. He had to get me home for supper and had some business at six. Innocently I asked him what his main business was. I thought I must have embarrassed him, but he remained cheerful enough, though vague. "I fix things up for anyone. But I work mostly for the family."

"For Uncle Semya."

"That's right. To do his buying and selling, his importing and exporting, he needs information. I'm a sort of liaison officer."

I understood how Shura's connections with the bohemians and

their connections with the underworld could prove useful for a businessman wishing to keep his finger on the pulse of the city. My admiration increased for Uncle Semya's good-hearted pragmatism. Rather than force Shura to take a regular job in the office, he paid my cousin to be his contact with the people he obviously could not deal with personally. People who would not trust him even if he did approach them. I asked Shura how he had first found Esau's. He said that it was instinctive; he had grown up in the area. He had had to earn his own living for years. His mother, like mine, was a widow. When he was ten, she had run off to Warsaw with a farm-implement salesman. She must have felt, as he put it, that he was old enough to live on his own. I commiserated, but he laughed and patted my arm. "Don't fret for me, little Max. She was my only dependent. When she went, I became a rich man."

I said nothing about Uncle Semya. It was obvious that our uncle had taken pity on Shura as he had taken pity on me. He made the most of Shura's talents as he planned for me to make the most of mine.

As we went by the parks and lawns, the trees and fretwork dachas of Fountain, we smelled the last of the acacias. Unspoiled beaches, cliffs yellow with broom, like scrambled egg; the white Gothic mansions of industrialists; the more modest houses of people who had retired to Odessa for their health. There were famous artists living there, too, said Shura.

In the square Shura left me outside Uncle Semya's. He was anxious to keep his appointment. It was about five. I had time to wash and change into my more familiar clothes, speak a few words to Wanda and ask when we were to eat. She said about six. I could go downstairs to the parlor, if I wished, to see Aunt Genia. The window was no longer quite the lure it had been that morning so I decided to do as Wanda suggested.

I knocked on the door of the parlor. Aunt Genia's pleasant warble bade me enter. The room was full of light from the street. In it were books and magazines and newspapers of all descriptions. There were potted plants and photographs and deep chairs. A mirror, into which were stuck dozens of postcards, mostly from Vanya, hung over a modern Art Nouveau whatnot. There were pictures on the walls, mostly romantic scenes of the provincial Ukraine. Aunt Genia put down her book. She invited me to sit in one of the comfortable chairs opposite her (there was no stove in the room, but there were radiators near the window and the far wall) and tell her how I had liked Odessa. I told her, of course, all I could, leaving out some of the parts which I thought might alarm her. I told her about the tram ride to Fountain and she agreed that it was a very beautiful district, that she might like to retire there herself one day, "if God spared her." The district had originally possessed a spring which supplied the whole of Odessa with water. Nowadays, half the houses were unoccupied during the winter. Since she was a girl they had come more and more to be used for holidays. There were, she said, too many restaurants and pleasure gardens. Had I seen Arcadia? I said that I had. That, she said, was the worst. A gong sounded. She rose with a sigh. "Dinner." There were also, she said, too many children at Fountain in the summer and not enough in the winter, while the limans on the other side of town had nothing but old people trying to prolong their lives by a few miserable months. "Women of that sort seek immortality," she said, "in baths of mud or the arms of monks. There's not much to choose between them." I wondered if this was another reference to Rasputin. Odessans, for all that they lived close to many representatives of the Czar, had extraordinarily loose tongues.

Uncle Semya had also changed for dinner. He now wore a dark suit and his hands were free of ink. Wanda served the three of us and then sat down to join in. Uncle Semya spoke of "consignments" and "bills of lading" for a while as he enjoyed the delicious cold yushka of the sort we used to call "country style." During the pickled herring, which Wanda went to fetch, he complained about "Moscow crooks" who had bargained him out of most of his profit on some barrels of olives. By the time we had reached the main course, which was boiled beef in horseradish with potatoes in butter, he had mellowed enough to generalize about the progress of the War. I was unable to concentrate on my great-uncle's soliloquy because I was overwhelmed by the food. Course followed course. I thought I had eaten my fill of the soup. Then I had found room for the herring. Now I was having to force my way through the beef. It was the first time in my life I had been embarrassed by too much food. And this, it appeared, from the way Uncle Semya was treating it, was an ordinary meal.

"You're tired," I heard Aunt Genia say to me. "You've no appetite. Overexcited, eh, Maxim?"

I nodded. I could not at that moment speak. I felt that if I opened my mouth a potato would pop out again.

The worst happened. Uncle Semya stopped speaking of the military skill of the Germans, the superiority of their equipment over ours, and noticed me: "What have you been up to, today?"

I grunted. Uncle Semya smiled quietly. "I hope Shura isn't leading you into bad habits. I warned him you had been respectably raised, that you have been a recluse in Kiev. He didn't take you to that casino . . . ?"

I shook my head, anxious that Shura should not be blamed simply because I was too afraid to speak.

"Or that house. What's her name?"

"We went to the harbor," I said. "And Fountain."

"Oh." Uncle Semya seemed almost disappointed. "So you saw the sea?"

"Mmm." Still the potato did not come out. "First time."

"It's easy to get used to. And yet, living on the edge of the ocean as we do, it keeps our brains sharp. Not just the invigorating air, of course, but the sense of the world. Keeps perspective. Makes you aware, moreover, that you're only too vulnerable. To the elements, let alone your fellow man." He enjoyed this. "We are prone to forget that we are mortal, we city dwellers. But the sea reminds us. To the sea we came and to the sea, at length, we shall return." A fruit compote was put in front of him. "Mother to us all."

This was my first encounter with my uncle's mild pantheism. At that time I thought he was expressing some sort of evolutionary theory.

After the meal Uncle Semya went into his study and I sat with Aunt Genia and Wanda, reading a scientific article in *Zanye* (*Knowledge*), which because of its radical associations had never been allowed in our home. There were several copies here. All had articles I would normally have found inspiring, but I was still too full of my impressions of the day. I would read a paragraph or two then discover I was thinking about warm bodies and laughing mouths, of bawdy songs and comforting companionship. That sense of belonging to something at last was what chiefly obsessed me. Odessa was Life and I had been accepted by it so easily.

FOUR

In the days which followed, Shura was to introduce me to scores of new delights, and against these I had absolutely no protection. My mother had warned me about revolutionists but not about the real attractions and dangers of Odessa: the gay, sardonic company of those slangy bohemians who did not give a damn for Karl Marx or the Czar, who believed that their city was the world and that nowhere else on Earth was so beautiful. They were in many ways right. Very quickly I began to assume the tastes and manners of my friends. Odessans were regarded by the rest of Russia much as Californians are regarded by New Yorkers. The bright clothes we wore were natural to us, natural to the rosy light which made the city glow, and only appeared vulgar when removed from their locale. Even casual thievery in Odessa was not looked upon very seriously. It was almost as if property in that city were already communal, save that it was up to a person to hang on to as much of it as he could but not be resentful if he were outwitted and parted from it. Of course, not everyone shared this spirit. Such people were usually officials or immigrants of some sort, anyway: like the pompous burghers in their seaside cottages, or the holiday makers who came to swim and lie in the sun. The women wished to flirt with sailors and our Odessa boys.

Odessa boys had dark eyes and white teeth and brilliant scarves.

They wore painted ties, displayed a great deal of cuff with elaborate cuff links, sported stickpins and monstrous rings and cocky hats and chocolate-colored spats; their waistcoats were of yellow mohair or Chinese brocade. Odessa girls wore feathered hats and dark, Ukrainian shawls, crisp, white blouses and light, swinging skirts. They patrolled the promenades in little, giggling gangs during the day and occupied the gardens, lit with strings of tiny electric bulbs, in the evenings. Then the huge Odessa moon would make the sea look like mercury, as volatile and indescribable as the Odessan character, while accordions or orchestras would play the tunes of the moment, as well as the latest songs from France, America, even England and Germany. Through the crowds would stroll soldiers and sailors, arm-in-arm with their lady friends; gigolos on the lookout for the wives or widows of self-satisfied merchants; merchants on the lookout for girls; pickpockets, confidence tricksters, photographers, hurdy-gurdy men and postcard sellers. Here, too, were families of Hasid Jews, conspicuous in their dark clothes, shawls, pe'os and other paraphernalia, who were an embarrassment to all, bourgeois Jew and Gentile alike. Yet they were tolerated, these fanatics, as they would not be tolerated elsewhere, in spite of the fact that members of the Black Hundreds, who had begun the pogroms ten years before, almost entirely comprised Odessa's city council.

Shura introduced me to girls. They kissed my cheek and said that I was "lovely" and "a duck," which was not quite the impression I had hoped to give them. I was learning the rich, elusive speech of the city, however, as I had learned other foreign languages, and was soon proficient in it. It was this ability, which I gradually lost as I grew older, which helped me in many of my future situations. Where language was concerned, I was a chameleon.

Shura was very pleased with my progress. He took me up to the limans, those strange, dark, emerald-green shallows, full of mud and minerals. They are half wild: the haunt of game fowl and blind fish, where reeds wave and peculiar shadows move beneath the glinting, agitated surface. They are half tamed, where the large hotels and health resorts crowd close together. Here I learned to run errands for rich women. There was a great deal of commission involved, for one was tipped by all parties involved in the transactions. At other times we would engage in business by the docks where there were always ships: steamers, sailing boats, schooners, loading and unloading. Cargoes of fish, fruit, wine, cloth or even coal were often sold directly as they were landed. Traders were omnipresent and would pay for information of many kinds. Shura was well known and I became almost as familiar to them by my slightly Frenchified nickname of "Max the Hetman." Also, my relationship with Shura guaranteed me a place in the bohemian inner circle. There was already a small legend which suggested I was "something hot in Kiev." Soon it was possible for me to wander freely about the district without Shura to guide me, and I made acquaintances of my own. I never went to the docks without him, however. That grey world of overhead railways, derricks and worn-out dray horses had a sense of danger to it. It was where most of the revolutionaries came from.

In the meantime, of course, I tried to obey my mother's wishes. I continued to study in the evenings (though they became shorter as my days grew longer) and to stay in the fresh air enough to show an improvement in my skin color, so as to placate my aunt. Uncle Semya seemed to expect nothing of me save that I "learn a little of the world before going back to school." I am grateful to his philosophy and experience which made me appreciate education all the more. But the wine and the euphoria could not sustain me indefinitely and sometimes I was forced to spend whole days in bed recovering from the excesses into which my enthusiasm led me. On one of these days a grinning Shura came to see me. "I heard you weren't too well. I warned you about that rich Armenian wine, didn't I?" He picked up one of my journals. His lips moved as he tried to read the German words in the text. "What's this?" He pointed to a paragraph about Oddy's work on chemical isotopes. It was the beginning of the end for practical science. Together with Bohr's atomic theories, Oddy's came to seem more like the mad abstractions of "modernist" paintings, whose authors were part of the same mutual admiration society. I explained to Shura that it was probably nonsense. His reply was to laugh and say, "I see. You can't understand it, eh?"

"Well enough to see through it," I replied. "Why are you here?"

Shura rubbed his nose. "I thought you might like to come out to Arcadia today. You need to get yourself a girl."

"I've no energy," I told him. "I can't even think."

"You need a doctor."

"Nonsense."

He was sympathetic. A little reluctantly, he drew something from his waistcoat pocket. Throwing his scarf back over his shoulder he opened a fold of newspaper and held it out toward me. "Don't breathe too heavily, Max. You'll blow a lot of money away."

I looked down at the small quantity of white powder which lay in the newspaper. It was like the stuff one took for dyspepsia or headaches. "What is it? For a hangover?"

"Exactly." Shura went to my dressing table and put the fold of paper carefully down. Then he took a ruble note from his wallet and rolled it until it made a tight little tube. I was mystified, amused. "What on earth's all this ritual?"

He brought the packet back, with the rolled ruble. "Do you know how to take it?"

"I don't."

"You sniff it into your nose."

"But what is it?"

"It's cocaine. You use it to pick you up. Everyone does."

"Like you get in hospital?"

"Exactly."

In those days there was little association in the popular imagination with cocaine and addiction. It was not illegal to use it or to sell it, but it was expensive and therefore tended to be the prerogative of the wealthy. As I inexpertly drew the first crystals into my sinus I felt not that I was doing anything particularly wicked but that I was party to yet another luxury hitherto reserved for my betters. At first there was nothing but a little numbness in my nostrils and I was disappointed. I told Shura that either I was immune to the effects or that I needed more. He continued to leaf through my books. Slowly a feeling of ecstatic well-being filled me. Good cocaine does not merely give one a sense of one's whole body coming alive; there is at the same time an aesthetic delight, a love for the drug itself, a love for the world which can produce it, a love for oneself and for every other human being, a supreme confidence, an exquisite sensitivity, a profound understanding of the tensions and forces controlling society. An habitual cocaine user (whether he injects or sniffs) should learn to distinguish the reality and the fantasy, to marshal the energies released by the drug, but at that time I was as much in its power as I had been in Shura's. Of course, I felt utterly my own man. "It works very well," I said. "I feel a hundred times better."

"I knew you would. Coming to Arcadia?"

I thought of the pretty girls I would see there, of the fine impression I would make. I thought of the foreigners I could meet and speak to, the inventions I could create, just lying on the sands. I dressed myself in Vanya's best (along with one or two extra items which I had purchased for myself). "What's the time?"

Shura shook his head and laughed aloud. "Oh, dear, Max, you're certainly a joy to know. It's about noon. We'll have lunch at Esau's first."

We never reached Arcadia. Instead we spent most of the afternoon in Esau's and I talked of all the things I knew, in all the languages I could speak; of all the things I was going to do; and my most attentive audience was little Katya, a year or two younger than myself but already a well-liked whore, who led me, still in a daze of cocaine dust, by her tiny warm hand, out of Esau's and along an alley and up into a sunny attic room with a window looking toward the smoky heights of Moldovanka and Vorontzovka, inland toward the ancient steppe, and here she took away all my clothes and exposed my body and admired it and stroked it and removed her own little silks and cottons and lay upon her white bed and taught me the trembling joys of manhood so that to this day the pleasure of cocaine and copulation are mingled together in my mind. I have been a regular user of the drug all my life and apart from some mild trouble with my sinuses I have suffered no ill effects. While I frown upon reefer smoking and opium taking, because they dull the wits and the will to *do*, which is the supreme human quality, I know many great men who have made use of cocaine to help them in their work. Of course, it can be abused —Bolsheviks and pop stars, for instance—but that is true of all the gifts we have on this earth.

After my experience with Katya I slept very deeply. Next morning I found that she was still there, still as tender as she had been, but anxious for me to leave because she stood to lose business. I asked when I could return. She said that I could come and see her the next day, when she had restored her routine. It might seem strange to my readers that I did not feel jealous toward her customers. I never sought to analyze my feelings. My love for Katya, with her small, boyish body, her wealth of black hair, her humane and profoundly benign eyes, her delicate lips and fingers, was one of the purest loves I ever knew. Even when I saw her with her "friends" I felt nothing but comradeship toward her. I do not think, in spite of what was to happen, that I managed to discover quite such a balanced relationship again. My life with Mrs. Cornelius was altogether more complex and her role toward me, in the early days at least, more maternal.

My meeting with Mrs. Cornelius came only a day or so after my first experience of sexual intercourse. My toothache had grown worse and Uncle Semya said I must have the best dental treatment. Again the name of the dentist, Cornelius, was mentioned. Wanda must take me at once to Preobrazhenskaya (one of Odessa's most fashionable streets) where the tooth would be pulled. My debauched life had left me pale, with bloodshot eyes. I think he believed my toothache to be worse than it was. He did not want the responsibility of telling my mother that I had, perhaps, poisoned my jaw.

In a smart Steiger, the driver a stiff silhouette on the seat in front, Wanda and I drove through foggy, autumn streets. By the time the cab turned into the long, straight avenue of Preobrazhenskaya I felt extremely lordly in my new three-piece suit, with white shirt, stiff collar and cravat, like a Count on his way to visit a Prince. My nervousness of the dentist had partly been offset by a soupçon of cocaine, taken just before we left, and partly by a sense of my own elegance. We disembarked outside an impressive building (it was in the district close to the Theater and University) just as sunlight began to fall again upon the city. We entered a lobby and took a flight of curving stone stairs up to a door which bore a brass plate announcing H. CORNELIUS, DENTIST.

We were expected, but there was another visitor in the well-appointed waiting room. She seemed very much a lady of fashion, in her mutton-chop sleeves and her hat with fruit and flowers on it, with a little veil. She smelled of expensive perfume. She was, I now realize, only about Wanda's age. But she had a romantic, foreign air to her.

She had not, it seemed, been expected. The dentist's receptionist was saying as much when we entered. I cannot reproduce the lady's wonderful English so will leave that to someone else. She seemed very confident as she stood in the middle of the room, holding her salmon-pink sunshade in one hand, her matching reticule in the other. She was dressed almost entirely in pink with some white decorations and, of course, the various colors of her hat. She was a picture from one of my French or English magazines. The feathers swept round, like the train of a savage monarch, as she turned to look at us. She had blond hair (not in those days very fashionable) and a pink-and-white face, with a little paint on it. She smiled down on us, although she was not particularly tall, and it might have been the Czarina herself condescending to notice me. She was speaking English, as I say, and seemed a little put out by the stupidity of the receptionist who had addressed her in German and then in French.

"I told yer. I've come ter see me cuz."

I recognized the English words, if not exactly the sense of what she said. "The lady is English," I informed the girl who, in apron and uniform, looked like a baffled sheepdog. I removed my hat. "Can I be of assistance, mademoiselle?"

The English girl was delighted. She seemed to relax. "Could you inform this stupid cow," she said, "that I am 'ere ter visit me Cousin Haitch—Mr. Cornelius. It is Miss Honoria Cornelius, who he'll doubtless remembah as the little girl 'e used ter dandle on 'is knee. I 'ave been stranded in ongfortunate circs—circumstances—and need ter see 'im in private—"

"You have not come to receive his professional ministrations, my lady?"

"Do what?" I remember her saying. This puzzled me. She added, "Come again?" I gathered she had not understood me.

"You have nothing wrong with your teeth?"

"Why the 'ell should I? Every one a bloody pearl and sound as a bell. 'Ow old d'yer fink I am?"

I spoke directly to the bobbing receptionist in slow, clear Russian. "This lady is related to his excellency, the dentist. Her name is Mademoiselle Cornelius. She is, I believe, his cousin."

The receptionist was relieved. She smiled and escorted the English lady into another, even more luxurious, room. With a "Ta very much, Ivan," to me, Mrs. Cornelius vanished. I was to learn from her much later that the dentist was not in fact a relation at all. She had come across his name in Baedeker's at a nearby bookshop and had decided to visit him. She had been traveling with a Persian aristocrat, a well-known playboy of those years, when they had had a difference of opinion in their hotel (the Central). He had left on an early steamer, having paid the bill only up to that morning. She was unable to speak a word of Russian, but even then she was making the best of things. She had been very grateful to me, it appeared, because she had almost been at the end of her tether. This was how she recognized me when we came to meet again. She had given up hope of finding an English-speaker anywhere in Odessa and I was "a godsend," even if, in her words, I "talked like a bleedin' book."

After she had gone, and Wanda and I were seated, the English lady's perfume (crushed rose petals) was all that remained of her. I was called into the surgery. Wanda still accompanied me. She was curious, I think, to see the inside of a dentist's workshop. A handsome middle-aged man, murmuring in what I supposed to be Dutch, peered into my mouth, clucked his tongue, put a mask over my face and made his receptionist turn the tap on a nearby cylinder. A strange smell replaced the scent of roses. I was gassed. A peculiar humming began in my ears— *zhe-boo, zhe-boo*—and black-and-white circles became a moving spiral. I felt sick and dreamed of Zoyea and Wanda and little Esmé, the warm, comforting body of my Katya. All were dressed in the salmon-pink costume of the English girl who was cousin to Heinrich—or was it Hans?—or Hendrik?— Cornelius.

I remember leaving with an emptier jaw and a fuller, throbbing head. When I asked what had happened to Mademoiselle Cornelius, Wanda giggled. "Her cousin seemed only too pleased to be of assistance." I was reassured.

With regular supplies of cocaine from Shura and from other sources, I was able to continue with my studies and with my new adventurous life. I developed a firm, regular friendship with Katya. Eventually, I fell in love with her almost as deeply as I had with Zoyea. The holiday seemed to be without end. Uncle Semya had assured me that I was welcome to stay until my place at the Polytechnic was "firmly arranged." There was no certainty when this would be. I was awake sometimes twenty hours in the twenty-four. Sometimes I did not go to bed at all. My letters to my mother were regular and optimistic. Nor was my whole life given over to adventure. Uncle Semya and I regularly visited the Theater and Opera (usually just the two of us). He proved an astonishingly tolerant host.

Aunt Genia was inclined to fret over me, feeling that, quite rightly, I was overdoing things. But at dinner Uncle Semya would laugh and say: "Wild oats must be sown, Genia"—this in spite of his standing in the community (high-ranking officials would often take dinner with us and on these occasions it was usual for Wanda and myself to eat in the kitchen with the cook).

Of course life with the pleasure-loving bohemians of the Odessa taverns was not without its problems. There were fights—or threatened fights—almost every day. In the main I was able to escape trouble, either by assuming a friendly or neutral stance (something which became second nature to me) or by talking myself clear. But I was not always able to avoid the revolutionaries my mother had warned me against.

In the main any political talk would send me away at once, unless it was the simple irreverences of Odessa small-talk, but when my engineering experience and scientific skills became known I was courted by more than one socialist. There was a particular scoundrel who might have given me trouble: a morose and introverted Georgian "on leave," as he put it, from Siberia. He wanted me to make him some bombs for an attack he planned on the Odessa–Tiflis main train. I trembled with terror at the very idea of being overheard, let alone involved. If my mother had known, it would have killed her. But I could not merely walk away from him. This sinister bandit with the unlikely name of "So-So" had a low, persuasive voice and smoldering eyes staring from a heavily unshaven and pockmarked face. These aspects alone were enough to make me address him with at least superficial politeness. I said I would look into the problem of producing the bombs. I planned to complain next time I saw him that it had been impossible to obtain the materials. I thought it wise to return to the tavern when I had promised, but to my huge relief he was not there. I never saw him again. Perhaps he was arrested. Perhaps he was shot by the police. It was even possible that, like the man who had double-crossed Misha the Jap over some morphine supplies, he wound up being fished from the Quarantine Harbor. There was only a certain, limited sort of honor amongst the thieves of Moldovanka. Anyone who broke his trust was submitted to sudden, swift justice of a kind which, if the Czar's police had been prepared to dispense it in a similar fashion, would have at once put paid to any revolution, Bolshevik or otherwise.

It is even possible that the Turks saved me from So-So's furious mouth. It was just the next day, when I was lying with Katya, that I was awakened from a wonderful, drowsy half dream by a whistling scream and the sound of a distant explosion. I thought there had been an accident in one of the factories or that a ship had blown up. But the screams and explosions became regular and, as I ran downstairs with Katya, a skinny friend of mine called Nikita the Greek dashed past in the street shouting that the Germans were shelling the city. Into the fog we went, with some idea that it was dangerous to stay inside, through a tiny, tree-lined plaza like an Impressionist's painting of autumn, and still that unreal, fascinating death (such things were new to us then) went whistling on. Everyone was panicking. It was terrible to see so many frightened people appearing and vanishing in the fog. Most of the shells had been intended for the harbor and the Allied ships there and soon Odessa's defenses came into action. The damage was chiefly in Persuip, the industrial district by the sea

where the shipyards were. The enemy was driven off with compara-
tive ease. The following morning we learned it had been the Turks
who had shelled us. Turkey was not at that time officially at war with
Russia. A couple of days later we declared war on the cruel and
cunning Moslem.

Until this raid I had been entertaining thoughts of remaining always in Odessa and going to the engineering school there (which was
very good, though it did not have the prestige of St. Petersburg's). I
do not think Uncle Semya would have objected had it not been for
that bombardment, which showed how vulnerable Odessa was. "The
sea is reminder enough of our death!" he said feelingly, that evening
at dinner. For the first time I was allowed to join him and two of his
guests. One was a local police chief and the other the captain of a
French ship which had been slightly damaged during the shelling. He
regretted, Uncle Semya said, that he could not take his whole family
to Kiev or even to Moscow. His business affairs were so complex that
they could not safely be left in other hands. This made the police
chief laugh. Uncle Semya was displeased, but gave a faint smile. He
said that he had thought of going into the entertainment business,
into kinema displays. It was the sort of thing people wanted during
wartime. Everyone agreed that the "kino" was the business of the
future. In America, fortunes were already being made. "It would suit
me," said Uncle Semya, "to be at least in one respect a patron of the
arts." He had considered opening a theater, but the investment in
these troubled times was a bit uncertain. Kinema equipment could be
moved, however, from place to place. You could give shows in barns,
in the open air at night if need be. He visualized himself and Aunt
Genia in a horse-drawn caravan—"a gypsy life on the open road"—
with his projector and stock of films, going from town to town. "How
popular we should be. How pleased people would be to see us."

"People are always pleased to see you, Semyon Josefovitch," said
the police chief. "You perform so many important services to the
community."

"To the world at large," said the captain, representative of inter-
nationalism. "You are well known in Marseilles and Cardiff. I have
heard people speak of you."

"What, in France and England?"

"To my certain knowledge."

Uncle Semya was extremely glad to hear this. "They find me an
honest merchant, I hope."

"Oh, indeed, I am sure they do!" The police chief discovered more cause for baffling laughter. I remain confused to this day by much so-called humor. I had every respect for the man's rank, but I found his red, puffy face, his grey-mottled beard, his sly smiles, rather unattractive, particularly after he had had more than a few glasses of wine. The captain was much more pleasant. He carried a private, circumspective manner with him, as if he only attended the dinner from a sense of duty, or because he had to deal with Uncle Semya on business. It could be that he was as upset as I was by the police chief's coarseness.

The following morning I received a depressing letter from Esmé. Her father had contracted influenza and had died quite suddenly in hospital. She said my mother seemed happy, though missing me. Esmé had gone with her and Captain Brown to the theater once or twice. They had watched some kino pictures of the War. She reported that our soldiers were driving the enemy back on every front. The specific news from Kiev now seemed very provincial. I read the letter with a certain sense of superiority. Esmé said she had decided to try to become a nurse at the front. I wrote back at once before going to Katya's, telling her that I thought this would be a perfect occupation for one of her temperament and character.

Before I could take the letter to the post office, Uncle Semya called me into his study. He asked if the letter from Kiev had been sent by my mother. I told him that it was from Esmé, a childhood friend. He seemed relieved. "I am wondering at the sense of keeping you in Odessa. The experience has been good for you so far. It has helped you grow up and so on. That, frankly, is what I wanted. You would not have survived much longer in the world, tied to your mother's apron—"

I came to the defense of my mother, but he raised a neat hand. "I am not criticizing poor Yelisaveta Filipovna. She has done very well by you. Rather better, I would say, than other members of the family who have had children. Vanya has his virtues, but I have no son to be proud of as she is proud of you." I warmed with pleasure. "That's why I am so anxious you should not be in danger. It is still taking a little time to approach the appropriate persons in Petersburg, but I think we are nearing success (you will have to be photographed). So it is not certain you will be able to begin classes in January as we originally planned. I am wondering about my duty. Should I let you continue your 'life studies' here in Odessa—I gather you have made many friends—or should I send you back to the safety of Kiev?"

"You think there will be another bombardment, Semyon Josefo-vitch?"

"The Turks took us by surprise. They will not be able to do that again. We are probably all right. But your mother will hear of this. What will she say?"

"She will want me to return, naturally."

"And you think you should go?"

"Not until absolutely necessary. I am happy here."

He was satisfied. "Genia Mihailovna and myself were both saying how much you had changed, how much brighter you have become. More self-confident. You'll be able to perform services for me, I hope, in Peter, when you go there."

"Of course, Uncle. I would be honored."

"We have a man on our hands, I think." He frowned. "You must be careful of the girls, Max." It was the first time he had used this diminutive. "There are diseases. You know of these?"

"I think so." I knew very well the dangers of venereal disease, always present in a port like Odessa. I took the necessary treatments, recommended by Katya. We had so far escaped any evident problems.

"And you have been to the casinos?"

I admitted that I had.

Uncle Semya became almost jolly. "I used to enjoy the casinos. The trick is never to play with your own money. Invent a system and then offer to cut someone in for half the profit. You'd be surprised how many investors you attract. If you win, they are pleased and continue to invest. If you lose, well, you have lost their money and must admit that the system needs improvement. It is how I got my first real capital."

I was astonished at this frank revelation, even a little shocked. But I realized my uncle had relaxed enough to offer me "man-to-man" advice. It was an announcement that, in his eyes at least, I had come of age.

Uncle Semya seemed distracted then. He sighed. "We had thought of emigrating. Less than a year ago we planned to go to Berlin where I have a brother. Now we shall have to wait and see what happens. I heard a rumor we were forming a new alliance with the Germans against the Turks. Yet they don't fear the Turks in Peter as much as they fear the Germans. We should move nearer to the middle. Perhaps to Kharkov. It's safer in the middle of any country. But there are reasons—" He waved a mysterious hand. "Let's see what your mother has to say." His sharp, mild features clouded. He said something, I thought in German, about the Jews, but he spoke so softly it was impossible to understand him. He reached into his desk. He took out a passport, smiled at it almost wistfully, then replaced it in the drawer.

Feeling that I had been given even more freedom than before, praying that my mother would not be alarmed by the news of the bombardment (though I knew she would), I returned to my room. After I had reinforced myself with a little of my own supply of co-caine I went to call on Katya, to see if she would come with me to Esau's. When I arrived at her place (which was over a hardware shop) her mother, who occupied the back first-floor room and was also a whore, said that she was busy. With habitual tact I left a message and went on my own to the tavern. I had expected to find Shura there, but he was about some business, and I fell into conver-sation with a couple of dancers from one of the cabarets. A man and a woman, they had just done a tour of the provinces and were com-plaining about Nikolaev, which they described as a "one-tram town."

Shura came in shortly afterward. He greeted me with a slap on the back and one of his winks. "Going to Peter, I hear."

I said that it still wasn't entirely settled. He ordered a glass of tea and drank it thirstily. He nodded. "When you get there, you want to keep in with all those well-connected young ladies at the university. They're the daughters of rich men. I talked to a girl yesterday. She's on holiday at Fountain and liked the look of me. Her father's a factory owner from Kherson. He sent me packing when he caught me giving her the eye. But he's the sort. An industrialist who'll back your patents." Another wink.

I said that it sounded as if he were recommending a con game, and he laughed. "Isn't it all a racket, Xima, dear? What if the War lasts forever? What if this is to be the world we'll know for the rest of our lives? We must protect ourselves."

I shared the general opinion that Germany and Austria-Hungary had bitten off far more than they could chew. The Hapsburg dynasty, for a start, was rotten through and through.

"And you don't think it's true of the Romanoffs?"

I had heard more scandal about the Czar and his family in Odessa than previously I had heard in the whole of my life. I had to agree that it looked bad. The Czarina and most of her court, I had heard, were drug addicts. The Czar's ministers and military high command were all corrupt. It was easy to believe these things in the atmosphere of Odessa. I let the subject drop, however, in deference to my mother. I merely said: "Russia has the strength to beat anyone."

A group of our friends entered and made toward our table. "Oh, we certainly have more cannon fodder than anyone else." As the boys and the girl seated themselves around us Shura looked toward the bar. There a young woman was singing a frenetic song to an accordionist's accompaniment. She was slim and neurasthenic while her musician friend was burly and dirty, looking as if he had come straight out of one of the more miserable shtetls I had read about and, thank God, never had to experience. "But, as the Vikings used to say, free men fight better."

I told him that there was no such thing as freedom, that in my view it was a revolutionary's idea of heaven. He was amused. Nikita the Greek (who was only Greek in name) pushed his workman's cap back on his head and leaned across the table, giving one of his strange, menacing grins. "Only a man without a soul is a free man," he said. "It's possible to live a free life, but only if you renounce your immortality. That's what I think." Nikita had been trained for the priesthood until he had run away from Kherson. He added: "One cannot have God and freedom."

It was pretty much what I had said. I glanced triumphantly at Shura, but he had lost interest and had his shoulder up. He was insouciantly chewing sunflower seeds and staring at the emaciated singer. Behind Shura's back, Nikita widened his big eyes and jerked a thumb at my cousin, as if to indicate that Shura was showing unusual interest in the girl. I grinned. I was to remember that grin with some bitterness, but at the time I said, "All the Turks have done is to wake us up to the real danger. Now we'll fight properly. Nothing can destroy Russia."

Lyova, the painter, came back with a handful of drinks and lowered them to the table. His dark hair fell over his eyes and he pushed it back. "That's what they said about Carthage. They were probably going about saying 'Carthage is indestructible. It's one of the oldest civilizations in the world.' Then look what happened. The Romans destroyed the whole thing overnight. And why? Because of a failure of imagination. They simply couldn't conceive of their fate. If they'd been able to do so, they'd have been here today."

"They are here," said Boris the Accountant, tapping his round spectacles. "Why do you think there are so many Semites in Odessa? The New Carthage."

"The New Gomorrah, more likely," said Shura, turning back and draining his tea glass. "Let's have some vodka." He seemed gloomy. He wouldn't look at me. I thought he must be upset at the prospect of our parting.

"Nonsense," said Nikita. He sneered. "Russians and Jews are all too innocent. They are still serfs at heart. We behave like kids, we're cruel to one another, because we are kids. We treat our own children badly . . ."

Grania, the curly-haired dancer with the heart-shaped face, would not have this. She made a disapproving sound. "Nobody loves children more than Russians!"

Boris said feelingly, "Cossacks aren't too finicky about Jewish children . . ."

"Careful what you say, Benya," Lyova warned him with a smile. "We have a Cossack hetman in our company." We all enjoyed this.

"We *are* children," insisted Nikita. "We love our 'Little Fathers,' our 'Batkos.' And it's why we're such materialists. Because we are poor, most of us, as children are poor. We have no power, no wealth, no justice save the justice of the autocrat. We are always quarreling about possessions. We must be the only race in the whole world to equate sentimental lyricism with emotional maturity. Our literature's full of trees and naïve protagonists. There are more trees in Russian novels than it took to make the paper they're printed on."

I do not think any of us followed Nikita's wild arguments too clearly. It was the first time he had expressed them. He was to become a journalist on a Bolshevik newspaper and disappear in the mid-thirties (I met his sister briefly in Berlin). Boris the Accountant seemed to agree with Nikita, however. "We are in the power of mad children," he said. "Russians will do anything to resist growing up. Thus they are easily ruled."

"And that's why we could lose the war," said Shura, giving Boris his talented attention and evidently making the accountant feel as if he had something profound to say. Boris merely developed the same theme:

"It's a vast, infantile nation. Its notion of maturity is a romantic youth's notion that he's mature when he becomes sentimental about general ideas like Love, Death and Nature."

We laughed as only sentimental youths, who had not really lost such ideas, can laugh.

I report these conversations, as I remember them, not because I believe they had any special profundity, but to give a flavor of the ideas current in Odessa in those days.

"It's the reason Tolstoi is so popular with the young and passionate," said Boris. "Natasha *is* Russia. Even the oldest, noblest greybeard is a kid. How else could they embrace Marxism so easily?"

At this mention of politics I was automatically on my feet. Most Jews like Boris were radicals and had to be avoided. Marxists, Kropotkinists, Prudhonists, they were all the same to me. They displayed a disease of the brain which could be highly contagious, for it was transmitted, as I once said of hypochondria, by word of mouth. Also I was still afraid of So-So. Talk of that devil might cause him to reappear. I decided to see if Katya's customer had left yet. As I got up, she came in. She dashed forward to throw her arms round me, kissing me in a way I found uncharacteristic. The bombardment had caused many of us to have second thoughts about our lives and, perhaps, put a slightly higher value on our relationships.

Shura remained in his strange mood. He was far from friendly to Katya and took a brooding interest in the singer, who had continued to pipe her peculiar Yiddish songs above the noise of our conversation. More vodka arrived. We all drank. We toasted the singer. Boris lost interest in politics when his fat girl friend arrived to let him know their parents had met and decided they should marry. He became quite pale and began to make calculations in the margins of his anarchist newspaper.

That was the day the Cossacks rode through Moldovanka and every Jew in the city shook in his shoes. The girl singer had stopped her wailing and we had grown rather stupefied. Katya had gone home, to prepare for her evening's business, but it was not yet dark. The sound of cavalry in a city is very peculiar to one who has not heard it before. At first we thought we were to be bombarded again, because the noise was unfamiliar, and that is why we fell silent.

When it is distant, the sound of cavalry in a city is like the wind which comes off the steppe, almost a hissing; slowly it grows louder and more irregular until it is a series of syncopated, broken beats, rising and falling, like water running at different speeds over rocks; at this stage it becomes suddenly much louder—the rushing noise of a clattering express train in a tunnel. And that is when it is galloping and you must get out of its way at any cost.

The Cossacks galloped past our alley and the bravest (or in my case the most curious) of us stuck our heads out of the doorway and watched the Cossacks charge through the streets of Moldovanka ghetto.

"They're frightening us because they failed to frighten the Turks," said Boris. "It's what they always do."

Shura mocked him. "They're just on their way to the garrison. It's the shortest route from the Goods Station where they disembarked. Look at them. They're not show cavalry or militia, those boys. They're a fighting unit."

It was true that the Cossacks had well-worn caftans and that there was dust on them. Their weapons looked as if they had been used in real action, rather than in the service of some pogrom.

"Nevertheless," said Boris, "the City Council had a reason for making them get off at the Goods Station and for telling them to come through here. Why are they galloping in streets? On cobbles? It's bad for horses."

We all shut him up. The Cossacks had done no harm (unless you counted the odd heart attack) and I for one had been inspired by them. With fighters like that we were assured of victory. And there were thousands—perhaps hundreds of thousands—of Cossack horsemen of half-a-dozen major hosts, not to mention all the minor ones— who would rally now that the Turk had dared attack us. I could imagine the joy in the Cossack villages when the news came that they would have another chance to kill Turks. I envied them. Only traitors and out-and-out Zionists could fail to be reassured by the sight of our wild cavalrymen of the steppe.

I had begun to develop one of the headaches which have since bothered me all my life, and so I made my excuses and returned home. The streets were unusually quiet, virtually deserted. I found the house absolutely silent. Nobody was in. I went to my room, thinking of having more cocaine, but I decided to lie in the darkness of the room, whose blinds had already been drawn, and try to sleep. There were disadvantages to taking stimulants. Sooner or later one's resources cried out to be replenished. I spent that evening in bed and went down to dinner, where I found Uncle Semya, Aunt Genia and Wanda. My uncle lacked his usual detached benevolence and Aunt Genia spoke brightly, but with even less substance than was normal. At one point she suggested we should all think of going to Kiev. Uncle Semya said that property was expensive there and we could not afford to live as we did in Odessa. After dinner I asked Wanda what the matter was. She said that it was nothing specific. The war news was depressing. Uncle Semya had taken them out to Fountain to look at a dacha he was thinking of renting for the winter. I found this in itself bewildering, for one did not rent summer dachas for Odessa winters, which were apt to be quite severe. He had decided against the idea, Wanda told me. A touch of war hysteria, I suggested. I had read about war hysteria. We had been warned against it. She said that was probably the case. She seemed sad as she sat in my room, but was reluctant to leave. I felt an urge to comfort her, but thought that any move I made would be misinterpreted. I said that I was very tired and that I must sleep. There would be no need to bring me any breakfast in the morning. I would sleep at least until noon. Usually Wanda was sensitive to my needs, but she continued to pass the time for a few more moments until at length she left. I began to wonder if she had fallen in love with me and that this accounted for her unusual behavior. Everyone was a little strange since the bombardment. They had taken it far more to heart than I had. Perhaps they had intimations of miseries to come.

For the first time since I had arrived in Odessa, I felt depressed and homesick as I went to sleep. I thought of lilacs in the summer rain, of smoke hanging over the steep yellow streets, of my mother's kindness and attentiveness, something which even my lovely Katya could not replace. This mood had left me when I awoke the next day, but it was to recur from time to time. However, I was determined to stay in Odessa as long as possible, even though winter was drawing on and the heavenly, unreal summer and autumn were giving way to a more prosaic, colder life.

I thought that Shura guessed my slight depression. He took to inviting me to parties (private houses tended to be the meeting places in winter) and to introducing me to different girls. It became harder to see Katya. At first I did not realize that I was seeing her only two or three times a week when before I had seen her every day. I became suspicious of her. I missed her comforting warm-heartedness. I became increasingly homesick.

There was a little light snow in November. It seemed to me that the whole of Odessa had been covered with cocaine. By early December I was using about two grams a day, most of it supplied by Shura. My mother had written to me to say that she thought I should return. I had written to say that the news had been sensationalized and that I was safe. I would go home "at about Christmas time." She did not write to Uncle Semya and I was able to tell him my mother was reassured. Then, on the morning that the first real snow came, I received a letter from Esmé telling me my mother had influenza and that Esmé had moved in with her, since her father's pension had stopped with his death and she could not, anyway, afford the rent on his apartment. This seemed an ideal solution. I was glad that my mother had companionship and someone as competent to look after her as Esmé. I wrote back to say that I would visit Kiev "some time after Christmas," that studies and so on were keeping me in Odessa and that Uncle Semya was anxious that I should get the maximum benefit from my stay. None of this was a lie, but the prospect of poverty and simple food over the holiday was too much to contemplate. I could have done very little for my mother in Kiev. Indeed, with myself and my mother to look after, Esmé would have been hard-pressed. Of course, I did not know that the influenza was a very bad attack or I should have returned home at once.

A day or so later, Shura asked me if I would like to go aboard an English steamer. I said that the idea was very attractive. Shura needed an interpreter in some business he was transacting with the mate of the ship. The captain was not aboard. He had gone sick and been put ashore in Yalta. I assumed that because of this the mate was interested in off-loading whatever his cargo was and taking on something else. There were fewer and fewer foreign merchant ships in Odessa, due to the winter and Turkish control of the Straits. I believe, too, they were taking different routes, to avoid German submarines. There were, from time to time, Australian warships in the harbor, but we rarely had any contact with their crews. I was glad of the rare chance to try out my English. That night we went down to Quarantine Harbor and showed passes Shura had obtained. Then we were met by two seamen with a ship's boat and were rowed to where the S.S. *Kathleen Sisson* was anchored, beyond the mole. She was not much of a ship; typical of the tramps trading along the coasts from the Aegean to the Sea of Azov. After Turkey entered the War, these began to disappear so rapidly that as a mercantile city Odessa went from riches to rags almost overnight. I think the *Kathleen Sisson* had been recalled to her home port of Piraeus and possibly her officers, who were the only Britons aboard, wanted to get out of the theater of war. The rest of the crew consisted of Greeks and Armenians who would have made a company of lascars seem savory.

We went below the bridge, to the captain's quarters, and met Mr. Finch, the mate. At the time I found him a pleasant, quietly spoken

Irish gentleman, but I suspect I would see him differently now. He was tall and dressed in a grubby white uniform. He offered us a drink of what must have been arrack, but which I foolishly thought would be Scotch whiskey. It tightened the muscles of my throat, making it hard for me to speak properly for several days. We sat down around a chart table and Mr. Finch began the conversation, asking Shura if he had brought the money. Shura told me to tell Mr. Finch that the money was on deposit and would be paid over at a mutually agreed time and place. Mr. Finch seemed displeased by this but became reconciled, giving us some more "whiskey" (I have never drunk much real whiskey since that day). Shura asked to see a sample and Mr. Finch took him away while I waited, impressed by the cabin with its wealth of instruments, charts and general seafaring paraphernalia. It was my first experience aboard a ship and even a run-down tramp was absolutely enchanting.

Shura and Mr. Finch returned. Mr. Finch told me that if Shura were satisfied we should agree on a time and place to meet "on neutral ground." Shura suggested a seaman's club near the harbor. This was a favorite of English and American sailors. Mr. Finch would feel at ease. The mate agreed and he and Shura shook hands. Mr. Finch said to me that it had been "a long haul from Malacca" and that he would be "glad to be back in Dublin." I expressed surprise that he had sailed all that way, and he laughed. "I joined this old kettle at Trebizond. I've been in damned native trains since Basra, worrying myself sick every minute I was on land. I started the whole deal before the War, see. Now I wish I never had."

It was not clear what the deal had involved. I began to suspect it must be illegal. Shura was inclined to sail a little close to the wind, but this was something which could land us in trouble with the police. We got back to the harbor and I said good-by to my cousin. I was glad the venture was over for me. Shura came to the house two days later and gave me "enough cocaine to last you through the season." He seemed even better disposed toward me than usual. I guessed he must be feeling guilty for involving me in something dangerous. The cocaine was of prime quality. This was probably what Mr. Finch had been carrying all the way from Malacca.

FIVE

The fog in Odessa grew thicker and colder, muting the slow moans of the last ships in the harbor. People occupied the streets less frequently. They put on their long coats, their mufflers, their fur caps. Christmas approached and the better shops were filled with light and wonderful displays; posters started to appear for Winter Balls and entertainments, many of them to raise funds for the War effort; ice-cream sellers gave way to chestnut sellers under the hissing gas lamps, and the stevedores on the docks put on quilted jackets and gloves, their breath mingling with the thick, low-lying steam from the ships. My mood grew steadily worse. In winter Odessa became a fairly ordinary city. I was scarcely seeing Katya at all—she was tired, she said—and I was using cocaine in stronger and stronger doses to relieve an almost suicidal depression. I had overdone my adventures. I had packed years of experience into a few months. I had neglected my work at the very time I should have been concentrating on it. I tried to stay with my books and forget about Katya. It was impossible. I decided to get up early one morning and go to see her, to offer her anything if she would forsake her profession and see more of me. She was an intelligent, beautiful girl and could easily have gotten a job in an office, or in a shop. Uncle Semya would probably help.

I bought her a present. A few days before Christmas Eve I

wrapped it in silver paper, tied it with green ribbon (it was an orna-mental clown of the best Ukrainian ceramic, bought at Magasin Wagner) and set off for Slobodka. In my dark suit, white shirt, bow tie, dark-brown bowler and matching English topcoat, with the present under my arm, I must have looked the picture of a young man on his way to "pop the question" (although I was not yet fifteen). I bought an expensive imported flower (already becoming scarce) to complete the effect. I also carried a white ivory stick with a carved head. This had been a present from Shura about a week before.

I arrived at the broken-down house in the alley where Katya lived. The front, used by the ironmonger, had not yet opened, but I knew a trick of jerking the door open, even when it was locked. I entered the dark, cluttered interior of the shop and tiptoed through to the narrow stair leading to Katya's room. She would have gotten rid of any customer by this time, but I did not want to risk embarrassing her. Determined to go away if a man was with her, I crept up the stairs and opened the door a fraction. I saw a form huddled in the bed with its arms around my Katya. I suppressed my jealousy. Then I realized I recognized the shoulder. It was young. A boy's shoulder. It was, of course, Shura's shoulder.

I did not behave then as I would behave now. I lost all control. I screamed and flung the door back. I realized why Shura had shown me such kindness, why Katya's time with me had become so limited, why she and Shura never spoke when they met at Esau's. I had been betrayed.

I recall only the emotions; the way in which the blood became a drum in my brain, in which my hot hand gripped the cool ivory of the stick as I advanced on Shura. He scrambled up with a yell, laughed at me, became terrified, tried to protect Katya, threw a pillow at me. I raised the stick. His naked body flew at me and caught me below the waist. I struck his back, his buttocks. I fell over. The fight had no proper end. I lost the stick. We became exhausted. I remember Katya weeping.

"Can't you see I loved you?"

Shura sat panting against a wall down which, as if to witness the drama, cockroaches climbed. "She loved us both, Xima. I love you both."

I said the usual things about treachery, trickery, double-dealing. I have been betrayed too many times since then to recall anything specific. Katya wanted Shura's maturity and my innocence. Fundamentally, she was a whore. She could not resist any of us. There were probably other lovers, as opposed to customers. I think she was one of those kindly, slightly frightened girls who gives in to the slightest pressure then spends her life trying to reconcile everyone, far too afraid to tell the truth which would extricate her from such situations. It is a characteristic of our good-natured Slav girls, particularly in Ukraine. There are even Jewish girls who are like it. They are incapable of scheming, but weave the most impossible webs of deception. These girls are so frequently treated as *femmes fatales* when, in fact, they are the very opposite. None of this occurred to my fourteen-year-old self. Drained by a drug which in later years would prove beneficial; exhausted by an unequal physical encounter; weeping with misery at the terrible thing done to me by my little Katya, I lay in a corner and picked cobwebs and dust off my fine suit, while my cousin Shura, trying to mollify me, got dressed, and Katya wailed, wishing she had never met either of us.

Shura suggested we go for a drink. I accepted. We went to Esau's where Shura cracked and chewed sunflower seeds and talked about "the world" and how he had been going to tell me but that Katya had been afraid it would hurt my feelings. Slowly the onus was transferred onto the woman in the case. Two or three glasses of vodka made it seem we had both been badly deceived by a little bitch. Another two or three glasses and I was close to weeping. I told Shura I had nearly killed him. Shura said it was appalling how trollops like Katya could make two friends fight so savagely. We drank to the doom of all women. We drank to eternal comradeship. When the question arose as to which of us was to stop seeing Katya we were both insistent we had "no rights"; then insistent that each had "greater rights" because of "loving her more." And so it went on, with recriminations creeping back and Shura rising and turning his shoulder on me, and me deciding to go to see Katya to demand from her a guarantee she would dismiss Shura for good. We left Esau's. We both had the same destination. We stopped at the corner of her alley. A woman went past, leading two cows (still kept for fresh milk in cities in those days) and we were separated by them. Both of us dashed past the beasts and tried to reach the ironmonger's first. This ludicrous and undignified scene resulted in the pair of us reeling drunkenly into stacks of pots and pans which we knocked onto the cobbles. Out of the shop came the middle-aged Jewish proprietor, screaming and waving his arms and cursing the lust of men and the venality of women. Why had God decided that he, a respectable shopkeeper, must support his impeccably virtuous family by letting rooms to women of easy virtue? (I knew that an "extra" on his exorbitant rent was an afternoon every week with Katya's mother.) We demanded he step aside and let us through.

"To have my shop destroyed by drunks!" He took a great axe from his display. "To bring the police down on my poor head! Wonderful! Cossacks in the Moldovanka! Let's have a new pogrom, eh? Stand back, both of you, or I'll give the police fair cause to visit me. I'll split your heads and hang myself rather than let you in."

Katya's orange-haired sluttish mother appeared behind him. She was pulling on a grubby Chinese robe. "Shura? Maxim? What's the matter with you? Where's Katya?"

"We have come to see her," I said. "She has to choose between us."

"But she left half an hour ago."

"Where did she go?" asked Shura.

"To Esau's, I thought."

"Was she laughing?" I asked significantly.

"Not that I noticed. What do you want with her? You boys shouldn't quarrel over a girl. She likes you both."

"She's a deceiver," I said. "A liar."

"She's a bit weak, that's all," said Shura. "I told her—"

"I won't have such discussions in my street, outside my shop." The Jew advanced with the axe. We retreated.

Katya's mother shook her head. "Calm down. Go for a walk together. Go for a swim." She seemed unaware that it was winter.

"She was not frank with me," I said.

"Frank? What is frank?" asked the shopkeeper. He gestured with his huge axe. "Jews are not the bogotyrs of Kiev. They have no room for such podvig luxuries."

"They have a great penchant for hypocrisy instead," I retorted.

He smiled. "If we are here to indulge in some rabbinical discussion, some orgy of self-criticism, let us settle down around the book, my young Litvak."

Did he think I was a Jew? I was shocked. I looked at his dirty skin, his stringy beard, his hooked nose and thick lips and realized what a terrible mistake I had made. To believe that Jews could be my friends, that I could exist in their company without some of their traits rubbing off on me! I backed away. I began to run through the alleys of the ghetto, knocking aside old men and children, treading on cats and dogs, breaking down washing lines, kicking cans of milk, until I was back at Uncle Semya's house, bedraggled, my coat flapping, my hat missing, my ivory cane lost in the struggle at Katya's. Straight up the steps and into the front door. Up the stairs and into my room. I lay on my bed weeping and swearing never again to have anything to do with Jews, with the Moldovanka, with my cousin Shura, with coarse, corrupt, vulgar Odessa.

When Wanda came in, she found me recovered from the worst of my rage but still weeping, still dressed in what was left of my finery. "What happened, Maxim? An accident?"

I looked up at her warm, fat body, her plain, concerned face. I decided that Wanda was the girl I needed. Wanda would never make herself available to more than one man. She would be grateful that she had a man at all.

"Only in love," I replied heavily. "A girl turned out to be unfaithful."

"That's terrible. Dear Maxim!" Feminine sympathy seeped from her pores like sweat. "Who on earth could do such a thing to you? What a bitch she must be."

I remember a pang or two at this description, but when I considered the situation I decided Katya had been more cynical than I had guessed. I made some attempt to defend her, remembering Shura's words. "She's just weak . . . "

"Don't you believe it, Maxim dear. Not a word. Weakness is a wall women hide behind. And it's a wall, I assure you, as strong as steel. You've been deceived."

"By a Jewish harlot," I said.

This seemed to make her hesitate. I think she was a little upset that I had been sleeping with a Jewess.

"Never again," I said.

"She didn't give you anything . . . ?"

I shook my head.

Wanda sat on the bed and began to stroke my dusty hair. She helped me off with my overcoat and my jacket.

In time, as these things go, she helped me off with the rest of my clothes. Then she undressed and climbed into the narrow bed beside me. Her soft, yielding flesh, her massive breasts, her great, warm private parts, her bottom, like two comfortable cushions, her strong, engulfing legs and arms, her wide, hot mouth, all brought immediate relief to my anguish. I began to congratulate myself that I had not only recovered from my pain but that I would always have another woman waiting. So different was Wanda from Katya that it was almost like making love to a different species. Slender, boyish girls like Katya and huge, peasant girls like Wanda, each has her virtues. To know a hundred women is to know a hundred different forms of pleasure. I was lucky to understand this while still so young.

Rising from the damp and overheated bedding, Wanda said she had duties in the house. She kissed me. She asked me if I felt better. She told me she had been a virgin. She had always loved me. Now I would not need to go out for my consolations. With an awkward wink and a blown kiss, she left me. I slept for an hour or two and woke to find the room in cold, pale twilight. I thought, now that my temper had cooled, of going to visit Katya. The prospect of having two lovers, as she had had, pleased me. But I realized it would be hard to accomplish. Wanda was in a position to watch—and watch jealously—my every move.

I felt vengeful toward Shura. I had confided in him. I had told him I loved Katya. He had given me cocaine, white clothes, ivory, to distract me from his dark plots. He had pretended to be my friend and mentor in the ghetto and had exposed me to its worst aspects. All the while he had laughed up his sleeve. I could not beat him in a fight. He was too strong. I could not go to the police and say he was a criminal. I had been involved in some of those crimes, as had friends of mine in the Moldovanka. Not that I regarded them any more as friends. Probably they had all known about Shura's making a fool of me and been amused. I had been treated as a naïf. A village idiot. There must be half-a-dozen good stories about Max the Hetman all over Odessa. I had lost face. I wondered how I could in turn humiliate Shura. Nothing came to mind. He was too certain of himself. Anything I did he could turn to his advantage. There was only one person to whom he owed something, whom he respected (aside from Misha the Jap), and that was Uncle Semya. I grinned to myself. It would be nothing less than dutiful to go to Uncle Semya and "warn" him of Shura's involvement in crime. My uncle would be horrified. He would send for Shura. He would punish him. It was an ideal revenge because it showed me in a good light and Shura in a bad one.

I turned my attention to Katya. I might be able to involve her in the revenge by mentioning her to Uncle Semya as the hussy who had

led my cousin into evil ways. But Uncle Semya was not shocked by
such things. He was tolerant of young men who sowed their wild oats.
What would he think if I told him Shura was Katya's pimp? It would
not make Uncle Semya take reprisals on Katya. Somehow I would
have to work out my own revenge on Katya.

I am not very proud of those thoughts. But I was a hurt youngster
believing himself utterly betrayed by his friends and by a race. I
behaved in a bigoted fashion. I have not a bigoted bone in my body.
My dislike of Jews, my anger at being identified with them, was
because we Ukrainians were inundated by Jews. The Revolution
was directly inspired by Jews. To be a Slav in Odessa was to be in
a minority. As a member of a minority, I am anxious to disassociate
myself from those of Oriental origin who control our press, our publishing, our radio and television stations, our industry, our engineering plants, our financial world. How many Ukrainians occupy such
positions in England?

Katya could quite easily be reported to the police. But that would
mean her arrest and deportation (since she and her mother were
from Warsaw), possibly her imprisonment. Even in my most vengeful moments I balked at my little Camille of the ghetto going to
prison. Also I wanted a more personal revenge.

I remembered the clown from Magasin Wagner which now lay
smashed on her floor. I would send her another Christmas present.
From an unkown admirer. I knew she hated spiders: spiders horrified
her more than anything. I would collect together a huge box of them
and I would send it to her, wrapped in wonderful paper. She would
open it on Christmas Eve and her screams would bring the whole
Moldovanka down about her ears.

In the meantime I was distracted from my vengeance. Lovely,
simpering Wanda brought me tea and cake, stroked my body and
made herself familiar with my private parts as if she saw them as
being quite independent of me, as if she played with a tame mouse, or
a snake, which she would kiss, fondle and laugh at. She had something Katya had never possessed: while Wanda made love to me I
could continue to exist in my private mind, keep myself to myself. It
is a great advantage of such girls. I have always valued it.

Another advantage to Wanda, of course, was that she had slept
with nobody else. She was clean. I did not have to take precautions
with her. This was a relief. That night I did little but scheme against
Shura and Katya. Uncle Semya had to go out to dinner, so I was not in

a position to betray either Shura or myself. After our meal, Aunt Genia played some popular Jewish melodies on her gramophone. Wanda and I made an excuse and retired early. I was in a far better position with her than I had been with Katya. With Wanda, the relationship between Katya and myself was reversed. I became the teacher, instructing my wonderful, passive pupil in every delicious debauchery.

My enjoyment of Wanda nonetheless left me with a passionate determination for revenge. I began to collect the spiders for Katya's Christmas present. Soon I had about a dozen in an old tea box. But I wanted more. So that they should not fight and devour one another I found various insects and fed the spiders every evening. Wanda did not know what I kept in the box. I refused to tell her. In the meantime I purchased gifts to present at Christmas Eve dinner. My uncle did not celebrate the Season elaborately. Like my mother he had little use for formal church services. The day before Christmas Eve I asked to see Uncle Semya in his study. He was rather distracted. The War, of course, was making his business difficult. The partial blockade had delayed certain important shipments. I determined to get my revenge on Shura as quickly as possible. Uncle Semya stood behind his desk, his back to the window. He wore a heavy black frock coat and a black cravat.

"I have distressing news, Semyon Josefovitch," I began. "It is my duty to tell you what it is. You, of course, must take whatever action you think fit."

This amused him. His mood of distraction appeared to lift. He asked me to sit down in one of the hard, cane-bottomed chairs he favored. He leaned back in his own leather-padded chair and lit a Burma cheroot. The room began to fill with heavy, oily smoke.

"I hope you are not in trouble, Maxim."

"I hope so, too, Uncle. My mother would be horrified if she learned what had happened."

"Happened?" He became more alert.

"Or almost happened, I suppose. I believe Shura to be involved with crooks."

He was surprised. He put his cheroot into his brass Persian ashtray. He scratched his head. He produced a thin, puzzled smile. "What makes you think so?"

"He is mixed up in the rackets. He could be working with Misha the Jap."

"Misha the what?"

"The Jap. A notorious bandit in the Slobodka district."

"I believe I've heard of him."

This was no surprise. Misha's exploits were the raw material of all the popular papers in Odessa. He had even been mentioned in the Nick Carter and Sherlock Holmes dime novel pulps we had in those days.

"He is a kidnapper," I said, "a holdup man. He forces local people to pay him protection money. If they don't, he shoots them or burns their shops. He deals in drugs. In prostitution. Illegal alchohol. He owns cabarets, taverns. He bribes police inspectors, city officials, everyone."

Uncle Semya became amused again. "Such a Jew should join the Black Hundreds."

"And he recruits young lads," I continued, "of all races. Ukrainians, Katsups, as they call Russians, Greeks, Armenians, Georgians, Muslims, anyone. He has a web like a—" (I felt uncomfortable) "—like a spider."

"Heaven preserve us! Are you sure this bandit doesn't just exist in your Pinkerton magazines?"

I told him I spoke the truth. "And," I added, "he has Shura in his grip."

"I cannot believe it."

"Shura tried to recruit me, too. He used me as an interpreter. I went aboard an English ship. He bought drugs."

Uncle Semya turned his head away. He looked through the window. There was a yard with an entrance into the alley running between the houses. He watched a small child balancing on the wall. The child fell off and disappeared. He turned to look at me again. "I think you're mistaken, Maxim. Shura works for me."

"Of course he carries messages between the ships and merchants and keeps a lookout for good cargo when it's unloaded. But for the rest of the time he works with crooks, prostitutes. There's a place called Esau's. A Jewish tavern. Perhaps you've heard of it?"

"I don't often visit taverns in Slobodka."

"It's a terrible place. Shura has slipped into bad company. He tried to involve me, too. I refused and now he's angry with me."

"You had an argument?"

"I objected morally to his life."

"He's a young bohemian. You, too, have been living such a life."

"There's a difference, Semyon Josefovitch, between bohemianism and criminality."

"And young people do not always recognize it." He waved a tolerant hand.

I was disappointed. "I think Shura should be sent away from Odessa."

"To where? To Siberia?" He sounded the word slowly and sardonically.

"Possibly to sea. It would do him good. The education."

"Did he ask you to tell me this?"

"Not at all." Shura would hate to be removed from Odessa, from Katya. With Shura gone I should have both Wanda and Katya. Even when Katya opened the box of spiders she would not know it was from me. I could resume where we had left off. The notion of sending Shura to sea had been an inspiration.

"Shura isn't much of a sailor. Also, we are at war . . . " Uncle Semyon relit his cigar.

"Think what he would learn."

"Have you told him you were coming to me?"

"No, Semyon Josefovitch."

"It might have been more manly to have done so?"

"He needs an adult to tell him."

"And you've mentioned this to no other adults?"

"Only yourself."

"I will speak to Alexander. But you must keep this a secret, Maxim."

"Because of the family scandal?"

"Quite so."

He sighed. Perhaps he was grateful that at least one of the younger members of the family was honest. "Off you go, Maxim. If you see Shura, ask him to come here."

"I will, Semyon Josefovitch."

Not an hour later, as I went downstairs to find wrapping paper for Katya's present, I saw Shura arrive and go through the door connecting Uncle Semya's business with the house. I had only seen these premises once: dark-painted wood and little glass windows, and oak, mahogany and brass desks, with clerks sitting at them who might have been there since the days of Pushkin. I wondered why Shura should go into the offices rather than into Uncle Semya's study.

I waited on the landing, watching the door, but Shura did not emerge again. I assumed he had left through another exit.

Feeling mightily pleased with myself, I went to ask Aunt Genia for the fancy paper. She handed me a sheet, together with some scissors and ribbon. I was not, she said, to disturb Uncle Semya if I saw him. He was in an unusually difficult mood.

"Was it to do with Shura?"

She shrugged. "Perhaps. He doesn't seem too pleased with you, either. Have you been up to anything?"

"Nothing, Aunt Genia."

I returned to my room. I was just a little puzzled. I wrapped the parcel. I called Wanda in and asked her if any boys in the street could be paid to take a parcel to Slobodka. She said that she would see. I had marked the parcel with Katya's initials, and her Polish surname, which was something like Grabbitz.

"Who are you sending a present to?" Wanda asked. "It looks a very nice one."

I kissed her. "It is nobody I love. A friend of mine. Someone to whom I owe a favor."

With a few kopecks, she took the box downstairs and eventually returned to say one of the street urchins from the square had agreed to deliver it. Now, if Katya asked who had given the boy the box, Wanda and not myself would be identified as the sender.

Wanda and I made love very briefly. I was not really in the mood. I was still wondering what had happened to Shura. The way my luck now ran, he could be on the next ship out of the Quarantine Harbor.

I had asked Wanda to leave me alone for half an hour and was reaching for the drawer where I kept my cocaine when the door opened softly and closed. I expected Wanda. To my horror, it was Shura. He was grinning at me in a very menacing way. He had abandoned his tie and shirt and was wearing a laced peasant blouse with a loud, heavy scarf tied around his throat; over this was thrown a fur coat whose surface had worn away in patches. In his hand was a three-eared cap. He looked almost pathetic.

"You little stool pigeon," he said. "You stupid, silly little Kiev-gilt goyim. You wouldn't have it out face to face. What a crook I am! That's a laugh. Uncle Semya's the biggest crook of all."

I was familiar with these revolutionary arguments. "Capitalism isn't a crime."

"Isn't it? Well, your plan misfired. I'm not to be sent to the galleys.

I'm merely to be more cautious about what I let green little sneaks see."

"Did Uncle Semya say that?"

"Not exactly. But it's the substance."

"I can't believe it."

"You don't have to. I thought we were friends, Max."

Shura spoke as if I had betrayed him! I now remember him with nothing but kindness and have long since forgiven him, but at that moment the fact that Shura considered himself a victim was almost laughable. I smiled. "Shura, it was you who broke the friendship."

"You idiot. I was sleeping with Katya before you even turned up. I asked her to be nice to you. I slipped her money. Why did you think it went so easily for you?"

"She loved me."

"I suppose she did. As much as she could. She's been my girl friend for years. Ask anyone."

"You're lying. It's despicable."

He went bright red. His face was a match for his cropped hair. "You don't have to take my word. Katya will tell you."

The door opened slowly. Wanda came in. "What is it, Shura?"

Shura told her to leave. I nodded in agreement. "This is between us."

"Don't start fighting, or I'll call Aunt Genia."

"I wouldn't touch him," said Shura. This relieved me.

"At least you've made it clear how you feel," I said. "What about me? My rival's a Jew-loving lout who can hardly speak his own name. A crook."

"Jew lover?" He laughed. "And why not? Do you know what our name originally was?"

"Your father's, you mean? I'm surprised you know it."

"Coming from you, that's rich."

We were hurting each other quite unfairly, as only those who have been close can wound. It was I who turned my back first, refusing to continue. If Shura was going to flout the fact of being half-Jewish, that was his own affair. It only confirmed what I thought.

"I feel sorry for you," he said. "You could have been happy here. You could have had friends here. People liked you. But not now. I advise you to get out of Odessa as quickly as possible."

Was it a threat? I said, "Odessa has no further attractions for me."

He opened the door, drawing his moth-eaten fur about him. "You won't say that when your sneg runs out." Sneg—"snow"—was our slang term for cocaine.

Then he was gone. Did he think he had turned me into a drug fiend? I became alarmed, then reassured. I was not the type to become addicted. I have gone for months without touching the stuff. Indeed, in recent years, with prices the way they are, I have all but given it up. They made cocaine illegal before the Second World War. It was one of the silliest things they did. They should have made aspirin and gin illegal at the same time.

On the morning of Christmas Eve I was called again to my uncle's study. Concerned that he had not heard from her, he had sent my mother a telegram. A reply had reached him from Captain Brown. My mother had bad influenza. She was worrying about me. It seemed that providence had given me a perfect excuse to leave Odessa and escape any attempted vengeance from Shura. Uncle Semya agreed I should rejoin my mother as soon as the Christmas holiday was over, when the trains would be running as normally as could be expected in wartime. A place had been found for me at the Petrograd Polytechnic Institute. I would begin there in January. A full wardrobe would be provided for me. I would draw a small allowance from his agents in the city. They would also find me accommodation. In return, I might be called on to translate in matters of business or carry small parcels to other agents of his. I told him I would be honored to serve him.

He had confirmed my place, he said, by telegram. A number of telegrams had gone back and forth in the past twenty-four hours. He had spoken to Shura and had received Shura's faithful promise not to engage in acts likely to embarrass the family. My revenge was frustrated. There was no time to plot a fresh one. At least, I thought to myself, Katya would be opening her spiders by now.

I went back upstairs to tell Wanda what was happening. We decided to make the most of our time together. I gave her a little of my cocaine to help her stay awake. We spent as much of the Christmas holiday as possible in an orgy of love making.

When my suitcases were packed and my first-class ticket (a gift from Aunt Genia) was in my pocket, I realized I would miss Wanda. I told her I would come back to Odessa as soon as possible. She must visit me in Kiev. I never did see her again. She became pregnant, gave birth to a son, and was looked after by Uncle Semya until she vanished three or four years later in the terrible days of famine and revolution.

Wanda and Aunt Genia saw me to the Kiev train. The station was crowded with uniforms. I was already missing Odessa, with her docks and shops, her fog and coal dust and her vital, noisy life. I believe I wept a little. Wanda certainly wept. Aunt Genia wept. The train began to move away from the platform, heading inland once more. I thought I saw Shura standing near the gate, raising his hat sardonically, Katya at his side.

It was snowing heavily as the train pulled into open countryside. I sat back happily in the padding of the heated carriage. This was more comfortable than the last trip. I was already making progress. I wore a Petersburg suit, a good-quality fur cap, an English topcoat with a fur collar, and black patent-leather boots. Over the course of a few months, I thought, I had not only become a man; I had become a gentleman.

With my first-class ticket I was able to sit in a deep plush armchair with my books and magazines close by on a little folding table. Soon after we left Odessa we ran into a blizzard. The further north we went, the deeper the snow became. All I could see was undulating banks of whiteness, interspersed with the roofs, smoke and domes of villages, the silhouettes of trees, the occasional snow-drenched forest. I could almost smell the snow through the windows, though of course the carriage was insulated and the motion of the train so regular one might not have been traveling at all. Just for the pleasure of it, I took the "large breakfast" in the restaurant car. I ate cheese and cold meats and watched the snow clinging to the windows. Sometimes it built up a layer before the speed and heat of the train melted it away, to reveal the steppe again. I strolled into the saloon car, which bore the sign of the Romanoffs, the two-headed eagle, over the door. Here I remained, in a small chair close to the ornate stove, listening to the murmurings of generals and priests, aristocrats and fine ladies; they were already drinking, many of them, for prohibition extended only to the lower classes. Their well-bred tones would from time to time be broken by sudden, loud laughter. They were cynical, in the main, about the War news.

Being in the saloon and unable to join the occupants depressed me. I returned to my carriage, where an old lady dressed all in black took a fancy to me. She began to tell me how she was the widow of a certain general killed in the war with Japan.

She spoke in the slightly Frenchified accents of St. Petersburg. I was soon able to catch the sound and reproduce it. She decided I was well educated, a well-bred boy. She shared some of her chocolates with me. She asked where I was bound. I told her Kiev. I was to go on almost immediately to St. Petersburg. She said I should come to see her and wrote down an address in a small notebook. The other travelers in the carriage were a high-ranking military man who said nothing, studied maps, read *The Voice of Russia*, and sometimes left to go to the saloon car to smoke a cigar; a theatrical, rather haughty young woman who claimed she acted in Moscow and was soon to tour the provinces. She smelled of the same perfume as Mademoiselle Cornelius, whom I still remembered with great pleasure. This actress had none of that lady's character; she was a typical, neurotic Moscow "beauty." I doubt if she was an actress at all. Probably a general's mistress, traveling separately to avoid scandal. Her brocades and furs had the look of trophies rather than familiar clothing.

The snow did not stop. It became dark quite soon and the gas was lit in the carriages. So comfortable and warm was the train that I was more and more reluctant to have the journey end. I hoped for delays on the line, some minor disaster which would extend the adventure for another day at least. Lunch came and went, and dinner. I talked to my old lady, telling her of my ideas, my plans, my expectations of "doing good for Russia." She said I would love Peter. "It is really Russian there, not like this awful province. This is a land of Jews. They are impossible to avoid."

Feelingly, I agreed with her.

"But in St. Petersburg," she said, "there you will find the embodiment of all that is best in Russia."

The actress claimed that Moscow was "more Russian" than the capital. There were too many Europeans in Peter. The place had been founded by a Czar who had looked to Germany for inspiration. See, she said, where that had gotten us. Attacked by the very people we had courted, to whom we had shown hospitality. Half the Royal Family was German. They were the scourge of the Earth. She wished she could remain in Moscow all her life. No socialists there. No nihilists. No assassins. There were no Jews and no Germans, either. It was a true Slav city, not some imitation Berlin or Paris.

The old lady listened with amusement. Her husband had been just such a radical. A Pan-Slavist who wished to turn his back on Western Europe. "But Western Europe will not turn her back on us, my dear."

"No, indeed!" said the actress. "She comes toward us with hands extended. With a knife in one fist and a sword in the other. We should have expelled all foreigners years ago. Including those who call themselves Russians." This was a reference to our "German Empress" and a number of nobles in St. Petersburg who were of German origin and still had German names. Even some of the generals at the front and the ministers in the Duma were of recent German ancestry, including the prime minister. There were plenty of rumors of German traitors working against Russia from within; a tendency, especially in Moscow, to put the blame for our military failures on corruption in the capital; a suspicion that the Court had no real interest in the progress of the War, that the Czar might be inclined to negotiate a peace at any time. I make this clear to show how bad morale was. Russia has never started a major war. We had never wanted to go to war; Germany had attacked us. As a result of this, almost the whole of the civilized world was now in arms. Although I felt more patriotic than many at this time, I could understand why they were so aggrieved. It could be argued to this day that Germany, who gave the world Karl Marx, prepared the ground in which Marx's pernicious doctrines could flourish. Many believe the German race the creator of the terror and chaos which is our twentieth century. I do not agree with this depiction. The Germans were very kind to me in the thirties, by and large.

My wish for delay was in part to be granted. The train was late. Because of snow drifts on the line, precedence given to military trains, and the general inefficiency of the railway company, whose best men were now engaged in war work, we stopped frequently. The temperature never became absolutely uncomfortable but the saloon car with its stove grew crowded and eventually we put on our top-coats and returned to our seats. The actress remained in the saloon, drinking cognac. We were brought frequent tumblers of tea to console us. By dawn the old lady in black had begun to shiver. At last the train moved slowly forward between high banks of snow. It was impossible to see anything but snow. It was as if we traveled through a brilliant ice cavern, a tunnel whose roof was illuminated by glowing grey felt.

Even as we crawled forward (we were only a few miles from Kiev) the snow came down again. Great sheets of it fell vertically. There was no wind. I was very tired, but I went to the observation platform behind the guard's van and looked back at the line. There were two dark parallel tracks in it created by the wheels of the train.

Even as I watched, they began to fill. It was as if the whole of the past, the entire landscape behind us, were being erased. I had a feeling of freedom which quickly gave way to a sense of loss. I remembered Odessa in the summer; the quick, babbling people, the gaiety of it all, the wit, the kindness, the comradeship. This blizzard had fallen on that Odessan summer like a final curtain. The Frost Gods were taking vengeance on those who, for a few short months, had dared to be happy.

A little later, as if celebrating escape from disaster, we came steaming and whistling into Kiev. The station seemed bleak, though as crowded as ever. The great baroque pillars where pigeons nested, the stone walls and ceilings, the looming Renaissance bas-reliefs, all gave an impression of coldness. With my bag (containing new clothes and gifts) I stepped down onto the platform, bewildered once more by the rush of the porters, the shouts of the passengers, the sense of panic which seized everyone the moment the train had stopped. But now I had no Shura to guide me.

I began to walk as best I could through this press. I ignored porters, vendors, touts. I had some idea of getting the tram to Podol and from there walking or getting another tram home. As I reached the main entrance and saw people fighting for cabs, crushing one another to get on the trams, I felt a terrible regret at the absence of Shura and his comradeship. I was never really to know such warmth and spirit again. I went past the terminus. The roofs and streets were piled with snow. There were braziers on the pavements, bundled-up old snow sweepers, peasants selling hot tea and chestnuts, troikas going past. It was familiar. I hated it. I had, in a strange way, become a person without a context. We Russians will do anything to ensure ourselves of a context. If slavery is the only one offered us, we will accept it rather than have none at all. It is what Kropotkin realized. It is why the Red Napoleon, Lenin, and his gang were so successful.

As a stranger, I looked at the city which I had left a few months ago and in which I had been raised. As a stranger, I did not enjoy what I saw. The War had already begun to affect us. The people were not as friendly, or at least as gregarious, as those in Odessa. There were not the smiles, the rapid exchanges, the gestures full of ambiguous meaning. So I thought.

I made my way to what was then called Stolypinskaya. If I walked along this street, it would eventually lead me to Vladimirskaya and St. Andrews, where I would be able to get an ordinary tram all the way home. I was anxious to avoid the crowds. I had turned into Stolypinskaya, with its tall, yellow buildings which, with snow at top and foot, resembled a kind of unappetizing seedcake, when I heard a shout behind me. I gripped my suitcase and felt a touch or two of anxiety until, turning, I realized it was Captain Brown, a hobbling old bear in black fur, rushing after me. "Maxim! I thought I'd missed you. Didn't you get the message?"

He had sent a telegram to Odessa. Because of the War it had not arrived until I had left. I was to have waited near the gate of the platform where he would meet me. He had no transport, so we continued to walk along the Stolypinskaya together. He insisted on carrying my bag. He said he had been waiting several hours, because of the train being so late. He thought I must be exhausted, but of course I had been far more comfortable than had he. He looked older. His face had become almost a modern artist's idea of a face, all in bright reds and blues. But I was glad to see him, even if he did smell of vodka. My mother had been desperately ill. Between them, he and Esmé had nursed her to health. Now she was "sitting up and complaining," drinking soup and no longer "getting ready to meet the Reaper." I had had no idea, of course, that she had been so ill. I assumed her influenza to have been relatively mild. But there had been something of an epidemic in the poorer districts. Many had died, said Captain Brown. Esmé had not written to tell me this because she had not wanted me to worry. He had written to Uncle Semyon asking that I not be informed of the danger. She was much better now and anxious to see me. He commented on my fine clothes —"a little too smart for Kiev, eh?"—and on my complexion, which was at once healthier and "more mature." I had cut down radically on the cocaine. I now no longer used it daily. The supply in my luggage might be the last I was to find for some time. I must treasure it.

We took a Number 10 tram up to our district. The streets of Podol below looked meaner and dirtier, even with the snow, and the people were wretched compared to those I had known in the Moldovanka. My dislike of Jewish poverty, Jewish passivity, Jewish greed, Jewish pride, welled within me, but I suppressed it. I had been shown kindness, too, by Jews. There were, I'll argue to this day, Jews and Jews. In aggregate, however, they can be depressing. Our little street was piled with snow drifts taller than I. Through them channels had been cut to doorways, and along the middle of the road. It seemed horribly seedy. I felt depressed as we turned into the building where I had spent most of my life. We climbed stairs smelling of cabbage and overbrewed tea, of kvass and sour dumplings. We entered the apartment and its oppressive darkness—the blinds were half drawn—where my mother lay on her couch pulled close to the black iron stove. Esmé, pale and weary and as sweet as ever, ran forward to take my hand, leading me to my mother. Mother coughed the most horrible racking cough I have ever heard. She spoke in the croaking tones I had learned to recognize from past illnesses of all kinds; it was her "ill" voice.

"Maxim, my dear son. Such a joy! I thought we'd never meet in this world again."

I embraced her, letting her kiss me on my face while I kissed her cheeks. She smelled strongly of embrocation. She was swathed in layer upon layer of bodices and blouses and shawls and I must admit that I was, after the style and good living of Odessa, just a little repulsed. The room was extremely warm. I broke free, in the end, and patted her head. She winced. I stopped patting and said to Esmé, "You have been so good. I was sorry to hear of your father. You are a princess."

She blushed. It was almost as if she wished to curtsy to me. "You've become so manly, Maxim. Your manners! A prince, at least." She spoke with slight irony, but I was flattered.

A great, expressive cough came from where my mother was propped. "He must eat!"

"I have the broth ready." Esmé disappeared into the next room and came back with a pot which she placed on the stove. "It's warm. It will not be long."

I looked miserably at the old familiar pot. The smell from it was no longer appetizing. The pot had sustained me since I was weaned. It had been filled, as it were, by my mother's sweat. I recalled the turnips and onions and beets and potatoes which had gone into it. And I longed for that spicy, tasty, Odessa food. The variety of borschtes, and yushkas, the kuleshnik, the schipanka, the zatirka, kulish and rassolnik, the herrings and boiled sturgeon and sardines, the roast meats with sauerkraut and prunes and buckwheat hash.

"You must be hungry," said my mother.

"I ate on the train," I said. "There was a lot of food. I'm not hungry. Don't worry."

"There's meat in the soup," she said. "Chicken. You must eat." She began to cough again, from the chest, her eyes watering.

"I'll eat later," I said. "I brought you a present." I was embarrassed because I had nothing special for Captain Brown. I produced the black-and-red shawl I had bought for my mother.

"It's beautiful," she said. "Real silk. Is it from Semyon?"

"It's from me," I said. "I earned the money."

"Earned? How?"

"Bills of lading," I said. "A profit on cargo."

"You're going to work in Semya's office?"

"This was a private matter," I told her. "Here, Esmé. What do you think?"

It was a beautiful apron, embroidered with intricate stitching. It had come from Wagner's. Esmé clapped her hands with pleasure. Her blue eyes widened as she inspected the embroidery. I had chosen well. It went perfectly with her coloring, her blond hair. I found a packet of "Sioux" tobacco in the bottom of my suitcase. I was by no means a habitual smoker. I decided to give this to Captain Brown. He was delighted.

"This is the best imported American tobacco," he said. "Virginian. You don't often get hold of it. I have seen where it is grown, you know, in the Southern States of America. Miles of fields, full of niggers picking the weed, and singing. Beautiful music, particularly in the distance. I once crossed America from Charleston to Nantucket. By the railroad. I've seen New York, though I was only there a few hours. And Boston, too. And Washington. And Chicago, where I still have friends." He fondled the tobacco and I was glad I had given it to him. He was the most pleased of all. "It's strange," he continued, "that I should have wound up here." He began to say something in English in a low tone. I only caught a few words and part of a phrase which had something to do with "worthless relatives in Inverness." At some stage in his life he had written to his family asking if there was "a berth" for him. He had received no reply. He claimed to be the black sheep of his family, though it was hard to see why. He was the next best thing to a father to me and a loving husband to my mother.

"The War is producing many shortages." Captain Brown pocketed the tobacco. "Everything is hard to get. I suspect profiteers. Hoarders. Things are worse, I gather, the farther north and west you go. People from Moscow say we're lucky."

"They've always been envious of Ukraine," said Esmé. "Father believed the Germans were fighting the entire War just to annex this part of the Empire. We've the best industry, the most food, the best ports. It stands to reason."

"Your father knew what he was talking about, Esmaya." Captain Brown tried to lean against the stove without burning himself. "I speak as a soldier. They want Russia as far as the Caucasus, which they'll split with Turkey. You can be sure some power-drunk Hun and some scheming Mussulman have made that decision already. Why else should Turkey enter the War?"

"We fought back the Tartar hordes," I said. "It should be an easy matter to drive the Germans and Turks from our borders."

"God is with Russia," said Esmé. "We always win in the end. We always shall."

"I'm sure you're right."

This discussion was terminated by a terrible fit of coughing. My mother, her hair streaming about her white face just as if she were having one of her nightmares, flung herself half off the couch. Paroxysms of coughing threw her body this way and that. She gasped for something, holding herself steady on the floor with one hand, gesturing with the other.

"Water?" said Esmé.

"Medicine?" said Captain Brown.

I made to help her up. She shook in my arms. It was a peculiar, spasmodic shaking, as if at first she tensed herself, then released the muscles she had tensed. Her teeth began to chatter.

"Should we send for a doctor?" I asked.

"It sounds callous," said Captain Brown, "but he will only charge money to tell us what we know. Your mother has become overexcited at the prospect of her only son being returned to her. She speaks of you all the time. She is proud of you, Maxim."

"Proud," gasped my mother. "Have some soup." I could tell that she felt both concern and pleasure.

"You must sleep, Yeliseveta Filipovna," Esmé told her. She produced a bottle of chloroform, saying to me, "She has waited all night for you. You were expected sooner."

"The train," I told her. "The War."

Noisily, almost greedily, my mother accepted the spoon. Soon she had fallen back on her pillows and was snoring. I looked miserably around the room. It now seemed impossibly small and cluttered. I saw my shelf. I had once enjoyed sleeping on my shelf. Now I longed for a bed, no matter how tiny. A bed with a white sheet on it and white pillows.

For almost a week I was to live in that apartment while my mother alternately coughed and snored, or occasionally broke into one of her old familiar nightmares. Esmé, at least, slept on the shelf, while I had her mattress in the other room. It was not quite so bad as I had expected. At least I had a degree of privacy, though the cooking utensils and food were kept near me. Water was fetched from a pump on the landing below, but we had a sink and drainage. We shared a lavatory with the drunken couple next door.

I spent some of my first day taking a walk with Esmé. I retailed a censored version of my adventures. She was impressed. I elaborated some anecdotes: going aboard the English tramp, for instance, and encountering Greeks and lascars. In the main it was enough to tell her about all the wonders: the pleasure resorts of Fountain and Arcadia, the sideshows at the fair, more impressive than any we ever saw at the Contract Fair in Kiev; the myriad ships and races. Esmé clutched my arm so tightly and listened so attentively that I began to suspect she had designs on me. But that was a terrible thought. Esmé was pure; above such desires. At least, she was unaware of any desires and her gestures were innocent. I pulled away from her. We continued to walk. Kiev seemed small and provincial compared with Odessa, for all that this was our major city. I missed the sea, the sense of the world beyond the water waiting to be visited. I told this to Esmé when she asked if I were glad to be home.

"I want the opportunity for escape," I said. "My soul has the scent of foreign parts. I want to travel. I want to build machines in which we shall all be able to sail through the air. Remember when I flew, Esmé?"

"I remember."

"We shall both fly. I shall go to Petersburg and get my diplomas. Then I shall possess the authority I need to convince the skeptics. Then I shall go to Kharkov and get finance. Then I shall build all kinds of flying machines: passenger liners, individual planes, everything. And gyro-carriages. And sailing dirigibles which can land on water or fly, depending on the whim and needs of the pilot."

"You will be famous," she said. "Kiev will honor you. You will have your name in the newspapers every day, like Sikorsky."

Sikorsky was in St. Petersburg already. Having abandoned the ideas he had borrowed wholly from Leonardo da Vinci, he was no longer experimenting with helicopters. I had dropped a similar line of research as being impractical. Another idea, involving the use of a cyclist powering his own propeller, was taken up some fifty or sixty years later. Sikorsky never replied to my letter offering him fifty percent of the profits if he helped me develop the invention. His plans had become more grandiose. He was virtually the inventor of that terrible weapon, the bombing aeroplane. Too late, however, to give Russia the air supremacy she needed. We could have transferred the theater of operations into the upper atmosphere. We should no longer have had to depend on unreliable, untrained peasants whose empty heads were fitting repositories for Red propaganda. Stalin, the "Man of Steel," has been blamed for a great deal. But Stalin, like Ivan the Terrible before him, realized the worth of encouraging Russians to rely on purely Russian brains and skill. Sikorsky, in disgust, soon went to America to earn a fortune and an exaggerated reputation. Other Russians simply never got the credit they deserved. Stalin knew what Russian aeronautic expertise was worth. We needed someone of his ilk at the time of the First War. Then, ironically, we should not have found ourselves saddled with him later.

Of course, I said little of this to Esmé as we walked through the St. Kyril gardens, in the last week of 1914. I had a certain gift for predicting the development of engineering ideas, but I was no Cagliostro!

During the week I was at home I was pleased to see my mother improving. Soon she was able to move about the flat. Uncle Semyon, it seemed, had granted her a pension. "He wants a gentleman in the family." My mother flourished his letter. "He will do anything to see you succeed."

"Will you give up the laundry?" I asked. It was now a source of distress to me that my mother earned such an undignified living.

"I am drawing a small rent on it," she said. "At present I am too ill to do much."

"You'll make yourself worse by returning over-soon," Esmé agreed.

"You should go to Odessa in the spring," I suggested. "It is wonderful there. The sunshine will make a new woman of you."

This amused her. "You're not happy with the old one?"

"Not in her present condition. Stay at Uncle Semya's."

"And be shot by Turks? This is the worst time to be visiting the seaside, Maxim." She was almost accusatory, as if I had suggested she put herself into danger. "We'll wait, eh? Until after the War."

"It will be over by spring. See what a Russian winter will do to our enemies. We'll thrive on it. They'll die by the millions in Galicia. The corn will be nourished on enemy blood."

This raised a horrified "Oh, Maxim!" from Esmé, a small groan from Mother, and a chuckle from Captain Brown as he entered from the other room where he had been washing up. "You've become a Russian warrior, Maxim."

"We must all be warriors of some kind." I had read this in one of the newspapers. "Every Russian is a soldier, helping to bring Victory."

"Every Russian?" Captain Brown winked at me. He had accepted my manhood whereas my mother still considered me the boy who had left Kiev in September. "What about Rasputin, eh? Do you think he's doing his bit? If so, I'd like to help him."

He was drunk. My mother exclaimed: "Captain Brown!" and suggested he go for a walk until he felt better. Esmé was blushing. I was surprised at the old Scot. Normally, drunk or sober, he was a gentleman. Perhaps his consumption of vodka had increased lately. With a murmur of apology he made a little bow to my mother and Esmé and left. He did not return for several hours. In the meantime I sat at the table and did my best, as I had done since my arrival home, to refresh myself on basic engineering principles. I had a place at the Polytechnic, but I would need to go through a preliminary oral examination when I arrived. I wanted to be sure of passing it. I continued to study at night while Esmé and Mother slept. My little store of cocaine got smaller, but my store of knowledge increased rapidly.

As I studied, ideas began to come back to me. These were projects I had set aside when I had left for Odessa. I developed a method of building underwater tunnels to link various parts of Petersburg divided by the canals and rivers; I toyed with the notion of bridging the Bering Strait to produce a direct land link between Russia and America; naturally, new kinds of steel would be required, and I considered different alloys. I was beginning, in short, to settle comfortably into my studious and creative mood again. Sometimes I would go for walks alone: to the gorge, now deep in snow, where Zoyea's camp had been; to the Babi gorge, where I had flown. Once I visited the run-down house of Sarkis Mihailovitch Kouyoumdjian, only to discover he had given up his business. It was the matter of the bakery engine, apparently, which had made him decide to leave Kiev. Business had become harder to find, possibly because people were reverting to preindustrial methods as the War progressed, and he had gone to Odessa not long after me. From there, I was informed, he had left for England. He had relatives, said an old female neighbor, in Manchester.

As my mother's health improved she began to worry more about my impending trip. "Odessa was one thing," she said, "but Petersburg is another. In Odessa you had relatives. In Petersburg you'll have no one."

"It's not true, Mother. Uncle Semya has given me the names of his agents. They are a respectable English firm. From Messrs. Green and Grunman I'll draw my allowance and I can go to them any time I am in difficulties."

"Petersburg is the center of revolutionary schemes. Everybody knows that. Your father was never political until he went there. They started all the trouble. The arrests. The pogroms. It's easy for them. They're the sons and daughters of the rich. If they're caught, they get exiled and have to go to live in Switzerland. But we get shot."

"I shan't get shot, Mother."

"You must promise to do nothing to put yourself under suspicion," Esmé begged me.

"I've no time for Reds." I laughed at their fears. "Cadets or Social Revolutionaries or Anarchists. I hate them all." In those days the Social Revolutionaries, as opposed to Lenin's Social Democrats, were regarded as by far the most fanatical radicals. Lenin, needless to say, hiding away in some luxury chalet, had never been heard of by anyone. It was only later, confident that his dirty work had been done for him, that he was paid to come back to Russia by the Germans and claim the Revolution as his own. People like that exist in all walks of life. They let the real workers exhaust themselves, then stroll in to take the credit.

I have had exactly that happen to me, with my inventions. Thomas Alva Edison's reputation was based on the brainchildren of his assistants. Since this commonly happens in the scientific field, it is not surprising it should also happen in business and in politics. Many Germans have told me that Einstein stole all his ideas from his pupils. There is a young man in the pub who tells me he wrote all the Beatles songs and received not a penny in royalties. Even Sikorsky's much-vaunted helicopter experiments were preceded by the Cornu brothers' successful French attempt of 1907, but you did not read much about them in the Kiev newspapers two years later. In the worlds of science and politics it is the man who has the most luck, seeks the most publicity, meets the right people, who gives his name to cities and to great companies. I am reconciled to obscurity, but at least these memoirs will set the record straight.

Obscurity seemed impossible to the boy who told Esmé of his plans for the future; of his visions of great, elegant skyscraper blocks rising above the ruins of the slums; towns with moving pavements and covered streets, with aerial transport, food dispensers, genetic selectors ensuring that all children were in perfect health. We were developing the technology. That was how we should use it.

Esmé for her part talked of when she would be old enough to become a nurse. "It will be too late, soon," she said, "the War will be over."

"Pray for that." What would she do in the event of peace? She would still go into nursing. "I want to do something useful with my life."

I squeezed her hand in gratitude as we sat on a bench in the winter sunshine, looking down over Babi gorge. "In the meantime you are keeping a brave woman alive. I owe everything to Mother, Esmé."

"When one only has a single parent, one appreciates them so much more," she said.

I agreed. She had become sad, thinking of her dead father.

"He was a brave man," I said.

She became bleak. "Brave enough. But will there be justice in this clean, scientific world of yours, Maxim?"

"Justice is a scarce commodity," I said.

She smiled. "You could be a great teacher."

I had considered this. "I might decide to run my own laboratory, with assistants to whom I can pass on my knowledge."

"I shall become your resident nurse."

"We shall each do our best, in our different spheres, to improve the world."

It was rare for me to make the mistake of believing knowledge could be used in the service of sentiment. It is no more the job of the nun to be "of the world" than it is for a pure scientist to design more efficient soup kitchens. It is mere intellectual arrogance to believe that science can cure human ills. But in Esmé's company I was often temporarily infected with her own feminine sentimentality. And I am the first to admit that without such creatures, the world would be an even less tolerable one than it is.

On my birthday I received suitable gifts from my little family.

Books, pencils, paper, a rare German pencil sharpener and a proper attaché case, all of which I should need in Petersburg. My mother wept and coughed and lay on her couch, looking at me through sleepy eyes and begging Esmé and Captain Brown to tell me to be sure I did not fall in with Reds and loose women.

I told her they were very strict at the Polytechnic Institute. I had looked it up on the map. It was not even in Petersburg proper.

The next day I had a letter and some silver rubles from Odessa. My uncle told me to make the most of myself in Peter, to meet the right people and to make a good impression on my professors. He told me I should be known there as Dimitri Mitrofanovitch Kryscheff and he enclosed a passport in that name. My own photograph was on it. This was a shock. Because of the War, he had evidently had to pull strings, but I had not expected to enter the Institute under an assumed name. I might have to use this name for the rest of my life. It would be on all my diplomas. I had not at this time become used to the idea of changing names as one changed clothes. The Revolution soon familiarized me with that particular procedure. I knew from Shura that many people had identity papers in different names. Some had changed a dozen times. But these were criminals, radicals, who were forced to do such things. The passport was authentic. Uncle Semya reminded me to let my mother know the name I would be using.

I could not speak of this at once either to her or to Esmé. I put on my English topcoat and wandered out toward the park. Here, on the hill, I thought the problem over. I could see how it had all come about, of course. With the War on, places at the Polytechnic were hard to come by. Many Ukrainians wished to study in Petersburg. Obviously there were too many applicants. Presumably this Dimitri Mitrofanovitch Kryscheff had given up his place so that I could go. Possibly he had died. He might have joined the army. There were a dozen possibilities. If I wished to learn, I should have to learn under a pseudonym. It would make no difference to the quality of that learning. Perhaps later I could admit my real name and get my diplomas properly inscribed.

I have hated hypocrisy and deception all my life, yet all my life I have been victim to it. That is the terrible irony. Here I was having to live a lie not because I had done anything wrong, but because my Uncle Semya had been willing to go to any lengths to ensure me a good education. I had learned that the world is made up of lies.

I informed my mother. She was not surprised. She had had some hint, she told me, in Uncle Semya's recent letters. Kryscheff was a good, respectable name. It had a ring to it.

I think that she was distressed, however. It could have been part of her general distress. In some ways it was bad for her that I had remained so long at home. Even Esmé was of the opinion that although my mother's spirits and health had improved her nerves had deteriorated.

On my last evening, Esmé and I went for a walk. I told her that I was to pose as Dimitri Mitrofanovitch and that she must keep the secret of my real name. That secret was my parting present to her. She smiled and said she would treasure it. She was not especially puzzled by this sudden change of identity, either.

We held hands, like brother and sister, and Esmé reassured me that she would look after Mother, that I must dedicate myself to becoming a great engineer. If I became famous as Kryscheff, what did it matter? My mother would still be proud and I would still be able to look after her.

By the next morning I had managed to fit myself into the role and was D. M. Kryscheff boarding the Wagon-Lit which was to carry me in the comfort to which I had become accustomed to the capital.

Uncle Semyon had sent the ticket together with a sheet of instructions as to where I should go and how I should behave in Petersburg. He was anxious I should act like a gentleman in every aspect of my life. He was prepared to spare no expense to this end. I was deeply touched by his kindness. My mother was overjoyed. She had been too ill to see me to the station and for this, I must admit, I was somewhat grateful. It would have been humiliating to have been seen with a sickly, weeping mother coughing out her last good-bys. Instead Esmé and Captain Brown came. They helped me with my luggage, saw that the porter took it to the appropriate compartment.

I was overexcited. I had never slept in a special Wagon-Lit coach. As I entered the coupé I saw that the top bunk was already occupied. I was to share with another gentleman. This was usual, unless one were very rich, and I had known there would be very few spare places on the train. Almost the whole of it was occupied by high-ranking military men and their families. Never had I heard so much drawling, well-bred Russian spoken—or so much French, for that matter. The girls spoke French in preference. I think they even liked to pretend they were French. Their accents gave them away. I could tell this, even though French is not the language I speak most fluently. It is the language of love; the language which these same girls would be speaking in a few years time as they tried to attract Bolshevik protectors on the streets of Petrograd and Moscow.

The compartment astonished Esmé. She had never heard of such things. She had expected, she told me, a row of cots, side by side in the carriage: a mobile dormitory. She discovered next door the little wash basin, with its polished wooden top which could be a table when the basin was not in use. Even the lavatory was disguised to look like a chair, its livery matching the rest of the coupé. The whole effect was of dark pink and white, glowing in the snowy light from the windows. The upholstery was the color of a confection later sold in Paris as *Fraises à la Romanoff*, presumably because it had been popular with the Czar. The sheets were the purest white and the blankets matched the upholstery. There were small sets of drawers and tiny wardrobes. My fellow traveler had already established himself. A smell of cologne filled the compartment and he had hung up an elaborate Arabian dressing gown. I read the notices on the door. They were in Russian, French and German. They drew my attention to the bell, which could be reached from where one lay in bed, and to the various services available. We were required not to smoke in bed and to call the attention of a guard at the slightest hint of fire. The list included all the usual rules of rail travel.

Captain Brown said the compartment compared favorably with the best he had experienced ("in India and elsewhere") and that he would have enjoyed coming with me. Esmé agreed and said she envied me. I was now used to a certain amount of comfort, but to Esmé this carriage was more magical than anything she had ever seen. She could not stop touching the blankets, the sheets, the fixtures. She was almost mesmerized by them and asked me, "Was this what it was like at your uncle's?" I laughed. "It wasn't so different."

She looked at me as if I had been elevated to the ranks of the gods. "You must do well at the Polytechnic," she said seriously. "It is a great honor, Maxim."

I squeezed her hand. "Dimitri," I reminded her gently. "All this depends on my being Dimitri Mitrofanovitch, son of a priest from Kherson." (These details were in my papers.)

"I hope you don't meet any clerical friends from Kherson." Captain Brown patted my arm. "Make your mother happy, boy. It was her letters got you this. If she hadn't bent her knee to your uncle . . .

Well, he's the only decent member of that family. I thought my own was bad enough, but at least they don't pretend I'm dead."

I had not heard this before. "I don't understand you, Captain Brown."

He smiled sympathetically. "It's all right, boy. You're not to blame and neither is she. They disapproved of your dad. Made themselves judge and jury. It's the religion, I suppose."

I was to hear no more. The guard shouted that visitors should leave the train. Whistles began to blow. Captain Brown patted my arm, Esmé kissed my cheek. I returned the kiss and made her blush. They stood outside the window of the coupé, smiling and nodding and making gestures until the whistle blew, the carriage jerked, and I was once again steaming toward the white landscape of the steppe.

A large young man entered the compartment. He was flamboyantly dressed in a high-collared shirt, a lilac cravat, black silk waistcoat, tight-fitting trousers and a frock coat. His fair hair was pomaded and piled into waves on his large, handsome head. He had wide blue eyes and a thick-lipped mouth of a sort I would normally mistrust. But he was very friendly in his greeting. He held out his big hand to shake mine. He bent his body forward in a pose which seemed familiar. He must be, I realized as he spoke, connected with the stage. "*Bonjour, mon petit ami.*"

His accent was gushing, exaggerated. I replied with a dignified: "*Bonjour, m'sieu. Comment allez-vous?*"

"*Ah, bon! Très bon! Et vous?*"

"*Très bon, merci, m'sieu.*"

This ludicrous schoolroom exchange continued until names were presented.

"*Je m'appelle* Dimitri Mitrofanovitch Kryscheff," I told him.

He was Sergei Andreyovitch Tsipliakov and he was, he said, a day behind the rest of his "gang." To our mutual relief, we returned to Russian.

"Gang?" I said, amused. "Are you a bandit?"

He laughed for some moments. It was artificial, trilling. A stage laugh. "You could call me that. Can I say 'Dimka'?" It was the diminutive of Dimitri. He had dropped formalities rather more rapidly than I might have preferred, but there was nothing I could do. He was, after all, a far more experienced traveler than I. I agreed. "You can call me Seryozha," he said. "We'll be pals on this trip. After all, we'll be intimates for a long while. It's freezing, isn't it?"

I found the compartment rather warm. Again I decided it would seem more sophisticated if I remained silent, offering no opinions until I had the measure of my companion.

"My gang's the Foline Ballet." This explained his dandified clothes, informal use of first names and soft, gesticulating hands. I had heard of the Company. I had seen it advertised in Kiev. I felt flattered to be sharing a coupé with so eminent a personage. I said that I had been in Odessa for some months and had not had time to see a performance. He said they had been terrible. It was an awful stage, he said. But they had gone down very well. Was I, then, from Odessa? Or had I been traveling?

I said I had traveled a little.

"We've been all over the world," he told me. "Do you know Paris? You must. And London?" He made a face. He did not think much of London. "Philistines," he said. "New York is so much more cultivated. You wouldn't believe it, would you? All those cowboys! But then you've been to New York?"

I could not deceive him by so many thousands of miles. I shook my head.

"You must go there as soon as possible. Away from all this War. They appreciate art in New York. They are so starved of it, you see, poor things."

I had become almost as captivated by S. A. Tsipliakov as I had been by Shura. I was flattered by attention, by the friendly and direct warmth of my companion. I went with him into the dining room. He bought me breakfast and insisted I have a glass of champagne.

We returned to our coupé and sat side by side on my bunk while he told me of his adventures abroad, the disasters and triumphs of their company (a small one, but highly regarded in the capital). He complained that the "awful War" had cut down badly on their traveling. That was why they had been in Kiev. They had been scheduled to go to Berlin at Christmas. "We'd been so looking forward to it, Dimka, *mon ami*. Christmas in Berlin. The lovely decorated trees, the Christmas songs, the gingerbread. The Germans invented Christmas as far as I'm concerned. It's all so wonderful. Tinsel and velvet and everybody so happy." He blamed the whole war on a few Prussians and "those greedy Austrians." It was not, he thought, the fault of the Hungarians. "They love music and dancing and all the arts. The Austrians think the waltz is the highest thing anyone can aspire to!"

He complained he could not even go to France, except in uniform.

He rang for the steward and ordered a bottle of Krug. It was with almost fainting astonishment that I found the order accepted. Within a quarter of an hour we had an ice bucket from which emerged not Krug, but the dark-green neck of the finest, sweetest Möet et Chandon. "It's almost impossible to get Krug in Russia any longer," he said. "Luckily the railway companies have some champagne. If you want to drink it, you must travel everywhere by Wagon-Lit!" He laughed, rolling the bottle in the ice. "Every capital is closed to us, for one reason or another. Of course, people in the provinces are only too pleased to see us. We play to full houses wherever we go. We're probably making more money here than we ever made in the rest of Europe. But it's so dull. I like amusement, Dimka. I work hard on stage so I must find proper ways of relaxing. What do you think?" He lifted the bottle from the bucket. I held out my glass.

With a flourish, my new friend filled it. "We're going to have a wonderful time. Happy New Year." He drank his glass off in a single movement. He sighed and was about to speak when the guard knocked on the door and opened it. He had coarse, red features, greying mustaches, a thick, dark uniform covered in gold braid. He saluted. "I'm very sorry, your excellencies. I was asked to keep an eye on the young gentlemen by his parents. Any problems, just call for me." He closed the door.

Seryozha scowled. The guard was "an interfering old fool!" I was flattered by so much attention. My "parents" must have been Captain Brown. Doubtless he had tipped the guard to look after me all the way to Petersburg.

Outside, the snow continued to fall and Seryozha and I continued to drink. He told me about Marseilles and Florence and Rome and all those "wonderful warm places we shan't be able to visit for months." As he got drunk, his speech became looser. Luckily I was used to it. Indeed, I found the strain of being a gentleman somewhat relieved by Seryozha's company. I giggled at his jokes and told him some of my own, at which he laughed as heartily as he laughed at his. "We should have some music," he said. "What a pity the other members of the troupe took the earlier train. We have so many wonderful people who can play the guitar and the mandolin and the balalaika and accordion, you know. We could have a little party. With girls. Do you like girls, Dimka?" He smiled and put his large arm around my shoulders. "I suppose you are a little too young to know what you do like, eh? But you have the feelings?" He winked.

I assured him I had the feelings. He squeezed my shoulder and then my leg. He suggested we order another bottle of champagne "to keep us warm." He rang the bell. The guard answered it. Seryozha said impatiently, "I wanted the steward."

"He'll be along soon, your excellency."

But an hour passed and our champagne was finished before the steward arrived.

"Another bottle of this," said my friend. "Better make it two."

The steward shook his head. "All the champagne is gone."

"We've hardly been traveling an hour!"

"We've been moving for three, your excellency."

"And you've run out of champagne?"

"I'm very sorry. It's the War."

"Oh, it's a wonderful War, isn't it, when artists are no longer allowed to take the few pleasures left to them? You give the public everything and what does it give you? Champagne rationing!"

"It's not our fault, your excellency."

"Then bring me a bottle of brandy."

"There's no brandy available in bottles. We have to keep our stocks for the dining cars."

"You mean if we wish to have a drink, we must dine?"

The steward took out his pad. "Shall I book you a table?"

"You had better." Seryozha stood up, looming over both of us. He flexed his legs, his arms. "I shall be in agony by morning." He reached into the pocket of his frock coat, which he had flung on his bed. "Can't you get us just one bottle, steward?" He produced a silver ruble. The man looked at it as if he saw his child dying and was unable to save it. "There is no way, your excellency."

From where I sat, I noticed the shadow of the bulky guard behind him. He was keeping an eye on the steward to make sure he was not bribed.

"It's all right, Seryozha," I said. "We've had plenty of champagne. More than most people will be getting for a while."

The dancer slumped down again, waving the steward away. "When shall we have dinner?"

"From five o'clock on, your excellency."

"Then make it at five."

"Very well."

"And ensure we get an apéritif."

"I hope so, your excellency."

Seryozha rose in anger, but the steward scuttled off down the corridor. "Dimka, my dear, we must all suffer a little in the cause of the War." He gave me a strange look from beneath hooded, shadowed eyes. "You do not blame me?"

"Of course not."

"I did my best."

"I saw."

"I think I'll rest for a while, until dinner. Why don't you do the same?"

I was feeling sleepy. I agreed it might be a good idea. Seryozha clambered into his bunk. I could see his bulging outline immediately above my head. I lay, in my shirt and trousers, with my jacket and waistcoat neatly hung up, trying to sleep. But the general atmosphere of excitement which I had experienced a few moments earlier now gave way to something akin to depression. I had been looking forward to that second bottle.

A moment or two later I heard a rustling from Seryozha's bunk. He was now sitting cross-legged, judging by the shape in the mattress overhead. A little time passed. I heard him give one quick sniff and then another. It was a familiar sound. I got up, in time to catch him unawares, and sure enough he held a short silver tube to his nose. It extended to a little box, like a snuffbox. Deprived of his wine, Seryozha had resorted to cocaine. He looked at me and put the apparatus away. "You've caught me taking my medicine."

"You have a headache?" I spoke with deliberate innocence.

"Just a small one. The fizz, you know. And then that awful experience with the steward."

"You should sleep."

"I don't feel sleepy. Do you?"

"I'm quite drowsy." This was not entirely true. I thought it politic. I hoped to be offered some cocaine. I still had a little more than a gram in my luggage. I had decided to save it for an emergency, when my studies demanded. Now I had found a new source. I determined not to lose touch with my ballet dancer. I must be sure to get his address. From him I could contact a source of supply. One of my secret worries would then be quieted.

Seryozha put out a soft hand and rumpled my hair. "Don't worry about me, my dark-eyed beauty. I'm feeling better already."

I pulled away. At the time I had very little experience of the ballet fraternity, but some instinct warned me. I believe the guard and steward must have guessed Seryozha's intentions and had done what they could to thwart him. People today think that Seryozha's is a modern aberration. It has always been with us. Virtually everything characteristic of the present day—every vice, political theory, tyranny, argument, art form—had its origin in the Russia of my own time. The degenerates of St. Petersburg set the tone, one could say, for the entire century.

I dined with Seryozha because I had agreed I should, but I drank sparingly, almost calculatingly. When we came to retire he let me undress in the little washroom. I put on my nightshirt and climbed into bed. He disappeared into the washroom. I heard normal sounds of ablutions. Then he came out.

He was quite naked. This was not unusual amongst men in those days, who always bathed together nude. What alarmed me was the size of his penis swinging a few inches from my face as he seemed to have trouble climbing into his bunk. The train had begun to move a little faster, but this was not why he found himself floundering over me, his warm stiff private parts striking my neck and shoulder. He made a great show of apologizing. I, of course, in my confusion, told him I did not mind. He sat on the edge of my bunk as if to recover, steadying himself with a hand on my arm. "Oh, Dimka. What a shock! Are you feeling all right?"

I said I was fine.

His hand stroked my arm. "I'm so sorry. The last thing in the world I wanted to do was startle you."

"I am not startled," I said.

"But you are upset, I can tell."

"Not in the least."

"You have become so formal." There were tears in his eyes.

"You have no cause to apologize."

"Ah, but I have. I am a monster. You know the kind I am?"

"It is a perfectly honorable profession. Russians have always been great dancers."

This seemed to upset him. With a grunt he lifted his great body upright and climbed slowly into his bed. Shortly afterward I heard more noises and judged he had begun to masturbate. Feeling some stirring in my own loins at his I began privately to indulge myself, also.

I fell asleep.

I awoke with a sensation of extreme discomfort. The lights were out. There was a peculiar silence everywhere in the train. It had grown colder. I was wedged tightly against the wall of the carriage and realized that my companion was lying on my bunk. As I tried to move my arm, which had pins and needles, his thick, almost sluggish voice spoke from the darkness. I could feel stale breath on my face. "You seemed cold. I thought I'd warm you."

"There's not enough room for two in here."

"You'll freeze." He placed a hand upon my arm. He was sweating. I wondered if the drink and cocaine had caused a form of delirium.

"I'm extremely uncomfortable," I pointed out.

"I can cuddle you."

"Thank you, Sergei Andreyovitch. I would rather not be cuddled."

"It's my duty."

"It is not. Why is the compartment so cold?"

"The train is stuck. The heating has gone wrong. We have stopped in a drift."

I struggled up. He tried to hold me down.

"I appreciate your concern, Sergei Andreyovitch, but really I am in some pain."

"I love you," he said.

"What?"

"You know that you love me."

"All men are brothers, Sergei Andreyovitch. But we are almost complete strangers." I began to crawl over his body. My hands touched the carpet. I felt his hand on my back. It began to caress my bottom.

"You are beautiful," he said.

"I'll call the steward," I suggested. I stood up and reached for the gas. I lit it. "Some black coffee will make a new man of you."

"What do you know of men?" The light illuminated his heavy, sulking features. He glared at me from beneath hooded eyes. "Why do you play such games? Go on, call the steward. Have me put in prison."

"Prison?" I was mystified. "What for?" He could not go to prison for trying to keep me warm in bed. I had an inkling he wished to make love to me, of course, but I was not experienced enough to be sure.

He looked at me with lugubrious gratitude. "Thank you, at least, for that."

I had learned tact in Odessa, so I did not push the point. However, I wished to escape the oppressive atmosphere, so I donned my dressing gown and slippers and opened the door.

He gasped. "What are you going to do?"

"Stretch my legs," I said. "Get fresh air. I suggest you resume your own bed, Seryozha."

"Thank you."

As I left he was beginning to climb unsteadily back to his bunk.

Walking along the corridor and looking out at the grey banks of snow through the frost on the windows, I felt at once confused and elated. I appeared to have put Sergei Andreyovitch in my debt. I did not know quite how, but I was prepared to exploit the situation if the opportunity arose. I had no security. I would have to fend for myself in St. Petersburg, and the more well-connected friends I could make, the better it would be for me.

As I stood at the window I saw a shadow appear at the far end of the corridor and a young woman, wearing a red-and-green robe, with her dark hair bound on top of her head, came walking slowly toward me. She was a little older than I, round-faced and pleasant, with oval brown eyes and large even teeth. She smiled at me. "You can't sleep?"

"I seemed to be stifling." I nodded back at my coupé.

"I'm traveling with my awful old nanyana," she whispered. "She's a peasant, really, though she's from Scotland. But she has all these habits. Ugh!"

"Habits?"

"She speaks in English all the time. In her sleep."

"Scarcely a peasant habit." I was amused.

"In England, surely, it is?"

This encounter began to seem as illogical as the one I had just escaped. "They have peasants in England," I told her. "Although they are more refined than ours."

"You have been to England?"

"I am familiar with that country." This was true. I owed my familiarity primarily to *Pearson's* and Captain Brown.

I had impressed her. "This is the first time I have traveled. We are from Moldavia, you know. We have some land there. A house. The country is very pretty. Do you know it?"

I regretted that I did not.

"You'd love it. But it's dull. Father retired there. Before that, he had traveled, too. In England. That's where he found my nanyana. She's not a proper Scottish governess. She looked after me because Mother was frequently in poor health."

"Your mother is dead?"

"Certainly not. She's as fit as a fiddle. She had anemia. Now she's cured. She rides a great deal. She has started an English hunt. With dogs and horses and red coats and all that. But I think you need a different sort of fox."

"The English fox is a wary little beast," I said. "And much admired."

She drew a pendant-watch from her bosom. "It's gone midnight."

I was anxious to keep her company. "You are traveling on from Peter?" I asked.

"No. I'm to go to university there."

"At the Koyorsy?" I had familiarized myself with most of the other seats of learning in the capital. The Koyorsy was for women.

"Yes!" She was delighted.

"I am also a student," I said. "I shall be at the Polytechnic. Although rather younger than most, I have a special medal."

She was not impressed. Many people in those days saw a Polytechnic as a rather low-grade sort of academy. Science and engineering are still not regarded, in many walks of life, as suitable subjects of study for gentlepeople.

"The War," I said, "requires new kinds of weapons. And new kinds of men to develop them. That is why I have been called to Peter."

She giggled. "You're a boy."

"I have already flown my own aeroplane," I told her. "Perhaps you read about it last year? In Kiev. I flew for some minutes in an entirely new type of machine, which I designed myself. It was in all the papers."

"I remember something about a new kind of flying machine. It was in Kiev, yes."

"You are speaking to its inventor."

I had won her over. She said with some coyness, "I can't recall your name . . ."

This, of course, was difficult. I hesitated.

She raised a hand over her mouth. "I am so sorry. You are not allowed, perhaps . . . The War?"

I bowed. "I am not at this point my own master. I can only give you the name by which I am known in the world."

"Spies?"

"There is some slight chance of it, mademoiselle."

"My name is Marya Varvorovna Vorotinsky."

I bowed. "You may call me Dimitri Mitrofanovitch Kryscheff. It is the name under which I will go in St. Petersburg."

She was delighted by the romance. Quite without deliberate deception I had learned how to appeal to a lady's sense of mystery. I had turned my whole dilemma to my advantage—with this young girl, at least.

"Will you be able to visit me in Peter?" she asked.

"If you will write down your address, I shall try."

"Wait here."

I waited, my imagination making designs in the frosted windows, my breath adding a further layer to the cotton-wool whiteness surrounding us. Soon she returned with a piece of paper torn from the flyleaf of a book. I accepted the paper, bowed, and put it into the pocket of my dressing gown.

"You must not feel obliged," she said, "to visit. But I have hardly any friends, you know, in Peter. I hope to make some, of course, at the Koyorsy."

"I will do my utmost," I told her, "to make sure that you are not lonely."

"You will be very busy."

"Naturally. However, a beautiful, intelligent lady is forever irresistible." I flattered her partly from natural courtesy (I have always had a sense of courtesy toward the fair sex) and partly because I remembered Shura's advice to make contacts with young ladies whose fathers could finance my inventions. This motive might seem ignoble, but in one sense it was absolutely noble. I was prepared to sacrifice myself to further my work in the field of science.

She smiled as I kissed her hand. "Nanyana Buchanan is awake," she said. "She heard me tearing the paper. I must go."

"We shall meet again."

"I hope so—" she dropped her voice, "M'sieu 'Kryscheff.'"

She fled away down the corridor. I was feeling pleased with myself as I returned to my coupé. I had made two excellent and useful contacts already.

My mood was spoiled by the sight of a fat, greatcoated major with handlebar mustaches and a single glaring eye (the other was covered by a cap), stumping up from behind me and growling: "You should be in bed, young man. What's the matter? Think the Boche have captured the train?"

"I was wondering why we had stopped."

"Because of the snow. I've been to investigate. We'll be hours late. Cold's cracked a rail, apparently. Too many trains. They're doing what they can. They say. A lot of people working out there now. I'm supposed to be joining my regiment. They'll be at the front by the time I arrive in Peter."

As on the Odessa–Kiev express, I would normally have been glad to have spent as much time on the train as possible, but Sergei Andreyovitch's peculiar behavior had stressed my nerves.

With some reluctance I returned to my compartment. The dancer lay with his arms thrown out of the bunk, dangling down, a dead swan. I had to dodge past the arm to resume my own bed. I kept the light on for a while as I read an old copy of *Flight* magazine which Captain Brown had found for me. The main article was about Curtiss' experiments with seaplanes in America. The thought of a ship capable of traveling on air, land and sea had occurred to me before. Under the shadow of Sergei Andreyovitch's gently swaying limb, I fell asleep planning a gigantic vehicle, part airship, part plane, part locomotive, part ocean liner. The size of the *Titanic*, it would be capable of flying over obstacles (such as icebergs) and therefore be the safest vessel known to Man. I imagined my name painted on its sides. All I needed were a few industrialists with faith and vision, and I would change the whole nature of travel. No longer would trains be stuck in snow drifts, reliant on lines and the weather and workmen digging with shovels. At the touch of a switch they would be able to lift into the sky. Was it possible to produce a form of hot-air cannon able to melt the snow in front of a train? The old-fashioned snowplow blade was not very efficient.

Our Russian trains in those days frequently ran on time, no matter what the weather. The War had begun to affect everything very quickly. Or rather, I suspect, the War became an excuse for the inefficient, just as the Revolution was later to supply similar excuses. Now the excuses have somehow become incorporated into the system itself. Delays in trains are deliberate. Part of some five-year plan to make the rails rust from lack of use. And if the reader should wonder why all the inventions I dreamed of half a century ago are still not a reality, do not blame the inventors. Blame the fools who were too lazy to build them; blame the unimaginative bureaucrats who introduced politics into science and instead of developing, for instance, the Zeppelin range of airships, or comfortable flying boats, or high-speed monorail trains, chose to devote their energies to making useless economies. I sometimes think Icarus must have crashed simply because someone supplied him with substandard wax.

The train had moved forward a little by morning. At breakfast Sergei Andreyovitch stayed only to take a cup of coffee and then sauntered back to the coupé when his request for a glass of vodka was refused. I guessed he was going to avail himself of his cocaine. Marya Varvorovna gave me a lingering, conspiratorial look, which I found very pleasurable. She sat some tables distant, with her stiff-backed Scottish nanny: a woman who wore plaid as if she were going into battle at Culloden. It was loud enough to be a weapon in its own right. I imagined people were grateful when she wore her street clothes, which were of an ordinary battleship color. She had a long, red nose, fading red hair and even her eyes had a distinctive red glint. I was glad Marya Varvorovna thought it inappropriate to admit our meeting of the previous night. If the nanny had approached me, I believe I should have dived into a snowdrift rather than cope with that hideous creature. Even Marya was clad in a tartan dress, though of a less vulgar collection of hues. She wore what I later learned was "Royal Stuart." By special decree any non-Scottish commoner is allowed to wear this particular pattern. Nanny, I now know, wore the plaid of her own Buchanan clan. It emphasized the tight sallowness of her skin.

As I sat in the strawberry-colored luxury of the Wagon-Lit Internationales dining car on the Kiev–St. Petersburg express and filled myself with delicious croissants, marmalade, apricot jam, cheeses, cold meats, steamed egg, I was strongly aware of the admiring gaze of that lovely young Russian girl who had all but guaranteed me the sexual companionship I had begun to need. I reminded myself to get hold of Sergei Andreyovitch's address. If I could make contact with his friends I would know where cocaine was sold and might also have an entrée into bohemian life. Cocaine, Shura had once told me, was much more expensive in the capital. Most of it was actually imported via Odessa.

The train crawled forward a few more miles and stopped again. This time we waited in a siding while a long military train went past. This camouflaged train had armored coaches and huge steel plates protecting the loco. It flew various flags and had positions on the roof for machine gunners. On flatcars, sandbagged artillery was guarded by half-frozen soldiers in greatcoats and woolen caps, vast felt mittens gripping long rifles. Not a few of the passengers waved and cheered at the stolid soldiers, who did not wave back.

"On their way to the Western Front," said a young captain to his pretty wife. "That's the sort of stuff we're sending the Boche. He'll be done for in a matter of weeks."

I was heartened by this news. I reported it to Seryozha as he lay, fully dressed and shivering, in the compartment. He complained about the cold. "I'll never arrive on time. So many envy me. Foline's bound to give someone my best parts. That will be the end of my career. You don't know what a fight it is, Dimka, to make a name for oneself in the ballet. Particularly in Russia. It's easier abroad, where there's hardly any competition."

"Go to Paris," I suggested, "and astonish them all."

He gave me an odd smile. "I'd rather stay in Peter."

"It's likely every train will be late," I said. "For all you know the rest of your troupe is still stuck somewhere outside Kiev and we're ahead of it. That's been known to happen."

He told me I was a dear and I had a good heart and that he was grateful to me for all I had done. It was little enough, I thought, but I took the opportunity of asking for his address. He wrote down the address of a friend instead: Nicholai Feodorovitch Petroff. He said that he had not yet decided on permanent lodgings in the city. If all else failed and I wanted to contact him urgently, he would always be glad to see me at the Foline, God willing. They would be leaving for America, he hoped, in the spring. He prayed that America would not come into the War or there would be absolutely nowhere to go. "At least people are glad of entertainment in wartime. The number of new theaters and clubs opening in Peter in just the last month or two, I'm told, is incredible! It used to be such an unfriendly city, you know. Not like Moscow. I love Peter. It's the only civilized place in the whole country. But it isn't really friendly, even now."

I was disturbed to hear this. I had a feeling there was something Teutonic and arrogant about the St. Petersburg citizens. When we eventually began to pull into the station it was grey and smoky and somehow characterless. It was too big.

Sergei was in a hurry to leave the train and get to the company to ensure himself of his position. He kissed me on both cheeks and lugged his cases down the corridor while old ladies and generals grumbled at him. I was glad he had left in such a hurry, for I had acquired his snuffbox, which he had left in his bunk. He would easily be able to replenish it. But it would keep me going for a long while. I would return the box itself as soon as I had used the contents.

My first impression of that noble city, created by the founder of modern Russia, Peter the Great, was poor. It seemed like a mausoleum. The station was crowded enough, full of uniforms, but lacked the casual bustle of similar stations in Ukraine. There were comparatively few hucksters, the porters were smarter and considerably more servile than any I was used to. I had no trouble getting one. There seemed to be izvozhtiks aplenty waiting outside for fares. There were also motor-cabs which tempted me, since I had never ridden in one. They would be much more expensive, I was sure. The streets of the capital were enormously wide, but there seemed hardly any life on them. Everyone was dwarfed. Perhaps all the life was in the great suburbs where the workers lived. In a sense it was, like Washington or Canberra, an artificial city, very conscious of its dignity. The double-headed eagle could be seen everywhere. Portraits of Czar Nicholas and other members of the Royal Family abounded. The whole place felt like a series of extensions of the royal palaces. It seemed one could not even raise one's voice here, unless it was to berate a servant.

I was also astonished at the way in which porters, cabbies and others were treated. Sharp, commanding voices carried through the cold air and bags were loaded into carriages, horses were whipped into rapid trots (vehicles moved at an incredible pace in Petersburg, as if everyone were racing everyone else). Trams and motor-cars, even, seemed better-bred than any I had seen before. They hardly made a sound. And when I gave the address of Green and Grunman, my uncle's agents, to the cab driver, I had to speak to him two or three times before he heard me. Partly this was because of the vast fur cap he wore, with his scarlet coat-collar folded around it. Partly it was my soft "Southern" accent which was unfamiliar to him. The whip snapped, the horse picked up her feet, and off we went, trotting past tall buildings which seemed to contain nothing but bright electric light and no people at all.

I was much impressed by the width of the streets, the classic beauty of the buildings. Our capital had been called the "Venice of the North" because of the rivers and canals intersecting the streets, the palaces and public buildings, hotels and barracks laid out with precision to provide the effect of maximum grandeur. Odessa could not bear comparison in size or scope and seemed small, comfortable and welcomingly provincial to me. I regretted the trouble with Shura and wished I had elected to study in Odessa after all. I felt like a yokel. If St. Petersburg had this effect on everyone (save, presumably, indigenous aristocrats) it was no wonder she had become a hotbed of revolution. Such cities create more than envy; they create self-consciousness. And many who feel self-consciously inferior will resort to aggressive politics. There was something brooding and haughty, something distant about the city. The sky above was too wide. I could understand, at last, how the characteristic literature of Russia came to be written and why writers of light-hearted stories turned into melancholics as soon as they arrived at the center of our cultural life.

The cab came to a halt outside a tall, grey building. A haughty commissionaire stepped forward to take my bags and to help me to the ground. I paid the cabby what he asked and added a small tip. The commissionaire wore an elaborate blue-and-gold uniform. I was used to a preponderance of uniforms, for almost everyone had one in Russia, but I had never seen quite so many as in St. Petersburg. I told him to look after my luggage and I took an electric elevator to the third floor of the building to where the firm of Green and Grunman had their offices.

I knocked on a glass door. Behind it moved several shadows. There was a pause. One shadow loomed. The door was unlocked. A tall, white-haired man stood bending over me. He was one of the thinnest people I have ever seen. His hair fell over his face and almost reached his drooping white mustache, which in turn touched his chin-beard (known in those days as a "Dutch") which then appeared to blend naturally with his collar and shirt. He spoke good Russian in a whispering lisp, which I assumed was some kind of English accent. He asked if he could help me.

I told him my uncle's name. I understood that I was expected. He seemed relieved and ushered me in. He took me through two offices where girl typewriters and clerks were hard at work at small, wooden desks, and knocked upon a polished oak door. "Mr. Green?" he said.

"Enter," said Mr. Green in English.

As we came in, Mr. Green moved away from his bookcase toward his large desk. This was inset with panels of green leather. He lowered himself into a matching padded chair, opened his plump mouth and said, "*Dobraii dehn* (Good afternoon)." I replied "*Shdravstvyi-teh*," or "How do you do." He raised dark brows to the lisping, white-haired gentleman and said, "Does the boy speak any English?"

"I speak a little," I replied.

Mr. Green smiled and rubbed at his jowls. "Good. And French? German?"

"Some of both."

"And Yiddish?"

"Of course not!" One might wish to learn Hebrew, but not that ugly patois combining the worst features of all tongues. Moreover, there was no need for it in Petersburg where Jews, in the main, were banned.

He laughed. "Surely a smattering?"

"A few words, of course. How can one live in Kiev and not come to know them?"

"And in Odessa."

"And in Odessa."

"Excellent." He appeared amused and distracted at the same time. He picked up a grey folder. "And we're giving you the name of Dimitri Mitrofanovitch Kryscheff. A good Russian name."

"I hope so," I said. "Is he a real person?"

"Aren't you real?" Mr. Green's eyes held a wary kindness, as if I were an attractive animal likely at any moment to bite him.

"His place at the Polytechnic . . ."

"He gained it easily. With his gold medal."

"I hope you don't think me overinquisitive, sir. I wonder if you know a little more. After all, I'm supposed to be from Kherson where my father is a priest. I have never been to Kherson. I know very little about formal religion, my mother being a God-fearing woman but not a great churchgoer."

"An Orthodox priest. That was a stroke of luck. You couldn't get any more respectable, eh?"

"I appreciate the respectability of it, sir. The mystery, however, is hard to fathom. Won't I be asked questions?"

"Of course not. Dimitri Mitrofanovitch was educated privately, at home, by his father. He was a sickly child. Just before he was due to take his place at the Polytechnic last term, he fell ill. Influenza. The unhappy lad was already tubercular, do you see? The priest was a relatively poor man and at his wit's end. Your uncle's friends in Kherson were approached for a loan to send the boy to Switzerland. They did better than that. They paid for the boy to go to Switzerland, to an excellent sanitarium where he may be cured. He will continue to study, of course. In Lucerne under your name. You come to St. Petersburg under his. Everyone is catered for and everyone gets a good chance in life."

"It seems very complicated," I said. "And very expensive. After all, I don't think I'm worth—"

"You are worth it to your uncle, it seems. You'll be of great help to him later. You can speak all these languages. You have a grasp of science. You are good-looking, charming, personable. You have a bearing about you. Why you could be the Czarevitch himself!"

I was pleased.

"But healthier," added Mr. Green, and spread his hands. "Thank God."

"Where shall Dimitri Mitrofanovitch be living?" I asked.

"We had thought close to the Polytechnic. But that is such a long way from the center and it would be useful if we could get in touch with you sometimes, or you with us. So we've found you lodgings not far from Nyustadskaya. It's very handy for the steamtram, for the Finland Station and so on. The tram will take you to the Polytechnic. What's the address, Parrot?"

"Eleven Lomanskaya Prospect," said the white-haired Parrot.

It sounded excellent.

"We'll take you there immediately, I think." I had a vision of the fat Mr. Green and the thin Mr. Parrot escorting me through the streets, each carrying one of my bags. But "we" meant a member of the firm. "Will you see to it, Parrot?"

"Yes, sir."

"And the term begins in four days?" said I.

"Four days. Make the most of 'em."

"Thank you, sir."

"Mr. Parrot will show you where the tram leaves and will give you details of which professor to see. I gather there's some sort of oral entrance exam. A formality. We've spoken to the professor. There will be no difficulties. What's his name, Parrot?"

"Dr. Matzneff, sir."

"He was very obliging?"

"He was, sir. His son left this afternoon."

"Straightened out, now. You'll find Dr. Matzneff helpful to you, my boy." Mr. Green beamed and patted my head. I wondered at these cryptic references. My uncle's influence must be considerable. He had pulled strings in every department.

Rightfully I was up to gold-medal standard and had only been robbed of the medal by War and Herr Lustgarten's departure. It was satisfying to know I had received my fair deserts. Uncle Semya was a great adjuster of rights. It was a relief that my professor would be favorably disposed to me. St. Petersburg was no longer quite the threatening place it had seemed.

Mr. Green gave me an envelope containing ten rubles. I would collect my allowance monthly. I should make careful use of it. The fares to the Polytechnic were about twenty kopecks a day, there and back. There might be opportunities to "make the allowance up to more" in the future. I thanked him, put the money in my pocket next to Sergei Andreyovitch's snuffbox, and shook hands. Then I accompanied Mr. Parrot, now clad in a maroon fur-trimmed greatcoat and top hat, to the ground floor. Here my bags were recovered and a cab called for us by the commissionaire. It was snowing. The hood of the cab was raised. It was already dark, but this part of the city was brilliantly lit. Once again, I noticed that almost everyone in the street, civilian or military, wore some kind of uniform. We crossed a long bridge over the wide Great Neva, a forbidding stretch of ice. To my surprise I saw in the distance a tram apparently trundling over the surface of the river. Mr. Parrot told me that it froze so hard it was possible to lay lines on the ice in the winter.

We entered an area much more crowded and familiar to me. I suppose it was poorer. Here were ordinary people, gas lamps, open-fronted shops, crowded apartment buildings, stalls selling food, clothing, crockery, magazines, the smells of cooking, the sounds of street musicians, children, quarreling and laughter. There were flights of darkened steps, alleys, half-starved dogs. I was more nervous of the district than I might once have been; however, the street in which we found ourselves was fairly quiet and it was comforting to arrive at it. St. Petersburg was not going to be an easy city, I thought, in which to find my feet. There were far wider gulfs between the classes. Even in Kiev, where there were many snobs, where poor people could find themselves driven from parks or certain streets, it had not been so bad. I was going to need all my confidence and might require the extra courage residing in my stolen snuffbox.

SIX

The uniform I would wear to the Institute was not as magnificent as some: just a simple student uniform of dark-grey serge with silver buttons, a cap with the badge of the Polytechnic. There was much to be said for the practice. It would mean that my limited store of clothes would last much longer and it would not become evident that I was relatively poor. Most of the boys studying at the Institute were of limited means. The rich men's sons studied at various Military Academies where science and engineering were taught, or at the Science Academy itself. Their uniforms were correspondingly more splendid, with gold embossed buttons and braid. Even so, we had uniforms for summer and winter, greatcoats, regulation-issue gloves, boots, caps and so on. All these were supplied on the day after my arrival by the specialist tailor to whom Messrs. Green and Grunman sent me. Mr. Parrot was again my escort on a dark snowy day to the back streets of the Moskovskaya quarter where the tailor had his huge establishment.

The room in which I would board was in the house of a typical Russian lady of middle years. She was good-humored, a little stupid, a voluble speaker on all topics of scandal, an ardent antiradical (she did not even approve of the Czar's concessions to the formation of a democratic Duma and praised the recent curtailment of its powers): she could see no point whatsoever in the study of engineering. She hated the motor-car, the tram, the train, the telephone, and she was not altogether convinced that steamboats were above suspicion. She thought, in common with many who lived close to the Neva, that their smoke injured the lungs, in spite of the fact that she only coughed during the winter, when it was impossible for the ships to sail. The nearby Finland Station, the steamtram terminus, and various factories, also gave her cause for alarm. Within an hour or two of my arrival she had asked me what I was going to do about it. She was also able to blame me for the War. I had the impression that she would have objected to the wheel if it had just been invented and that she might also have had a great deal to say against the discovery of fire. For all this, she was a woman I grew to like.

Her house was one of those featureless terraced Petersburg houses, set a little back from the street, with a narrow courtyard and all the rooms of regulation size. My room was on the third floor. It was much bigger than my room in Odessa. It was equipped with its own little stove and washing facilities, a large comfortable bed which could be set against the wall and disguised as a sofa during the day, a desk, a curtained-off "dressing" alcove and so on. There was a lavatory one floor down. I shared the house with the lady, her two daughters, a maid and four other guests, all minor bureaucrats. We ate at a communal table downstairs. The food, I was to find, was heavy and indigestible by Ukrainian standards, but it was wholesome enough. The woman prided herself on providing good service to her customers. As the War went on and shortages became more evident we were given the choice of paying a little more in rent, allowing her to keep up the standard of food, or paying the same rent but taking poorer food. Having experienced the horse-flesh stews in the restaurants students used, I elected to eat whenever possible at Madame Zinovieff's (she was no relation to the notorious Bolshevik).

Apart from the fact that she wore a wig and thick rouge to hide the scars of some disease, there was nothing very remarkable about the widow. Neither were her daughters anything out of the ordinary. Olga and Vera attended a nearby school and were interested in Russian literature, a subject which had never meant very much to me. They were full of romantic talk of Tolstoi, Dostoieffski, Bahshkatseva and various poets of whom Ahkmatova (a woman) is the only one I recall. They read novel after novel, book of verse on book of verse, and they spoke of Lermontov's and Pushkin's characters as if they were real people. I found these girls often irritating and naïve.

They were also very plain. I was to learn later they thought me haughty and proud, like some character in a then popular novel, and they had been "a little in love" with me. Russian girls are always a little in love with someone. But predominantly their abiding love is for themselves. I admit that when a Russian girl falls heavily, she falls all the way. This, however, is much rarer in real life than it is in fiction, where passionate creatures are forever destroying themselves mentally and physically for the gratification of some inebriated cavalry officer or criminal-poet. I had never known a Russian girl to consider destroying herself, say, for a clerk in the Civil Service or a supervisor in an engineering works. One has to have no useful social function and preferably no money to win the hearts of such ladies. It is odd, therefore, that when they marry they tend to place much importance on the earning power of their dear one.

I was pleased when Olga elected the next morning, a Saturday, to show me something of the city. Thus far my impressions had been very vague. I had seen a few wide thoroughfares, a few alleys, the canals and quays, some municipal buildings, a girder bridge or two, some factory chimneys. I was more than pleased to take a tram with her over the Alexandrovski Bridge. There was no snow falling. The sky had cleared to a pale blue. This color was reflected in the ice below.

Very shortly we were in what she called the better part of town, on the Nevski Prospect, Petersburg's main thoroughfare. The traffic moved as rapidly as modern cars and was far more alarming. We descended at a tram stop halfway up the Nevski. Olga, her hands in her muff, told me we should be crossing to look in the windows of a great shopping arcade opposite. Beneath the shadows of its columns were windows full of glittering goods. Something else attracted me, a mechanical toy being demonstrated, and so I set off across the Nevski and was almost knocked down by speeding troikas and motor-cars. There was a whistle from behind me but I could not stop. In a panic I moved through the traffic and jumped to the far curb, panting. The glove of a "blue archangel" (a Petersburg gendarme) fell upon my shoulder. A white truncheon tapped my arm. This huge bearded old man shook his head in admonition. "There are less public ways of committing suicide." Olga came up. She explained to him I had only just arrived in the city. He accepted her explanation and continued on his way while I moved toward the arcade and stood beneath its canopy, looking at the displayed brass steam-locomotives. Olga shook her head and said I was lucky the policeman had been in a good mood.

The day was bright. The Nevski was emptier than I had expected. There were nothing but officers and ladies going past in carriages. And there were far more policemen than I had seen either in Kiev or Odessa. Olga showed me the main avenues and places of interest: the great Winter Palace of the Czar, the Peter and Paul Fortress, St. Isaac's and all the other buildings still to be found in the guidebooks. However I was irritated by the scale of everything, which made me feel even more insignificant. It was as if Peter had deliberately built his city for gods rather than men. We saw the famous shops of Fabergé and Gratchef, the Field of Mars, where ceremonials were held, the monuments and museums of the main Spasskaya district. Few of these interested me since I was more disposed toward the future than the past. Indeed, the city depressed me. Not because it was a collection of grandiose buildings surrounded by slums (most capitals are that) in which riches and poverty were contrasted to a degree which would be found crude in a novel by Zola, but because it was an artificial place, having no real function save to administer the rest of the country and to glorify its rulers. Like Washington, it was the product of naïve, eighteenth-century minds, imitating the fashions then prevalent in France and England. Both cities were named after the "modern founders" of their nations, but had no natural geographical ascendancy or place in the main lines of commerce (as New York or Moscow have). But what marked them chiefly was the soullessness of everything save that of which they are rightly ashamed, their slums.

Naturally, St. Petersburg's gentlefolk did not display a rudeness of taste I associated with the city. Our Russian aristocrats were amongst the most cosmopolitan in the world, traveling regularly to Paris and Berlin, Switzerland and elsewhere. A good many of them were not originally of Slavic origin, but bore German, French, Scandinavian and even British names. Because of the Czar's strong feelings, one did not find Jews at Court, but there were Armenians, Poles, Georgians and many more nationalities, all with Russian titles. These people had been encouraged to become Russian citizens since the days of Peter the Great. It at once strengthened and weakened our Empire. Considerable profiteering went on. The great merchant families, the industrialists, even many of the aristocrats, continued making their fortunes by diverting war materials to their own profit. They did not really believe that the Germans, Austro-Hungarians or perhaps even the Turks would take advantage of Russia. The War was a game, a chance to display their fine uniforms, to impress their womenfolk, to make histrionic self-sacrifice (if they were women) and to glorify the Slavic soul.

This in the first few months seemed the prevailing spirit in St. Petersburg. As our armies showed themselves to be ill-equipped (partly because of profiteering, partly because of a lack of attention to detail typical of the romantic Russian), and were beaten in battle after battle, just as ten years earlier we had been beaten on the sea by the Japanese, morale went from the euphoric to the melancholic. Only the professional soldiers were left to try to save something of the "Russian steamroller." They were too late.

My use of cocaine was for a while abated, due to the routine I was to follow for the next months. On the Monday I set off for my interview with my professor at the Polytechnic Institute. I traveled by steamtram from the Wylie Clinic terminus.

My first ride on a steamtram was an exhilarating experience. The trams were like small single-carriage trains, running on rails and drawn by a boxlike locomotive (possibly a Henschel or an English "Green"). These locomotives can still be seen on narrow-gauge lines. In the summer some of the coaches would be open-sided, but in the winter they were enclosed. The locomotive itself had accommodation for about ten passengers. It was always these seats in winter which were the most coveted. There was no heating on the other coach. Needless to say my first trip to the Institute aboard the Number 2 tram was in the rear carriage, close to the door. In my new uniform and my greatcoat I was comparatively warm as we drove through the industrial suburbs. The misty streets were full of huddled figures on their way to factories like the famous Putilov Works. We passed into semirural country where bare trees and wooden fences seemed stuck at random into dirty snow and a smell of urine and oil predominated until one reached the middle-class suburbs and eventually, after about three quarters of an hour, arrived at the Polytechnic buildings. These were unremarkable, institutional edifices and not in the least welcoming. Neither were the few students who watched my arrival. I asked the way to Dr. Matzneff's office and was directed through various cold corridors, past many bleak, closed doors, until I found one bearing his name. I knocked. I was told to enter a bare, dark-green room. I removed my cap, wondering if I should salute, for the professor wore a magnificent naval uniform. It was usual for retired military instructors to take positions in civil schools. Instead, I shook hands with him. He had a faded, sad-eyed look and was not the ogre I had expected. His hair was thin and grey; his mustache drooped and was snuff-stained. He remained standing near a small window which looked out across a courtyard. He could see above the green half curtain on its brass rail, but I was too short to know what, if anything, he stared at.

"You are Dimitri Mitrofanovitch Kryscheff?"

"I am, your honor."

"You expect to study here, under me?" He sounded deeply weary. For no good reason I felt sorry for him.

"I hope so, your honor."

"You seem a polite young man."

"I wish to become a great engineer, your honor. I am delighted to have the opportunity . . ."

He turned slowly, his sad eyes staring into mine. "You have a genuine wish to study here?"

"It has been my ambition. All my life."

Perhaps he was used to interviewing students who had failed to be accepted by better-class academies, who regarded the Polytechnic as a last resort. He grew a little more cheerful, though it was obvious he was not by nature a happy-go-lucky man.

"Well, well." He sat down behind his desk. I remained standing, my cap in my hand. "That, at least, is a relief. I am probably as puzzled as you are, you know."

"Puzzled, your honor?"

"You did not come here under conventional circumstances. You came on my recommendation. All being normal, you would not have a place here at all."

"I think I am qualified, your honor."

"That is commendable. And more than I hoped for. Do you wish me to examine you?"

"I am ready, sir."

He took a sheet of paper from his drawer. Reading from it he asked me straightforward questions on various scientific and engineering principles. I answered them easily. At the end of the session there was a faint smile on his face. "You are right, Kryscheff. You are perfectly well qualified for your place." I wondered why he was so surprised. He shrugged. "Since you're here there's a possibility you will benefit. But for what purpose?"

"I wish to be a great engineer, sir. To bring Russia many inventions. To increase her fame and her prosperity."

"You are an idealist?"

"I'm no radical, your honor."

"That, too, is a relief. My son . . . well, you were told, eh?"

"No, your honor."

"Well, then, it's confidential. Between your Mr. Green and myself. My son was not as sensible. I was grateful to Mr. Green for helping . . . he has been very kind. I am glad to return the favor."

"Your son is in trouble, sir?"

"He's traveling abroad." Dr. Matzneff sighed. He rubbed at his mustache. "There are hotheads at this Institute, Kryscheff. You would do well to avoid them."

"I shall, your honor."

"We all come under suspicion. Particularly with the War. It's not as bad as nineteen-five or -six, but it is still bad. People have been shot, Kryscheff."

"I know that, your honor."

"And exiled."

"I have an abhorrence, your honor, of politics. The only paper I read is *Russkoye Slovo*."

A deeper sigh than the last. "Read it and believe it, Kryscheff. All you need otherwise are your textbooks, eh?"

"My views exactly, your honor."

We shook hands. He looked forward to seeing me in his class next day. I took the steamtram back to my lodgings behind the Finland Station. I would discover from fellow students that Dr. Matzneff had been a radical in his youth. His son had followed in his footsteps. My uncle's agents had probably bribed officials to commute a prison sentence to one of exile. That was how I came to have a special mentor at the Institute.

Uncle Semya and his associates were responsible for more philanthropic acts then many public charities. It is encouraging that not all "secret brotherhoods" are revolutionaries, Freemasons or Zionists. In the spiritual teachings of Gurdjieff (himself an Armenian), Blavatsky (a Russian) or even the Christian-Jew Steiner (an Austrian), we learn of groups sometimes called "the White Ones": great, wise men and women party to the wisdom of the ages, who try to help mankind without ever interfering with the course of history. For a while I was a member of the Theosophists, then the Anthroposophists, and lastly a Gurdjieff group I briefly attended in London. Naturally, I cannot speak here of what I learned. It is against all their laws. I saw a man only recently who broke the Code of the Gurdjieffschini. He was mesmerized in a telephone box and has not woken up since (we shared a hospital ward for a few weeks when due to a typical administrative oversight I was thrown in with the senile patients). I will not go so far as to suggest that my Uncle Semya belonged to this "White Brotherhood," but he formed part of a network of international businessmen I simply call "the men of good will." It was thanks to them, and they existed in all civilized countries, that I received my higher education. And if I received it under a false name, well, that is all part of the necessity for secrecy, I think.

I was already becoming used to being Kryscheff and so adaptable was I in those days that sometimes I all but forgot my original name. I was soon Dimka to Mme. Zinovieff's daughters, and even the good widow herself would use this term of affection. I did not mind it when we were alone, but found it embarrassing when the other guests were present. I tended to keep myself to myself both at home and at school. Marya Varvorovna's address was still carefully preserved but I did not find time to see her. My regular trips on the tram were my only relaxation. On these I read fiction, usually H. G. Wells or Jack London in the cheap, red editions published by a London firm and sold in the English bookshop in Morskaya. They could sometimes be bought secondhand from street stalls if one were lucky. A good deal of my money went on such luxuries, but they were well worth it.

I had hardly needed any of my own store of cocaine, let alone what had been in the snuffbox (it was kept in ice on the window sill to preserve its efficacy). My studies were comparatively easy. The oral examinations with Dr. Matzneff had taken on the nature of friendly chats. Russian examinations are almost always oral, which is why we have such good memories for conversations and events. My professor had become increasingly well-disposed to me. He realized I was not only a serious student of science, but a clever one. I made very few friendships with other students. Most of them did not seem to like me much. I had once or twice been asked if I were of "foreign blood." When I said I came from Ukraine, I was even asked if I were not a "half-Jew." I became sensitive on the subject. Jews were only allowed beyond the Pale of Settlement by special permission. I had received no such permission because I needed none. I was a true Slav, through and through. This gave offense to the few Jewish students. Happily I escaped any major upsets because some of the other pupils sided with me and drove the Jews back into their little enclave.

My complexion was no darker than most. I was frequently compared by old ladies to the Czarevitch himself, the poor little boy whom Rasputin claimed to have "cured." It was not as if I had any Semitic characteristics, save my father's mark, that stupid operation done "for the sake of health." But the most damaging rumors spread magically. It is not always possible to stop them, however privately one lives. In Germany, I believe, the operation was already common and it became "quite the thing" amongst ordinary people in England and Canada between the wars. Doctors recommended it. The same is true in America. But certainly not in Czarist Russia! My dead father's curse follows me still. It will follow me, I suppose, to the grave. I could wind up in the Jewish Cemetery in Golders Green. That would be an irony. The rabbis would spin if they knew a Gentile lay next to them. My hope is that I will have the full Orthodox Service. I shall, as soon as possible, speak to the Archbishop of the Bayswater Orthodox Church, which I attend whenever my health allows. It is so moving, the Russian service; all the white and gold, the incense, the people standing about the priest while he blesses them: then the icons are carried in procession. I celebrated the main holy days with the Zinovieffs in St. Petersburg. This was almost the only time in my youth I was able to experience the wonderful feeling of acceptance and joy known to the true believer. It is a strange thing that the people which knows best how to worship God is today denied God in its own country!

My relationship with my fellow students left much to be desired but I had the comfort of the Zinovieffs, my regular letters from Esmé, and less frequently from my mother and Captain Brown; the close, enthusiastic interest shown in my progress by Dr. Matzneff, who soon made me his favorite. Since it was not possible for me to afford the long journey back and forth to Kiev every holiday, I spent the vacations in Petersburg and Dr. Matzneff would have me visit his own apartment which, although rather dark and empty, had the feel of a home that had once been happy and not unprosperous.

On only one occasion did Dr. Matzneff ask me anything about my past. He supposed I had become Kryscheff because of my "background." I said that it was true we had not been rich. My mother could not afford the fees of the recognized schools and colleges but my uncle was helping with my education.

"And your uncle is associated with Mr. Green."

"Mr. Green is his agent in the capital. My uncle is in shipping."

This seemed to enlighten Dr. Matzneff. "Of course, you could not get the necessary travel permissions, so you used another person's . . . ?"

I believed that my uncle, I said, had known Dimitri Kryscheff would not be using his place at the Polytechnic. Dr. Matzneff held up a tactful hand and said I need tell him no more. This was just as well. I had little else I could tell him. Thereafter, my professor showed me even more attention and needless to say I came in for almost exactly the kind of cruelty and name-calling I had experienced a few years earlier as a pupil of Herr Lustgarten.

Consequently, I did not mix with the other students. I was in one way relieved, for too many of them entertained the most cynical and bloodthirsty radical ideas. The Okrana, the political police, came to the Institute more than once. The ordinary "pharaohs" (a disparaging slang term for the police) also kept a regular eye on the place. I did sometimes miss the camaraderie I had experienced in Odessa. St. Petersburg, it seemed to me, was a place where healthy companionship could not be found. I had lost the will to visit Marya Varvorovna. All the boys of my own age at the fashionable military schools kept mistresses amongst the shopgirls and small-time actresses who were only too glad to give themselves to a "gentleman." Even the skating rinks and dance halls were in the main private enclaves for those with money. St. Petersburg sometimes seemed a series of castles behind whose walls privileged people engaged in every vice and pleasure. In the meantime, on the far island outskirts of the city, like some vast besieging army of the damned, the excluded, lay the camps of a more menacing enemy than any threatening from Prussia. The inner city contained the fortresses of light, of glass and diamonds and brilliant, beautiful people. The outer city, with its huge, bleak factories, its chimneys from which poured blood-red flames and sulphuric yellow smoke, with its filthy canals, with its sirens wailing like lost souls, held the fortresses of darkness. From them one day would issue the engulfing, defiling mob.

In spite of the War, the revolutionaries were out in force. Jews and Masons, saboteurs and wreckers, continued to incite the honest people to strike. Cossacks were from time to time forced to make a show of strength, though few people were hurt. Feeling against the Reds grew as the news from the Front became grimmer. More "brown coats"—political police—paid visits to the school. I was completely above suspicion. The fact that I was unpopular with the young radicals counted in my favor. Dr. Matzneff, however, was frequently questioned. He would sometimes emerge from these sessions looking pale and extremely distracted.

There were more and more soldiers coming and going in the city: marching troops, military trains, artillery teams clattering through the streets, large guns being transported on wagons to and from the station. The papers at one time made a great deal of Kiev being threatened and swore that the Germans would "never take our Mother City!." The War had almost ceased to be one in which various allies fought various other allies. It had taken on the nature of a Patriotic War, like the war against Napoleon. Increasingly the newspapers harked back to this. Since the Germans did not take Kiev, I did not worry very much and was in the main unmoved by the War news. Kiev could never come to harm and even if the Germans occupied it my mother and Esmé would not suffer. There was a good deal said of rape, crucifixion and wholesale murder and looting by German troops, but I did not expect such things to happen in Kiev, even if they happened elsewhere. The Germans, I knew, were an orderly, scientific people. I was not completely undisturbed by the thought of our Mother City being entered by Teutons. But the original founders came from Northern Europe in the first place. Better Teutons than Turks or Tartars.

The Petersburg spring arrived. It was greeted by the entire population as if Jesus had created a miracle! It was true that the famous "silver nights" of the winter were the only positive factor in favor of the months between October and April, but I, coming from the South, could hardly believe it when that pathetic Baltic spring filled the hearts of the citizens with so much joy. Wading through dirty slush in felt overshoes, having miniature green buds pointed out to me, being shown some already wilting flower as proof that summer was on the way, watching a demonstration of Futurists, in orange top hats and yellow frock coats, marching along the center of the Nevski holding placards announcing the death of art, the end of "the greater illiteracy" and so on, was one of the most disappointing times of my life. I had been led to expect a great deal more. For me, St. Petersburg was at her most beautiful in the mist. Then all but the great buildings were obscured and the trees looked like petrified, many-tendriled Martians forming a guard of honor for the few of us who chose to walk the boulevards and parks. The blocks of flats and offices, set back from the Prospects, became natural cliffs, orderly and quiet and completely devoid of life.

In this most artificial of all cities, this forerunner of the great housing estates and high-rise pseudotowns of the modern world, boredom seemed endemic. As the War went on, little theaters and cabaret bars proliferated and crime and vandalism, violent terrorism and morbid "modern" art were at their peak. Police and soldiers appeared in even greater numbers but revolutionary literature poured from secret presses. The police and soldiers had become as corrupt as their masters, and were everywhere held at bay, by profiteer and Red alike, by the greased palm or the threat of death. Jewish agitators knew how to wheedle their way round their "comrades" the soldiers; and Jewish speculators knew where to find the weaknesses in their "friends" the police and politicians. The Russian people were being sold back into slavery by the very men employed to protect them.

For my part, of course, I knew very little of this at the time. I studied. Even through the summer vacation I continued to study. It was a joy to learn from Dr. Matzneff. He evidently got great pleasure from teaching me. He swore to me that he would make up for the injustices I had suffered. He appeared to focus all his idealism upon me. I believe he made enemies amongst the pupils and staff as a result. He encouraged me in every field of learning. He encouraged me to think for myself; to speculate. As the end-of-the-year exams arrived, he told me I had no need to fear them, for I was bound to pass. And pass them I did (they were chiefly oral). I would leave the Institute with flying colors, Dr. Matzneff told me. If I kept up my studies as well as I did, a diploma was assured. I would be a qualified engineer and ready to begin working for a firm.

As groups of students, we visited factories. These were in the nature of "field trips." We saw foundries, with their scarlet crucibles of steel, their rivers of liquid metal, their sweating, dark-skinned workers. We went to locomotive plants. We saw how weaving machines and printing presses were made. Only the armaments plants were restricted to us. We went to see motor-cars reassembled. Most of these trips were of little interest to me. I had learned far more with my Armenian boss two years before than I learned here. In Kiev I had been expected to do the work, not watch it from a distance while scowling men made comments about "gentlemen workers." By the students of the military academies, who regarded themselves as the elite of St. Petersburg's youth, we were known simply as "blue meat." We were not, in their eyes, gentlemen at all.

I returned to Kiev for the Christmas holiday and found Esmé older-seeming, while my mother had made a good recovery. She was still something of an invalid and had continued to hire her interest in the laundry to a friend. Esmé now worked at the nearby grocery shop. She had hoped I would have stories to tell her of Petrograd as I had had stories of Odessa, but I had to admit I led a dull life, with my books, and that, with Dr. Matzneff's help, I was getting on well. She said she was pleased.

She had become very womanly. I asked her, as a joke, if she had a boyfriend as yet. She blushed, saying she was waiting for someone. I wished her good luck in her hunting.

The holiday was quickly over. I returned to Petrograd in a second-class carriage shared with one other student and several junior officers, all ex-cadets who had received their first commissions and were planning how to win the War. They were elated because we had recently made one or two victories in Poland. It seemed the German invader was on the run. The news from France was bad. Hundreds of thousands of people were being killed. It appeared to my fellow student (he was at University and rather superior about it) that the world would go on fighting forever until it was one vast battlefield and the world's population was eventually dead in a trench of gas or shrapnel wounds. I was not interested in defeatist talk and joined the junior officers in condemning him for his cynicism. He came quite close to being punched. For a little while I left the compartment and tried to get served in the restaurant, but the food was already exhausted. I had to go into the lavatory and eat the sausage and potatoes my mother had given me.

Because of the difficulties of traveling, I had been forced to leave Kiev on my birthday. Thus I celebrated it sitting on a wooden lavatory seat, in a cold, slow train which jolted over every sleeper, eating a piece of inferior salami and a half-frozen potato. Needless to say, I would not be the only Russian looking back on the Winter of 1916 as something of a Golden Era!

Arriving at my lodgings I was greeted by a weeping landlady and two grinning daughters. They had made their conquests and were officially engaged to their beaux: the elder, Olga, to a corn chandler called Pavloff, the younger, Vera, to a traveling salesman representing the Gritski Soft Drink and Mineral Water Company. Thus, within a year, they had given up dreams of Evgeni Onegin and had settled for a couple of wage earners with a potential future. What both these husbands did after 1917 I do not know. Presumably, if he was good, one would remain a manager in the State Corn Division (with an appropriately ugly name like Statcorndiv) and continue to short-weight his customers whenever there was corn to sell (which would not be often). The other might represent the Statminsoftdrink Bureau in Leningrad and the Novgorod district, coloring all beverages red. Since he would not have to sell the stuff because it would be the only drink available he would enter the Statminsoftdrink Information Bureau where he would praise the virtues of Communist pop over the decadent Capitalist kind. He would have no real work, a better bread ration, and would risk being shot by the Cheka if the Party Line on soft drinks changed and he was discovered to have praised the virtues of cherryade over raspberryade when it should have been the other way around.

All this was in the future. We still had another year of freedom. A year in which food rationing became more and more stringent, in which the life of the capital began slowly to prefigure the life all would lead under the Reds. At least by paying a little more money from my allowance I was saved the sickly taste of horsemeat. Mme. Zinovieff continued to serve the best she could and this was far better than most. She was helped, as so many others were helped, by Green and Grunman. They had once employed her husband. He had been killed on an errand for them in Denmark. My allowance was increased as inflation grew steadily worse. Dr. Matzneff continued to give me extra tuition. With the Zinovieff girls working and spending their spare time with their fiancés, I had precious little company. Because of my studying, I had lost the self-confidence necessary to write to Marya Varvorovna, although she filled my fantasies. Her address, as well as that of Sergei Andreyovitch, were still safely kept. Sometimes, when my eyes grew tired from reading by the light of oil lamps (both gas and electricity were often rationed and candles were quite hard to find) I would consider getting in touch with them, or even of asking Olga if she could introduce me to a nice girl. But I was too tired. If I stopped reading, I fell immediately asleep. I took the precaution of getting into bed as soon as I had had my supper, so that when I did go to sleep in the middle of a book, at least I did not wake up in the morning wearing my outdoor clothes.

The dreary winter of Petrograd was followed by a dreary spring in which there were further minor demonstrations, further scandal concerning Rasputin and the Court, further large gatherings of Cossacks and police in the streets. There were further visits of "brown coats" to our school, further news of defeats of our forces. I became incensed by the ludicrous public posturings of the so-called Futurist artists who celebrated the Age of the Machine. They could not tell one end of a bicycle from another, and would have been horrified if they had had to spend half an hour at work in the grease, fumes and soot of an ordinary factory. The snow turned to dirty slush; the miserable buds poked cautiously forth, the tram lines were taken up from the Neva's ice, the "white nights" gave way to nights with a peculiar, greenish tinge to them, and the Prospects, so frequently in darkness due to power cuts, were made scarcely more cheerful by pinch-faced girl thieves of ten years old or less selling withered bunches of violets for extortionate prices and, if no policemen were in hearing, offering their own dirty little private parts for a few kopecks more.

In my tired and somewhat depressed condition, I came to yearn for Odessa, for Katya or even Wanda (who had written once, claiming without proof that I was the father of her "lovely, healthy boy"), for the jolly company of Shura, who might now be unemployed because of what I had told our uncle. I began to feel homesick for Kiev, but I was determined to return home with all the proper credentials. I would practice as a fully qualified engineer with a good firm who would gradually learn my worth and give me a laboratory of my own. I thought of working for the State Aircraft Company, where I could easily have gotten a job at once, save that I did not possess the "official" scraps of paper proving my abilities.

Another Easter. Exchanges of eggs. "Christ is Risen!" The sonorous chanting in the church, the procession, the prayers for our Czar, for Russia in her struggle against Chaos and Barbarism. We were attacked from every side by Turk and Hun as we had been attacked for centuries. It seemed to me, as I knelt to pray between the Zinovieff sisters, that the great area of green which was the Russian Empire, one sixth of the entire globe, could be wiped out overnight, as that Carthaginian Empire had been destroyed. I rose to my feet wondering if it was my duty to join the army, to fight against our enemies, to ensure the future of the Slav people. The mood passed. I was still too young to be an ordinary soldier.

Any idea I had of serving my country as cannon fodder rather than as a cannon maker disappeared when I returned to the Institute after Easter to find a third of the students vanished and three professors summarily dismissed. The Okrana had visited the principal.

They had had a list of "undesirables" likely to damage the War Effort, who could be potential spies for the enemy. The outspoken Reds had all gone and for this, of course, I was grateful, but it was when I went into Dr. Matzneff's class I realized my own bad luck. Dr. Matzneff had gone. In his place was his rival, the black-bearded, bulky, dark-uniformed Professor Merkuloff, who told me to take a seat at the back of the room and pay attention, for I would be receiving no favoritism from him. My "friend Matzneff" was out of a job and lucky not to be in prison. I was shocked by the open aggression shown by Merkuloff. "You will have to study very hard if you want any sort of pass at the end of this year, Kryscheff," he added. He knew very well that I was the best student in the whole Institute, that I could discourse on virtually every subject taught there, and many more besides. But now I was faced with his blatant opposition to my advancement. Professor Merkuloff hated Dr. Matzneff and hated anyone whom Dr. Matzneff seemed to like.

Leaving school that evening, feeling utterly downcast, beginning to wonder if I had been foolish in all my ambitions, I considered going to see Dr. Matzneff at his gloomy flat. I knew this would be stupid. The "brown coats" would be on the lookout for any student who seemed to be hobnobbing with a suspected traitor. It would mean the end of my own schooling.

I returned to my lodgings, where Mme. Zinovieff handed me a letter. It had arrived, she said, shortly after I had left. The post, along with all other services, was in a state of partial breakdown due to the War.

The letter was from Dr. Matzneff. He told me he had been dismissed because in his youth he had shown sympathies with the ideas of Bakunin and Kropotkin, the anarchist-intellectuals. His son, as I knew, was in exile in Switzerland, still a violent and outspoken Social Revolutionary. It was only by a miracle he had escaped imprisonment or exile to Siberia.

Dr. Matzneff advised me not to contact him unless I was desperate. He knew I had no interest in politics. He would be with me in spirit. I should not be downhearted. If I worked hard there was no reason I should not still be the star pupil at the Polytechnic, triumphing over all difficulties.

It was a touching and heartening letter. I determined to show Professor Merkuloff that Dr. Matzneff's "favoritism" had been no more than recognition of outstanding talent. I would study all the harder, night and day if necessary, and win diplomas in every subject. I would cause them all to eat their words.

The days grew lighter. Fashionable people began to leave Petrograd not for the seaside, for the Crimea, as they had once done, but for their dachas in the country, closer to Moscow. I trained myself for the exams due at the end of the year. I would make it impossible for the authorities not to notice me. I began to ignore everything and everyone in pursuit of those studies. Of course, they became harder, the deeper into them I went. I had no great difficulty mastering the ordinary set problems, but I wanted to do better. I wanted to do so well they would have to promote me at least a year ahead, possibly grant me my diploma immediately. It would free me from Merkuloff. I would receive a higher standard of tuition from teachers who would not share his bias toward me.

I gave up fiction. I gave up my outings with the Zinovieffs. I gave up most of my sleep in order to study. I stopped thinking about Marya Varvorovna. I studied every textbook we had been sent. I studied the advanced textbooks listed in the bibliographies. I began to understand whole areas of science, whole principles of engineering, as my mind made intellectual leap after intellectual leap. I had, of course, to resort again frequently to my cocaine, but this aided me in making unique connections. I began to see the very structure of the universe. Whenever I slept (which was infrequently) I saw every planet in the solar system circulating about the sun; I saw the other planetary systems, the galaxies. The whole universe was pictured to me. And the world of atoms was mirrored in the picture. Into this great conception I could fit an ontological understanding of the world encompassing the sum total of human knowledge: and more. These were the visions, I realized with excitement, which had led Leonardo and Galileo and Newton to their discoveries. I was party to the secrets of Genius. I knew I must not reveal too much at once to my teachers, particularly Merkuloff. He was an ordinary man with an ordinary mind. Others at the Institute had good minds, but even they would not recognize the value of my innovatory theories. I was party to the knowledge of the Gods: I could write it down, but I could not, at that time, communicate it to the world.

I walked to and from the tram stop and felt like a giant striding between buildings barely reaching my knees. It was still very cold. The weather meant nothing to me. Before me I saw the stars and the lines of force combining to produce what we call "the universe." The nature of matter itself was just within my grasp. At school I attended lectures but I already knew their substance. I listened with polite impatience to Professor Merkuloff. He was a fool. I ignored the remarks of my fellows. I returned home and I studied more and more. But my supply of cocaine had begun to shrink. I knew I would need more if I were to continue with my work, which was now filling a number of bulky notebooks. I was at the peak of my powers. I could not afford to lose time. I hunted for the scrap of paper on which Sergei Andreyovitch Tsipliakov had written the address of his friend, where he would be staying. I decided to take the last of the cocaine and return the snuffbox. It would be an ideal excuse. I could tell him the box had been opened and all his "medicine" had been scattered. He would be grateful for the box, which looked valuable. I would find out where he bought his cocaine and I would buy some, too. I would spend the money on it which I would otherwise have spent on expensive imported fiction.

I took two trams to a street off the Nevski, near the Mikhailovski Gardens. I at last found the apartment building. It was not quite as grand as I had imagined, but far grander than anything I had visited before in St. Petersburg. The porter stopped me from entering until I gave the name of Seryozha's friend, Nicholai Feodorovitch Petroff. The porter made something of a grumble about the "succession of ruffians" he had to deal with and told me where to go. It was across the courtyard, near the top of the building, occupying a whole floor. It was very quiet and felt extremely prosperous. I rang the bell of the apartment. The door was opened by a young girl wearing little more than a Japanese kimono. She had a vaguely Oriental cast to her heavily made-up features and moved with peculiar gliding grace which was at once stiff and natural. Perhaps she was also a dancer. She said nothing after she had admitted me, but began to glide away toward the inner rooms. I took off my cap, closed the door and followed her. I found a large chamber furnished in the "Arts and Crafts" style, a kind of Russian Art Nouveau then fashionable. The place was full of peacock feathers. I experienced a slight superstitious frisson. I had been taught it was unlucky to bring peacock plumes into a house. "Are you a friend of Kolya's?" the girl asked.

"I had hoped to see Sergei Andreyovitch Tsipliakov."

It was then that she threw herself into one of the deep armchairs and let her kimono fall open. Her nipples were rouged. Her breasts were tiny. She had male genitals. It was a boy made up as a girl. I became confused, then the cocaine helped me rally myself and I remained superficially unimpressed.

The creature drew his kimono about him. He said off-handedly: "I don't think Seryozha and Kolya are on speaking terms. Are you a friend of Seryozha's, then?"

"We met on the train from Kiev."

"You're not the little yid he tried to seduce?"

I smiled and shook my head. "That must have been on another trip. Is he staying here?"

"He was. There was a row."

"He's moved?"

"Well, he isn't here. What did you want him for?"

"I have a snuffbox belonging to him."

"Any snuff in it?"

"There was never any snuff in it."

The youth gave a knowing sneer. Evidently this was a sophisticated "sniffer." It was no part of my plan to aggravate a person who could help me find what, in all languages, cocaine users once called "snow."

I said, "My name is Dimitri Mitrofanovitch Kryscheff."

"You're from the South."

I modified my accent to give it the sharp, Petersburg sound. "May I have the honor of asking your name?" I bowed with the sardonic courtesy one might extend to a lady of easy virtue. This pleased him. He stood up, making a gesture which could have been an attempt to curtsy. "*Enchanté*. You can call me Hippolyte."

"You are also connected with the ballet?"

"Connected, yes." Hippolyte giggled. "A drink? We have everything. Champagne? Cognac? Absinthe?" Absinthe had just been banned in France.

"I'll take absinthe." I had never had it and was determined to sample it before the apartment's owner returned. He might be more restrained in his hospitality.

With another artificially sinuous flirt of the hips, Hippolyte moved to a large cabinet and poured me some absinthe. "Water? Sugar?"

"As it comes."

Hippolyte shrugged. He presented me with a long-stemmed narrow glass in which yellow liquid shone. I do not believe I let my pleasure show on my face as I sipped the bitter drink, but from that moment I had found a new vice. It is one which, sadly, became harder and harder to indulge. Hippolyte was free with the absinthe. He brought me the bottle. It was called "Terminus." Modern readers will not remember the old advertisements which might only have appeared in good Russian shops. I never saw one, I think, in Paris. *"Je bois à ton succès, ma chère,"* says the Harlequin to his *fin-de-siècle* "Mucha" lady, *"et à ceux de l'Absinthe Terminus la seule bienfaisante."*

I settled patiently to wait to see what would happen. The worst would be an angry host who would give me some idea of Seryozha's whereabouts before he dismissed me. I could also go to the Little Theater in the Fontanka where the Ballet Foline was performing some piece of nonsense by that Grand Deceiver, Stravinsky. We were entering an age of brilliant conjurors posing as creators. They took the techniques of the traveling sideshow and transformed them into art. In time they allowed every "sensitive" young person to become an artist: all that was required was a gift for self-advertisement and the persuasive voice of a Jewish market-spieler.

Hippolyte inspected his kohl and rouge. The silver frame of the mirror was, like almost everything here, fashioned to resemble naked nymphs or satyrs.

The door opened and the master of the house entered. He was very tall. He wore a huge tawny wolfskin coat. I was immediately admiring and envious. One would not wish to give such a coat up, even at the height of summer.

The wolfskin was thrown off. "Kolya" was dressed entirely in black, with black broad-brimmed hat, black shirt, black tie, black gloves, black boots and, of course, black trousers, waistcoat and frock coat. His hair was pure white, either dyed or natural. His eyes had that reddish tinge associated with albinism, but I think overindulgence and a natural melancholy had created the effect. His skin was pale as the snowdrops in the hands of Nevski flower girls. When he saw me he drew back a step in mock surprise. With his black, silver-headed cane in one long-fingered hand, he smiled with such compassionate irony that, were I a girl, I should at once have been his.

"My dear!" he said in French to Hippolyte. "But what is this little grey soldier doing in our house?"

"He came for Seryozha," said Hippolyte in Russian. "His name's Dimitri Alexeivitch something . . ."

"I am known as Dimitri Mitrofanovitch Kryscheff." I bowed. "I called to return this to M'sieu Tsipliakov." I held out the snuffbox.

With an elegant movement of his arm (I could see whom Hippolyte imitated), Kolya plucked the box from my palm. He snapped it open. "Empty!"

"It is, your excellency."

I had flattered and amused this magnifico.

"You are a friend of Seryozha's?"

"An acquaintance. I have been meaning to return the box to him. But my studies interfered."

"And what are you studying? I see you are enjoying the absinthe. Sip it slowly and drain the glass, my dear. It is the last bottle." He spoke neutrally. There was no sidelong glance of disapproval at Hippolyte as I might have expected. I was in the presence of a real gentleman, a dandy of the old English sort, rather than a debauchee of our Russian kind. "Your French is good," he said. "Your accent is almost perfect."

Hippolyte was scowling, evidently not following the conversation.

"I have a talent for languages."

"And languages are what you study? Where? At the University?"

"No, no, m'sieu. I study science. I have already produced a number of inventions and designs for new vehicles. Methods of bridging oceans. Well, all kinds of things . . ."

"But you are exactly the sort of fellow for me!" Kolya seemed genuinely delighted. "I am obsessed with silence. You read Laforgue?"

I had never heard of him.

"An exquisite poet. The best of all of us. He died very young, you know. Of the usual sickness."

"Syphilis?"

He laughed. "Tuberculosis. My dear sir, I am ignorant. Will you give me lessons in the secrets of the internal combusion engine, the electrical landaulet, the composition of matter?"

"I should be happy to . . ."

"You will become my tutor? Really? You will supply me with images?"

"Images, m'sieu. I am not sure . . ."

"The symbols of the twentieth century, my dear Dimitri Mitrofanovitch. It is in science we must find our poetry. And we must give our poetry to science." He spoke, I must admit, as if he had rehearsed this speech more than once. I was in the presence of a Futurist, but not one of the vulgar fellows I had seen demonstrating in the Nevski. There was something about "Kolya" which impressed me in a way the Futurists and other modern confidence tricksters had not. Kolya had magnetism. Kolya knew at least a little of the sciences. If he was rich—and he seemed to be—he might pay for private lessons. In turn these would pay for the cocaine he would be able to supply.

Hippolyte was glaring at me now. I think he suspected a rival for Kolya's affections. This was ridiculous. I have occasionally been forced to indulge in certain minor affairs with members of my own sex. Who has not? I know this will not shock an English audience, for such things are the norm here. But my relationship with Kolya was to be one of the warmest friendship and regard. I had in fact found a patron!

"Are you fond of Baudelaire, Dimitri Mitrofanovitch?"

"The poet?"

"The poet, indeed!" Kolya strode to the window and drew back the shutters, letting in thin, Petersburg light. *"Les tuyaux, les clochers, ces mâts de la cité!"* He smiled. "The celebration of urban life. The greatest poets were never Arcadians, your singers of shepherds and their lasses. The greatest poets of the world have always cried the virtues of the streets, the slums, the alleys and the buildings, the things created not by God but by their fellow men. To be a true poet is to sing of the city. To sing of the city is to be a true revolutionary!"

It seemed a safe enough way of being a revolutionary. I was not unduly alarmed, although I began to have doubts concerning Kolya as an employer. I was already associated in the minds of the police with one radical and here I was falling in it seemed with another. But I needed the cocaine if I were to continue with my work, to win my diploma, to begin my career, to give the world the benefits of my brain.

"Villon, Baudelaire, Laforgue—even Pushkin, young Dimka. All celebrated the city. The innocent abroad in the gutters of the world, eh? It is our natural environment and it is natural for us to sing of it. Nature is the factory, the apartment building, the gas holder, the locomotive. Are they not more beautiful than fields and flowers? More complex than cows and sheep? If Russia is to rise: if the Scythians are to display their glory to the world—then we must cease our celebration of the veins on the leaf of the beech; the wonder of the crushed poppy beneath the foot; the subtlety of sunsets over Lake Ladoga. We must describe the yellow fumes of the factories distorting the bloody rays of the sun: making human art of what we always believed was the work of the Gods alone.

"Have you watched the sunsets over the docks, Dimka? Have you seen how red light is made more beautiful by the smoke and steam from the ships? How it illuminates the bricks of the buildings, the rusty sides of the ships, the wooden hulls, the sails? How it reflects from the oil lying on black water, producing a thousand images within one image? Have you noticed how a steam locomotive brings roaring life to a dead landscape, as the great primeval beasts once brought it similar life? How golden sun streams through fine coal dust? Do not all these things excite you, make your blood pound, your heart beat with joy? You, a scientist, must understand what so many of my fellow poets do not! For all they rant of rods and engines, they have no true imagination and therefore cannot see that these things are not the objects of their satire, but the inspiration of their humanity!"

Whether it was the work I had been doing, or the effects of the cocaine, I was, I admit, inspired by Kolya's words. He said in poetry all that I had been thinking. He inspired me to dreams of even greater intensity. I saw us, the Poet and the Scientist, changing the whole world. Those marching Futurists were only bragging journeymen. They had little in common with this wonderful individual.

"I should like to read your poems," I said.

Kolya laughed. "You can't read them. Sit down. Drink some more absinthe. I burned all my poems this winter. They were simply not up to standard. They were in imitation of Baudelaire and Laforgue. There was no point in adding second-rate verse to the mountain already immersing our city. I shall wait for the War to end, or for the Revolution to come, or for Armageddon or the Apocalypse. Then I shall write again."

He seated himself upon a great divan in the center of the room and reached for the bottle. "Would you have the last of the wine?"

"If there is no more—" I put a hand over the top of my glass.

"Enjoy it. Why shouldn't you? If this war continues, if the Apocalypse really comes, then we'll have no more absinthe anyway, merely the wormwood itself, if we are lucky." A black sleeve extended toward me, a black glove clutched the neck of the Terminus flask. Yellow liquid poured up to the rim of the slender goblet. "Drink it, my scientist friend. To the poetry you will inspire."

"And to the science you will inspire." I was fired by his mood. I drank.

Hippolyte vanished and, tut-tutting, emerged, it seemed only moments later, in a fairly ordinary, if somewhat dandified outfit, and said that he was "going down to the Tango" to find some company.

He was bored, he said. Kolya wished him an amiable farewell. Then, pausing by the door, Hippolyte said, "You'd better let me know when you want me back."

"Whenever you like, my dear!" Kolya was casual. "Dimitri Mitrofanovitch and myself will be discussing matters of science."

Hippolyte scowled, hesitated again, then left.

A moment passed. He was back again. "I might go on somewhere," he said.

"Just as you like, Hippolyte." Kolya turned questioningly to me. "Would you like to visit the Scarlet Tango? Or are you bored with such places?"

I suspected the Scarlet Tango would be like the bohemian cafés I had frequented in Odessa, where cocaine was always available. I must have seemed eager when I replied that I did not think I would be bored.

Kolya said to Hippolyte, "We'll see you there in an hour or two."

The door slammed. Kolya sighed. "Beauty is cheap in Peter, these days, Dimka. But it seems always to be accompanied by bad manners. It's a pleasure to meet a scholar for a change."

I was fascinated by this black-clad ghost, this Russian Hamlet. I had relaxed completely. Doubtless the absinthe made me reveal, almost at once, the nature of my quest.

"You are a sniffer!" He was amused. "Well, well, the good things of life are spreading amongst the people. The Revolution is with us, after all!"

"I should point out," I said with some dignity, "that I am a rather unusual student at the Polytechnic, and not a very popular one. My experience of life has not been entirely of the schoolroom."

He apologized with grave good manners. "And where were you, before the Polytechnic?"

"In Kiev," I said, "where I flew my own machine."

"And so young? Where's the aeroplane now?"

"It was not an aeroplane as such. It was an entirely new design. It was reported in the papers."

"And you flew to Peter?"

I laughed. "I crashed. I still need time to perfect the design. But perfect it I shall."

"And after that? Where did you go?"

"To Odessa for a while. I had already gained some practical engineering experience. In Odessa I developed a liking for cocaine and the pleasures of the flesh."

I must have seemed a little naïve to him, but he did not show it.

Since then, I told him, I had given up such vices and was concentrating on my studies. I mentioned my new problems. I was determined to succeed in spite of all. To this end I had begun to use a stimulant again. My work was proceeding well on all fronts. I had developed theories which would astonish any true scientist. I did not expect them to impress the staid and orthodox hacks currently teaching at the Institute. I had hoped to get more cocaine from Sergei Andreyovitch.

"You are not a friend of Seryozha's?"

"An acquaintance, that is all."

"So your interest is in 'la neige' rather than the place from which it falls?" He smiled kindly.

"Exactly."

"Well, it will be nothing to find you some. Particularly with the War on. God knows how they can supply all the warriors, poets and scientists with what they need to get them through this conflict and famine. You're not interested in morphine?"

"I've never indulged myself with the distillation of poppies. The world of dreams is not an escape for me. I intend to impose my dreams upon the world."

He was pleased by this turn of phrase. He poured me the dregs of the absinthe. "I hope you will not disapprove of me if I say I have injected the occasional dose. When I have needed to retreat from society. The drugs can be complementary, you know."

I did not fully realize then what I know today: Cocaine is a stimulant, but morphine is a killer. I have never made use of depressants. It is not a very large step from the world of sleeping hallucinations to the cold world of Death; from Heaven on Earth, as it were, to the genuine article. The road away from Hell, as the Poles say, is the road that leads there.

I sipped the last of the absinthe. "I must point out that I do not use the drug for pleasure. I need it to keep my brain alive and my body working."

"Are you afraid you'll go mad with so much work?"

"It is possible, but I have the necessary control."

"Inspiration and madness are very similar, I think." He crossed to the cabinet where he kept his drinks and opened a porcelain dish whose lid was in the shape of a white pierrot peering at a half-moon. "I have some here. I think it is good quality. These days one must be careful. So many customers. As a consequence, so many rogues who will dilute the crystals with anything which comes to hand. You must be careful. In Odessa, before the War, you would not have known such dangers, eh?"

"There are a few crooks in Odessa," I joked.

"So I have heard."

He was bringing me alive again, as Shura had brought me alive. More. For Kolya was a sophisticated man of letters, a theater critic, a writer of essays in the thick journals, a man of taste, dignity and discrimination, who recognized intelligence and creativity. I was to discover that he saw himself more as a publicist of talent than as a talent in his own right. He was one of those great and necessary people who encourage others to aspire to do their best, whatever that best may be.

His whole name was Count Nicholai Feodorovitch Petroff and he was related to the famous Mikhishevski family, one of the chief aristocratic Petersburg clans, whose ancestral estates were in my native Ukraine. Nicholai Feodorovitch had visited rural Ukraine occasionally but had no experience with the cities or of that particular shore. He knew the Crimean coast well, however. "It is even warmer. We should go there," he said, "this summer. If the War ends." I enjoyed the fantasy. I asked if he had not stayed even briefly in Kiev or Odessa. He laughed. "I find them both attractive as ideas, Dimka, but that is all. The dark, romantic Jew has always intrigued me as a character, you know. I have every sympathy with Shylock. Haven't you? Or even poor Fagin, who is the liveliest of Dickens' characters? Or the noble Isaac in *Ivanhoe*?"

I was familiar with none of these English books then. Of course I had seen reference to them in my set of *Pearson's*. The English were inclined to take a tolerant attitude to Jews. One of their most honored writers, in those days, was Israel Zangwill, and they had, as we all know, a Jew as their Prime Minister. My friend continued in praise of the English poet Shelley, whose character Ahasuerus in *Hellas* inspired Kolya a great deal, he said, if only for the single speech he was fond of quoting:

> What has thought
> To do with time or place or circumstance?
> Wouldst thou behold the future? Ask and have!
> Knock, and it shall be opened—look, and lo!
> The coming age is shadowed on the past,
> As on a glass.

Politeness made me refrain from telling Kolya what I thought of such high-sounding rubbish. The English have many virtues. They are excellent engineers and practical scientists. As storytellers they give their novels good, strong, exciting plots. But as poets they have done more damage to the world than any others. The ideas of Byron and Shelley have probably caused more young men to lose their lives in hopeless, idiotic, romantic causes than the ideas of Karl Marx. Romanticism is the disease of the Modern Age. It is the direct result of increased leisure amongst a certain class. If one does not believe me, one has only to look around at the so-called hippies and "dropouts" who always complain of poverty yet find time to bargain with me for coats worth twice the price I am charging, and pay in the end with money donated to them by the State!

Perhaps, as some say, the world is no more decadent now than it always was. But what the so-called decadents of my days in St. Petersburg had was a sense of style, of taste, of social position and, indeed, a good education.

Education, of course, can also confuse. Nicholai Feodorovitch was a great Slav, a true Slav, a believer in the Slavic Renaissance, but his love of romantic verse was also his blind spot, for he was morbidly philo-semitic, as so many of his heroes had been. Even as we left the apartment, on our way to the Scarlet Tango, he put an arm around my uniformed shoulder and quoted some nonsense from Byron about "tribes of the wandering foot and weary breast." I owe the lines (for I would not otherwise remember them) to Mrs. Cornelius, who was educated at the Godolphin and Latymer School in Hammersmith, where only the very best pupils are accepted.

> How shall ye flee away and be at rest!
> The wild-dove hath her nest, the fox his cave,
> Mankind their country—Israel but the grave!

A sentimental streak of this sort is often the attribute of a dandy. It is as if they allow themselves one weakness. With some it is a liking for dogs or horses to whom they are inordinately kind. Nicholai Feodorovitch had a weakness for Jews: the very people who were at that moment scheming the destruction of him and all his caste. That was one of the ironic tragedies of life. I have noticed similar ironies wherever I have gone about the world. Even the Wandering Jew himself could not have witnessed as much as I have witnessed in my day.

The Scarlet Tango was not far from St. Catherine's Catholic Church. It was in a side street mainly occupied by little jewelers and confectioners. It was part beer hall, part bohemian café of the kind one used to find in Montmartre, full of dazzling mirrors and crystal lamps, crowded with circular tables and gilded metal chairs on which sat young men and women chiefly distinguished by their bright clothes, their pale faces and their intensely glittering eyes; make-up was in use with both sexes. Both sexes smoked cigarettes, often of European brands, in long holders. Upon a stage at one side, a Negro four-piece orchestra played the latest syncopated jungle tunes: the rag, the cakewalk, the coon dance and the slow drag. Was there a war in progress? Were there bread shortages? Was light becoming as scarce a commodity as fresh meat or hope? H. G. Wells' time-traveler visiting the Scarlet Tango might have believed that the world was at its happiest and most prosperous. Copies of the most outrageous revolutionary and artistic journals were being openly read: *Truth, Freedom, New Worlds, Apollon* and *Cosmic Manifesto*. The place had much of the atmosphere of Esau's, though on a larger, grander and more elegant scale. Its atmosphere of friendliness, laughter and argument attracted me as I had been attracted before. There were famous names to be found here. Names associated with all that was called the "Russian explosion" in the arts. It was an explosion as welcome to me as the bombs which fell on Notting Hill during the Second World War.

At the time, helped by Kolya's absinthe and his enthusiasm for what he called "Modern Experience," I developed at least an ability to parrot the names of their pantheon: Stanislavski, Diaghilev, Kandinski, Malevich and Chagall, Blok, Mandelstam, Akhmatova, Rabinovitz and others. Kolya, of course, could quote them all, could name pictures, even hum tunes, if tunes they were. He had enjoyed the company of Sergei Andreyovitch largely because of the latters' ability to interpret modern music. "But like most ballet dancers, he had only a limited imagination. You will find that a dancer has about six things he or she can do well: a good leap, perhaps, or a pas de deux or perhaps one of those writhing movements they favor so much. And they do them over and over again, in every ballet, whether 'free' or choreographed with rigid discipline." I had to take his word for it. Ballet is another art which has never much attracted me. My experience of ballet dancers has not been particularly happy. Their egos are such that they are quickly gratified with praise. Their talent becomes as stultified as their muscles if they do not exercise. There were a good many dancers to be found at the Scarlet Tango.

Later, we went on, full of absinthe, arm in arm, to another, less impressive place called the Wandering Dog, where Kolya had friends with whom he seemed more intimate and relaxed. My own recollections are vague. I had become almost incapably drunk. Doubtless I made a horrible fool of myself. I recall a small, not very pleasant young Jew lisping lines about Ossian and Scotland, moon and blood. Though in Russian, they might as well have been English, they were so derivative. A few lines remain with me, for they are the lines which always come out whenever I am inebriated (which is rarely, these days):

> I am reminded of the hills
> Where Russia finishes suddenly
> Above a black and barren sea . . .

If ever I was going to develop a taste for modern poetry, I would have done so in Kolya's company. Very late into the first night I found myself on the doorstep of my lodgings watching a carriage jogging off back toward the twinkle of the city while I fumbled for the bell. I was admitted by a desolate Mme. Zinovieff, who exclaimed about the state of my uniform and then, realizing I was drunk, cried out that she had betrayed me and let me fall into bad company. I explained to her I had been dining with a famous Count and this, of course, mollified her a little. When I could not recall his name, she began to mutter and complain. She was not angry with me, but she had promised Mr. Parrot I would come to no harm. She was responsible for my moral welfare. I assured her this was a unique occasion. I had had to accept the Count's invitation. It would have been bad manners to have done otherwise.

She helped me to bed and out of my uniform. I fell asleep so heavily that if the next day had not been Sunday I should have missed school. I awoke with a hangover. A sense of depression was relieved when I discovered in one of the top pockets of my uniform jacket a screw of paper filled with two grams of the finest cocaine. A little of this snuffed into both nostrils and I was a new man. I was too late for breakfast, as a smiling, head-shaking Mme. Zinovieff informed me, so I took one of my books on electrical engineering and enjoyed a glass or two of weak tea at a nearby café. I read the chapter on the

Lundell Protected Ventilated Six-Pole Motor which even by that time was outmoded. The trouble with textbooks is that they tend to reflect what their writers learned twenty years before. This was for me, however, light reading compared to the abstractions I had been absorbing through most of the week. The chapter gave me some ideas for a development of the conventional hoisting motors then coming into use on some battleships; this in turn led me to theorize about aeroplanes which could be launched from ships without needing a conventional runway. In that little café in Viborgskaya behind the Finland Station on a spring morning in 1916 I invented the modern aircraft carrier. It was nothing more than an exercise. When I had made my sketches and worked out all the mechanics involved, I crumpled up the paper and threw it away. Later I would return to the idea and make better plans, but it will give my readers some hint of how prolific I had become, how casually I had learned to treat advanced conceptions. I returned home for lunch and spent the afternoon studying the specifications of Waygood and Otis Electrical lifts with Rosenbusch Controllers, with a view of the building of a hydraulically operated deck which could be lowered when not in use and raised when the planes came in to land. I also developed a method of mooring airships at sea, also by means of electrical winches, so that the dirigibles could be towed until needed, then carry out bombing raids far beyond their expected range.

If I had taken my plans to the War Office or the Admiralty at that time, the whole course of the War would have changed. Russia would have emerged stronger and triumphant, a leader in modern military and engineering science, the greatest Power of her day. The British converted tractors, the "tanks," would have been as nothing compared to our airship bombers and aircraft carriers. I think I already guessed not only that the people who ran the ministries were corrupt or conservative, but that they were actively interested in making a separate peace with Germany. Had they been able, they would have capitulated eighteen months before the Bolsheviks gave away vast areas of our country. These were not recovered for years, in many cases not until after the Second World War, when the old Russian boundaries were restored. In 1916 green and pink areas on the map represented the two largest empires the world has known. The Russians almost lost theirs through the agency of the Duma and the Jews. The British lost theirs through laziness, self-contempt and an exaggerated idea of the ability of savages to understand the principles of

Christian decency. Two Empires have been destroyed forever. Only a few vestiges of their culture remain in corners of the world as yet uncorrupted by sentimental liberalism and a wish to placate at any cost the wily, unscrupulous Oriental.

SEVEN

Now I reached the most intense period of my whole creative life. During the week, I attended lectures. I read books years in advance of what was being taught on the official syllabus. In the early evenings I took the steamtram home and made my own notes. Then, at around eight or nine at night and with some gesticulating and lip-pursing from Mme. Zinovieff, I would join Kolya at his flat or at one of the cabarets we favored. He would recite endless poetry in French, English, Russian and abominable German. I would tell him how a Zeppelin was constructed, or the principle allowing the tank to function, or how electricity is generated. I believe he sometimes paid as much attention to my lectures as I paid to his poetry. I had become a sort of mascot of the New Age for him, but he was always polite and never at any time was he rude and he would never allow anyone to offend me. At the Scarlet Tango and the Wandering Dog, bohemian artists, foreigners, criminals and the *crème de la crème* of revolutionaries who would soon be serving with Kerenski or Lenin, all met together to talk, to listen to music, to find sexual companionship and sometimes to fight. This particular admixture of experience was ideal for me. I at last discovered a source of women and Marya Varvorovna was forgotten. They were prepared to treat love as cheerfully as my Katya had treated it. I had male admirers and was flattered, but did not succumb to them. There were

many girls or older ladies who found it exciting to quote the porno-
graphic ravings of Mandelstam and Baudelaire at me, then take me to
their wonderful beds. There I could lie upon silk. There I could
wash myself with warm, perfumed water. I became increasingly self-
confident again. I found it was possible to reduce the amount of my
reading. Now there was hardly a field in which I was not profoundly
conversant.

By the time the Summer Vacation came I was ready for a holiday.
With Kolya, Hippolyte, a girl who called herself "Gloria," after the
English fashion (though she was Polish), and a couple of "poets," we
visited the Summer Gardens and broad quays of the Neva, took the
rare steamer up the river, enjoyed picnics on the banks, or lunches at
those magnificent wooden establishments on several floors, not unlike
Swiss ski lodges, which catered for the steamer trade and by now
were pleased to welcome any sort of customer.

Empty of the *haut monde*, St. Petersburg filled up with wounded
soldiers and sailors, with nurses on leave from the Front who sought
consolation in the arms of healthy civilians (there were all too few of
us left). This wealth of femininity even distracted agitators like
Lunarcharsky, who became Commissar of Education under Lenin,
or Onipko, the notorious anarchist, who had helped spark the abor-
tive 1905 revolution. For obvious reasons these were ineligible for
the army. Happily, Kolya had few intimates in this latter group,
though the proprietor of the Wandering Dog (one Boris Pronin who
saw himself as a kind of Russian Rudolphe Salis, of Chat Noir fame),
seemed only too pleased to welcome these incendiaries, bombs and
all!

I should make it clear here that I was no hypocrite. I aired my own
views frequently and often found others who supported me, particularly amongst the "Pan-Slavic" group. Even those who disagreed
seemed to treat me with the best possible humor. If I had not had the
lesson of my father, I might have been caught up in their infantile
enthusiasm for destruction and change. I drank absinthe in the company of beautiful whores. My compatriots were revolutionaries,
vagabonds, poets. They nicknamed me The Professor or The Mad
Scientist and bought me more wine and listened to me as few have
listened to me since. These same people were to survive the Revolution only at the expense of their humor, their irony, their very souls.
They became the grey men of Lenin and his successors. Some died
early—Blok and Grin—and did not live to see the destructive conse-

quences of their foolish hopes. Most, like Mandelstam, were to see all their visions decay, all their hope fade, all their courage and generosity become a weapon turned against them to insult and degrade them. This was, indeed, the last year of their Revolution, that year of 1916, for their enthusiasm lay in the dream of Utopia, not in the reality which was to trap me as much as it trapped them. I was lucky to escape. Some (Mayakovski, for instance) escaped only through suicide.

The Wandering Dog was closed by the police, but the bohemian life continued. The War appeared to be improving and victories were reported. British armored cars and Russian Cossacks plunged through the mud of Galicia and forced the Uhlans and the Austrian infantry to retreat. But bread became harder to obtain. The lines of miserable working people, their faces shaded by caps and shawls, as if in mourning, became familiar irritations: To the poets who spoke of the pathos of it, to the revolutionaries who foretold the risings, to the ordinary middle-class public, called in Russian slang the "boorzhoo," who had become increasingly the prey of thieves robbing them of their groceries and their money. The War was draining us. They should have spent money on food and distributed it free. Then we might have averted Chaos. But the Czar's ministers were too obsessed with War, and the revolutionaries actually wanted people to starve so they would rise. The boorzhoo could think only of their own families; they had been called upon to give up everything to help with the War, to supply the soldiers at the Front. There is no need here to go into the whys and wherefores of the Revolution. Too many émigrés; too many historians; too many Bolshevik revisers of the past have done that already. We have had a thousand versions of *Ten Days That Shook the World*. Perhaps we should have at least ten versions of *A Thousand Books That Bored the World*. I shall not add to all that. What happened, happened. We did not really believe it would happen, though so many warned of it. Poetry, when it becomes reality, rarely pleases anyone, least of all the poets.

Pronin opened a new establishment called *Prival Komendiantoff* (The Retreat of the Harlequinade). It is difficult to translate the exact sense of the name. Comedian's Halt, perhaps. We all found it very appropriate and praised Pronin when he appeared, leading a mangy mongrel by a piece of ribbon ("all that is left of the Dog") and promising that this establishment would be even finer than the last. It was certainly more elaborate. Negro boys dressed to look as if they had come from the Court of Harun al-Rashid served at the tables. Murals of a blatantly radical nature covered the walls and ceilings. From the walls stared Negro masks, the lighting issuing from their eye sockets. The same Negro band played the same raucous music whenever we were not having to listen to another new poet or *petite chanteuse*, or watching the posturings of some Pierrot mime while a horse-faced woman in a long purple dress droned on about the moon. Black female inpersonators sang jazz songs. Female impersonators were the rage of Café Society. At odds with all this avant-gardism were girls in peasant costume; tablecloths made of bright peasant handwoven fabrics; "folk-art" ceramics, to remind us that this was, after all, Russia; that we were not Frenchmen or even Germans. The cellos groaned and the mime artistes twisted their silly bodies into parodies of the human form. The jazz band wailed. The little song-stresses sang in tiny, toneless voices about the death of birds and mayflies. We talked and drank and whored. Sometimes it would be dawn before I (nowadays wearing a velvet jacket, red Ukrainian boots, riding trousers and a Cossack shirt) would stagger out into morning sunshine over the Field of Mars.

Here, colorful soldiers still paraded above the heads of our "menagerie,'" which, as usual, was in a series of cellars. Hussars and streltsi trotted and marched in polished leather, in carefully brushed serge, in brass and gold braid, and we would wander past, some of us hardly able to stand, staring in astonishment at these vestiges of the old world. We would be moved along by policemen who seemed, more frequently, to share our attitudes. Futurists would pause in their constant bickerings with Acmeists (there were as many opposing artistic camps as there were political). Social Revolutionaries would stop in midsentence in an argument with Tolstoians and watch opened-mouthed as a band struck up or a column of blue-coated, red-hatted soldiers wheeled and turned to the sound of patriotic marches. I was infected by the general cynicism. I think there was hardly anyone in Petrograd by that time who was not. I think if we had stumbled out of the Harlequinade one morning and seen German troops parading, we should scarcely have noticed. If we had noticed we should not have cared. The artists would have announced the coming of the Germans as the first sign of a "new age" in Art. The revolutionaries would have said this was a sure sign the people would rise up at any moment. The cynics would have said that German efficiency was better than Russian incompetence. And that would have been the end of it. We half-believed that this strange dream would continue until we all died the early, romantic deaths we expected to die in a sufficiently distant future. Nobody took anything very seriously, I think, except Kolya, who, with Tolstoi, had faith in the natural divinity of the human spirit. My faith was in the triumph of Man's ingenuity over all the vicissitudes of nature, including human nature. Both of us, I am sure, were as guilty as everyone of adding to the rhetoric of despair. It was easy to be smart and drink champagne and toast the triumph of the working class. One forgot the slow transformation taking place everywhere. St. Petersburg, an unnatural city, easily blockaded, cut off from her supplies by virtue of her physical geography, pretended to herself she was not under siege and that Victory was a month or two away. By the autumn, when it seemed we were completely beaten, as we had been beaten by the Japanese at Port Arthur, the fashionable carriages were fewer than ever in the Nevski. Merchants and landowners saw Moscow as a safer wintering place than Peter. And Kolya, with some amusement, quoted Kipling, of whom he was also very fond:

The Captains and the Kings depart!

Rome, he said, was being evacuated, for the Hun again threatened. "Byzantium! Byzantium!" he sang, as he escorted me home in his carriage one late August morning. "They are all fleeing East. Wait until the Czar goes to Moscow, Dimka. Then you will know it is the end of us."

"The Czar will never give up the capital."

"The Czar scarcely occupies it now. How often have you seen the Royal Standard flying over the Winter Palace?"

"Tsarskoye Selo is not too far from the center," I reminded him.

"There's no proof he's there. The rumors are that he, his family, Rasputin, are already packing their bags and plan to stay with the Kaiser. They're related, after all."

Our carriage stopped at an intersection as a marching column of cadets went past. The drums rolled, the trumpets blared, the fifes piped and the cadets moved as one creature. Kolya smiled sadly. He was as usual dressed all in black. The only white was the white of his hair beneath his hat. The paleness of his face was relieved by his slightly pinkish eyes. He put his chin upon his fist and shrugged. "Did you know I was once a cadet, Dimka?"

"I suppose you must have been." It was natural for a member of the aristocracy to attend a military school.

"I ran away. When I was fifteen. I ran away to Paris because I wished to meet poets. I met a good many charlatans and was seduced by a few of them, men and women. But I don't think I met a single poet until I returned to Peter! Now all the Russian poets, all the artists, all the impresarios, are going to Paris! Is that an irony? Should we follow them, Dimka?"

"The Germans will be beaten soon," I said. "The newspapers are confident. They haven't been so confident for ages."

"A sure sign of impending defeat!" He laughed.

"Our allies won't let it happen. England, France, Italy—even Japan—will come to help."

"They are no better off than we are. The Germans have all but taken Paris."

"Then we had better stay here," I said.

"Until the War is over, at least. You should be reading only German science and philosophy and I should be studying Goethe. I shall go to—where? Munich? Or study with the Moravian Brothers, as George Meredith did. There I shall become a proper, mystical German intellectual. In the new German Empire—the Holy Roman Empire—we shall become good Goths. We shall forget Paris. Paris and Petersburg alike will be provincial towns. Berlin will become the capital of the world. Art will flourish there, nurtured by our Russian genius, as it flourished in Berlin before the War. We will be like the Chinese, Dimka, and let ourselves be conquered, only to conquer secretly by means of our superior culture, our Slavic heritage. No longer shall we imitate the French and the English and the Italians. We shall become the architects of the new Empire. We shall present plans for a Kremlin in Berlin and our very energy and freshness will impress the German Caesar so that in time everything will take on a Russian tinge. Why should we worry about military victory when our greatest weapon lies in our Slavic genius! And you, Dimka, will show the world what Russian science can accomplish, because you are Russian at heart. As Russian as me!"

I presumed he was referring to my Ukrainian background. Sometimes he could make mysterious pronouncements which completely confused me. But I was never able to interrupt Count Nicholai Petroff in these soliloquies and rarely saw any point in trying. It was like listening to inspiring music. To interrupt him would have been like interrupting our Russian hymns, like shouting a contradiction in the Alexander Nevski Cathedral in the middle of a *Kyrie Eleison* or *Pomychlayu denya Strachnya*.

By September Kolya and I were possibly the closest we had ever been. I had returned to school to continue the impression of an attentive student. St. Petersburg began to smell not of apathy any longer, but of fear. It was tangible, even as I traveled into the suburbs on the tram. Neighbor was beginning to distrust neighbor. Gangs of pinch-faced men in black coats and hats moved between factory and working-class suburb with a silence holding more menace than complaint. Mme. Zinovieff became harsher in her criticism of me, of the girls and their fiancés, of the urban world in general. On my monthly visit to Mr. Green I was warned to "tread carefully" and advised to purchase a money belt in which to keep my allowance. He said that Uncle Semya had written to him to ask him how my studies went. I said extremely well. I was bound to jump a year in my next class. Mr. Green said I must soon use my gift for languages and my "knowledge of machinery" to pay a visit abroad for Uncle Semya, who was considering importing farm machinery. I asked for more details. Mr. Green would tell me nothing more, save that my education "would be put to some use at last." Did Uncle Semya have a job waiting for me when I left the Polytechnic? I enjoyed the prospect of going abroad.

As if to counter the fear in the city, the military displays became grander. Golden banners, portraits of the Czar, rattling drums, shrilling trumpets daily filled the city. The National Anthem was played on every possible occasion. It was at this time, to escape the empty display, that I took to wandering about the docks, a book under my arm, looking at the ships and gear which would begin to disappear as the Neva froze. I wondered where Uncle Semya was sending me. I watched the donkeys hauling fish from the little sailing boats. I admired the steam launches with their short funnels and strange, busy motion. Beyond them the great ironclads and the few passenger ships of the Baltic Shipping Company lay at anchor, a picture of tranquillity, or stasis. Sometimes a wild, banshee wail would come from one or another of the ships. Occasionally it was possible to watch an old-fashioned brig or schooner in full sail, leaving perhaps for Finland or Norway, or even heading out toward England. I was sure that England would be my own destination. It was not more than two or three days away from here.

Surrounded by the bustle, the creak of the hauling gear, the putter of the engines, the shouts of the dockers, I found peace. The docks stretched for miles along the Neva. They were one of the few areas not radiating that peculiar atmosphere of terror found everywhere but in the bohemian cafés.

Yet even some of those girls, whose apartments I visited, no longer offered me quite the retreat and escape I had first found. They seemed neither so warm, so carefree, nor so soft. The apartments themselves were as comfortable, cut off from the outside world; they still swam with the scent of Quelques Fleurs and were draped with Japanese silks and white towels. The girls broke the unspoken pact, and referred increasingly to their nervousness. Women are more sensitive to the *Zeitgeist*. They are the first to consider emigration during troubled times and they are nearly always right. They are the first to warn of treachery and cowardice in our ranks. They have this sensitivity, I believe, because they have more to lose than men. Sadly, I was too young to appreciate the feelings of these various Cassandras. I became, instead, impatient with them. I gave up sleeping with intellectuals and girls of good breeding. I sought the company of ordinary whores whose job was to mollify, to console, to keep the world at bay. I think quite a few of us dropped the beauties we had once courted and contented ourselves with brainless, good-natured creatures whose paint, dyes, cheap furs and cheaper satins became increasingly attractive as we grew tired of thinking. Thought meant considering the world and its war. The world was too full of fear to be any longer palatable. Because of this mood, I suspect, my second encounter with Mrs. Cornelius did not develop into an amorous affair.

I had heard of the "magnificent English beauty," a favorite of Lunarcharsky and Savinkov and their radicals, but I had not associated her with the girl I had helped briefly in Odessa. The revolutionaries had their own haunts. It was those with literary or artistic pretensions who appeared infrequently at the Harlequinade.

On 5 September 1916, I saw her again. She was the only female at a table where bespectacled, mad-eyed men in ill-fitting European jackets plotted the reorganization of the poetry industry. She seemed more than a little drunk. She was dressed in a beautifully cut and simple blue gown. On her blond hair was a small hat of a kind just becoming fashionable. It matched her dress. It had a cream ostrich feather following the line of her hair and neck, half curling under her chin. She was drinking the Georgian champagne we were all by that time substituting for the real thing, but she gave every appearance of relishing it. In a holder blending the colors of her hat and her feather, she smoked a Turkish cigarette. Her skirts were lifted a little so that her sheer silk stockings were revealed above blue suede boots. She was the only woman in the café who gave any appearance of enjoying herself. All the others wore the painted smile of the harlot or the nervous grin of the intellectual. I was sure she would not recognize me as I raised a hand. She frowned, sat back, asked something of her fiercely arguing companion (Lunarcharsky, I think: he had one of those goatee beards they all wore). He looked up, glanced in my direction, shook his head and returned to the fray. I lifted an eyebrow and smiled. She grinned, saluting me with a glass of champagne. I heard her familiar tones drifting through the general din:

" 'Ere's lookin at yer, Ivan!"

It was Mademoiselle Cornelius to be sure. I began to rise, to join her. She shook her head and pointed at an empty table. It was close to the stage where the Negro violinist squeezed discords from his instrument which would have horrified the maker. She joined me there. She still smelled of roses. She put a friendly hand on my arm with none of the ambiguity I had come to expect from Russian women. "Yore ther lad from 'Dessa, ain't yer?" She spoke in her usual English. I bowed and said that I was. She commented that it was "a turn up an' no mistake." It was an even smaller world than they said it was. She was doing nicely in Peter and had learned "Russki" enough to get by. When she gave me an example, it was perhaps the worst example of grammar and the most romantic accent I had ever experienced. I could see why she had so many admirers. I asked her how she had come to the capital and what she was doing with Lunarcharsky. Did she not know they were all wanted by the police?

She said they were a more honest bunch of crooks than some she had met. She had a feeling that they "knew what was going on." This was not true, she added disapprovingly, of the rest of the idiots in this bloody country. She had left Odessa with one of Dr. Cornelius' patients, an aristocratic liberal who had been holidaying there. When their affair ended, she had fallen in with the radicals, whom she found amusing and, as she put it, "good sports." She also had an eye, I believe, to the future, but her taste in men, together with her sense of humor, would often bewilder me. I am the first to admit, however, that I have never understood many jokes and that her taste was to serve both of us well in the years which followed.

She told me that I was looking "peaky" and if there was anything I needed in the way of grub I should ask her. She had a few contacts. I said I was eating better than most. I was studying hard for my examinations. She wished me luck. She said that she wished she had stayed at school, but there had not been much point "in the Dale." She referred, I learned, to Notting Dale, her birthplace. She had later moved to Whitechapel where she had "met a lot of Russians." These Russians were actually Jewish immigrants fleeing the pogroms. When Mrs. Cornelius suggested we go "somewhere quieter" so that I could tell her how I was getting on, I was reluctant to accompany her. I had been picked up by too many women during that period. I had become sated and wary, even of her.

I said I needed an early night. She laughed. "Don't we all? I'll see yer abart, Ivan." She patted my arm and got up to return to her party. I immediately regretted not taking her up on her offer. I do not believe, now, that it was sexual. She had wanted exactly what she had said she wanted, a quiet chat.

My friends congratulated me on my "conquest" and one of the well-bred beauties leaned over and asked me loudly what "the English whore is like in bed." Offended, I left the Harlequinade's Retreat.

The autumn term was remarkable only because we were allowed to wear hats, scarves and greatcoats in classes. There was no fuel allocation for heating the Polytechnic. The lectures were if anything duller than ever. As the world grew colder, life took on an entropic aspect. Social energy was running down. Within the first week of my return to the Institute the steamtrams were replaced by horsetrams. These were driven by haggard, pallid figures swathed in dark felt and serge from whose heads thin white fumes occasionally escaped. The men had been brought from retirement and were like the coachmen of the dead. Their horses, lean, sickly beasts, would eventually fill the stomachs, perhaps, of orphans—the first *bezhprizhorni*—who now swarmed about the railway stations and filled the parks. Displays of pomp and glory continued. We were advised to suffer all our discomforts because the War was almost won. More and more wounded men appeared on the streets. The theaters thrived, but many restaurants could not find enough food to make it worthwhile remaining open. Even Donan on the Moika Canal, that favorite of the *jeunesse dorée* and the Apollon group (who shared the building) had to close at lunchtime and became more of a bar than a restaurant. The sturgeon in mushroom sauce, the white partridges with klufka jam and bilberries, the other delicious Donan specialities, gave way to horse meat in sauces which could not disguise the unpalatable odor of what Kolya called "long cow." We would joke: recommending the "stuffed sparrow" or the *"chat meunier,"* not quite realizing what was to come. Together with the orphans and the wounded in the streets came a plague of rats. Newspapers reported the "scandal" and suggested they originated from foreign ships, but the wild dogs and cats, released by owners no longer able to feed them, were unquestionably our own. In not much more than a year the same people who had let them go would be hunting them again for the pot. It would be like the days of the Paris Commune.

There was a steady decrease in our food supplies and an increase in illicit alcohol. Everyone lacked sleep. There was horrible tension in the air, a morbid sense of doom, longer bread queues, longer rows of wounded waiting for transport or a hospital bed, larger crowds of beggars, hucksters and prostitutes on the quays and boulevards. So many aristocrats had left for Petrograd's old rival, Moscow. Newspapers increasingly resorted to references to the Patriotic War against Napoleon as if preparing us for guerilla action with invaders on our own soil. Many people felt we were already defeated. The air of melancholia spread even to the Scarlet Tango. The Negro band played "Swing Low, Sweet Chariot" and "Nobody Knows de Trouble I've Seen," while thin young ladies with painted cheeks recounted gloomier jingles concerning death and the cooling of love.

I took to writing longer and more optimistic letters to my mother, to Esmé, to Captain Brown: Life in the capital was full of good cheer; the Czar and his family appeared in public every day; the Germans were bound to retreat soon; this winter would see the end of them. Because of difficulties with transport it was unlikely I would return at Christmas. They should not be surprised, though, if I did especially well at the Polytechnic. I wrote in cafés and restaurants. I wrote at school. I posted the letters sometimes twice a day. I was feeling homesick for the ordinary discomforts of Kiev. Petrograd's filthy, uneven pavements, piles of refuse, menacing beggars, were all the worse for being unfamiliar. I received replies which were as optimistic. My mother said her health had improved. With God's help and a mild winter she was looking forward to returning to the laundry. Esmé said she had applied to train as a nurse. She would soon leave the grocery. Captain Brown's vaguely Anglified, sprawling letters, in which Russian characters took on the appearance of modified English ones, insisted that "Johnny Turk" was on the run. He was

only good at "defensive tactics." "Fritz" was useless without his officers and there were precious few of those left alive. British armor
would soon shift the Hun from his ratholes. This would improve the
morale of the "Frogs," who had no real stomach for War, as they
constantly demonstrated. He supplied maps in which military positions were described. He demonstrated how we would "smash
through" the German positions on a narrow front, with the Rumanians closing on them in a pincer movement. None of these battles
ever came to be fought. Indeed, the trench war was interminably
boring. Larger numbers of men were killed and wounded. It seemed
Summer would never come again. Fimbulwinter and Ragnarok were
actually with us.

Along the Nevski a few high-stepping horses still pulled fine carriages. As snow fell and rivers froze and ice formed on the streets
some troikas appeared. But along the gravel walks between the main
pavements and the roads, there hopped a variety of cripples. They
had missing legs and arms, bandaged faces, peculiar, rolling limps;
they wore uniforms and frequently paused as if expecting a friend
to approach and offer help. They lined up beside newspaper kiosks.
They stood talking in low voices as they leaned against the railings of
parks and private gardens. The *Petersburgskaya Vedomosti*, a special
copy of which was printed on vellum every day for the Czar, always
referred to these wretches as "heroes" and would show pictures of
them waving, smiling, saluting: the very essence of courage and
hope. Charitable institutions could not deal with the numbers. Thousands of deserters sneaked back with the wounded. Some were caught
and shot.

Stories of Rasputin grew increasingly bizarre. One afternoon
Kolya took me to a great Petrograd house overlooking a more pic-
turesque part of the river. Various members of the Mikhishevski
family were gathered for tea. Clearly neither I nor the Count was
particularly welcome. The overfurnished house contained a bewildering mixture of old, heavy sofas and tables and the very latest modern
furniture from France and England. Here I met my first aristocrats
"at home." They seemed a rather ordinary group of people. They were
richly dressed, had perfect manners and the china from which they
drank their tea was very thin, but their conversation was not as brilliant as I had hoped.

When the older relatives had left, two girls and a youth, cousins of
Kolya, who appeared to be their hero, gathered about my friend and

discussed the Court gossip. Rasputin had strengthened his grip on the Czarina. As a result the Czar, who doted on her, was losing interest in the War. Only his honor, and the Rumanian alliance, made him refuse to consider making peace with Germany.

I paid very little attention to what was said, so I cannot report it faithfully. My interest was in the Fabergé *objets*: a frog carved from Siberian jade, several Easter eggs, a little model of a policeman, also carved from stone and tinted with colors impossible to distinguish from the natural hues. The intricacy of the work intrigued me. The rest of the room had the usual naked nymphs supporting lampstands, mirrors, bon-bon trays and flower vases, all of which might have been more suitable to a bordello. It was a sign, I suppose, of how decadent Russian aristocracy had become. Less liberalism, and we should have a Czar on the throne to this day.

I was distracted by the voice of a pretty young girl with all the animation of a true "Natasha," whose light auburn hair hung in heavy curls to her shoulders. She was dressed in a yellow-silk day dress trimmed with sable. "Anna Virobouffa says we must follow Rasputin's example and find redemption through debauchery."

Kolya was amused. "Really, Lolly, I don't feel redeemed yet!"

"Oh, Kolya!" She brandished a cigarette which was lit for her by her brother, who wore the uniform of a lieutenant in an engineering regiment.

"She says it was a wonderful experience. It freed her spirit."

"I've heard the phrase. I knew a political assassin who claimed the act of murder also freed his spirit. Have you been to Rasputin's séances?"

"One, yes. Mother wouldn't let me go to another."

"Were you redeemed?"

"Lolly" simpered. "Of course not. It's a salon, you know, full of wonderful perfumes and fabrics. You sit at an ordinary tea table and have an ordinary afternoon tea. But he talks all the time to you. His eyes!"

"What does he smell like?" asked Kolya. "I heard he never bathes."

"He smells like—" Lolly blushed.

"Like a dirty peasant," said the young man. The girls laughed. "It's true! He smells awful. Of sweat!"

"Dishonest sweat. How valuable it can be." Kolya looked to me for appreciation of this, but I did not understand the witticism. The young engineer, however, laughed.

Lolly continued. "He talks about God and the world, you know. About our souls, our bodies, our need for experience not usually associated with the kind of lives we lead even—even with our husbands . . ." She sighed. "He's so convincing. He's in touch with the common people."

"He cured the Czarevitch." This was the other girl. She wore a red dress.

"The poor boy's still dying," said Kolya.

"While you're with him," Lolly went on, "he transports you from all cares. We were allowed to ask him questions, you know. He was like a wonderful, simple father. And then he just took one of the ladies—I shan't say her name—and they went into the next room. After a while he came back alone. The lady leaves by another door. Or stays on until later. Whatever he tells her."

Kolya frowned. "You aren't disturbed by this behavior?"

"It *is* spiritual, Kolya. He shows you Light in Darkness. The Divine Light."

"You'd give up everything for him?"

"Everything. He's holy, Kolya. He *pretends* to be a charlatan. He sometimes says he is. He has the most wonderful sense of humor. There's something about him. I've studied Madame Blavatsky, of course, and the Theosophists. This is so much more real and intense."

"He hypnotizes them," said the lieutenant. His name was Alexei Leonovitch Petroff and he seemed anxious to impress his older cousin. He ignored me and made me feel uncomfortable. "What do you think, Kolya? Anna Virobouffa says they obey him absolutely. He drugs them, I suppose. The more there are together, the more they vie to display their obedience to him. Haven't there been some suicides?" He touched his mustache and sought inexpertly for a fallen monocle.

Lolly dropped her head. "So Anna Virobouffa says."

"They kill themselves to show devotion?" Alexei laughed. He sought Kolya's approval. His eye caught mine and shifted.

"I don't think that's the reason. It's spiritual," said the girl in red.

"The canals are full of young women who at this moment are discovering the truth of Rasputin's spiritualism. Isn't it a sin? Don't they go to Hell?" Alexei Leonovitch was goading her. I found his sneering tone unpleasant. He was only a year or two older than I, but seemed to regard me at once as an inferior and an interloping superior.

Kolya stopped him. "Grigori Efimovich has abolished Hell in the afterlife, Alexei. Hell has now come to earth. Hadn't you heard?"

"You're an abominable cynic, Kolya." The monocle was screwed, at last, into the appropriate eye.

"I'm a realist. Why should people believe in the conventional God? There's no evidence He any longer exists. Rasputin could well have the right idea."

"You're being terrible, Kolya," said Lolly.

"I'll stop if you wish. I was speaking to a soldier only yesterday. Not a poor muzhik who never knew why he'd been recruited, but a young man. He had been a cadet and had become a lieutenant. Like you, Alexei. He had only one arm, only one eye, only one leg and part of his right ear was missing—"

"Kolya!"

"I'm training to fly," said the lieutenant, "so this doesn't really apply to me."

"I'll stop," Kolya offered again.

"Go on." Lolly used a tone, mixed sympathy and morbidity, typical of Russian women to this day.

"He was glad he was out of it because he might have run away if he'd been returned to the Front."

"Not a gentleman, then," said Alexei Leonovitch.

"Perhaps not any longer." Kolya looked tolerantly at his cousin. "Just a wounded soldier. He said this kind of war is like one's worst dreams. Terrible things happen but you can't move. You can't do anything to help yourself or anyone else."

Again Alexei interrupted. "The air war isn't like that. Chivalry still exists—and action."

Kolya continued patiently, "It's not the same as the old cavalry charges, the old advances, old battles like Borodino, where issues of some sort at least are decided. This war is strange. First you fear it; then you come to be mesmerized by it; then you become so tired by it you can watch a comrade die before your eyes and not believe it's real at all."

"People mauled by lions are said to feel nothing but the most beautiful euphoria," said Lolly.

"But what's this stuff about the Front got to do with Gregori Efimovich Rasputin?" said Alexei. He was distressed and awkward.

"Oh, quite a lot, don't you think?" Kolya gave his teacup to a servant who had come to clear away. He stood up. "Make sure the mangy old lion doesn't maul you," he warned Lolly. "You know I never agree with your mother about anything. But I agree with that. The *starets* is exploiting the grief we can't admit and won't admit until the War reaches its end."

None of us understood my friend. He was in a peculiarly introspective mood as we left the grand house and took the carriage back to his apartment. I left him to himself. I had been disappointed by my afternoon in High Society. Perhaps the best of the family had not been present. However, I had been erotically moved by "Natasha" and what she had been saying and realized how much I had come to miss the company of unspoiled, uncynical girlhood. I decided it was time to visit Marya Varvorovna. I walked to the building overlooking the Kryukoff Canal. On the canal, barges had been replaced by sleds dragged by emaciated mules. The towpaths were patrolled by so many policemen I began to suspect an important criminal was to be arrested. The concierge, an old "gentlewoman" of Polish extraction and like most Poles thoroughly bad-tempered (they never got over the shock of being conquered first by us and then by the Germans), insulted me by making the sign to ward off the evil eye: "No Jews!" she cried. When I pointed out loudly that I was Ukrainian, of Cossack stock, she complained what horrible people the Ukrainians were and what the Cossacks had done to her poor country. All her estates had been confiscated. Chopin himself had been a relative. A familiar enough litany. I listened as patiently as possible before losing my temper. "All I wish to know, Panye, is whether Marya Varvorovna Vorotinsky is at home." I had already noted the girl's card, together with another lady's, on the door of the building.

"Of course she isn't. She's studying. She won't be home until six. Who are you?"

I bowed. "I am Dimitri Mitrofanovitch Kryscheff. I am currently staying with my friend Count Nicholai Feodorovitch Petroff." I gave Kolya's address. "And can be contacted there."

She was mollified. She apologized. Or rather she offered some unlikely rationalization for her bad manners. She said she would give Marya Vorotinsky my message. If I wished to call again I should almost certainly find her at home. I could not be there that evening, since I had arranged to have dinner with Mademoiselle Cornelius and some of her friends. I said I would hope to call the next evening.

I dined at a place called Agnia's, run by a hard-faced widow incapable of smiling at anything. It was the sort of café which had American cloth on the tables and a general atmosphere the bourgeoisie like to think is working class. It was, of course, occupied entirely by bourgeois revolutionaries plotting, without any evidence of irony, the downfall of their own kind. I was unhappy about going to the place, which was in the Petersburgskaya and not that far from my lodgings. There was a chance the place might be raided by the police. I found the food uneatable. The company (Lunarcharsky and his friends) was boring and rude and Mrs. Cornelius was desperate for conversation which, much as I tried, I was unable to supply. My only interest was in Science. I had no casual conversation. Amongst Kolya's friends I would be asked for information, for a scientific opinion, which I could always offer cheerfully, keeping silent when there was nothing to say. Mrs. Cornelius was beautiful, of course, and I enjoyed her ambience, but my anger at the nonsense being spouted by her companions was countered only by natural tact. I left early. I hoped to see her again. She understood my situation, I think, and felt a little guilty. As I left she kissed me on the cheek, wafting roses, and said softly, "Ta ta, Ivan. Don't do anything I wouldn't do."

In some trepidation I walked back through the wretched streets of our besieged capital. I paused on the Sampsoneffskaya Bridge to watch men breaking holes in the ice, which was still too thin here to use as a thoroughfare. They were like tramps. The only thing which identified them as anything else was their uniforms. Why they were smashing at the ice, with pieces of wood and old railings, I still do not know. Perhaps they were hoping to fish.

At school the next day I was singled out for attack by Professor Merkuloff. He had a horrible cold and his nose was bright red. His eyes glared from beneath a ridiculous woollen hat which reached to the top of his glasses. The lecture was on something simple, the construction of a dynamo. He sarcastically asked me if I knew what a dynamo was. I replied quietly that I did know.

He asked me to define an ordinary dynamo and the principles by which it worked. I gave him the usual definition. He seemed disappointed. He asked if I knew anything else. I described the various sorts of dynamo then in general use, who the manufacturers were. I then talked about current experiments with new types, the kind of power it could be possible to generate, what machines could be run off such and such a source, and so on. He became flamboyantly angry. He screamed at me, "That will do, Kryscheff!"

"There is more, your honor."

"I asked a simple question. I need simple answers."

"You asked me to elaborate."

"Sit down, Kryscheff!"

"Perhaps you would like me to prepare some kind of paper on the development of the dynamo?" I said.

"I would like you to sit down. You are either insolent or you are a bore, Kryscheff. You might simply be a literal-minded idiot. You are certainly a fool!"

This was exactly what my envious schoolmates wanted to hear. His sarcasm drew an easy laugh from them. I had it in mind to face Merkuloff down; to demonstrate his lack of intelligence and imagination. He was a time-server. He only had his job because of the War. But it would mean my dismissal from the Institute and I could not afford it. I would be spitting in Uncle Semya's eye. I would kill my mother. So I sat down.

This was when I finally resolved to display the profundity and complexity of my knowledge. I would eventually show the whole school that I knew more than teachers and pupils together. I would wait for the best chance. When I did this I wished to show Merkuloff up for the opinionated cretin he was. Our examinations, as I have explained, were chiefly oral. There would be a main end-of-term exam before the whole teaching board of the Institute. That was when I would take my revenge.

I was oblivious of the snifflings and jeerings of the other students as I boarded the horsetram for the slow, freezing journey home. I read an article on Freycinet's work on reinforced concrete (he had built the famous airship hangars at Orly). I also found a reference to Einstein which I could not at that time completely comprehend. Now I know we were both working toward a very similar end. He was formulating his General Theory of Relativity while I was planning to astonish my professors with my own ontological ideas. Such coincidences are common in science.

Later that evening, wearing my suit, I returned to the house overlooking the Kryukoff Canal. I was greeted this time by a simpering concierge who said Mlle. Vorotinsky was looking forward to entertaining me. If I went through the courtyard and took the staircase up to the first floor I would be welcomed by the young lady herself. She regretted, in a voice like poisoned honey, her duties made her stay at the front of the building or she would have been honored to show me the way. I crossed a courtyard heaped on all sides with filthy snow. A skinny, tethered Dalmation barked at me. This was an older type of building and rather pleasant. I immediately felt safe here. I wished my own lodgings had the same air of security.

I found the appropriate landing and the door on which Marya Vorotinsky and her friend Elena Andreyovna Vlasenkova had placed their neatly hand-lettered nameplates. I turned the key which rang a bell on the other side of the door. I waited. Then a small girl, very pretty, with huge blue eyes and brown wavy hair, wearing a simple brown velvet dress we used to call "convent best," offered me one of the widest, most open smiles I had ever received and bowed me into the apartment. "You must be M'sieu Kryscheff? I am Lena Vlasenkova and very pleased to meet you."

I kissed her hand. "I am enchanted, mademoiselle." I spoke in French.

She said in delight, "You are not Russian!"

"I am Russian through and through."

"Your French is perfect."

"I have a talent for languages." I removed my hat and coat and gave them to her. We entered a light, airy room heated by a beautiful Dutch stove, each tile individually painted and fired, showing scenes of Netherlands country life. There were peasant fabrics everywhere. The pictures on the wall were fine, conventional prints of Russian rural subjects. The place was a wonderful haven. I immediately conceived a desire to stay there forever. Then from the next room emerged, in a dark-green dress trimmed with French lace, my oval-eyed acquaintance from the Kiev–Petrograd Express. "My dear friend! Why take so long to call on us?"

She stepped forward and shook me warmly by the hand. She did this, I suspected, to impress Lena Andreyovna, whose face still wore the same broad, merry grin.

"I have had reasons for not making myself too conspicuous. It has been impossible . . ."

"Of course. We understand absolutely."

Both she and Lena Andreyovna seemed to know more about my "secret life" than I did. I wondered if I had said anything on the train which I had now forgotten. I became fairly cautious.

"The day is not far off now," Lena Andreyovna murmured as she seated herself on the couch, smoothing her skirt under her.

"No, indeed," I said.

"You will have some tea, M'sieu Kryscheff?" asked Marya Vorotinsky. "I am sorry we have nothing else to drink."

"Tea would be most welcome."

"It's ready," said Lena Andreyovna. "I'll fetch the glasses." She sprang up and returned rapidly with a tray on which were three glasses in wicker holders. The big, copper samovar steamed on the stove.

"You look tired, tovarich," said Marya. "You've been working hard?" She used a term which was in general use at the time, but was particularly popular with revolutionaries of the Social Democrat and Social Revolutionary parties. However, it had no particular significance. As I sat upon the couch and sipped the excellent tea, I nodded. "I have had a great deal to do."

"You know you can count on us for any help," said Marya intensely. "We're entirely at your service."

I was impressed by the generosity of her statement, the passion with which she made it. "I'm much obliged to you." I wondered if they shared a bedroom. It was likely. I found them both attractive not so much for their physical looks as for the quality of youthful enthusiasm and innocence I had been missing. They were already offering to help me when they had absolutely no idea what my work could be.

"You must not be afraid to tell us to be quiet," Lena was earnest, "if we say the wrong thing. We respect what you are doing."

"I am obliged to you for your discretion."

"Have you been traveling abroad?" asked Marya. She sat on the rug at my feet, her tea glass beside her. "Or have you been in Russia all this time?"

"Russia," I said, "chiefly."

"You can stay here if you need to," Lena said. "We have discussed it. We think we should let you know that. It could be of use."

"Again, I am much obliged." It did not really matter to me what they thought my work was. They were offering me everything I had hoped to find. I could not believe my good fortune. I guessed that they thought me some sort of special courier for the military, some engineer working on a mysterious secret weapon, or that I was an envoy for the Czar himself. It did not matter. If I wished I could come here, spend whole days here. Possibly, in time, I should be able to spend nights here. I wondered to which girl I should show most attention. One should always be seen to be courting the girl one does not actually want. Both had their merits. I decided it would only be polite to pay most attention to my original acquaintance. It would be far safer for me then if Lena succumbed. She knew even less about me than her friend. I luxuriated in their attention for two or three hours. Then, remembering I had agreed to meet Kolya at the Harlequinade's Retreat, I made reluctant excuses. I left their innocence, their security, their admiration, behind me. I walked on air as I headed for the cabaret. That night, I decided, I would take the best girl in the house and enjoy myself so thoroughly she would not be able to move a muscle by the morning. I felt like the Czar as I descended the steps to be greeted by the usual friends.

I had some bad absinthe but a very satisfactory whore. With a new supply of cocaine in my velvet pocket, I returned to my lodgings, entering with the key Mme. Zinovieff, after much persuasion, had given me. I found four letters of different dates waiting for me in the little black tin box decorated with painted roses, which my landlady had hung on the wall for guests' correspondence. I was replete and had not felt so physically well for days. In my room I tested my lamp to see if any oil remained. I decided to wait until morning to read the letters. I slept better than usual and I awakened early. I opened the letters, laid them before me on the quilt. The first two were from Esmé, the third was from my mother. The fourth, surprisingly, was from Uncle Semya. Esmé was at a nearby hospital treating our wounded, as well as German prisoners on Darnitsa across the Dnieper from Kiev. She said they all seemed alike, pathetic and shocked. It was hard to feel the Germans were anything but wretched slaves, forced to fight by rapacious masters. Our own Russian soldiers, she said, were "splendidly courageous and always cheerful, true Russians through and through." The letter from my mother said her health had improved. I was not to worry; she had a slight chill, but doubtless that was the winter. The river was frozen, she said. She hoped that food supplies were easier to obtain in Petrograd. Since Brusilov's advances against the Germans she had expected improvements. I was to eat, she begged, anything I could. I was to eat "for her." The letter from Uncle Semya was cryptic. Everyone in Odessa was fine. The War made things difficult but the "Rumanian decision" (to change sides) had improved morale all round. There had been minor pogroms by private groups, but nothing like those of ten years before. Happily the wrath of the people was turned against anyone of German origin. It was surprising, he added with his characteristically dry humor, how many more Russians now occupied Odessa than before the War. Dr. Cornelius had managed to leave the country. Things seemed to be improving, he said, but there must still be contingency plans. He might need me to journey abroad on his behalf. He would arrange all necessary papers. He knew he could call on me when the need arose.

I wrote back immediately. I owed everything to him. I was doing "brilliantly" at school. When the time came for the end-of-term examinations I should impress everyone, as Pushkin was said to have impressed his teachers at the Tsarskoye Selo Lycée. He could expect an appropriate oil painting of me in due course! Naturally I was always at his disposal and would await news of the service I could perform. Mr. Green had told me to expect something of the sort. I was looking forward to my first trip abroad. Could he, through Mr. Green, let me have some hint of where I would go?

I wrote a brief letter to Esmé. Things went very well in Petrograd. We made sacrifices with the rest of the country, but very soon we should sweep the barbarian back to his lair for good. In the meantime she could help the prisoners by teaching them Russian. It might be the language they would be required to speak after the War! I wrote to my mother. I am ashamed to say I asked no specific questions about her chill. Instead I said I was glad she was "basically well." I was sure she would soon be over her sniffles; besides she had a nurse about the place now. My mother, I should say here, was a woman of fundamentally excellent health. She complained of poor health, like so many of us, when she needed a little extra sympathy. I preferred to give her my love, respect and understanding. This was more dignified, I felt. She understood. She said that as an intellectual, I could not always display the "direct emotions" of ordinary people. In this she showed her usual perspicacity.

If I were to travel abroad, I would have to study harder. I reduced my visits to the Tango and the Retreat. I stopped going to the theater and the kino with Kolya. I cut down on my visits to the whores. Instead I went more frequently to the flat I called privately "the virgin's nest." Here I was allowed to read, to write, to remain night and day, if I wished, being fed with relatively wholesome food and with all the tea and coffee I could drink. Marya's father had been a well-to-do beverage merchant, originally situated in Yalta before moving to Moldavia. Lena's father, she said with some disdain, was a "factory owner" in Minsk. My interest in Lena increased to the degree that I came close to proposing marriage to Marya. However, neither of these virgins was approached by me. Though they would often purr around me like cats wanting cream, I displayed very little

amorous interest in them. I was keeping them for security and tranquillity. Their sexual favors could wait until I was ready for them.
When I slept there, I slept on the couch. I rarely let them see either
what I read or what I wrote. Not only did they humor me, they
became confused if they should accidentally move a book or even
glance at a page.

It was only bit by bit I began to realize they considered me a
foolish young Bakunin, plotting the downfall of the Czar (the event
which they sometimes toasted in tea, in low voices), and in one sense
I was delighted by their misconception. It gave me even less respect
for them. I felt no guilt about making use of them. Knowing as much
as I did I was able to drop the odd revolutionary's name. This meant
far more to them than it did to me: here, some of those who had
bored me so badly in the cafés were heroes. They were merely two
typical middle-class Russian girls prepared like so many of them to
throw away their careers, their freedom, perhaps their lives, for
someone who was not only a worthless troublemaker but coldly
schemed their ruin. Better they should devote themselves to me, who
had a genuine cause. The flat came to be full of *Iskras* and *Golos
Trudas* and inflammatory pamphlets. They kept them about, I believe, to impress me. In the end I had to explain that it was bad to
"call attention to certain facts" and that it would be best if they kept
their anarchist literature elsewhere. They were full of apologies. The
ill-printed, ill-written manifestos and declarations soon disappeared.

My work continued. I visited Kolya, but more frequently at his
home (where Hippolyte still resided) than at our old haunts. He was
becoming distressed with the progress of the War. He claimed we
were as good as done for. I think the Petrograd winter had brought an
earlier than usual melancholy. He said the Czar was doomed. Feeling
against Rasputin was high. The Czar's running of the War (he had
taken personal command of the army) was as inept as his running of
the country. Many officers, including some of the "old guard," felt
Nicholas should be replaced. "The Revolution," Kolya said, "will not
come from an uprising in the streets this time. It will come from
within."

Kolya smiled at me. As usual he wore black. His face seemed paler
than ever, his hair all but invisible against the white light from the
window. "What we really need," he said, "is a new Napoleon. French
or Russian. We have no generals of genius. They can't understand
the terms. They have no precedents and that, Dimka my dear friend,
is what destroys them. They are so used to relying on precedent."

"You mean tradition?"

"I mean precedent. Precedent is a simple-minded way of imposing apparent order on the world. Yet it robs whoever employs it of his need to reach a personal moral decision. A decision which suits the situation."

"You've been reading too much Kropotkin, Kolya."

"Even Kropotkin calls on 'history' as a model. History will destroy every one of us, Dimka. Soon there will be no more history at all! Analysis. That might have saved us. The basis of all modern science, eh? Analysis, Dimka, not projections. You're prone to project, as you know, when you get excited—"

"What! I'm a pure scientist." I realized he was probably joking.

"Marx, Kropotkin, Engels, Proudhon, Tolstoi—all use precedent and so they are completely unscientific. Kropotkin might be the most scientific. He has the proper training. But the radical young already treat him as some sort of Old Testament prophet, quoting his words rather than applying his methods. Is that all we are to have? Substitutes for past orthodoxies? Is the language of science to replace the language of religion and become a meaningless litany in support of authority?"

"There are already such narrow-minded scientists," I agreed. "But there are others, as there will always be, who oppose them, who are constantly, as am I, generating new theories, new analyses."

"And they are accepted?"

"Eventually. I'm staking my life on it."

"Eventually? When their words have been incorporated into the litany."

"Science is less subject to decadence. It thrives upon change. But is it a better world in which nothing is considered worthwhile if it's more than a day or two old?"

"It could not be more boring."

In those months before the Czar's abdication, the streets became even worse. The broad pavements were dirtier and more depressing. Peter was a city of death and desolation. The War reports suggested tremendous advances until in early December, just before I was due to undergo my examinations, came the news of the taking of Bucharest. Rumania had capitulated. We had lost an ally overnight. Even more wounded filled the city. France and England were rumored to be preparing to ally themselves with Germany against Russia. Even I, obsessed with my dissertation, could not ignore the fact that we were in great danger.

Then it came to me that all my examiners would be sharing this mood. In the course of speaking, I could tell them of certain personal inventions which might help win the War. I would not go into details which would frighten those poor, unimaginative souls. I would merely mention my ideas in passing. Psychologically, it would be a perfect moment to display my knowledge and ensure myself of the highest marks.

It was not a plan conceived with cynicism (though, of course, I had the motive of wishing to startle both Professor Merkuloff, the rest of the academicians and the other students) but I knew it might stand me in good stead with my attempts to achieve a government appointment.

I tested some of my speeches out on the two girls. They were impressed, though most of what I said went well over their heads. I tested other ideas on Kolya who said that I was "brilliant" and laughed with joy to hear me expound my scientific theories. I wrote letters home explaining I should soon be sending good news. I wrote to Uncle Semya. He would have a nephew of whom to be more than proud. To my landlady and her daughters I became, as they put it, "unbearable" because my confidence was so great. I think they had preferred the shyer Dimitri Mitrofanovitch of his first year in St. Petersburg. As the day of the main examinations came closer I grew more excited. I saw pictures of myself addressing the professors and examining board. I saw my fellow students listening with stunned wonderment or leaning forward with sudden, ecstatic understanding of what I was really saying.

In the first days, one merely saw various professors and answered simple questions. I went through the examinations patiently, letting drop hints that my knowledge extended rather further than the questions demanded. In the middle days, I began to lard in more information, making casual reference to certain modern inventions, to specific kinds of materials and manufacturers, to current research findings and advanced theories. On the last day, when it was my turn to give my main dissertation before the class, in the great hall, I decided to pull out all stops. I had learned, like many others in those times, to inject myself intravenously with cocaine. I gave myself a strong solution shortly before I boarded the tram. By the time I arrived at the Polytechnic neither the cold nor the anxious looks of my fellows could touch me in the slightest. I was ready for everything. I remember flinging open my coat as I crossed the misty quadrangle to the main hall, showing the same contempt for the weather as I felt for them.

I waited impatiently (even some of the examiners noticed this) while four others gave their pathetic, faltering speeches on this or that tiny aspect of technology. Then at last my name was called and I strode up to the dais on which, around a curved table, sat the entire staff and governors of the Polytechnic. Over their heads was a large portrait of a benevolent Czar Nicholas; before me were the assembled students. I noticed some of them giggling or making comments about me. I was able, with stern glances, to quell these easily.

Professor Merkuloff's sarcastic tones came from the table. "Well, Kryscheff, and what are you going to speak about—assuming you have absorbed any of your studies?"

I turned and laughed in his face. It was not an insolent laugh. It was the laughter of one who shared a joke with an equal (or an inferior, in actuality). "I am going to speak on the ontological approach to the problems of science and technology," I told the examiners, "with a particular emphasis on technological aids to the winning of the present struggle."

"A rather large subject," said Vorsin, one of the senior professors. He was a small old man with a yellow, wrinkled skin. "For someone in your year."

"It is a subject, your excellency, I feel quite at ease with. I have been doing certain studies in my spare time. The reason I was sent to your Institute was in one sense simply to complete a formality. I required academic information not generally available. I also wished to learn something of academic disciplines. I believe that this is what impressed Professor Matzneff and aroused the animosity of certain other professors. I am deeply grateful to your excellency and to your staff for the help you have given me, however."

Vorsin seemed impressed. He smiled at his colleagues.

"Now, your excellency, if I could begin . . . ?" I bowed with considerable dignity.

"Begin," said the old man, and he moved his hand in a gesture which displayed magnanimity and kindness. He leaned over to murmur something to Merkuloff. I knew that he was asking about me and that he would receive a biased opinion of me from Merkuloff. But I was amused by my professor's stupidity and presumption.

I began my discourse almost at once. I disdained notes. I addressed the assembled students. I turned occasionally to speak to the professors, who almost at once began to show astonishment. It was as if Jesus had sat down with the Elders in the Synagogue. Indeed, I felt somewhat godlike. This was partly due to the effects, I suppose, of the cocaine. If I was not a Messiah to the Age of Science, I felt at least I might be His Baptist!

There was no denying the immediate effect of my words. I discussed the problems of Newtonian science in relation to modern knowledge. I discussed the most recent developments in the field of extra-strong materials, which would enable us to build entirely new types of machines: gigantic aeroplanes and airships. I drew their attention to the possibilities of rocket propulsion, as opposed to the limitations of the conventional internal-combustion engine. I spoke of gas-operated aeroplanes. This would involve a system of superheating by which certain gases could be brought to an appropriately intense temperature. I spoke of a kind of Gatling gun which could be operated by means of compressed air, which would shoot thousands of needles into the enemy's ranks. Each needle could contain a hollow tip in which was concealed deadly poison. No matter where he was hit, the soldier would die almost at once. Failing that, a narcotic drug could be used and we should have wars without death. This would be far more efficient than gas canisters which anyway could be counteracted by means of gasmasks. I also described monster machines, a thousand times bigger than the largest tank. These could simply crush their way through the enemy lines, physically burying all who stood against them. I brought into question our whole understanding of current technological developments. I was about to go into more abstract matters, concerning electrical atoms, when Merkuloff—that jealous mental dwarf!—sprang up and cried:

"I think we have heard all we need, Kryscheff!"

"I have hardly begun," I said calmly. "There is much more."

"Sit down."

I explained that they had not realized these were merely my opening remarks.

"We realize all we want to realize." Evidently overwhelmed by his own conscience, knowing to what extent he had misjudged me, he was speaking gently. Perhaps he wished to spare my energies? At the time, however, I felt he was trying to thwart me.

"If you are to award the appropriate marks," I said, "it is only fair I should give you a fuller picture. These are times when information itself is a weapon."

The old man, Professor Vorsin, cut me off. "Possibly your ideas are of interest to an enemy? Any spy . . ." He gestured out into the hall.

I followed his meaning, but I had anticipated him. "That is the reason, your excellency, that I have made no specifications in this dissertation. If the government wished to see my plans, I should be happy to meet with the appropriate person at the proper time. I have only skimmed the surface here."

"We are much impressed," said Vorsin.

Merkuloff spoke. "You are dismissed from the hall, Kryscheff." Could the man still be envious? Was he determined to crush me? It was unbelievable. But I misjudged him, I think. I was not sympathetic to his own confusion. His senior forced him to resume his seat. Vorsin was plainly upset by Merkuloff's attitude. He addressed me respectfully. "My dear Dimitri Mitrofanovitch, I am sure you have been doing a great deal of demanding work. But you have brought up so many fresh ideas that it is hard for us to digest everything at once."

I nodded as I tried to hear what he said above the uproar from the hall. The students were acknowledging my genius. It was a great moment. I could see that the other professors, too, were stunned by my dissertation. I decided to ensure myself, there and then, of my future. "Can I therefore be certain of a diploma this year?"

"Absolutely," said Vorsin. "We will make a Special Diploma for you."

This was beyond anything I had hoped for. "A Special Diploma is not necessary, your excellency." I showed, I think, proper modesty and self-discipline.

"It will have to be a special one," said Merkuloff, capitulating at last. Never have I experienced such wonderful elation. I had not really expected quite this success. It was very sweet.

"Very well, your excellencies. I accept." I bowed to them. I bowed to the shouting, stamping crowd below. I raised a hand to silence them. "But I shall continue here at the Polytechnic, at least until I am offered a government post." I saw no point in crowing. They had had the grace to accept defeat. I would show grace in my victory.

"Of course," said Merkuloff in a strained voice. "Next term, we shall sort all that out."

"And the Diploma? Is it to be presented before Christmas?"

I could guess there would be the usual red tape involved. I was not surprised when Professor Vorsin shook his head. "It will take time to prepare. We shall have it ready when you return."

I was satisfied. And Merkuloff, judging by the way he sat with his head in his hands, was at long last thoroughly bested. Dr. Matzneff was vindicated. How pleased my mentor would be when he, in his exile, learned the news.

Triumph was to be added to triumph. Vorsin personally led me from the stage. Students pressed around me, clapping, whistling, cheering, even laughing with delight. The senior professor raised his palm to silence them. But the noise continued. Behind me, like a conquered tyrant, crept Merkuloff. With his own hands Professor Vorsin put my cap upon my head. He ordered Merkuloff to "fetch the troika." I asked if there was anything I could amplify for him. "All that can come later," said the generous old man, "when we both have more time and when you are rested." I assured him I had no need of rest. I had not felt so well for many a month. I suppose that it was impossible for him to believe that such mental expenditure was not automatically accompanied by physical exhaustion. Needless to say, I was sustained by the injection of cocaine and would eventually need to sleep, but not at that moment.

I was taken out into the quadrangle. Vorsin's personal horse and troika stood ready. Students were still cheering. I heard snatches of their phrases: "It's the great Kryscheff!"; "He's Galileo and Leonardo rolled into one." I bowed. I waved. Again they cheered me. Again the kindly Vorsin tried to silence them. I was flattered by his thoughtfulness. He apologized for not being able to accompany me himself. My own professor would see me safely home. It was obvious that Merkuloff was reluctant. He frowned. He began to remonstrate. He was not "qualified" to go with me. This was a change of tune! It was my turn to show magnanimity. It would be a pleasure, I said, to have his company in the troika. In awe, he climbed in to sit beside me. With a friendly acknowledgment to the senior professor, to the noisy students, I gestured for the driver to whip up the horse. Then we were off at the old St. Petersburg lick, bells jingling, moving almost as swiftly as my thoughts, while I enlarged on my ideas to the open-mouthed Merkuloff. He could still not find the words to tell me how he had misjudged me.

"The Special Diploma will, of course, be very welcome," I assured him. "But my future interest will chiefly be in government work."

He said he was sure the government would supply my every need.

I was pleased with his perspicacity. "It is materials and supplies I require. Then I can begin to build."

He said I should try to look after myself. I was overexcited.

"That's hardly possible at the moment," I reassured him. "My dilemma is whether I should remain at the Polytechnic, perhaps to help with the teaching, or whether I should lend all my talents to the War Effort?"

This was something, he said, which had to be carefully considered. Perhaps it could be discussed next term "after I had rested." I pointed out, again, that I was at my peak. It would, however, be convenient to have more time to myself. He agreed. He suggested I take a sabbatical while the necessary meetings were held at high level. There would not be time this term to go into every detail. The staff would have to meet government representatives the following term. He suggested I wait until I heard from the Polytechnic. This fitted in with my plans. I agreed. "It will also allow time to prepare my Special Diploma."

He had been thinking of much the same thing. We galloped through glowing mist. A white night was looming. As we neared Petersburg proper, he asked me where I lived. I decided not to give him my poorer address. I told the driver to go to the house by the Kryukoff Canal where my virgins lived.

At the entrance, I was greeted with more fawning by the old Polish woman. Now she addressed me as "your honor." Evidently she astonished Merkuloff. He still had his cold, and was blowing his nose heavily. He explained that I was overtired. She should make sure I rested. He said someone, perhaps himself, would come to make sure I was all right. I told him this would be unnecessary. The Polish woman was puzzled but said I might be her own son. Professor Merkuloff's attitude toward me had at last completely changed. He said that she was a good, kind woman. I had delicate sensibilities. I must have every comfort. I must rest my brain as well as my body. If a doctor were needed, the Institute would send one. I patted him on the shoulder, to show that I appreciated his magnanimous acceptance of defeat. "The girls are like sisters," said the Polish hag. "They will know what to do."

She escorted me to the apartment door. Lena answered the ring. Her face brightened when she saw me. The "panye" explained I had been brought in a troika. My professor asked that I be specially cared for. Lena led me into her feminine nest, assuring the concierge everything would be done. I was still, of course, on top of the world. We entered the main room. "Are you on the run?" she was excited. I flung an arm around her shoulders and embraced her. "It has been the best day of my life." I realized she was mine. I could now celebrate. I kissed her gently upon the lips. She whispered that Marya was not yet home. She drew away from me, but I held her little wrist. I told her that I loved her. It was true. I loved everyone at that moment. I had astounded the school with my brilliance. I had come home in the senior professor's own troika. The entire Polytechnic had been in an uproar. She asked if I had done anything "politically dangerous." I laughed. "It depends what you mean, Lenushka. I showed them the Future. I showed them the Age of Science. I showed them all the possibilities for change in this old world of ours."

"And you convinced them?"

"They applauded me."

"Everyone?"

"Everyone."

She could not quite understand. I embraced her again. I kissed her with more passion. I needed this culmination. This reward. Little Lena was ideal. A virgin. Her breasts began to rise and fall, her hands touched my back in an embrace. Then she had pulled away, blushing. She would make me some tea. I flung myself on the couch. It was covered with a peasant quilt of most intricate patterns. It was faintly, deliciously perfumed. I watched her body in its rustling frock as she moved about the apartment. At length she brought me a glass of tea. I accepted it, gesturing for her to sit beside me. Again that sweet, uncertain movement. Then she was with me, cradled in my arms. We sipped the tea together. I began to make love to her very slowly. I stroked her arms, her face, her thighs. A little later, I picked her up and carried her, weeping, into the bedroom. She made to resist, but no woman could have resisted me that day. My hands moved under her clothes and found flesh, then her sex, and she gasped. But, for all her feeble, birdlike flutterings, she was mine. I undressed her. Then I undressed myself. Her face was at peace, her eyes were like the eyes of a gazelle which had fallen in love with a leopard. She would willingly die for one touch of my paw, one movement of my mouth on her flesh. My body sang with the controlled agony of delicious passions and heightened senses. Then I was upon her. I took her fiercely. She wept and groaned and shrieked. I clawed her so that blood came. I bit her. I plunged into her and more blood came. And still I was not sated. I rolled away from her. Her eyes had turned to burning copper and her hair was a halo of flame, her body a lattice of scratches, of little bites and voluptuous, spreading bruises. Now she wept deeply, for the pleasure, for the release of her weeping, and I took her again.

As I rolled back, Marya entered the room. "Lena! Dimitri?" She was horrified. She shivered in her little fur cap, with her muff still on her hand. She was gasping. I smiled. I gestured to her to join us. I could easily have satisfied them both. She closed the door and had gone before I could suggest it. I laughed. Lena lay there staring vacantly at the closed door. I took her for the third time. My sperm filled her anus like liquid steel. She was once more overcome by her passion. Marya was unimportant. Let her disapprove. Lena agreed. She had become wild; a wonderful animal. We kissed and nibbled and stroked one another's warmth and youth. We were about to make love for the fourth time, when Marya again opened the door. There was gaslight now behind her. It had become quite dark. She had removed her street clothes. She was in distress. "I thought you loved me," she said.

"I love you both. Come." I offered myself.

"This is wrong. Can't you see?"

"There is nothing wrong in being alive."

"We'll be out soon," Lena told her. "We'll explain."

"Your body! What has he done to you?"

Lena had not been aware of the love marks. Now she looked at her breasts and her thighs and first she smiled, touching them, then she lost some of her elation. Foolish Marya had entered Eden. She had done what Lucifer did to Adam and Eve. She had made us suddenly self-conscious. The little idiot was the snake bringing sin to the Garden. I was furious. I leapt up. I jumped for her. I caught her by the hair. "Free yourself from all these preconceptions!"

"This isn't freedom—it's—" She burst into tears. She tried to struggle away from me. But I held her. "Join us, you bitch! Be a woman!"

Then it was like a wheel. A gigantic flywheel on which we were all spinning. And Lena was shouting. Dancing naked between us. I was tearing at Marya. At her clothes, her hair, her body. Round and round we whirled, unable to control anything. We were crushed in a machine which was white hot and yielding but which had the pressure of the hardest alloy. The cogs were ripping us to fragments.

Blood sparkled. Slowly the squealing and wailing grew louder. It was unbearable. I looked at the girls. One was completely naked, the other had her clothes in shreds. One breast was exposed. Both were weeping and bleeding. They were begging me for something they refused to accept. They begged me for forgiveness, for death. They begged me for my love and for the ignorance they had lost. They begged me for the Faith I had given. Which now they thought they had lost. They begged for God, for the gentle, punishing Christ who had come to them in that hour of revelation. I was suddenly weary. I felt only contempt for them. They resisted everything they most desired. They resisted enlightenment. They refused to trust me. In that refusal they showed themselves for stupid little masturbating creatures. They had been prepared to entertain fuzzy romantic notions about free love and revolution, even assassination. Now they could not relinquish their poor, unformed identities. They would take no risks. I drew on my clothes. I laughed at them. They wept and bled in each other's arms. They pleaded with me to become again the illusion I had let them create. I buttoned up my jacket. I owed them nothing. They owed me everything. My clothes became my armor. Their knight had offered them the salvation of their senses: the celebration of their own femininity, and of their primal sexuality. They had rejected the gift. I strode out of their apartment. They became Bolshevik whores, I believe, during the Revolution, and morphine addicts. Stalin doubtless cleared up what was left of them. It was only the stupid or the mesmerized who ever perished in those camps. Nobody was ever forced to die.

I paced through the night, beside the frozen canal. I pushed the crippled and the starving from my path. I hoped to see Kolya at the Harlequinade, but they told me he had gone home. I went to his apartment and let myself in with my key. Hippolyte was in bed with him, lying amongst furs. Kolya himself was asleep. Hippolyte was petulant. "Get out."

I crossed to the cabinet to pour a drink and look for more cocaine. I found some Polish tawny vodka and tossed it off. I opened the Pierrot jar and took a pinch of white powder. I tasted it, sniffed a little into my nostrils to experience the delicious numbness. Hippolyte had risen. He was whispering at me. "What are you doing?"

"I came to see Kolya."

"What's wrong with you?"

"Nothing."

"You're mad."

"Inspired, perhaps. I'm not here to interfere." I reached out a hand to stroke him. "I love you, too." I loved the world.

Then Hippolyte grinned his little, mindless, harlot's grin. "Oh, I see."

Kolya's naked body was gold crowned by silver as he came into the room. "Good evening, Dimka. It's late, eh?" He took the vodka bottle from my hand and poured some into a glass. "How was your dissertation?"

I had become calm. I had no wish to boast of my achievement. "I think it was successful."

"Good. I expected you would have come over to the cabaret."

"I had some women to see."

"Celebrating?" said Hippolyte. He was confused.

"Trying to."

"The women didn't suit you?"

"They were too young. I offered them the mercy of my body, the salvation of my pain, my triumph. And they refused it."

"Oh, I know what you mean!" Kolya laughed with Hippolyte. "They're timid little things, on the whole, girls." He leaned against me, as if drunk, and began to unbutton my coat. "Did they hurt your feelings, Dimka?"

"Not at all. They made me impatient."

"They haven't the stamina."

Hippolyte loosened my scarf and the jacket of my uniform. I was feeling languorous. I yawned, appreciating the attention, enjoying the passivity. Kolya and Hippolyte led me back toward the bedroom, strewn with the skins of wolves and panthers, foxes and tigers. I was fully prepared to let them worship me. This was what I had wanted all along from the girls. Marya and Lena had not understood. Kolya and Hippolyte instinctively knew what to do. There was more vodka. There was more cocaine. I was magnificent. They told me so with every touch. I was a pagan God. I cannot explain. It was not perversity. I was Pan. I was Prometheus. I was Prometheus in a world which did not fear me. How those stupid little girls had feared me. Silly mice. I was a bronze Titan, a Lord of Thebes, an Etruscan nobleman, an Egyptian god-king. An Emperor of Carthage!

It is vague, the rest. I slept for a very long time. Kolya brought my clothes from my lodgings. He was very gentle with me. I do not think Hippolyte was present. I was tired. Kolya's goodness was Christlike.

It was too much. For a while I attempted to emulate it. But his goodness was a virtue of the nobly born, of the privileged. It was nothing I could afford, in the end.

There was a letter. I did not open it until I had slept again amongst the wolves and the foxes, with Kolya as my guardian angel. He did nothing that was unnatural. He helped me. I opened the letter on a morning. Much refreshed, I relived my moments of conquest. I felt a certain foolishness in exposing myself to the girls. I would not be able to return for a while, until they had calmed down. I knew they would not betray me because it would mean betraying their idealism. The packet was sealed with red wax. I broke the seals, and here was further proof of my victory over my past. A vindication of all I had been through. A passport. And a letter from Mr. Green. I was to leave for England after Christmas. I was to go to Liverpool to conduct some business. I must call and see Mr. Green as soon as possible. He would give me the details of my journey. I had a passport. I had a Special Diploma. I had recognition. And all in a rush. That is frequently how things happen, of course. Frequently, too, all the bad news comes at once. But I will not taint this reminiscence with any note of sourness. I am not one to brood on what might have been. My fate is in God's hands. Heaven is my reward. I have sinned. I admit it. But I gave my knowledge and my innocence to the world, and if the world did not reward me as I hoped, it was because it was temporarily conquered by my enemies. Few would disagree that they were God's enemies, also. The world is in the power of the Antichrist.

Kolya said that until I left for England, I should stay at his apartment. This suited me very well. After that first night I received no further attentions from Kolya and few from Hippolyte.

Rasputin was murdered. Shot, stabbed, poisoned and pushed under the ice, yet still he lived and roared. He was Russia. Tainted Russia, mystical and vibrant, and refusing to die. But for rejecting the cleansing of science and modern knowledge Russia paid a terrible price. She did not have to give up her soul. There must be equilibrium. Neither "salvation through sin" nor the massive "Russian steamroller" could rescue us. By then it was hopeless. We could not be redeemed by our divine irresponsibility under autocracy, by our magnificent Slavic wholeness of sentiment, by the careless bravery of our Cossacks, nor by our trust in a defeated Christ. Christ slept and Russia was stolen from Him.

There was no point in returning to Kiev for Christmas. The trains were in confusion. There was a threat of the enemy occupying White Russia and parts of Ukraine. My letters and telegrams reached my mother in time. To my mother: DISSERTATION GREAT SUCCESS. HAVE RECEIVED SPECIAL DIPLOMA. WHOLE SCHOOL CELEBRATES. YOUR LOVING SON. Through the good offices of Captain Brown came the reply: CONGRATULATIONS. LOVE FROM ALL. WE ARE VERY PROUD. BEST WISHES FOR THE SEASON. To Uncle Semya I sent a similar message, but I added a few extra words. GOVT. POST LIKELY. THANKS FOR ALL CONFIDENCE. WILL SERVE YOU ANY WAY I CAN. GOD BLESS THE CZAR AND GOD SAVE RUSSIA.

This meant that all members of my family were able to celebrate the season with great delight. I spent it quietly with Kolya. Happily we were able to find some decent food in our City of Disaster. The ghost of Rasputin, the threat of civilian strife, of Revolution, hung like mist over the streets and canals. The food was horribly expensive. Hippolyte did not join us. He had taken to leaving the apartment for days at a stretch. Kolya reassured me this was nothing to do with me.

We remained close, but not sexually. Indeed, that act on the night I had won my Diploma had not been carnal. It had been an act of love and celebration. I have sought religious advice on the matter. I have been reassured I committed no sin in the eyes of God. Never has God been better understood or more passionately loved than in Russia. Never has He been obeyed and honored so thoroughly. Russia was God's noblest creation. But He slept, wearied by War. Christ was betrayed by Lucifer. Russia was stolen. And nowhere else in the world, save in the Greek churches, have I been able to find Him. His gentle Son was accepted in Constantine's Byzantium, which we call Czargrad, the Emperor's City. He saved the Roman Empire. His gentle son, crucified by resentful Jews, offered himself to Russia, and was accepted. Christ is Greek. Christ is God. They are a unity. The Jewish God is false. The Jews betrayed God and betrayed Russia. They brought us madness and despair and ruin. The Czar drew a line across the map. He said "Jews, you shall not pass beyond this point." But they crept through and they pulled the Czar from his throne. They killed him. They gave Russia to the Devil. Christ was distracted by so many dying souls. Christ was sleeping, lying with the millions killed by War. And when He woke, Russia had been stolen from Him. How can these be the opinions of a Jew? I reject that Jewish God. I accept Christ. No Jew could do that.

Carthage came out of the Orient and threatened Rome. Carthage came out of Africa. Ancient, prehistoric, savage blood. Carthage was the ghost who rode with the Tartar Khans, who razed Kiev and brought Moscow to her knees. Those Khans will come again. Why else do honest Russians remain wary of their "Chinese comrades"? Do they share the same delusions? Perhaps. But they do not share a blood or a culture. Let the Chinese call us "foreign devils" if they like. We know who the Devil is and who serves him. Russia remains in readiness. She has turned her back on Christ, but Christ has not forgotten His Slavs. Let the Jews continue to lend tainted ideas as they have lent tainted money down the generations. Both will be destroyed. The signs are there already. Even under Stalin they began to get back more interest than they expected on their ideas. Stalin learned. Stalin would have begun the cleansing of Russia if he had not been poisoned. Do not think I forgive Stalin, that renegade priest. But in old age he came to understand his errors. He was gathering his strength for the war against the ghostly Semitic Empires, against Babylon and Tyre, Phoenicia and Carthage, against Israel, against the Eastern hordes who dreamed of the glories of Genghis Khan come again . . .

Rasputin deserved his death. He preached ignorance, not knowledge. True Faith is gained through wisdom alone. He corrupted the Czar. God punished them all, perhaps as they deserved. The Czar was deceived. When he came back to Christ, Christ was sleeping. It was too late. In despair, the Czar abdicated. His prayers had become garbled and thickened by the teachings of a womanizing charlatan who was possibly in the pay of International Zionism. The Czar was responsible only to Christ, and Christ could not advise him. So Nicholas abdicated, precipitating the Terror, destroying the Future, robbing me of so much.

Unaware of this, I was very excited about my forthcoming travels. I was in love with England. For me it was populated by beautiful ladies and fine, haughty gentlemen. All my impressions came from popular Russian stories and from my *Pearson's* magazines. I knew poverty existed, from reading Wells, but it was not like our Russian poverty. It was a comfortable poverty. Nobody in Britain or America has ever witnessed true poverty as we knew it. I see nothing wrong with poverty, either. Give the baby too much milk, and he has nothing to strive for, as they say in Siberia.

Again, I began to read everything I could find in English. I spoke

English with Kolya (whose grasp of ordinary speech was not so good, but who knew far more about literature). I polished my vocabulary and my grammar. Not a day went by without my taking out my new passport, which included my photograph, supplied by Uncle Semya (it was another of those which he had had taken in Odessa) and delighting in it.

The passport was in the name of Maxim Arturovitch Pyatnitski. Things had become rather overcomplicated, but I was in such a good mood nothing really bothered me. As soon as possible I visited Mr. Green. He told me I should be going to Liverpool, via Helsinki. I would take the train through Finland, get a ship from there, and probably return by the same route. I might have to travel via Göteborg, or even Denmark. Merchant shipping was having trouble with German submarines.

I did not worry about the risks. The prospect of seeing my beloved England outweighed anything else. As it happened I would not see England until Bolshevism and Zionism, ironically, had taken root in the mental soil imported from my own country.

Throughout January I relaxed. Then I became concerned as no news arrived from the Polytechnic about my Diploma. I grew agitated. Next, Mr. Green told me that the international situation had become difficult. The package he had originally wanted me to deliver was lost. It would be a little while before he could get another. Inaction distresses me. My attempts to see Lena and Marya were rebuffed. The silly minxes had become frightened of me. Lena had a bruise on her face. She told me I had caused it, but I certainly had no memory of hitting her there.

Mr. Green at last informed me that another package was ready. I could not leave just then, because of a sea battle between the English and German fleets which might ease the blockade. He said it would be best to wait a couple of weeks. The package contained secret letters between my Uncle Semya's firm, Mr. Green's office, and the firm of Rawlinson and Gold, who had a branch in Liverpool. Their main offices, I was told, were at Whitechapel, London. I wished I might be going to Whitechapel. Mr. Green said it was important I got to Liverpool and returned on an early ship. I would be a "secret courier" for him, traveling as a student searching for émigré relatives. Soon, of course, I expected secret couriers to be carrying my own plans between friendly governments. I wrote to Professor Vorsin asking about my Diploma. I received a courteous note telling me that the

Diploma was in preparation. They were writing to my father to inform him of my success. My "father" was, of course, the priest whose son was currently undergoing TB treatment in Switzerland. It was to be hoped he would know how to respond. Now I had a letter which at least confirmed my right to the Diploma. I began going out again with Kolya. But an increasing number of revolutionaries were taking over our favorite cabarets. I saw Mrs. Cornelius once or twice. She said she was getting "fed up" with everything and would like to leave Peter. I told her I would soon be visiting Liverpool. She suggested we travel together. She knew Liverpool, she said, "fairly well." This was good news indeed. I told her what my route would probably be. I promised to find out about train and sailing times.

More and more strikes took place, particularly in the industrial suburbs. There were by now far too many voices raised in sympathy. I heard my landlady had had trouble (her house was on the Vyborg side where armed deserters were not above holding up "boorzhoo" women and robbing them). Wounded soldiers with bitter faces talked quite openly about the state of the War, complaining against God and the Czar, and nobody arrested them.

On 14 February 1917, I received another letter from Professor Vorsin. The Diploma would be prepared and sent to me. He was not sure the Polytechnic could teach me anything further. He would be pleased to meet me there or at my lodgings to discuss the matter. I wrote back saying I would appreciate the talk. It might be best if he recommended me for a government post at once. I received a rather brief reply, signed by his secretary. The contents of my letter had been noted. The professor was giving it his earliest possible attention. I was much cheered up. By the time the Czar left for Mogilev, to supervise the progress of the War, I was as good as ready to hold the Petrograd fort for him.

There is no need for me to describe what happened later in February 1917. In spite of all, we were taken by surprise. Strikes, mutinies, the Czar's abdication, the setting up of Prince Lvov's Provisional Government, the wild rumors, the wholesale chaos in the streets. Our enemies, Reds and Jews alike, celebrated their wonderful achievement while the people went on starving and the soldiers went on mutinying, and crime ranged the capital unchecked. Professor Vorsin fled Petrograd with half the staff of the Polytechnic. Mr. Green was winding up his office. He told me he now planned to take the package to England himself, "not that there was a lot of point now."

Kolya joined the Socialist Revolutionary Party. I was left alone and bewildered.

Petrograd became an alien, crazy city. Every day there were demonstrations and meetings. People were openly rude to their superiors. Decent men and women could not go abroad without being molested. Here was democracy and socialism in action. Everything was pulled down. The Czar was living in virtual exile with his family. Those who had any sense were already taking their money abroad. And still the Provisional Government claimed it could continue to fight a War. They were anxious, of course, not to lose the friendship or loans of countries like England and France. They knew Russia would fall apart without them.

I visited the Polytechnic and found Dr. Matzneff back in charge. This, at least, was something. I told him of my problem. He assured me that he knew of my case and would do all he could to see I was properly looked after. Many records had become lost. He suspected some of the academics of destroying them. It would probably be better if I went home for a while until things became normal. Eventually the Institute would be functioning as usual. I could return and he would help me sort everything out.

"I was promised a Special Diploma," I explained. "Can I still expect it?"

"Of course. But the times are so uncertain. With the paper shortages it's hard to get things printed."

"It is important to me. I had a letter from Professor Vorsin. He assured me the Diploma was being prepared. I had hoped to show it to my mother."

"Well, the letter will do, eh, for the moment?"

I agreed the letter was absolute confirmation. I would leave my address with him (I gave him my proper name) and would wait until I heard from him. I would be prepared to make a special visit to Petrograd to collect the Diploma. It would be unsafe to trust the mails in the present crisis. I had heard of postmen, for instance, dumping their bags into the snow or the garbage at the announcement of the Czar's abdication. I think my old friend Matzneff also had some intimation of the difficulties lying ahead and was trying to save me from the worst. Within a few months the Bolsheviks would be in control. Civil War would be laying our vast country waste, wreaking far more damage than anything the Germans might have done.

I shook hands with Matzneff, wished him luck, hoped he would be able to run the Polytechnic through what he termed the "interim confusion." I repeated my offer, as I felt I should, to help teach if necessary. He said he appreciated this but that teachers of routine experience were what were currently needed. He was trying to attract Vorsin and a few of the others back. They had lost some of their nervousness and might return.

I am glad I decided to take his advice. If I had not, I should almost certainly, like Vorsin, have become a victim of the Cheka. I bade him an affectionate farewell. I returned to the apartment to say good-by to Kolya. He promised to send for me as soon as things were stable. He had acquired sudden political influence. When he was Prime Minister, he said, he would appoint me Minister of Science. It was a consolation. Even if the revolutionaries had taken over, it was as well to have well-placed friends. Things might not be so difficult in the long term.

I went to the Harlequinade and asked after Mrs. Cornelius. The place was packed. Some mixture of poetry reading and political meeting was taking place. Red bunting was stuck everywhere. It was a madhouse. I pressed through the crowd (I had already learned to address all and sundry as "Comrade"). I searched for Mrs. Cornelius. She was not there. I left a message with a mutual acquaintance. My English trip was delayed. I would try to contact her soon. In the streets there were groups of students waving huge red flags. "La Marseillaise" was being played on every sort of instrument, on gramophones, by military bands. Trams and buses trundled by, full of yelling students and drunken soldiers. It reminded me of the Paris Commune. I remembered what had happened to that particular "social experiment." I prayed Kolya would have the sense to moderate his views and policies.

I stayed the night in Kolya's apartment. There were political newspapers and posters, all the junk of Revolution littered about. My friend was attending a meeting of the Duma and did not return. In the morning I packed my bags, borrowed Kolya's supply of cocaine, two bottles of Polish vodka, and a few silver rubles, and walked to Mr. Green's. I found the office in complete confusion. Everyone was leaving. Only Mr. Parrot was to remain. He looked unhappy. I told Mr. Green I needed some money. He was evidently reluctant to part with what he had, but gave me some paper rubles. He said they would be enough to get me to Kiev. I must write direct to Uncle Semya if I needed any more. I thanked him for his help. I still had my passport and would be glad to act as his courier if he needed someone in the future. He nodded and said he would remember my offer.

Through misty snow I walked to the station. It was in complete chaos. Deserters, released prisoners, cripples, touts, pimps, honest artisans, bohemians, aristocrats, businessmen and students were all trying to flee the city. There was no question of a luxury journey home. By paying three times the proper price I was lucky to get a third-class ticket. I found myself crowded into a carriage which already had one window broken ("for some fresh air," as an unshaven soldier told me). There were tiers of smelly bunks. These were full of gypsies, Jews, Tartars, Armenians, Poles and drunks making the compartment reek of foul tobacco, cheap vodka and vomit. I clung on to my bags, forced myself to be agreeable to an old Jew in a black overcoat and a young soldier with one arm, who was also trying to get to Kiev, and squeezed in between them.

Eventually the train moved slowly from the station. St. Petersburg was a miserable shadow, occupied at last by the forces of Chaos. We left it behind us. Then a white wind blew through the broken pane, making it impossible to see the countryside beyond. I consoled myself that, after all, I had achieved far more in the capital in a shorter time than I had thought possible. I would be returning home with some honor!

EIGHT

Four days later the train arrived in Kiev. By the time I struggled from the freezing compartment into the afternoon gloom I had been robbed of some books, a couple of inexpensive figurines bought for my mother, and a pair of gloves. Luckily I had some fur mittens of Kolya's. I put these on before gripping my bags and setting off on foot in the direction of Kirillovskaya and my mother's flat.

My city was occupied by every kind of scum: deserters who had killed their officers, peasants who had murdered their masters, workers who had stolen from their employers; all had come to Kiev to spend their gold on drink and women. On the train I had met a great many Petrograd businessmen, nobles and intellectuals, and similar individuals in flight from Moscow. They were hoping to get to Yalta or Odessa or anywhere on the coast. I do not know where they expected to go from there. Turks and Germans blockaded us on every sea. Perhaps those places were less infected with Revolutionary madness. Here red banners hung between buildings; there were proclamations on walls (some in Ukrainian, which baffled me); meetings were carried on at every corner; and bands were playing Shevchenko's "The Ukraine Will Never Die" as well as "La Marseillaise." The floors of the train had been filthy with sunflower seeds and with every other sort of inanimate and animate rubbish. There was no difference here, either on pavements or in parks. Incompetents had taken charge. Kiev had collapsed as a civilized city. Trams had ceased to run on time; cabs had disappeared; bands of drunken brigands in sailors' uniforms and army greatcoats roamed about at will, demanding money, drink, food, cigarettes, from passers-by. Because the democratic Rada had not defined it, police and Cossack militia were uncertain of their authority. Should they try to arrest the brigands? Should they merely ask them to leave other comrades alone? Should they shoot on sight? Should they simply ignore the activities of the new aristos? The deserters and convicts were armed to the teeth, cheerfully willing to kill anyone who frustrated them: a typical situation in all Russia's cities during Kerenski's days. It would get worse. The Bolsheviks would merely legalize the terror and give it moral justification. Every murder victim became a liquidated bourgeois just as nowadays they are all listed as traffic accidents. It looked as if half the city was drunk and the other half sunk into dejection. I passed by Podol. The whole ghetto had turned Red: the Jews were celebrating their conquests. I bought a *Voice of Kiev*. It had already taken on a nationalist note.

By the time I reached our quiet, unlit street, I had realized I must support any authority, even if it were socialist. My arms and back ached horribly. I tugged the bags up the dark, smelly staircase to our landing. I knocked at the apartment door. There was silence. I went up a flight and pulled Captain Brown's bell. Soon the old Scot stood quivering in the opening. His breath was heavy with homemade vodka. His eyes were scarcely able to focus.

"It is I."

He coughed in surprise. He wiped at his untrimmed mustache as if it were a piece of food he had found adhering to his lip. "Your mother will be very pleased."

"Mother isn't in."

"Bring your bags." He gestured a welcome. "Thieves everywhere. You might have been murdered. The envious wretches will kill anyone with a hint of refinement." He stumbled down after me and tried to pick up a suitcase. He failed. I had never seen him so helpless. He was old and pathetic.

We entered his hollow flat. Through all my childhood it had been a piece of the Britain I loved: trophies on the walls, English pictures and books. Even the carpets had seemed English. Now the captain had sold everything of value. I was appalled. I wished someone had warned me of his decline. He sat on a bare table and apologized. "Hard times. The War. Your mother works late at the laundry. They had to release half the staff. Others have gone off God knows where. Into the countryside, probably, to join the looting. The government's trying to stop it. Could be worse. The first days were horrifying." He poured cloudy vodka into a glass. "A dram?"

I accepted. It looked poisonous. He said, "With luck things will soon be normal. Prince Lvov isn't interested in Ukrainian independence and Kerenski wants us to go on fighting the Germans."

I smiled and sipped the awful stuff. "You've been infected by politics, Captain Brown."

"It's a political world." He slumped. "Esmé went to Galicia. Did she write?"

I was disappointed. "When did she leave?"

"Two weeks ago. Mixed force. British motor division and Cossack cavalry. A lot of desertion. Hope the little girl's all right." He became hazy. Again he wiped at his mustache as if bewildered by it. "They're not kind to women, are they? The conscripted peasants. And Mongols?"

I began to worry. "The nurses should be recalled."

"Won't come back. Too noble."

I explained to Captain Brown that I needed rest. Could he let me in downstairs? He regretted there had been an incident. He did not remember it clearly, but he had insisted afterward that my mother take back his set of her keys. There was now a spare at the laundry. I did not have the energy to walk to the laundry so I remained seated on one of the captain's last decrepit chairs. The vodka made me light-headed. I had no desire to greet my mother smelling of cheap alcohol, but the stuff jolted me awake whenever I began to doze. Captain Brown had lapsed into English. He was telling a story of Pathans on the Northwest Frontier, mixed with almost identical tales of the Malay Archipelego, and of coal mines in Welsh valleys, where dynamite had caused subsidence, destroying villages. Dynamite was the common feature of all three tales: its misuse by people who did not understand it, its need to be properly placed, to be fitted with the correct detonators. Captain Brown kept confusing the various locations. Pathans appeared in Merthyr Tydfil and Celtic pit-men in Sourabaya.

At length I heard a sound on the landing below. I went to the banister and looked down. My mother, straight-backed as ever, with her marvelous hair piled neatly on top of her head, wearing a smart, black overcoat, black dress, and black boots, was opening our door. "Mother!" I descended.

She turned. She began to weep. She made no attempt to come to me. I was unable to move toward her. Perhaps she had reconciled herself to my disappearance or even to my death. Now she could not believe her son (elegant and poised, if rather tired) stood before her. Eventually I reached her and embraced her, kissing her hand as she kissed my forehead. She asked me if I would be staying for a meal. I assured her I would stay for some time. Shaking with emotion, she took me by the arm and led me into the flat. I found the place homely, simple and comforting. With a sigh I paused and looked around me. I smiled. "It is good to be here."

"Oh, my dear son." Again we embraced.

She began to engage herself with the stove, with the samovar, with the soup pot. Captain Brown knocked lightly on the door before dragging my bags in. I explained I had bought presents which had then been stolen. They commiserated. Captain Brown collapsed onto my mother's couch. He said I had been lucky to arrive with so much. How were things in the capital? I said they were not good. Captain Brown had heard that Americans were arriving in huge airships with some kind of ray to kill thousands at a stroke. "It might conclude the War and let the Czar restore order. The end of trench fighting. But the buggers seem to have become attached to those holes in the ground. You'd think they were all bloody Welshmen!" He laughed heartily at this obscure racial joke. My mother had not realized he had sworn. In her presence he never swore in Russian. One Russian oath is worth twenty Greek ones. In the company of men, Captain Brown could have won any argument in any tavern in Kiev by sheer force and color of his vocabulary. Now his head fell upon his chest and he began to snore. He had left his bottle behind but its effects remained with him for an hour.

My mother hurried about laying the table, heating the soup, cutting the bread, complaining it was like sawdust. She had found two cockroaches in the last loaf. She had had to queue for those cockroaches the best part of an evening after work, in the freezing cold. She knew of several women who had caught bronchitis or pneumonia and died in bread queues. It was ridiculous when everyone knew Ukraine was the breadbasket of Russia. This sounded almost like the cry of a nationalist. I said we were luckier than people in Petrograd, but there were some living better than the Czar in parts of Siberia and the Caucasus. Supply trains had been diverted and they had to eat their produce or let it rot. (All those nationalists ever aspired to was fat bellies and brainless contentment. I still see them with their silly banners and hunger strikes near the Russian Embassy. I laugh at them. If I were in the embassy looking out I would think what idiots they were. Their "nation" is more independent now than it ever was. I wonder why they will not return. Could it be they prefer life in a country where they can complain freely as they fill themselves up with soup and meat every day? At home they would not see so much as a cabbage or slice of goose from one week's end to another. I long to be buried in my native soil. It is Russian soil. But the Bolsheviks have long memories. They hanged Krassnoff, then over seventy, because he had been Hetman of the Don Host. They found him in Germany in 1945. They had his name on their list of enemies. He had done nothing except lead his Cossacks into honorable battle and write good books about the Russian problem. But the Reds took this doddering, harmless old fellow from his flat and hanged him. I, too, have attacked Bolshevism.)

Captain Brown woke to seat himself at the far end of our table. He stared for some while at the bowl of soup before he picked up his spoon and then, as one unused to the exercise, began to eat. My mother watched him affectionately. "I haven't been able to feed him properly."

Considering her long hours and hardships, I thought she looked well. She agreed. Something had brought out the best in her. She had gathered her strength. Doing the work herself was easier than supervising those girls. She had been more like a Mother Superior, sometimes, than a laundress. Captain Brown laughed at this and splashed some of his soup. He apologized. Placing his spoon neatly in the plate, he lapsed into sleep again. "He has not been well," said my mother. "The drink's at the root of it. I've been too tired to cook for him every day, you know. We eat our main meal at the laundry to save time. I come home," she shrugged, looking about her, "as you see, to sleep." It was true the flat had a neglected air, but I preferred it. Flat and Mother both seemed more relaxed. "Of course, I miss Esmé." She sighed. "Such a beautiful girl." She asked me when I intended returning to Petrograd.

"I was advised to let things settle down a bit," I said. "A month or two and I can collect my Special Diploma. It will be useful. I'd hoped to serve the government, but now I'll try for a job, perhaps in Kharkov, with a good firm. I have plenty of ideas to be patented. It's even possible I could work independently."

"What shall you do until you get your Diploma?"

"Sleep." I patted her shoulder and bent forward to kiss her cheek. "You shall have Esmé's bed," she said.

NINE

I was soon more at ease in a chaotic Kiev than I had been in Petrograd. I knew my city's streets, its alleys, its shortcuts between buildings. I knew the areas hooligans preferred and where I could avoid the worst of them. I knew houses where I could hide. Our district, being a suburb, was relatively undisturbed. It was poor, offering very little for the wandering riffraff. We were also lucky in that Podol was a main target for the looters. As the Dnieper ice began to break up, sending huge creaking, groaning and snapping sounds echoing throughout Kiev, I found I had developed something of Mother's resilience. The ghost of my father had been laid to rest. My mother, as the widow of a martyred revolutionist, could not now be more respectable. Things might get worse, but it would make a change, as we used to say. In fact things improved for me. I decided to try taking over some of Sarkis Mihailovitch Kouyoumdjian's old customers. Engineers were in short supply. I had met one or two people who had asked desperately after my ex-boss. Since he had left Kiev half the local machine shops no longer operated. I had only a tenth of the Armenian's practical experience and his feeling for broken-down engines. Even so I knew I should have plenty of business.

I did a few small jobs for the Podol Jews who had been Kouyoumdjian's main customers. They were overwhelmingly grateful.

They paid almost anything I asked. Like my former master, I became a jack-of-all-trades, fixing electrical equipment, steam engines, internal-combustion engines, all devices not powered by man, child or beast. Indeed, I was willing to do what I could with anything containing cogs or levers. Thus, I soon had a fair bit of money with which to buy myself more sophisticated tools and some to set aside at home (the banks were not trustworthy). I used Captain Brown as a part-time assistant. With a job to do he became more sober during the day. My mother could have given up her laundry work, but she, too, was enjoying herself. It would have been pleasant to have seen Esmé from time to time, since we had been such good friends. She would have relished my success. There were more than enough women to satisfy my sexual needs. With money in my pocket, I became a very popular fellow in the cabarets where I spent an evening or two a week. The only shadow on my mind was the fact that I still had not heard from Professor Matzneff about my Diploma. Until I had it, I could not write off to the important engineering concerns applying for the job which would also help keep me out of the army. I had reduced my cocaine consumption to almost nothing, though our "Mother City" became one of the main supply centers. Several of the women I saw were old friends from Petrograd. There were poets here, and painters and entertainers who knew me. My social contacts became very wide and useful. I took to dressing in expensively fashionable suits. Spring grew warmer. I bought myself a straw boater with an English-style band, and a silver-topped cane. I could go into any shop in Kreshchatik and purchase what I wished. I could hire carriages. And all this with honestly earned money. By day, and sometimes by night, I was a mechanic, in dirty blue cotton covered in oil. When I visited the center of Kiev, I became the most elegant of youths.

The Foline Ballet Company arrived in Kiev and with it my old friend Seryozha Andreyovitch Tsipliakov. He greeted me elaborately when he came, at my invitation, to a private room of the Hotel Arson. The place had been renovated and taken over by Ulyanski. It was decorated in bizarre, explicitly sexual murals which never could have been tolerated a few months before. I found it convenient for a number of reasons. I chose to turn a blind eye to its vulgarities. It had become one of the main artistic and émigré meeting places in Kiev. Seryozha was impressed by my elegance and surroundings. He hugged me to him. I returned his embrace with affection. If it had not been for him I should never have met Kolya. We sat down to dine. I asked him if he had seen our mutual friend recently.

He told me Kolya had become too proud and had dropped everyone, that he was now a Prince and involved in the Arts Ministry but was unwilling to look after his old friends. Seryozha said he was planning to leave the Foline and go to America at the first chance. He asked where he could find some little boys and some cocaine. I told him and we parted. I had become oddly homesick for Kolya and Petrograd. I even considered returning there. But the fanatics were steadily gaining the upper hand in the government. The "Bolshevik coup" of October was a natural consequence and everyone had expected it. Kerenski unleashed the whirlwind and was consumed by it. It is a shame Stalin could not have taken over at once, but History, that mystical force Bolsheviks invoke in place of God, was against him. He would never be able to rid himself of the Tartar Lenin and the Jew Trotsky sitting on his shoulders, whispering into his ears, even though he had killed them both.

While I worked as a jobbing mechanic I continued to develop a stream of inventions, drawing up detailed plans on proper graph paper, giving every sort of accurate specification. When I applied for work in Kharkov or Kherson, I would be able to make the best possible impression. The summer was a good one. From Saint Alexander's I could look across at Darnitsa, where the big German POW camp was, and see the prisoners bathing. They were in dreadful condition. They had endured hardship during the fighting and we could not afford to feed them. They were eating lice. I had a plan for them. It involved interesting local industrialists in certain patents I had. The Germans could be used as workers to develop them. They would be happy to work for food alone. But materials were short as well as men.

I also had a particularly exciting scheme: a machine to concentrate light. This was an admittedly primitive precursor to modern lasers and masers which are revolutionizing medicine and astronomy today. I planned to harness invisible light (what is now called "ultraviolet"). With proper equipment and more faith from those nervous Ukrainian businessmen, at that time interested in getting their money out of Russia rather than investing in our War Effort, I might have turned the tide of conflict. The machine had drawbacks and would have been difficult to transport, but would have done more to spread alarm amongst the enemy than the most dashing and effective of cavalry or tank charges.

Mother began to display an informed intelligence which surprised me. My simpler ideas induced quite specific questions. I told her about my compressed-air machine gun and my pilotless "fireship" dirigible which could carry an enormous bomb, be towed into position by aeroplane, released over its target, then deliberately shot down. I was pleased to explain to her what was involved. I had even more schemes than I had had in Petrograd. Now I possessed the time and confidence to clarify them. I anticipated among other things the communications satellite (for which I have never received a penny in royalties), the television, the radio-printed newspaper, the war rocket and the transport rocket. Domestic automata were another idea of mine (the Czech word for serf, *robot*, had not yet been popularized by the leftist writer Čapek). I was also working on a scheme for pilotless aircraft controlled from the ground by radio signals. I realize now that I spoke too much and too freely. Not only in Russia, but also when in Germany, America and England, where many of my schemes were "borrowed" by unscrupulous men claiming my inventions as their own and selling them, needless to say, to Jewish firms who are still making fortunes from them. I need not name names here. It is enough to say that Marx and Spenser did not invent, I think, the underpant.

Looking back on those strange Kiev days, I suppose I must have seemed a peculiar figure to people who knew me. My mother, however, was not at all disturbed by my entering our flat as a grease-spotted mechanic and leaving as a man about town. I was gaining experience in every way. Primarily I confined my activities to Podol. There was more than enough work in the ghetto. The Jews would do anything to keep their sweatshops going. I rarely had to travel more than a few streets. The trams had begun to run roughly on time. It seemed to us that things were settling down.

In my white suit, my boater, with my silver-headed cane, I would take a Sunday stroll along the banks of the river. I would hire a carriage to go for picnics in the countryside with Mother and Captain Brown. Esmé returned on leave, looking exhausted and thinner than I remembered. For once I was able to be of use to her. Rather than have her suffering the discomfort of our apartment, I decided she must stay at a good hotel, the Yevropyaskaya on Kreshchatik. She was welcomed as a countess and received every courtesy. She was delighted. She hugged me and kissed me and said it was a wonderful present. She was pleased about my Diploma and full of questions. I could see she needed sleep so left her in that elegant summer room, full of silver and gilt and silk. I would call for her in the evening. Meanwhile I had a variety of clothes sent round to the hotel and ordered a four-wheeler to be outside by six o'clock.

At six she was wearing a perfect blue dress, a fashionable matching headband, feathers, "tango" shoes. She wore little make-up, and her large blue eyes looked lovely in their setting of pink and gold. I was proud to be seen with her as our carriage took us to Czarskaya Square and one of the best restaurants in Kiev. She tasted course after course, but was unable to eat very much because of the excitement. "They told me everyone was starving at home!"

"Not everyone," I said. "The food is simply not getting to the soldiers. So it has to be eaten." I told her I knew of people who made special trips to Moscow and Petrograd with just a couple of baskets of provisions. They came home almost millionaires.

"Is that how you're living?" she asked.

"Good God, no! I'm doing proper work." I was rather hurt by the suggestion. She became apologetic. I poured her more French wine and calmed her. "I've taken over Sarkis Mihailovitch's business. The profiteers, you could say, are giving me my profits. But mostly they're honest enough. Everyone buys and sells something. Have you seen the markets? Bessarabskaya? A Contract Fair going all year round! Peasants bring their produce to the city because no one can get to the country. They drive whole herds into Kiev. And you can obtain literally anything in the Bessarabskaya." I was too delicate to do more than suggest my meaning, but she understood. Working amongst soldiers had evidently given her a knowledge of the world.

A band started to play. It was gypsy music, very sad. Esmé began to relax. She was immensely beautiful now, in her prime as a girl. I still considered her a sister. I could not regard her as a sexual partner. I wished her to keep her virginity. I could now help her marry well. I was a brother and a father to her. I wanted to do for her what her father would have wished. A number of my friends and business acquaintances saw us together. I was winked at more than once and when Esmé was not in earshot I was congratulated. I explained nothing. It suited me to be seen with her. When the War was over I would need to give dinners to great industrialists. Esmé would make a perfect hostess. I could employ her in my firm. I had begun to evolve what the Germans call a "lifeplan." I would model myself as far as possible on Thomas Edison, the American inventor and entrepreneur. My name would become as famous throughout Europe as his was in his native land. It would become a synonym for progress and enlightenment, possibly mentioned in the same breath as Galileo and Newton. But I would be practical. I would keep control of my own patents. I spoke to Esmé of this and of certain details I had already worked out. "You will be a full partner," I told her. "It is only fair. Your encouragement, and Mother's, made me what I am."

She looked down at her plate and she smiled a little. "I had aspirations to become a doctor," she told me. "I think I have a vocation."

"And perhaps Captain Brown could become a laundress!" The humor was meant to be harmless. The image of my feminine Esmé in mannish suits, carrying a doctor's bag, was ludicrous. "Why not? Anything is possible in the New Russia!" I parodied a popular phrase of the Provisional Government. I changed the subject: "There's talk of mutiny. Will you be safe at the Front?"

She looked up and laughed spontaneously. "Safer than walking up Kreshchatik. Dear Maxim. The soldiers are like children. You get the odd agitator, of course. But their loyalty depends on respect. If they like an officer, or a nurse, they'll do anything for them. Conditions are unspeakable. They're so grateful if you merely wipe the sweat from their foreheads. They're honest, decent, Russian lads."

"All the virtues you mention can become vices overnight."

She did not want to listen. She frowned and shook her head.

"Children can turn against you," I said.

"We're their nanyanas. They trust us. They know we suffer as they do. They know we volunteered to help them."

I called for the bill. She had reassured me a little. But she was still innocent.

We took the carriage through the steep Kiev streets. There were lights of sorts burning, candles and oil lamps. I wished we had been able to paint the town red in proper style, the old style, when Kreshchatik would have been full of electrics and gaslight; the pleasure gardens along the river would have had different-colored lanterns glowing in the trees. German bands would have played waltzes. Then I should truly have enjoyed my triumph and her enjoyment.

Esmé said she felt guilty. So many were now homeless, sick and crippled. I told her that I was not oblivious to the misery. I spent my own money freely, giving to beggars and to various church institutions, to organizations set up for the aid of the needy. Even the Jews of Podol knew me for one who could be relied upon to put a coin in a collecting box. Meanness has never been one of my vices. When I had money, I would give. And, of course, I was saving. I had a duty to my mother, to myself, to all those I loved, to make sure that political events would not affect them. The day would come when Mother would be too frail to work at the laundry. A man can live as he chooses, I said, so long as he is insured. Freedom is based on a sense of responsibility. That is what the Bolsheviks never realized. The only slogan I ever hoped to see strung out on a banner over any street was "Live and let Live."

Esmé asked where I intended taking her next. I mentioned a popular cabaret. It had one of the usual names: The Purple Monkey or the Chartreuse Sioux. She asked if she might visit the flat instead, to have a quiet glass of tea with my mother and Captain Brown. Captain Brown would have had more than one quiet glass of vodka by now and if not asleep he would be singing some obscure Glaswegian shanty, but I understood that the high life could be exhausting. I had no hesitation in ordering the carriage up Kirillovskaya to our own little street. Esmé's instincts had been good. Suddenly I was at ease again. Here so little had changed: the woods and gorges, the mixture of houses, the distant barking of dogs, the quarreling of couples. We might have been the two happy children who had attended Herr Lustgarten's school. So little time had passed since we had tried out my first flying machine. Now her father was at rest and, oddly enough, my mother seemed mentally at rest.

Though I had a key, I knocked on the door. It was opened at once. My mother had seen Esmé earlier, before I had arranged the hotel, but she hugged her as if greeting her for the first time. "What a beautiful girl. You are still an angel. Look at her, Maxim!"

I looked at her. "Were you expecting us then, Mama?"

She became flustered. "Was it a good restaurant?"

"The best. You must come there."

"Oh, I always get too nervous. I have indigestion before I take a bite of bread!" It was why I had given up trying to take her out.

Esmé sat down in her usual chair and removed her shoes. She hitched up her skirt and scratched a perfect calf encased in pale blue silk. I was used to women, of course, and most of them had no modesty at all, but I expected different behavior from Esmé. This was stupid of me. She was, after all, amongst family and she had been serving at the Front. My mother put lumps of sugar and pieces of the fresh lemon I had bought that morning into Esmé's tea. "I've brewed it strong. You've gotten used to strong tea, eh?"

"Not any more." Esmé did not elaborate. "It's very good, Yelisaveta Filipovna." She looked at me, smiling. "The best thing to pass my lips all day."

"I have wasted a fortune!" I said in mock despair. I settled down into a chair and accepted a glass of tea.

"You are not eating properly," said my mother to Esmé. "The food is bad?"

"Not as bad as what the soldiers get."

"Weevils in the bread, eh?"

"Sometimes."

"Mother," I said, "you've become a critic!"

She shrugged. "They let us criticize now, instead of eating."

Esmé was amused. "We're all turning into revolutionists."

"We bend with the wind," said my mother. "What is the alternative?"

I knew her thoughts. My father had never learned to bend. He had stuck zealously to his religion of anarchy and violence. Strangely, now that chaos threatened on all sides, my mother had lost her anxieties.

Esmé made it clear she did not want to discuss the War, "at least not tonight." We talked about a letter my mother had received that day from Uncle Semya. It was one of several he had sent. All the others had gone astray. "He's well. He says they're making the most of the lull. They've taken a villa in Arcadia. Is that a nice place, Maxim? It sounds it."

"It was," I said. "Perhaps it still is." I wished we could all three be there at that moment, enjoying the warm, salty air of an Odessa evening. I yearned for that southern magic, the smell of rotting flowers mingled with brine, the simple fellowship of Shura and his friends which had appeared so sophisticated and now seemed pleasantly provincial. "Shall we all go there tomorrow? Take the train?"

"Is there a train, anymore?" My mother brightened.

"There has to be. It's a main line."

"It's a wonderful idea." But she was hesitant.

Esmé drained her glass. "I have to be back in two days. You could go."

I became obsessed. "What about compassionate leave?"

Esmé was regretful. "Not fair. There are only a few of us."

"She has her duty, Maxim."

"Yes, Mama."

"And I suppose we have ours." Mother collected the glasses. "Without me, the laundry would collapse. The ladies would receive gentlemen's collars and the gentlemen would be going to bed in ladies' nightdresses." She giggled. She had to pour herself another glass of tea and sip it before she could stop. We both laughed with her.

"It's like the old days," said my mother, and her face became set and sad.

"The future will be better," I said. "We'll buy a house of our own. On Trukhanov Island. We'll have a yacht. We'll sail up and down the Dnieper. We'll have a motor and visit Odessa whenever we feel like it. And Sevastopol. And Yalta. And Italy and Spain. And Greece. We'll take the waters in Baden-Baden, which by then will be part of Russia, and we'll go to England for the Season. Paris will be our second home. We shall hobnob with the famous. You, Esmé, shall be courted by dukes, by the Prince of Wales. I shall attract a circle of titled ladies who will fight one another for my affections. And you, mother, will be Queen of a Salon!"

"I should become bored very quickly."

"I shall invent a new method of cleaning everything. A universal laundry. At the touch of a switch, you'll make the whole world shine!"

"I could run the Salon and this world launderer at the same time?"

"Why not!"

We laughed again. Those were moments which were to be amongst the happiest I have known.

My mother told me Uncle Semya was very pleased about my Diploma. If I needed any assistance finding a good job in Odessa he would be happy to offer it. He suggested, however, that there were opportunities "elsewhere." She took him to mean I might find greater scope abroad. I wondered if he still wished me to travel to England. The thought excited me. Since I had become such a man of the world I could go anywhere with complete assurance. The passport remained one of my most important treasures. It was an "open" passport, the hardest to obtain, particularly during the War. I could leave and enter the country at any time. I could visit all countries friendly to Russia. I could go to England, America, France. If peace were made, I could even go to Berlin should the spirit take me. At the age of seventeen I was a person of considerable substance. I already possessed virtually everything I had ever dreamed of save the resources to build my own inventions. I took Esmé back and on my way to my own hotel I continued my internal debate.

I had written once or twice in the past month to Professor Matzneff. Probably the letters had not reached Petrograd or perhaps he had left the Institute. I had given other letters to friends who felt it safe to return. It would be a little while before I had any reply. Telegrams were no longer reliable. I had made one or two attempts to deal with representatives of the Kiev Technical College but they were too busy with their politics to take an interest in my problem. One man, with pince-nez, a grey beard and all the appearance of a typical *ancien-régime* supporter, told me mine were "Russian qualifications." If I wished to receive a diploma in Kiev, I must retake the examinations in Ukrainian. I had given up in disgust. In the meantime I was still rising in the world. Peasants, workers, deserters, refugees, men of affairs, poured into Kiev, demanding services often operated by machinery. Thus I enjoyed the benefits of the influx as well as the inconveniences. I could see that science and technology were to be Russia's salvation. Putilov, the visionary industrialist, shared my view. So would Stalin, for that matter. We needed no revolutions. We needed, I suppose, word from God that He approved of science.

The Germans took Riga and even more people came into Kiev. Livonia had begun to claim "nationhood," so in a sense the victory was not on Russian soil, but all true Russians saw the defeat of Riga as a terrible blow. Of course the Jews did not care who won. They might have felt, speaking Yiddish, that life would be better for them under the Germans.

Soon I would be eligible for the army. I was determined not to be thrown away as cannon fodder. I wrote out a number of copies of the letter in which Professor Vorsin had mentioned my Special Diploma. Each copy was clearly marked "Duplicate." It would not seem as if I were attempting a crude forgery. I sent these off, together with a letter of my own, to various establishments in Ukraine, offering my services. My only problem was that the letter had addressed me as D. M. Kryscheff whereas my new name was M. A. Pyatnitski. This was the sole substitute I made. Professor Vorsin's writing was very precise and formal and easily imitated. I produced, after several attempts, a facsimile which was honestly what he had written, but which now called me by the same name as the one on my passport. This might seem a petty trick. It should be understood that I was determined to get justice. It did not seem wrong if I corrected the balance, since events threatened to rob me of everything I had achieved. With the help of a local printer, I reproduced the stationery of the Petrograd Institute of Technology. It was on this that I transcribed the professor's promise of my Special Diploma. After it was done I felt many doubts lift from my mind. I became confident that the wind would soon turn and bring me what I deserved. Through an acquaintance in the Podol underworld, I had two copies of my passport printed, complete with photographs. One was in the name of Dimitri Mitrofanovitch Kryscheff, so that it would marry with my Diploma if it came in the wrong name. The other was an exact copy. Captain Brown introduced me to a British Tommy in hospital in Kiev. He was due to return home via Archangel. He had lost his right leg. I offered him a good sum if he would carry a passport home with him. I asked him to put it in a safety-deposit and leave the key in London for collection by me. He winked mysteriously as he pocketed my gold rubles. "Don't worry chum. I'd be doing the same." He said if I got to London to go to St. Martin's Lane Post Office where I should find my key. I only half-believed him. But Captain Brown assured me he was a thoroughly reliable fellow. He had also agreed to take a letter which he would post to the captain's relatives in Scotland as soon as he arrived in Blighty. The young soldier's name was Fraser. He was to become quite a success as a shoe-shop proprietor in Portsmouth. I still wonder if he began by selling all the odd shoes of his own pairs. There must, after all, have been many men needing only right shoes in postwar London.

I had been wise to take my precautions. In September 1917, when Kiev was at her golden best, Kerenski made himself premier and declared Russia a republic. Hubris! He had overstepped himself. He was obsessed with his own mission to "save Russia." He underestimated Lenin. Almost at the very moment when we might have won the War, when the first American divisions were arriving to help us, Lenin and his gang became the rulers of Russia, ready to make a separate peace with Germany. This merely confirms my contempt for Comrade Bronstein as a strategist. There was no need for peace at all. We had almost won. It was a typical Bolshevik decision. It pretended to have anticipated and planned for the chaos it itself created. History? Men were deserting from the army faster than they could be sent to the Front. So the Bolsheviks said this was part of their scheme. They were to change their tune very shortly afterward. Most of the population rose up against them. They had to create a Cheka and a Red Army to terrorize the people they claimed to be saving. On the day of the first important tank battle, at Cambrai, our Ukrainian Rada declared the province a republic. We were suddenly no longer Russian citizens. At least we were not subject to the Bolshevik madness. Although my links with Petrograd were almost completely cut off I felt we had gained breathing space. We still had a free-enterprise system enabling me to continue working and saving.

The snows covered Kiev. The river began to freeze. The armistice was as good as made. It was signed officially by the Bolsheviks. This did not mean an immediate end to the fighting. It did not improve the lot of the ordinary people one jot. Such paper agreements rarely do; but soldiers came home and with them Esmé. I think the city was kept warm during that winter by the agitation of large crowds, by bodies pressing together in the squares, by the hot air issuing from every mouth. Esmé declined to stay at an hotel. I let her live with my mother while I went to the Yevropyaskaya, which was full of delegates of one sort or another. It was impossible to find peace there. Eventually I moved to the more expensive Savoy. Even here I was to be plagued by politicians. I gave up after a week or two and returned to Ulyanski's. It had ceased to be the Hotel Arson and was now the Cube; the last word to describe a ramshackle building of imitation Gothic turrets and imitation Kremlin domes. Still, the mixture of architectural styles did not clash on the outside nearly so much as the mixture of artistic styles within. Acmeists, Futurists, Constructivists, Cubists; poets, musicians, painters and journalists drank quite as much as the politicians. They talked almost as much as the politicians. They certainly fornicated as much, if not more; but at least they left one alone. I had worn out a lifetime's supply of different cockades during my couple of weeks at Kreshchatik hotels. Once established at the Cube I began to feel as if I were back in Petrograd in the good old days. I had a small top-floor private suite looking out over snow-covered parks and bare trees to the Dnieper.

I still worked as a mechanic. I kept my tools and overalls at Mother's. Esmé was relieved to see the evidences of my honest work. She continued with her nursing. She now served at the Alexander Hospital, not very far from where I lived. Occasionally I was able to give her lifts in a cab. When cabs became scarce, we sometimes shared a tram ride. As fuel and lubricating oils disappeared, my Podol customers began to go out of business or adapted to more primitive manufacturing methods. I would shortly be in the position of a doctor whose patients were all dead, so I cast around for larger game. It was not hard to find. Some of the main engineering firms, a few stores with private generators, hospitals and public offices, all needed me. This was far more to my taste. Gradually I became a diagnostician until I did little of the ordinary physical work myself. My knowledge of more sophisticated machinery was at first almost wholly theoretical. It did not take me long to get experience, though at cost, sometimes, to the customer. Soon I exchanged my overalls and tools for a sober dark-grey suit, a grey homburg and grey overcoat with a fox-fur collar. I must have looked ridiculously young in that fine suiting, but I knew what I was doing and could easily instill my own confidence into those seeking my help. Sometimes a machine had nothing wrong with it. Its operators had simply lost heart. I was able to cure it with a few mystic passes and taps. I told my mother how my career was improving. She wondered if I were not moving "too far, too fast." But I was getting what I could while I could. There was no telling how long our Ukrainian Republic would stand. Both Bolsheviks and Germans were greedy for Ukrainian corn and raw materials.

I gave my mother the best holiday of her life. We had a Christmas Eve dinner in a room at a fine restaurant where I managed to get her to take a glass or two of champagne. She enjoyed herself immensely. The waiters treated her like a queen. Esmé and Captain Brown sang Christmas songs and we exchanged gifts. It was marvelous. I never feel guilty about my mother. When it was possible I compensated her for much of her suffering. That night she knew a taste of heaven. As we drank liqueurs I told them my great plan. I was going to start a proper business. No longer just a consultant, I would be head of a firm of engineers.

"Whatever happens to Kiev in the future," I said, "there will certainly be a demand for us. We shall design new factories, install machinery, give advice. If Ukraine booms, we shall boom. If she is in trouble, we shall help her in her trouble."

My mother seemed taken aback. Her face clouded. "And what will you call yourself?"

"All-Ukraine Engineering Consultants," I said. "It has a suitable ring to it."

She became reconciled. Esmé grinned at me as if I had somehow pulled off a coup requiring both nerve and intelligence. "And your own name?" she asked.

"Pyatnitski, for the moment."

"Your father . . ." began my mother. But then she nodded. "It would be better. You'll be careful?"

"The times have changed," I said. "I have changed with them. I was born to be part of these times."

"You've an eye for the future," murmured Captain Brown from behind his champagne glass. He toasted me. "A Happy New Year to you!"

My mother began to cry. Almost at the same moment, Esmé began to chuckle. It was a strange experience. I did not know to whom I should respond. At length I went to comfort my mother. "Why are you crying?"

She said she was crying from happiness.

TEN

The Bolsheviks sold Russia off and Ukraine again became a republic. I remained in prison where the Reds, for reasons of their own, had put me. The Rada did not see fit to release me. I had done nothing. Eventually I was able to explain myself to the Varta security police of Hetman Pavlo Skoropadskya; to help them identify the genuine troublemakers. Then I was free. Trudging back over the bridge I saw my rescuer himself, leading a parade. Skoropadskya looked every inch the Cossack, with his white riding coat, white shapka, silk trousers, decorated red boots, English stallion and silver-hilted saber. The Germans believed he had his hand on the pulse of Ukrainian thought. He was an infinitely better alternative to the socialists and anarchists. He was able to police Kiev with our German allies and restrict the bandit gangs of the rural areas. These killed Uhlans as cheerfully as they killed Varta. The Exalted and Glorious Excellency, Pan Hetman Skoropadskya, as he was called in official proclamations, had half the intelligence and twice the swagger of Mussolini. But he had sweeping Cossack mustaches and he shaved his head in the old Zaporozhian fashion. He reminded us of what Cossacks had stood for: self-reliance and courage. My only quarrel with the Hetman was his apparent wish to destroy all signs of the modern world. The three terrible weeks of Bolshevik occupation had lost me a good many of my best business connections. So many had been killed. But the Germans were interested in keeping our factories going. Skoropadskya could not afford to alienate them.

I found myself naturally falling in with the Germans who were in the main practical, good-hearted fellows. The peasants were the chief cause of all our frustrations. The Germans had been promised grain. But the canny Ukrainians defeated our attempts to wrest it from him. He had learned to hide whole fields of corn, whole herds of cattle, as easily as he had hidden away his gold and his icons. German requisition teams, with official orders from Hetman Skoropadskya, searched barns and houses and found not so much as an egg. Used to threats, the peasants would confuse them, display their poverty, claim that Makhno's guerrillas or Hrihorieff's bandits or some other force had already taken everything. It was an easy claim to make. Makhno in particular was displaying considerable ingenuity in his attacks. He flew the black banner of Anarchy and seemed to come and go faster than an express train. A favorite trick was to dress in Varta uniform, claim he was chasing himself, enter a Varta garrison and then shoot down the occupants. To many he had already become a Robin Hood or Jesse James and dozens of legends were current about his daring exploits. It was forbidden to mention him in anything but a bad light in the newspapers. More folk heroes were not needed in Ukraine. There was a need for order, proper transport, proper communications.

In Kiev, at least, there was now a semblance of Law. German businessmen began to come to the city to trade. I was able to discuss my new company and what it could do. It was important to increase production for export and home consumption. I mentioned new British and American machinery likely to outstrip anything we had. I discussed plans for new plants, new kinds of generators, new manufacturing machinery. This impressed the far-sighted Germans. They were by this time hard-pressed themselves. Many of them confided to me they thought Germany might not win the War. There would be a need to build their country up again very rapidly if it were not itself to fall into the hands of socialists. They suggested I consider locating a branch of my firm in Berlin. The sooner our countries were back to normal the sooner the Reds would be thwarted. Through my business friends I made the acquaintance of top-ranking officers and through these I came to meet the elite of Kiev society. I would now give my name automatically as Pyatnitski: I had been born in Tsaritsyn, my family had been killed by peasants in 1905, I had been brought up by relatives in Kiev, Odessa and Petersburg. This was, of course, fundamentally the truth. To have mentioned our rather ramshackle suburb to the *crème de la crème* would have raised too many eyebrows and closed too many doors. My mother's family, of course, had been well born, so I had an innate ability to mix with the very best people. Many of Kiev's nobility were envious of my "Petersburg manner." They attempted to imitate it. Quite often people made gestures I had made only a moment or two before, or repeated little remarks of mine. I considered adding the title "prince" to my adopted name, but this would have been inappropriate, given the volatile political situation.

I still saw women friends at the Cube, but I had moved back to the Yevropyaskaya, where many of my German acquaintances also stayed. I preferred the classical elegance of silver and gold, of big, clear mirrors, of plush and crystal, of properly dressed waiters and clean, white linen. All this had returned as the Bolshevik butchers departed. The Germans appreciated it, as did the latest wave of Russian émigrés.

If Kiev were becoming packed again, at least it was packed with a better class of people: people with money, common sense and concrete notions of how to counter Bolshevism. Factory owners from Petrograd and Moscow had always argued for faster and better industrialization. They had foreseen the Revolution and blamed the Czar for his short-sightedness. They said the "socialist experiment" would last about as long as Cromwell's Commonwealth. It would be a bad time: a time of destruction and intolerance. Cromwell had killed the King, torn down churches, destroyed cathedrals, but there were still kings, churches and cathedrals in England to this day. It was a powerful argument and an encouraging one, but it was a delusion. Now I know all that can save the world, to paraphrase Lenin, is God plus electricity.

My mother found the changes alarming. While the Bolsheviks had occupied the city and red flags had flown and I had been in prison she had seemed cheerful and content. Every vicissitude had been met with a joke. Esmé and I had marveled at her courage. She had bluffed the Reds away from a search of her home. She had wheedled them into providing her with extra rations. She had become personal laundress to a Chekist commissar. She knew the names of many minor Bolsheviks. She praised Comrade Lenin to the skies. She casually dropped the names of Zinoviev and Radek as if they were old friends. She had almost certainly delayed my execution and thus saved my life. But the strain had taken its toll. As the Bolsheviks retreated, she had had an attack of her old bronchial trouble and had gone to bed. By the time the Hetmanate was established, she was still coughing but insisting on going to work. She began to smell of sal volatile and carbolic soap. The flat was returned to its previous impeccably clean state. She kept apologizing for her "selfishness." She said she had been a "bad mother" to me, that it was her fault I had no father.

"I should never have gone with him," she would say. "He was bad for me and I was bad for him. We were never suited. But it was ten years. And they were not all miserable."

I found her reasoning difficult to follow. She had overtired herself in every way. She became worried by the new wave of pogroms in Podol. I assured her the fires would not spread. Then she said she was afraid the Hetman's army would conscript me. I set her mind at rest. My friends would look after me.

"You were never any trouble," she told me one evening at supper. "Everyone said so. They envied me. 'He's so good. How do you do it?' You were always good. From a baby. You're too kindhearted, Maxim. Don't let some woman hurt you."

"I won't, Mother. I'm only eighteen . . ."

She smiled. "The girls love you, eh? Esmé! Don't the girls all love him?"

"They must do," said Esmé. "He's quite a dandy."

"Remember when you and Esmé used to sleep here? You over the stove, Esmé in her room?" She became excited. "Didn't we all have fun?"

I did not remember anything in particular. But I could not bring myself to say so. "It was great fun," I said. I had to leave then, to do some business.

It was still light as I turned the corner into Kirillovskaya and began to walk down the hill toward the city. The summer evening had a lazy yet unsettled quality to it. There were fewer factory chimneys smoking. Many of the smaller concerns had completely closed down. There was a darker mass of smoke over Podol. The sounds were muted in the streets, yet I heard the wail of a riverboat quite clearly, as if it were only a few feet from me. Gold-and-green domes of distant churches had a dull, deep shine; yellow brick was warm, it seemed to radiate heat; and the smell of grass, trees and flowers from the wooded gorges mingled with scents of soot and oil and that hint of leather always associated with a large occupying army. I could smell horses, too. Here it was as if the town and country met and blended in almost perfect harmony. I wanted to pause, perhaps hoping a tram would come by, but I knew better than to make myself prey for the gangs occupying some of the outlying parks. I glanced automatically up at an embankment. There was nothing but evening haze on hedges. As I walked down the hill into the city, I had a definite sense of God's biding His moment. What puzzles me, to this day, is in what manner we failed. The churches, both Orthodox and Catholic, were never fuller, from morning to night, than in that uncertain summer.

I returned to my hotel to enjoy a second dinner with a Prussian major, an Austrian colonel, a Ukrainian banker and two émigrés recently arrived from Vologda where, they said, anyone with a vocabulary of more than two hundred words was liable to be shot by the Cheka out of hand. I heard stories of Bolsheviks capturing "government" officers, of stripping them naked and cutting their rank insignia into their living flesh before killing them. The days of the French Revolution, the days of the Commune, were as nothing compared to the years and years of the Bolshevik Terror. And what did we have to counter it? Humanity? Religion? All we had was *pazhlost*, that grey, half-dead spiritual state one is in during the winter, when nothing is worthwhile and one can only hope to survive until spring.

In those days ordinary military operations did not exist; the entire pattern of war had gone crazy. It was gradually to become our Civil War. In the Northeast were Czechs and Japanese, Russian Whites and small numbers of Americans and British. Finns, Letts, Lithuanians, Baltic Germans, Poles, French, Greeks, Italians, Rumanians and Serbs were all fighting somewhere. Few of these groups, even if they had been allies against the Germans, were able to agree either strategy or a common aim. Out of China, across the border, there were even raids from mixed groups of Chinese and renegade Cossack bandits bent entirely on looting and pillaging whatever they could get away with. It was like the Middle Ages, only worse.

My mother took, in the coming weeks, to sending me notes in which she apologized for disturbing me, told me not to visit her and insisted I look after myself and be careful. The notes were brought by various means, often left at the hotel by Esmé on her way to work. Sometimes she would enclose a message of her own, insisting I stay away "for your own sake and your mother's." My poor mother was suffering from hysterical exhaustion. She would soon recover. I continued to feel extremely uncomfortable.

My days and evenings were spent advising people on the installation, siting or repair of machinery. For these services I was paid in a variety of ways. Sometimes they were direct cash transactions. Sometimes shares or bonds. I was able to invest some money in France, Switzerland, England and, of course, Germany. Without even possessing an office, living entirely out of the hotel, I was becoming a man of means. I knew this could not last forever. I had still not received decisive backing for my main projects. The political climate remained too unsettled for anyone to consider serious investment in Ukraine. There was, too, a certain amount of "pogromchik" activity in Kiev and outlying regions. This made the German financial people nervous. Many of them had Jewish connections of their own: Jewish masters to whom they were liable. I considered traveling to Berlin, but my mother's health stopped me from coming to a proper decision.

As the evenings grew darker and colder, we began to hear rumors of heavy German defeats, of revolutionary activity similar to the kind which had sparked the Petrograd risings. It was obvious that my German acquaintances were wondering if they themselves would have a country to which they could safely return. In the meantime, Ataman Petlyura was gaining strength. His Cossack cavalry and his Sich riflemen were joined by many irregulars and it seemed he represented a more popular and stronger force than Skoropadskya's. The Germans were thinking they had backed the wrong man.

The Hetman should at least have made some pretense of deferring to peasant demands, but he was too honorable to do anything save obey his own conscience and God's will. And so he fell. Winter drew down upon Kiev and my hopes were dashed. Almost overnight, my German colleagues left, my Hetmanate contacts deserted me, and the politicians drove me again from the Yevropyaskaya Hotel. Germany's Hindenburg Line had been breached. The German Chancellor proposed to accept an armistice plan drawn up by the Americans. The British refused to consider the idea. They wanted blood. By November a Communist Soviet was established in Bavaria and revolution broke out in Berlin itself. The Kaiser abdicated. Prince Max of Baden, the Chancellor, relinquished his position to a socialist. Germany became a Republic and was no longer an ally against Bolshevism. Maps were taken out and lines were redrawn. We had lost our Crimean territories to Tartars. In spite of the treaty signed with the Don and Kuban Cossacks we had not gained a real ally against the socialists. Just before Christmas 1918, Petlyura was back in full command promising, in Ukrainian, a secure national future. Not only Russians found his posturing dangerous, a good many Ukrainians decided it would be wiser to give up the struggle. Half the industrialists vanished. During the festive season I again entertained my family at a good hotel; again I spoke of my plans for my engineering business. But it seemed I had achieved little beyond making some money, most of which I should probably never be able to claim. Even my work was likely to be curtailed by the socialists. I had no Special Diploma. I had no career worth speaking of. There was hardly any working industry in Ukraine. I was unable to read most of the newspapers because they were suddenly in an alien language. I had trouble filling in simple forms. I was insulted if I did not ask for my tram fare in Ukrainian. I had again become some sort of second-class citizen. I thought of going to Odessa where at least now it would be possible to book passage on a ship. But I would bide my time for a little while, until the Greens settled in. I moved back to my mother's flat. She was cheerful and well again. This was a relief. But her moods remain a mystery to me to this day.

Esmé had continued nursing through at least three different regimes. She was beginning to look drawn. It was Esmé, I thought, who suffered from exhaustion now. My mother devoted herself, with maniacal quixotism, to learning Ukrainian from the badly printed books available. New schools and universities had been established. All, of course, taught in Ukrainian. There was no longer a chance for me to work as a teacher. I had not received a single reply to my requests for a position, though it was generally accepted amongst my friends and the business community that I had done brilliantly at Petrograd. I admit the impression was useful. I was often, these days, addressed as "Doctor" and more than once I was called "Professor." I found this comforting. It did no harm. When I received my Special Diploma I could go on to receive a proper doctorate almost anywhere. I want no one to think I made these claims for myself. But life is often hard. If people wish to have illusions about one, then it is sometimes foolish to spend unnecessary energy denying them. Doubtless because she was overworking, Esmé could sometimes be condescending and irritatingly sharp when I wanted to discuss my plans for the future. On the other hand my mother would sometimes call me "Doctor" just for the sound of it. She would stand on our landing and say, for instance: "Well, well, Doctor, here's our old friend Captain Brown to see us."

Captain Brown was beginning to decay almost by the day. His face was blotchy and his hands had an obvious drunkard's shake. His craving for alcohol was pathetic. Sometimes I was tempted not to pander to him. But Esmé would say, "What else has he to live for?" and I could not argue. His stories became more confused, though substantially familiar. He was baffled by what he called "this fake language with its fake government, its fake bank notes and its fake history." We hushed him when he uttered such sentiments in Russian. It did not matter when he spoke English as he did most frequently now. Esmé had learned a little English from me, but not enough for her to understand him clearly. Once, she told me, he had been found in Bessarabskaya market where he had gone up to one of Petlyura's Sich riflemen and asked him which circus he belonged to. He had spoken first in English, then in French, then in German, then in Russian and then, it seemed, in Polish. The soldier had either misunderstood him or had not bothered to take exception to the insult. A couple of friends had brought the captain home.

I visited Bessarabskaya myself. Cocaine was plentiful and cheap there, though not of particularly good quality. I was building up a supply for a rainy day, as they say in England. The market was booming, with old family heirlooms to be purchased for a mere *chag* or two. Chags and *karvovantsis* were the new monetary units. The notes were so easily forged nobody bothered to check them unless it was in the post office. Inflation was running at a ridiculous rate. At least for a while the prostitutes became younger and prettier. Two of them actually turned out to be the virgins they claimed to be. I was again in a mood to take my pleasures as they came, in case they should not come too frequently later.

If only all Cossacks and those claiming Cossack freedoms had managed to work together in one huge host we would easily have driven the Reds back to Moscow (now their capital). Trotsky, Lenin, Stalin and the rest would have ended their days as querulous old exiles. The genuinely humane people would have encouraged a Russian renaissance. Our country would have been the most glorious center for the flowering of art and science the world had known since the days of the Italian Medici. Everybody says so. What drove Sikorsky away? Bolsheviks. What drove Prokofiev away? Bolsheviks.

My mother blossomed under Petlyura even more wonderfully than she had under the Bolsheviks. I offer no interpretation. Admittedly things were quieter in the outlying suburbs. There were no more fires burning in Podol. My mother was distressed by inhumanity of any sort. When people expressed their dislike of Jews she always became upset, refusing to join in. The usual talk was harmless enough. But she would say "God has designed a role for each of us. It is not the race or the religion, it is the man or the woman that is important." I was thus brought up in a more tolerant atmosphere than most Kievan children. It has helped me understand people, encouraged my humanity, allowed me to mix, without feeling uncomfortable, with all sorts, black or white, high or low. When we heard that French Zouaves had occupied Odessa, in support of Denikin, that the city was "colonized by black men," as the papers put it, we were all horrified. But Mother made a joke of it. "It will be lovely," she said, "to see a bit of extra color in Ukraine." I began to understand how she and my father had come together. She had a broad, humane and trusting faith in the beauty of the world, of people's natural tendency to help one another. He shared her ideals but felt betrayed by those he had sought to support. People were far more complex and yet far more ordinary than he wished to believe. The socialist utopia did not spring from the ground overnight. He began to attack those whom he regarded as responsible for threatening his hopes. The simple fact is that my mother was mature, in the way of women, and could see that the best way of improving things was to lead a good, clean, kindly life.

Revolutionists almost invariably attempt to simplify the workings of the human heart. This planet of ours is full of generous, warm-spirited, good-humored and intelligent women supporting raving, idiotic fools like my father. All that was ever betrayed was his own humanity. How long can a woman live with a jealous man? That is the simple question in which lies the answer to my own background, I think.

Those months of the Directorate became relatively easy. I began to move into the world again. Many of the new politicians were sympathetic to my schemes for mechanization and industrialization. "We must use the wealth of the Ukraine," they said, "to make ourselves strong and independent." So, for the time being, I became a nationalist, couching my arguments in terms of the province rather than the country. Luckily the letterheads and cards I had had printed—ALL-UKRAINE ENGINEERING CONSULTANTS. *Managing Director Dr. M. A. Pyatnitski*— still had the appropriate ring and the hotel Yevropyaskaya, having become something of a headquarters for Petlyura's henchmen, was a perfect address. I moved back into my old suite. I began to entertain as I had done before. Inflation, the retreat of the Germans, a lack of faith by Russian and Ukrainian investors in Petlyura's reforms meant I had to augment my income again. It was easy enough to do. I had contacts in every part of the city. But it was irritating, for instance, to be a courier for someone who did not want it evident he sniffed cocaine; or to arrange girls for some under-Minister anxious that his wife should not find out; or to act as a go-between for a factory owner needing certain forms stamped in a hurry; but it continued to help me keep my way of life and my friends. I was an agent of change, a catalyst. Much which was good about Petlyura's government was directly or indirectly to do with help and advice I had been able to provide.

I was not distracted, now, by notes from my mother. I did make use, though, of Esmé's free time. With her strawberry-blond hair and her superlative taste she made a perfect hostess for my special evenings. Everyone complimented me on Mme. Pyatnitski if they were under the impression we were married, or on my "fiancée" or on my "cousin." To intimates I let it be known she was my half-sister. I think that spiritually she was my sister through and through. It was no lie to claim a little blood, too. We had mingled it, often enough, in our childish games. Esmé found enjoyment in what she called my "farces." She would cheerfully lend her energy and her imagination while always insisting that her world outside was "real." This was because she was a nurse and saw so much of the disease, malnutrition and physical destruction. Gangs of homeless children, *bezhprizhorni*, were beginning to become a serious problem. They had the courage of the pack, the hunger of starving dogs. Cripples and wounded in the streets were impossible to count. Beggars were given public handouts but there were far too many for the system to accommodate. A strong police force was badly needed. Haidamaki militia were inclined either to sudden savagery or absolute laziness when it came to maintaining the Law. There were attempts to recruit former police officers back into the service. But this was only partially successful. In time, Petlyura might have modified and improved conditions, and even rid himself of the hampering burden of nationalism. He did not hate Russia, he said. He hated the "enslaving institutions." He also, I know, hated the Orthodox Church. He had been raised a Catholic, like so many Ukrainians, and here was a fundamental difference few were anxious to touch upon. We were witnessing a low-key religious war.

We had a taste of the old rivalry between the Roman Empire of the West and the Hellenic Empire of the East. Kiev saw as many emperors come and go in as short a time as Rome or Constantinople when those Empires fell apart. As my mother said in her merry way: "At least under the Rus or the Tartars people had time to get used to their rulers. These days it's impossible to know who you're supposed to cheer." But she liked Petlyura and his white horse and his gaudy Haidamaki with their baggy trousers and fancy waistcoats and scalplocks. The Haidamaki had saved Ukraine from Polish oppression in the eighteenth century. They represented another calling on the past in support of a hoped-for future. Ends are defeated by means. The future will always be defeated by the past. The past is a useful metaphor but it is a terrible precedent.

My mother hoped the laundry would be nationalized. As manageress, she would have security without the same responsibility. Petlyura's brand of socialism, she said, seemed fair enough. Petlyura needed to court what remained of the business people. Again I found myself rising in the world. I knew everyone. I was invited to various high-level meetings. I was called "Doctor Pyatnitski" by everyone and regarded as a scientific *Wunderkind*. I was allowed to expand on the possibilities of Ukrainian monorails, Ukrainian civil airlines, Ukrainian garden cities for the workers. My ideas no longer struck people as fantastic. All Ukraine's potential was to be used. I mentioned special kinemas, education centers, aerial guard-ships which could protect our frontiers from Bolshevik aggression. We should soon have the cream of Russian genius, I pointed out, back in Kiev. Kiev could become the capital of a new Russian Empire (diplomatically I termed it "an expanded Ukrainian state"). I spoke of my dreams and I helped others to dream. That was my gift. I offered it to to government and at last the government began to accept. I had no official position. I thought it foolish to accept one. I was only just nineteen years old. At last I had found a ready audience for more complicated ideas, such as my invisible-ray device. I made no large claims. Such machines could, however, form a defensive ring ("an iron ring of light" as someone said) about a city, making it almost invulnerable to attack. This was the nearest thing to the recent force-field notions of the Americans.

We needed something quickly. We had the Poles attacking from the West, Whites from the South, Reds from the North. There were Rumanians invading Bessarabia. French and Greek forces had been landed in Odessa. A variety of Cossack and pseudo-Cossack insurgent chieftains (atamany) and Anarchist brigands, such as Makhno, changed sides almost as rapidly as the regular units, a few of which still supported Skoropadskya. Ataman Hrihorieff (sometimes called Grigoriev in English) had turned against the Directorate to join the Bolsheviks. He took with him a large rabble of so-called insurgent cavalry; looters and pogromchiks to a man. We in Kiev believed no rumors whatsoever. If Bolsheviks were said to be occupying the Left Bank Dnieper, we cocked our heads. If we heard no unusual artillery or rifle fire, we continued about our business. At that time Petlyura seemed likely to drive the Bolsheviks out of Russia altogether. Then he allowed the farce of "Ukrainianization" of the Church. Suddenly Orthodox services were performed in Ukrainian and half the Church's intellectuals were dismissed from their offices or actually killed by their parishioners, simply for arguing the unchallengeable fact that there was no such thing as a Ukrainian Church, since all were subordinate to the Patriarch of Constantinople. The nationalist mania was spreading.

It was to destroy my homeland, the birthplace of Russian culture.

ELEVEN

One evening in the middle of January 1919 I was invited to dinner at the Savoy Hotel by a group of industrialists, educationalists and politicians. They said the meeting was to be of considerable importance. My presence was absolutely necessary.

I arrived at the hotel dressed in my best. I wore my heavy fox-fur overcoat, hat, gloves and my felt-and-rubber galoshes. I carried my silver-topped cane. All these were left in the foyer. The manager apologized that the elevator was temporarily out of action. In a dark three-piece suit, with a conventional collar and tie, I made my way up the wide staircase to the first floor. I stopped outside a huge door which I assumed led into a ballroom. I was admitted by a uniformed servant. It was, in fact, the master suite of the hotel. It put my little suite at the Yevropyaskaya to shame. I walked along a short passage which was entirely mirrored on sides and ceiling. A green curtain was pulled back to allow me into the main dining room which, with its crystal and gilt, had not changed since Czarist days. It was occupied by cigar-smoking men. Some were in evening dress and some wore uniform. Others were dressed as I was in what were in those days recognized as tastefully classless suits. I was greeted by the journalist Elanski. He had the reputation of being a pro-Bolshevik and a terrorist. He was a mild-looking man with spectacles and a goatee. I had met him at the Cube where, because I kept my peace, I was considered a socialist sympathizer. Elanski introduced me to a variety of men whose names I knew. They shook hands with me and thanked me for sparing the time to come. They evidently believed me an important figure, but I was not sure what my importance to them was. Shortly after I had arrived, the green curtain was swept back and our self-styled Supreme Commander, Semyon Petlyura, came in. He was shorter than I had guessed, with the pink, smooth skin known as "typically Ukrainian," a small mustache and a birdlike way of moving his fingers together when he talked. He wore a green-and-gold uniform. I addressed him as "Pan," which was a term used only in Ukraine and Poland. He said he would prefer to be known here as Comrade Petlyura. He smiled. He said it made him feel more relaxed; that he was amongst friends. He, too, thanked me very deeply for finding time to join the meeting. We sat down to dinner. To my surprise I was given a place on Petlyura's left, while Elanski occupied his right. Next to me was a general and opposite the general was a high-ranking minister in charge of the Civilian War Effort. I was called "Comrade Pyatnitksi" throughout the dinner and found the fact privately amusing. I understood during the meal something of the euphoria of holding powerful political office. It made me more determined than ever to keep out of politics in future. All the men there were worried about Bolshevik gains. Without proper allies our lines of supplies and communications would soon be cut off. Kiev would have to be abandoned. The insurgents were unreliable. Most of them had little idea of the importance of railways and telegraphs. They tended to fight only for local territory, often with the intention, Petlyura thought, of setting up tiny nations along old Cossack lines. He was even uncertain of his own Zaporozhian forces once they had gained what they wanted. "We have plenty of cavalry, plenty of infantry, a fair number of machine guns, plenty of trains, no aeroplanes, little artillery worthy of the name, no tanks or armored cars. In fact, we are only slightly better equipped to fight a modern war than Stenka Razin." While we laughed at this, Petlyura's small face became stern. He made a movement of his lower lip, which had the effect of strengthening his jaw. "And that is why, Comrade Doctor, we have asked you to let us know your views."

I was taken aback. "I'm no strategist."

"But you are a scientist." Elanski leaned forward. "And a brilliant one. Everyone speaks of you. I've met people from Petrograd, from

Moscow, from Odessa. All say you're one of the most far-sighted men of our day. A child genius, who built his first flying machine at the age of eight."

I smiled, holding up my hand. I wore rings, now, of Ukrainian filigree silver. They gave me a vaguely nationalist air without actually identifying me as anything in particular. "Stories of that sort are apt to be exaggerated. I have a number of inventions, many theories, some practical ideas. But without proper materials I am unable to make the necessary experiments. Thus, gentlemen, comrades, you find me in Limbo."

"Can you give us aeroplanes?" asked the general. His name was Konovalets and he was scarcely older than I, though his face was set like limestone.

"Not without proper plants and expert men. You must know this already. French aeroplanes are your best hope."

Petlyura spoke in a small voice. "We need to buy time against Lenin and Trotsky."

I looked questioningly at Elanski, who shrugged. "They won't guarantee us anything."

I was still cautious. Should the Bolsheviks enter Kiev next week, Elanski might be singing a different song. His type was becoming familiar in modern Russia.

"We had heard about a kind of ray. Like concentrated sunlight." Someone spoke from the other end of the table. "Have you developed this ray?"

Now I laughed aloud. A few months ago nobody had taken the idea seriously. Tonight they ignored practical mechanical conceptions and grabbed desperately at a notion which every one of them would normally have dismissed as cheap fiction. But now the Reds were knocking on Kiev's gates. Some there, I could tell, were still a little doubtful. There was no way in which I could convince them. I did not intend to try. I could make no claims until a prototype had been built. "Ray-cannon are not easily developed. A good deal of money and equipment is required."

Petlyura was impatient. "You can have what you need. Doctor Braun," he indicated an elderly gentleman, "is a scientist from Kiev University. He can put all their resources at your disposal."

"When I have heard the young man's idea," said Braun in a deep voice. He gave me a stare.

"I have done some research," I said. "I believe it's possible to concentrate a ray of light until it is so powerful it can cut through steel."

"It is not an unfamiliar theory," Braun agreed. "I don't see how you can apply it."

"A special vacuum tube would be needed. Like a very large radio valve. Shall I describe it as simply as possible?"

"For my sake," he said. The old man had a sardonic humor lacking in most of his colleagues. Perhaps he had less to lose. I described how mercury would be introduced into a tube and boiled to drive out air. The mercury vapor would then be trapped while the tube was sealed, with wires extruding. Low voltage could be applied to a heating element in the tube. Once it reached a temperature of 175° Celsius a high voltage would be applied to the electrodes, producing an electrical discharge in the mercury vapor. The excited mercury ions would then emit a light beyond the spectrum perceived by the human eye.

"I call this Ultra-Violet light," I said. "Mirrors or quartz lenses could be used to focus it."

"And how much electrical power would you need?" Braun was impressed. He frowned over some notes he had made in pencil on the tablecloth.

"Obviously, the better the source of power, the stronger the beam."

"It is violet in color, the ray?" said someone else.

I began to explain, but Petlyura gripped my arm. "How many of these ray machines could you build to give us, say, a month before help arrived?"

"There would have to be an experimental model first. After that, it should be fairly easy to manufacture more. If the generators were available to power them."

"Would the generators in the electricity stations do?" Petlyura inquired.

"I think so." I had not expected such an offer. This meant he was willing to divert Kiev's entire power supply. I was flattered. "Cables would have to be laid."

"Where would the machines best be sited?"

"On the heights." General Konovalets was adamant. "That gives a sweep, you see. If they were used in the outlying suburbs they would be too cumbersome to move quickly, eh?"

"The machines themselves would be transported in the normal way of artillery, but the power sources are the problem." I admired his quick grasp. "One can't go dragging huge cables all over Kiev. The people, as well as the streets and the houses, would get in the way."

"They always do!" Konovalets spoke with mock despair. "St. Andrews would be one good site."

"You mean the observation gallery, near the dome?" I considered this. "The only thing I wonder about there is—" I hesitated, not knowing whether to bring the question of religion into a discussion with socialists, many of whom might be militant atheists.

"Sacrilege," said Petlyura. "Is that what you're worrying about? You're a believer? And a scientist?"

"—the problem of diverting power to such a high point."

"There is no sacrilege," said Konovalets quietly, "in defending ourselves against Bolshevism. They are sworn to destroy all religions."

I saw at once that he was right. Indeed, it was almost as if God were providing us with a site from which we could defend His faith.

"We'll construct the experimental model in St. Andrew's." Petlyura lit a cigarette as waiters took away our dishes. "Power is easily diverted?" He looked toward his Minister.

"Not that easily, Supreme Commander."

"But it can be done?"

Braun said, "It might be best having some sort of emergency source. A small petrol-fueled generator, or banks of Voltaic cells."

"Voltaic cells are a bit old-fashioned." I smiled.

"I've always found them reliable. They don't break down."

"But they're hard to operate. The connections?"

Braun shrugged. "I still advise a separate source of energy. If, in the middle of fighting the Bolsheviks, they capture our electricity stations, then we have no weapon."

I was forced to agree. I now understood his logic. My mistake, as usual, had been to miss the practicalities as I became obsessed with the pure idea. The very term "death ray" was unpalatable to me. These days we have such words as "anti-personnel devices," which keep the entire thing in perspective.

I had been elevated from my rather ambiguous status in the scientific and business community to a full-fledged member of the socialist Petlyurist group. I was nervous. I asked Petlyura what my powers were.

"Whatever you need to fulfill your task." He was expansive. "You may requisition whatever you want—men and material—so long as you do not actually interfere with our current military operations. We have Russian and Polish chauvinists to contend with. And Denikin is likely to prove a highly unreliable ally, if he actually is an ally. He, too, is a chauvinist, but at the moment he hates Trotsky worse than me. What will become of him if the French decide he is an embarrassment?"

"Let him go to Turkey with a hundred riders," said Konovalets. "Things are so bad there, he'll be able to conquer the whole damned country in a week and have himself crowned Czar of Constantinople."

Petlyura raised his champagne glass. "Death to the enemies of Ukraine!"

I sipped a reluctant toast. As a "Russian chauvinist," I was not in complete accord with our Ataman.

"Twentieth-century methods will produce a twentieth-century revolution," said Petlyura. "And it will impress the superstitious peasants with the importance of science. I hear you are a linguist, Comrade Pyatnitski?"

"I know English, German and some French," I said, "as well as Polish and Czech."

"And Ukrainian?"

"The local dialect?" I experienced a moment of terror.

Petlyura changed the subject. Then I thought him a gentleman, whatever else he stood for. My diplomacy had not worked, but neither had it misfired. Official Ukrainian was a form of Galician not easily assimilated even by Kievans who spoke their own patois. The language was about as authentic as the average Republican bank note.

We were all of us in that candlelit room speaking, needless to say, purest Petersburg Russian. Petlyura said, "I would imagine the French would pay for the secret of your ray?"

It had not occurred to me. I think Petlyura saw this in my face. He smiled reassuringly as he patted my shoulder. "It is all right, citizen. You would not be here if I took you for a traitor. But I shall dispatch a courier. We'll tell Freydenberg we're in the process of constructing a secret weapon. He must move their forces up quickly or it will fall into Bolshevik hands."

"That is strategy." Konovalets was approving.

"It's diplomacy," said Petlyura. His pink cheeks beamed. "And we thought it would be so easy to save Ukraine."

"I shall need authority," I said.

"Give him a rank, Konovalets." Petlyura spoke carelessly.

Konovalets shrugged. "You are now a major in the Republican Army."

And that was how I gained my first military title. Quite legitimately, but without having once spilled a drop of blood.

"You'd better have that confirmed," Petlyura told an aide. "Is there anything else, Comrade Doctor?"

"I have been expecting papers from Petrograd," I said. "They were held up. They're probably destroyed now. A Special Diploma."

"A Russian diploma? They're useless here. Professor Braun?" Petlyura had these people hanging on his every word. The professor understood as rapidly as had the general. "You need what? Some sort of diploma? We could give you an honorary degree from the University."

"It would not be the same." I explained what had happened in Petrograd. "My dissertation warranted a Special Diploma, you see. The equivalent of a doctorate." I reached into my pocket and produced my wallet, handing him a copy of Professor Vorsin's letter.

Braum read the signature first. "I know Vorsin. This is his. If the Comrade Secretary—Ah, Pan . . ." He looked up at Petlyura as if suddenly uncertain of himself.

"Is it important to you?" Petlyura asked me. He took the letter from Braun. He read it. "Well, it confirms what we have heard. Is that your price, Comrade?"

"There is no price," I said, "for resisting Trotsky and Antonov. It's thanks to them I have nothing on paper."

"This letter is certainly clear. Isn't it, Braun?"

"Absolutely. We can—we have diplomas—" The professor spread his hands. "If a Doctor of Science is in order . . . ?"

Petlyura made a quick movement of his head and stared directly into my eyes. Then he looked at his napkin. "Will that suit you, Major Pyatnitski?"

I sighed and reached for my crystal goblet. "These are insecure times."

Petlyura called down the table to his old comrade, Vinnichenko, another pro-Bolshevik. "Do you approve of this now, Comrade President?"

Vinnichenko, a literary man with very little stomach for what was happening, looked tired. He said sourly: "Certainly, Comrade Supreme Commander. If the Praetorians have agreed."

Konovalets scratched the back of his neck. "This is silly. The Sich riflemen are loyal. We don't wield power."

I thought I was to witness open argument amongst the various Directorate factions. Vinnichenko said wearily, "I apologize, Konovalets. But you're the only one the French seem to trust at all."

"It's because they've never heard of me." The general smiled.

I laughed politely. Konovalets had the look of someone who might well be taking the reins of power soon. This was not to be the case. Colonel Freydenberg, in charge of the French, found it impossible to tell one socialist from another. He had been insisting, I was to learn, that all "reds" be dismissed from the Directorate. Petlyura, Vinnichenko and the others controlled the Directorate. Freydenberg's ultimatum was tantamount to demanding the dismissal of the whole government before he would come to the relief of Kiev. To Freydenberg, Petlyura and his gang were no more than bandit warlords. His only sympathy was for Denikin's Whites. The Russian Volunteer Army was larger, more reliable, and represented the Czar.

Konovalets' Galician sharpshooters were the Directorate's strength. This was why Vinnichenko had called them Praetorians. They were grouped in the outlying suburbs ready to meet Bolsheviks moving toward the city. No newspaper reported this fact. I was equally unaware of the immediate danger after I had left the meeting. Kiev seemed very quiet. The winter was cold. The snow was hard. I could not believe very much would change until March. In the meantime I had achieved both my Doctor of Science, and the rank of Major. As I had once dreamed, I had been honored by an entire government. It was ironic. I could not abide their idiotic politics but I admit I was momentarily seduced by the chance, at long last, to work on one of my inventions.

I had a note sent to Mother, briefly outlining my good news. She replied via the same messenger. I was to be careful. I was not to worry about her. It seemed every time I tasted success she became frightened. She had been too long with her head down, I suppose. It was hard to blame her.

Next day a diploma from the University of Kiev was delivered to my suite. Maxim Arturovitch Pyatnitski was a Doctor of Science who had graduated on 15 January 1919. Shortly afterward an officer of the Sichovi Striltsi arrived to salute me, address me as "Major" and hand me an ordinary paper envelope containing all necessary insignia. I was expected, apparently, to provide my own uniform. I would have a special white one. I thought the matter over again seriously. I put the envelope in a drawer of my escritoire for the meantime. I was becoming identified with a specific political group. If the Bolsheviks arrived I was likely to be rounded up and this time I would certainly be shot unless I was very careful.

I prayed my so-called "Violet Ray" would be effective against the Reds. Petlyura had given me the idea of taking the secret as soon as possible to Odessa. The French garrison would put the device at Denikin's disposal. The entire fate of Russia lay in my hands. I received another message: A note from Petlyura confirming every assistance, giving me carte-blanche powers. The monks and priests had been ousted from control of St. Andrew's. I was now the new proprietor. This caused me some uncertainty. But God has His own methods. And surely my light beam issuing from the great blue-and-white tower would fill even the Bolsheviks with an awe of the Almighty?

Work began that day on producing a suitable vacuum tube. We were hampered on every side. Desertions at the glassworks; promises of copper wire which failed to have any substance; engineers suddenly disappearing; Russian mechanics hearing of some Bolshevik or insurgent victory and trying to get to Odessa or Yalta before all escape routes were cut off. The chaos in the streets returned. Petlyura's forces were melting away. The French were right not to trust him. In the meantime the bell tower of St. Andrew's became the housing for my equipment's alternative power source: banks of Voltaic batteries, connected with heavy copper wire, operated by a monstrous Nife Switch. In the chamber below I discarded tube after tube, mirror after mirror. Power cables were carried through the sacred corridors and up the steps of that wonderful building, ready to connect to my machine when it was ready. The monks were bewildered but had been convinced by Petlyura of the necessity for using the place in the war against the Bolsheviks. The tube was secured in a sturdy tripod frame of aluminum and wood and looked makeshift. The mirrors were large at the end nearest the tube and shrank to smaller sizes, tapering almost to a point. Quartz lenses would have worked much better. Some were "being requisitioned," but did not arrive. We looked down over the Podol ghetto. I could almost see my own street, higher up the hill. As one of the soldiers remarked, "If we can't wipe out Antonov, we can finish off a few Jews before we leave."

With the help of some cocaine, I worked rapidly at the device. Petlyura himself came to see me three times. On the third I was able to demonstrate some of the machine's potential by directing the fluorescence onto a sheet of newspaper which almost immediately burst into flames. He was impressed.

"But will it burn Bolsheviks?"

"It's a question of power," I said. "It should have limitless capacity so long as it has enough electricity."

Petlyura seemed not to have slept. He was sallow. His eyes had a withdrawn look. "I shall give you the entire city, the entire Ukraine," he told me, "if it will work. This will offer the people heart. This will bring the soldiers back."

He had become desperate. I began to wonder what my next move should be. At the first opportunity I had my official car take me to Mother's flat. There I warned her of the possibility of the Bolsheviks reoccupying the city. She laughed at me.

"The Bolshviks were here before. And we are still here. So what is there to worry about?"

"It might be necessary, Mother, to go to Odessa. The French are in control there. We shall be safe in Odessa."

"Safe in Odessa?" For some bizarre and mysterious reason she began to cackle.

I waited until Esmé arrived and told her my news. It was getting late. I was due back at my equipment. I could not afford to offend Petlyura, especially since he was becoming obviously overtired. I gave her an outline of what was happening. I begged her to be ready to leave with Mother and Captain Brown, if he would go.

She was confused. "The countryside is full of bandits. I have my work."

"There'll be as much work for you in Odessa as here."

She saw the point. "When should we leave?"

"It might be wise to go before me. I can send for you if things quiet down. I am working . . ." I held my tongue. "There is some hope."

"I will not go to Odessa," said my mother. "I have never been to Odessa."

I took my watch from my pocket. It was getting too late. "What harm will come to you? You can stay with Uncle Semya."

"Semya has been very kind. I don't think Evgenia would like me there. She wrote a funny letter about you. And some girl. I burned it. She's always been jealous."

"Mother, the Bolsheviks could take Kiev any day, unless my work is effective. I am asking you to be ready to leave. Once they are here, it will be impossible to get on a train."

"That's true," Esmé agreed. "You should do as Max says, Yelisaveta Filipovna. We love you."

"My laundry," she said, "is my life. I would be foolish to go to Odessa. Am I to retire to a seaside dacha?"

"You could," I said. "You would enjoy it."

"I would not."

I had no more time to coax her. "You must promise to take Mother and Captain Brown. When you get my message." I looked into Esmé's wonderful blue eyes. I kissed her on the lips before leaving.

Kiev was not so much a city under siege as one which seemed already to have fallen. Haidamaki had looted Podol with such efficiency they had hardly time for their normal pogromist activities. No fires were started, few Jews were killed, unless they seriously interfered with the business at hand. Shadowy groups of men with sacks and rifles dodged back and forth across the street as my motor, flying Petlyura's official flag, rolled over cobbles which had not been cleared of snow for days. I was glad to return to the relative security of Kreshchatik. It was protected by more disciplined troops. At the half-deserted Savoy I quickly went to the main suite to report my progress to an anxious Petlyura who laughed, turning to Vinnichenko. The curtains were closed. Vinnichenko was peering through them like a spinster at a neighbor. "Are we going to hear any more of 'cooperation' and 'evacuation'?" Vinnichenko shrugged. He was probably disappointed not to be able to greet Trotsky, Stalin and Antonov personally. Petlyura asked me, "How are things in the city?"

"Troops are looting it, Supreme Commander."

"We should never have trusted the ones who came over from Skoropadskya."

"We should never have thought we could hold Kiev." Vinnichenko turned his back on us both. "We should have stayed with the peasants and not thrown in with Russians and Jews."

Petlyura clapped me on the back. "Do not let anyone tell you I have anything against your people."

I smiled, feeling my power over him. Was he trying to placate the Russian "Katsapi" billy goats he had so despised? "You don't hate us anymore?"

"It's the peasants," he said. "Russians and Jews own all the shops, all the factories, all the machinery." His voice had begun to rise. He controlled himself. "Is the ray ready for final tests?"

It could not be tested until I had more power. I thought it would be pointless to requisition civilian electricity and harm public morale until the last possible moment.

Petlyura became immediately calm, as if responding to morphine. He stroked his mustache and gave me an encouraging wink. "Off you go, then, Professor."

The Savoy echoed. Some of the mirrors had been removed, as if the entire building were being made ready for shipment. There were very few shops open in Kreshchatik. Many were boarded up. I was tempted to drift down to Bessarabskaya and find myself one of the really young girls who were now working there. I had developed a taste for them. I was certainly a better customer than most they could expect. But with some weariness I directed the driver to return to St. Andrew's and the tower, which was full of light, like a beacon in the darkness and confusion. Climbing the stairs to the top of the church, I heard distant noises from the city: gunfire, shouts and screams. All these had become familiar. I wondered if I would miss them if they were stopped.

Some new, larger tubes had been delivered. I admired the workmanship. The corporal who was helping me said that they would probably be the last we would get. I asked why.

He grinned. "They looted the glassworks about two hours ago, that's why."

"What do they want with glass?"

"They thought they'd find gold."

I inspected my tubes. They were excellently made. I began carefully to unscrew the clamps holding the smaller tube on the swivel stand. I replaced it with a new one. "Gold?"

"They guessed the Jews were making gold," said the soldier. "Because of the crucibles and stuff."

"The glassworks isn't Jewish." I connected up the wires.

"They got even angrier when they found that out." The corporal laughed.

I stood back to admire the machine. Once the mirrors were properly aligned and more power diverted, I thought it would be possible to try out the ray on one of the trees near the yacht club. It still stood, deserted, on Trukhanov Island, on the other side of the icebound river. I lit a cigarette and then, in a democratic mood, handed one to the soldier. He was impressed by the gesture. "Thanks, Comrade."

"What about Bolsheviks? Will we beat them?" I felt it was important to know what a regular soldier, with some experience, thought. He was more reliable than Petlyura.

"It depends. They're nearly all Russians. They look down their noses at Ukrainians. It keeps them together. But Ukrainians can't even agree on what to call their commanders."

I nodded. "They'll side with anyone, it seems. The Hetman, Petlyura, Hrihorieff, Trotsky, Korniloff . . ."

The soldier drew on the long paper tube. "This is good tobacco. Is it Turkish?"

"I think so."

He made a gesture toward the suburbs and beyond. "Those poor bastards out there have nothing. They don't believe in governments —nationalist, Czarist, Bolshevik, Polish, French. They believe in freedom and owning a plot of land."

"To nurture their own gardens," I said.

"If you like."

"Voltaire," I explained.

"I know." He was amused. "That's why they put me with you. I'm the intellectual of the division." He began to laugh. "I did a year at technical college before I was conscripted."

"You were at the Front?"

"Galicia."

"You'll fight the Bolsheviks when they attack?"

"You're crazy," he said. He patted my tube. "This will fight the Bolsheviks, Comrade Professor. I'll be running like fuck for the nearest train."

I laughed with him. We were of an identical mind.

I left him on guard when I had lined up the available mirrors and tested the projector once more on a paper target. I had slept only a few hours during the whole week but I still did not feel like going to bed. I directed the driver to Bessarabskaya. He told me it was four in the morning. From all around I heard cackling laughter, breaking windows, the creak of handcarts bearing away loot. We returned to the hotel where I found a mesesage from Esmé. A train departed for Odessa in the morning. She would do all she could to be on it, but she needed extra papers, travel permits. I telephoned a good friend of mine in the appropriate ministry. I was impossibly lucky. He, too, was not sleeping. Within an hour, I had documents for myself, my mother, Captain Brown and Esmé. I put my permit with my passport, summoned a soldier from downstairs, and sent him to Esmé. For once I was relieved that neither Esmé nor my mother was resisting me. I fell asleep suddenly and was awakened at noon by a nightmare in which I, several years younger, was writhing in the mud, the only figure on a vast, deserted battlefield. There were bullets in my stomach.

I did not immediately open my eyes because I thought for a second I was in Odessa again, listening to the sound of the Arcadian surf. My eyes were filled with yellow light, like blood. I realized that the sun was out. It was the first sunshine I had seen for a long time. I rolled over and looked about me. My apartment was insane. I had not noticed before that it was so untidy. Yellow blood from the sun. It ran in a series of canals, cut across the steppe. It ran swiftly and could not be navigated or crossed. The booming continued. It was, of course, artillery fire. It might have been our own. It had been impossible to distinguish friends from enemies. They battled over Kiev. They came and went. They all said they were saving us. Some cities are fated to become symbols. In those days we lived symbolically in a symbolic city. The mad universe of the Symbolists had for a while become reality. Had all those people I despised in *Petrograd* been prescient? Or had they created this world because it was the only environment in which they felt at ease? It was a madman's world. Someone was standing in the room. A young corporal in a Cossack coat. He held his sheepskin hat in his gloved hands. I think he said the situation was urgent. Yellow blood still filled my eyes. I got up. I was wearing my clothes.

Hannibal's Numidian cavalry drove deeper and deeper into Spain, that pious land; drove deeper toward the shrine of the Holy Virgin. And the steppe was broken by black trees. Burning bronze ran through the Kiev gorges. And I was on fire; and my mother's black clothes were on fire. "A train?"

Cossack: "They thought you'd been killed. The enemy is close. You are needed, Pan."

He spoke with a strong Polish accent. My Polish was weak; from Mother. She had taught me once. And I had listened to her nightmares.

"Has the train left? The morning train for Odessa?"

"The emergency train. Yes."

"Was it well protected?"

"Armored, I think."

I went with this Polish Cossack. There were little girls singing a huge chorus in my mind. Pure, Russian voices. There is no sound like it. And still I blinked away the sun's blood. It was Liszt. I had heard it at the Opera House in Odessa with Uncle Semya. Dante. I could not. My mind was weak. Something had attacked it as I slept. There is no purer sound than that of little Russian girls singing. *Magnificat anima mea Dominum!* Into Purgatory. So much for the *Divine Comedy*. I was surrounded by them. Had I wronged them? I could not have wronged anyone. I took what others would have taken. I am no priest. I have never claimed it. It was at the Albert Hall. I should never have gone. Layers and layers of red, all circling down to the hell on the stage; that Bolshoi chorus. But I was lonely. I had lost everything. Some would have adopted a dog. I was tired of dogs. We had had too much of dogs in my Russia. And children never trusted me. Did they know? I am not an uneducated man. The Cossack put me in a red carriage and I was taken up the hill to Andreivska. That red hell of the Albert Hall. I remember the lights. The little girls in their white dresses. They had to take me home in the end. I wanted to hear those voices, even though they sang in Latin.

Rome and Rome and Rome. They said Britain was the New Rome. All she inherited was the patrician. Moscow inherited the priest. Rome and Byzantium, Kiev and Moscow. The voices are still as sweet and I did them no damage. I was clean. I was cleaner than the others. We got to the church and Petlyura himself had arrived. He was furious. "Sleeping, Comrade?"

"I worked late into the night."

"And so has this fellow?" It was the soldier with whom I had shared a cigarette. He looked bleak. Petlyura had evidently been screaming at him. There were various generals standing about in coats with elaborate frogging. Some had no insignia. Some had removed their epaulettes. I had learned to recognize such sights. It was almost as good as waving a white flag. From below in the church the priests were holding a service. It was the Kiev part-singing of Diletski. I think it was *Khvalite imya gospoden', aliluya!* It was an omen, I thought. Church and Science were coming together to destroy the Red Jew.

"My machine is as good as ready," I said with dignity. "I was awaiting instructions."

"Antonov's forces are moving in from all sides." Petlyura scowled. "We've no time to set up further stations. This is the only one we can use. Tonight we shall direct it over there." He pointed roughly toward my own home. I was glad Esmé and my mother had gone. There was no more sun. I blinked at Petlyura. He said, "You are certain the light is invisible?"

I reassured him.

"It will weaken their morale. It will give us time to put the rest of our plan into action."

"You are going to counterattack?"

"Look after the scientific matters, Professor."

The soldier glanced cynically at me. I avoided his eye. I wanted no trouble. My head was aching. I had forgotten my cocaine. I asked permission to return to the hotel for medicine. "Have some of mine," said Petlyura. He handed me a small golden box containing cocaine. I was not surprised. That entire Revolution, that entire Civil War, was fought on "snow." It was the fuel, far more than politics or gunpowder, of the entire affair. Revived, I noticed the soldier smiling at me in an insolent way. "You think I don't know what I'm doing?"

"I think you might be the only one who does, Comrade."

Petlyura said sourly, "You could be shot, Corporal."

"I think I stand a fair chance of it today, Comrade Supreme Commander." The corporal had no fear because he had become so tired. I felt sympathy for him. We were being outmaneuvered. Even Scipio had needed an army to destroy the Carthaginian elephant. It was all sunshine in those days. The battles were fought in heat, not snow. Only Hannibal had known snow and that was the kindly snow of the Alps. It had not been Russian snow. Ragnarok come again. Entropy. There is so much evidence in Russia. We are lucky to have our brief moments of warmth and life. It is why we worship God.

Petlyura was mumbling at the corporal. He could afford to shoot nobody. His army might only now consist of the silent generals, the corporal and my ray machine. He said something in French to the only man apart from myself in civilian dress. But Petlyura's accent was so abominable I think no one understood. The civilian might have been the French consul. He nodded. Petlyura asked me to position the lens toward the woods of Trukhanov. "Could you hit those trees?"

"Of course. But I must have the power."

"It's being diverted."

I directed my machine toward the Dnieper ice. As I pressed the appropriate switch I drew a thin line of heat across the white surface. "I have melted it. Think of the civil applications of the machine."

"Cutting ice seems hardly the purpose . . ." said one of the generals.

"It could be of use on ships," said another. They all spoke like automata. It was as if they had drawn their energy and inspiration from Petlyura, a source which could no longer supply what they needed. My device meant little to most of them. They did not know why they were here.

"You burned the ice?" Petlyura borrowed some field glasses. "I see the crack. Excellent. In itself, this will be of use when they try to cross. It will be like Alexander Nevski. Our enemies will perish in our river."

He gave me the field glasses. They were of no use to me. A general leaned forward and, with a peculiar smile, retrieved them. "Thank you," he said slowly, as if I could not understand Russian.

The priests were still singing for their congregation. The sound grew louder and louder. Petlyura found their voices disturbing; I was glad of them. Even then, without realizing what I was doing, I was receiving God's inspiration and not Man's. I was to remember that moment, when I alone, in the assembled company, had strength.

"Those peasants," said Petlyura. "They are brutes. They are treacherous, stupid. They betrayed me. They are primitive beasts."

"We're all that, Comrade," said the soldier. He leaned against the parapet, looking toward the window. "But some of us are innocent beasts. That's the only difference. You didn't spend long enough with the herd."

Petlyura was sucking at his weak lower lip. His pale eyes looked from general to general and found nothing there but blankness. "Korishenko," he said, "you will ensure all power is directed to the professor's machine."

Glad to be on his way, Korishenko saluted and departed.

"We'll wait until nightfall," said the Supreme Commander. "Will there be any danger? No backlash from the machine?"

"It is unlikely."

"And what if people get in the way?"

"Tell everyone to stay in their basements," I suggested. "Just in case."

"We don't want to slice some poor Jew in two," said the corporal.

Petlyura and his henchmen were already leaving the tower. Petlyura had begun to speak in his appalling French. I heard the civilian say, "What of the Jews? Is there another pogrom?"

"Naturally, there isn't."

"We have Jews in France."

The men disappeared into the swollen voices of the chorus and I was left with my corporal.

"Did he say anything to that Frenchman about retreating from Kiev?" he asked.

"No."

"What did he say about the Jews?"

"Nothing."

The corporal lifted his arm as if to knock over my machine. "I have no prejudice, but I warn you . . ."

"What are you saying?" His gesture continues to haunt me. Did the fool think me a Jew because I had an interest in science? I agreed with Petlyura and the peasants' point of view on that score. The Jews in Ukraine and Poland turned the very earth white, they bled both countries. The black earth was drained so deep that only blood could bring it back to life. Blood and the sun and our wide rivers which the Reds claim to have harnessed. Who can tame a Russian river? It is eternally free. They tried to make European bourgeoisie of us all, but they failed. We are not naturally middle class. We are intellectuals, we are workers, we are peasants. Let the Jews find their Zion elsewhere. They shall not have Russia. Only Slavs survive on Slavic earth. The Tartars failed to survive. The land destroyed their khanates. They are the same: Phoenician trader or Zionist fifth-columnist. I know this as I know the Devil is in all men. As the Devil is in me. I offered the soldier a cigarette.

The afternoon sun was beginning to sink. Kiev was silent. Everything was still. Trains steamed away from the city. I could see their smoke. I saw figures on the ice. I did not know who they were. The singing had stopped from below. I felt lonely. I could have wept. I wanted a girl. I wanted comfort of any kind. I remembered Kolya. Was he now in prison in Petrograd? Emigrated? With Korniloff or Denikin, fighting their way back to the center of power? Why were Poles invading Ukraine? They wanted their Empire back. No wonder the Germans came to fear them, as they feared the Czechs. Czechs were famous for their courage and fighting skill. They fought their way home across Siberia. Teutons fear Slavs, just as the decadent

Latins feared the Vikings. If only the Empire had stayed together. A Slavic Empire. We should have had a neo-Hellenic world by now. We are the inheritors of the Greeks. It is our Slavic blood, not Communism, which unites us. The Anglo-Saxons and the Chinese have had their day. They have achieved the stability of death. Negativity was never a Slavic trait. We would always rather be doing something than nothing. If the Poles had looked to Germany for their territory, we should not have had another War. Nationalism goes against all rational progress, all the findings of science, all the experience of mankind. Israel! A fresh joke, for now the Jew becomes a "nationalist." That is when we have to fear the worst.

As it grew darker I could tell the requisite power was being diverted. The corporal went to fetch us some food. He returned with the news that everyone had been warned to stay in their cellars. Some thought there was to be a Zeppelin raid, others had heard a story of my "Violet Ray." It is astonishing to what extent information spreads in a city under siege. Gossip, as they say in Ukraine, takes the edge off hunger. My emergency Voltaic batteries were also prepared. I connected these to the transformer in case of a sudden failure of power. The darkness brought relief to me. My eyes were hurting. I could not dismiss the images of death, of blood, which filled them. At least Esmé and my mother and possibly Captain Brown were away by now, racing down the line to Odessa where French order existed, where there was hope. If things became worse, Uncle Semya could help them leave the country for a while. I assured myself that as soon as I knew exactly which way the wind blew I would use my ray to demonstrate its power, pack it up with the aid of the corporal, and be off with the basic apparatus to the French. The next train to Odessa would be carrying myself and my invention. The next ship out would be taking us to Paris.

There were no lights burning anywhere, but the artillery fire had begun. There were flashes of light from Trukhanov. I directed the projector at the island. The corporal asked me for one of my cigarettes. I handed him the case. He removed one of the papyrussa and put the case back in my pocket. He began to smoke. I wondered if any Bolshevik field glasses observed his red tip. If so, what did they make of the silence and darkness? The guns continued to fire from time to time. I heard a few yells, the sound of motor-engines, of horses' hooves on the wooden blocks of streets where snow had melted beneath the wheels and feet of the Petlyurist army. I pressed the switch of my projector. I saw a flash of light. I think I destroyed a gun. I turned to the corporal so that I could enjoy my success with him. He had gone. The entire church was deserted. Kiev had filled up with ghosts. I trusted the corporal's instincts more than Petlyura's or my own. I called to him, but it was too late. He had gone to join the Bolsheviks or return to his village. I was about to dismantle my projector when I heard boots on the steps. I was in such a state of terror I was sure I should see ghosts or Antonov himself. But it was Petlyura, in his green uniform, with his black shapka on his head, a riding crop in his hands. He had a more dapper appearance than the Hetman. He sought an aristocratic image which simply made him look ridiculous. A character from *The Prisoner of Zenda*.

"Have you used the ray yet?"

I told him I had destroyed a gun.

"One gun isn't enough."

"The machine has to be aimed. It consumes a great deal of energy with every shot. I have done well so far."

"You raised my hopes. You betrayed them."

Two generals stood behind him, together with a few soldiers of lesser rank. All wore different uniforms: some blue, some white, some green.

"I told you what I could do. With another day or so."

"Antonov is almost in Kiev. He's moving troops up rapidly. We're going to have to evacuate the city. You'll hold off their advance with your ray."

"Alone?"

"You're a major in the Republican Army, Comrade. You can be shot for disobeying orders."

Someone grinned. "That's true."

"And you're leaving?" I could not believe such perfidy.

"We're withdrawing from this position. We still have a great deal of support. I think we can rely on Hrihorieff. There's a strong chance the Entente will lend us troops. Denikin and Krassnoff will have to throw in with us. It's to their advantage."

"How shall I leave if the Bolsheviks find me?" It seemed a fair question.

"You'll be able to slip away," said a captain. "You're wearing civilian clothes."

I wondered if I could get back to my hotel and pick up my bags or whether they would have been stolen already. I saluted in military fashion. "Then I shall do my duty." That duty, naturally, was to my dependents and to myself. There was no chance at all of the Ultra-Violet Projector standing off the entire Bolshevik army. Petlyura had miscalculated everything. I asked him where I should meet the rest of the army.

He hesitated. "You'll hear."

He expected me to be captured. He did not want to risk my revealing his position. Some of his generals looked openly sympathetic to me. Others were smiling. I seemed to have become a bone of contention amongst them.

"What if Antonov captures the ray?" I asked.

"You'll destroy it first."

I thought he was placing a great deal of trust in my loyalty to a cause I had never supported. "If they capture me before I can destroy it?"

Petlyura turned. With a gesture of supremely arrogant impatience he struck with his whip at my apparatus. I was horrified. The tripod wobbled but held. "They'll never guess what it is. They have no money. They can't pay you. Take it to the French. They'll give you what you ask." He was accusing me of something. He was mad.

I became confused and distracted as I attempted to right the machine before the precious vacuum tube was thrown out of alignment. But Petlyura had already done his worst. The machine would take hours to reset. I told him nothing of that. "You asked me to build this."

"And it doesn't work!"

"You have not given it a fair trial."

"Very well. Use it now. Sweep Trukhanov."

"I will do my best. You have probably made it impossible . . ."

"Destroy Trukhanov."

I shrugged and pointed the projector in the general direction of the island. I began to move it as a man might move a machine gun, spraying from side to side. Nothing, naturally, happened.

Petlyura was laughing. "I'm in a hurry, Comrade."

I noticed from my instruments that not enough power was going through the transformer. "The power has been diverted. I must use the Voltaics." I pointed up the narrow stair to where they were arranged. "Someone must pull that large switch all the way down when I give the word."

Petlyura was staring at me as if he believed himself crazy. "Will it work?"

"Pull the switch!"

Some fool went clattering up to it, all spurs and frogging; a military genius who could sit on a horse without instantly falling off and was thus a general in Petlyura's idiot army. He pulled the switch, of course, before I gave the word. The Voltaics began to arc. The soldier came stumbling back. There was noise and light everywhere. Petlyura screamed and was gone, his men behind him, while I battled with what was left of my equipment. It was impossible to do anything. I opened one of the straw-filled ammunition boxes which had brought my vacuum tubes. The case still contained a tube. All I needed were the lenses. I began to dismantle them as quickly as possible. Someone returned. There was a pistol shot, the tube on the tripod burst and as I covered my eyes I felt pieces of glass strike my hands and forehead. Another shot was aimed at me. Petlyura evidently wished to ensure the Bolsheviks gained no advantage. It seemed at that moment to be a bizarre act of vengeance. I thought it was Petlyura himself firing. I suppose I was mistaken. I saw flashes of pistol fire and a dark silhouette. I moved behind one of the columns, onto the outer balcony. All six shots were discharged before the figure ran away. Something was on fire. It was my straw. I tried to pull at least one of the tubes to safety but there was every danger it would overheat and burst and then I should be killed. Electricity still sputtered. The connections had been badly made. My worst danger was from the fire in the straw. I did not save a single lens, a single tube. I moved cautiously down the steps, trying to hear any sound of the assassin. But he was gone. I heard some cars going away. Monks with tapers came and looked at me. They were accusing me. I tried to ask their forgiveness with my eyes but they turned their backs to me. I was too cautious to speak. I still found it hard to believe such hatred and violence had been directed at me. I slipped from the church. A Jew in a skullcap ran past. He was panting. He held something to him. A bundle. It was a baby, I thought. But it was probably a family heirloom he hoped to save from the new invaders.

I moved nervously back towards Kreshchatik, but I was hardly bothered at all. The inhabitants had taken to their cellars. All the Haidamaki had gone. I reached the Yevropyaskaya and walked through undefended doors. I went up to my room. There was no one about. My room had been searched. Nothing of any note had been taken. I slipped my diploma, passport and other papers, together with some gold, into a special secret pocket of my trousers. I packed my notes and realized that most of my designs for the machine, together with written descriptions of processes, had gone. I put little packets of cocaine into prepared places in my jacket and waistcoat. I wondered if Petlyura himself or one of the others had decided to sell my plans to one or another of the opposing forces. There was nothing I could do. I no longer had any concrete proof I had built and tested my "death ray." I had been thoroughly and cynically betrayed. After some thought, I decided to take what I could and head for the station. It would be dangerous at night. I would wait until dawn before venturing out. I went to sleep in all my clothes because the heating had been turned off in the hotel. I heard shots. There was yellow blood in my eyes. I writhed in mud. My mother burned. Bronze bubbled through the gorges of Kiev. Suns rose and set over a battlefield which was the whole world. Years went by as I searched for something.

In the morning I looked out of my window and saw Red Army cavalry riding up Kreshchatik.

TWELVE

It was like a flood of brown and red mud in that wide, cold street. Remorseless and orderly, it flowed to the drone of engines and the trotting of horses; it flowed into the buildings, as disciplined as Germans and as fearsome as Haidamaki. I was looking at a real army, at last, and I was terrified. This was what Trotsky and Stalin and Antonov had built from our old Czarist army: they had fueled it with Bolshevik fanaticism and fired it with promises of land and utopia. A dream worth killing for. And it was a Russian army. It was singing. The men on horseback, or in cars, or those who were marching, they were laughing in that easy, desperate way Russians have when they fight. Not a single Nationalist or Republican flag could be seen in the whole of Kreshchatik. Not a single shop was opening into the thin sunshine of that February dawn. There was only ice and Bolshevism in the streets. Without much hope, I began to finish packing. I dressed in my old "classless" suit, of black and white. I was able to light a cigarette before the door handle rattled and a tired voice asked who occupied the suite. I went to the door and opened it immediately. "Good morning, Comrade," I said. "I'm glad to see you at last. I am Pyatnitski."

It was a Chekist commissar in the leather jacket they all wore (many still wear such jackets, as easy to spot as Special Branch anoraks). He had yellow hair and a wide, prudish mouth. There were three Red Army guards behind him. They wore sailor uniforms, with red stars and bandoleers. They carried long rifles with fixed bayonets. The Chekist held the hotel register in his hands. He turned the pages. "You have stayed here frequently, Citizen. Is this your home?"

"I lost my own home," I told him. "It was looted by the Hetman's people and by Petlyura."

"You don't seem to have lost much." He came into the room.

"I was poor. I worked with the Soviets. Pyatnitski?" I hardly knew what lies to tell. I was desperate to talk my way clear of this terrible man.

"You've stayed here and left, stayed here and left. Why's that?"

"I was in prison," I told him.

"What had you done?"

"Nothing. Bolshevik sympathies are enough to get you jailed in Kiev."

"You weren't here during our previous occupation?"

"I was in Kharkov, visiting comrades."

"And who do you support? The Kiev group?"

I knew no more about the different factions of the Party than I did about the sorts of flowers one might discover on a country walk. "I was nonaligned," I said. "My sympathies are with Moscow. I had made attempts to get back there."

"Have you any papers?"

I knew better than to give up my real papers, but I still had a spare set in my luggage. I opened my suitcase and took them out. "You'll see I'm a scientist."

"Doctor Pyatnitski, is it? You're very young."

"I did well at Petrograd, comrade."

"Your degree is from Kiev."

"I was transferred. That's why I found myself here in the first place. You'll discover that Comrade Lunarcharsky is an acquaintance of mine. He'll vouch for me."

"You're well connected." He was sardonic. "One meets a lot of well-connected overnight Bolsheviks."

"I knew many comrades in Petrograd. Before the Revolution. I had a reputation. There are people there who know me."

The Chekist sighed and scratched himself under his chin with my papers. He replaced a wide-brimmed hat on his head and looked at me through green, almost sympathetic eyes. They were the eyes of a man who was about to kill me. He turned away. A ritual had begun. "You'll let these comrades search the rooms?"

"If you think it necessary." There was a growing scent of death. I had smelled it once or twice before. I would learn to identify it easily in the months and years which followed.

"You've been living very well."

"I've been lucky."

"How have you earned your money?"

"As a mechanic."

He sniffed. I wished I had stayed at Mother's or had risen early enough to catch that Odessa train. "My working clothes aren't here, of course."

He removed his hat again. One of the sailors found an envelope in a drawer and brought it to him. "We still need skilled mechanics, Comrade." He emptied all the Petlyurist military insignia into his hand.

I began to laugh.

He rounded on me. He was one of those unimaginative men who finds laughter baffling. I stopped. "I was offered a commission. Of course, I refused it. That's a souvenir."

"A major?"

I would normally have become impatient at this schoolmasterly malice, the stock in trade of so many Chekists and, indeed, policemen everywhere. They have no wit, but they have power. The worst abuse of that power, in my view, is in its employment to make bad jokes.

"Is it major? I'm impressed." I was frightened.

"Why did they offer you a commission?"

"They wanted my help with their industrial problems."

"Running factories? Or motor cars? Or what?"

"Advice. I've helped keep most of Kiev going."

He rubbed at his light-colored eyebrows. He drew his puritanical lips together as if he had remembered a particularly unpleasant sin, either of his own or someone else's. "You wouldn't have had anything to do with the fire in that church? It was like a damned beacon. It helped us move in last night. I heard Petlyura or the French had installed a secret weapon up there. It had gone wrong. Was that you?"

"It was," I said. "I sabotaged it."

He smiled.

"I was fired at by Petlyura's men," I said, "while I was doing it. I'd been asked to work with it. I agreed. It was about to be turned on our forces when I set the sights out of alignment. There was a fight. It exploded."

"I think we'd better shoot you," said the commissar. I had irritated him. Over the months he had been doing his job he had evidently ceased to listen to words. He listened only to the sounds his victims made. He had learned to recognize desperation and anxiety and to identify these, as the simple-minded always will, with guilt. I could only continue to repeat the names of certain Bolsheviks whom I had known slightly in Petrograd. These names produced what Pavlov calls a "conditioned response." It made him hesitate. He probably hated uncertainty, but he would hate those who made him uncertain, so it was a dangerous game I played. These Moscow leather-jackets were famous for their snap decisions: a look at the clothes, a glance at the hands to see if they had done manual work, a quick check to ascertain "bourgeois background," and off to the firing squad. Some-one has since mentioned that the whole of the Bolshevik leadership could, by this yardstick, have been shot by the Cheka. My hands were not soft. I held them out toward the Chekist. I was mute. He frowned. I held my hands out to him, showing the fingers and palms callused by the mechanical work I had been doing. He hesitated. He coughed for a second or two and drew a cigarette from a cardboard box he carried in one of his pockets. He had to shift his holster to get at the cigarettes. He struck a match. I looked around for my own cigarette. I had dropped it, but nothing was on fire. My papers went into his other deep pocket. "You're wasting my time. You're under arrest."

"House arrest? What have I done?"

"This room's needed."

There was a sound of feet in the passage outside. A woman's voice. Mrs. Cornelius came in. She was wearing a loose, one-piece dress made of bright red silk and she had a red cloche on her head. Her lips and cheeks were carmine and emphasized the blue of her eyes, the gold of her hair. When she saw me she stopped dead and began to laugh.

"'Ullo, Ivan!" She embraced me. "Yore a proper littel bad kopeck, ain't yer!"

"You're with the Reds?" I said in English.

"Been wiv 'em all ther time, ain't I? Lucky fer me, eh? Well, they're more fun than the ovvers. Or were. I've got a noo boyfriend. 'E's ever so important."

The Chekist was now looking firmly at his polished boots and frowning. He said something very sharp to the sailors. They began to carry Mrs. Cornelius' trunks into the room. She glanced round. "I'm not kickin' yer art, am I? They'll do anyfink fer me. But it's too much, reelly. Sort o' musical chairs. Yer never know 'ose bed yore gonna sleep in next, eh?" She threw back her head and bellowed with laughter. She giggled. She put a soft hand on my arm. "Yer gotter larf, incha?"

I did my best to smile and to adopt an easy stance which might convince the Chekist, who remained in the room, that I was one of the party elite. "Is Lunarcharsky here?" I asked.

" 'E stopped bein' any fun ages ago. And 'is wife or somefink got stroppy. Nar. I'm serposed to be wiv Leo, but 'e keeps goin' ter ovver places. I jest can't catch up wiv 'im at all. I don't reelly mind."

"Leo?"

"Lev," she said. "You know. Trotsky. Littel trotty-true-ski I corl 'im. Har, har, har."

"You're his—paramour . . . "

"Lovely of yer ter say so, Ivan. I'm 'is bit o' all right, if that's wot yer mean. Well, it's fer the best. I'm tryin' ter get back ter ther sarth. Is that wot you're doin'? I couldn't stand anuvver winter 'ere, could you?"

"To Odessa?"

"Seemed a good idear. 'E don't speak a word o' English," she confided of the commissar, who was looking very sourly at both of us, "and 'e 'ates me. 'E don't seem too bloody fond o' you, by ther look of it."

"I don't think he is. You are going to the coast, then?"

"I've orlways liked ther seaside." She winked. "Funny time ter pick fer an 'oliday, innit?"

She knew I was in trouble. It was a knack she had. "Wot's ther service like 'ere?" she asked casually.

"It depends who you are."

The leather-jacket said, "Would you mind speaking Russian, Comrade? When in Rome . . . "

"Russki?" Mrs. Cornelius replied in her abominable and attractive Russian. It was easy to see how, with her beauty and her spirit and her accent, she had won the hearts of the top Bolsheviks. She baffled the Chekist far more than I had. She laughed. He turned away to hide his scowl. "If yer like, Ivan." It seemed she addressed everyone by the same name. "This is a very good comrade. He is on his way to Odessa to work for the party there. He is known to many leading comrades from Petrograd days. I think you will find he and Comrade Stalin are old friends." The so-called Siberian Bolsheviks had more weight with the rank-and-file at that time. Stalin was then just a name to me, associated with various rather incompetently waged Civil War campaigns and not popular with the Jewish intellectuals who controlled Party policies.

I said, taking out my watch, that I had probably missed the Odessa train. The Chekist went to put his cigarette out in a spittoon. "It was stopped. It's being searched at Fastov."

"That's all right, then." (I make no attempt to imitate Mrs. Cornelius' Russian.) "You can send a telegram and tell them to hold it up a bit longer."

"But how can I get to Fastov?" I asked a reasonable question.

"Same way as the troops," she told me. "By motor."

"I am not fortunate enough . . ."

She slapped me on the shoulder. She began to pull on a huge fox-fur coat with a matching hat. "Daft!" she said in English. "We'll go in *my* bleedin' motor, won't we!"

On her instructions, the sailors picked up my bags. They took them down to her large Mercedes which was still parked outside the main doors. There was oil on the snow. I thought it was blood. " 'Op in," she told me. I climbed into the back seats. I had never experienced a car like it. It felt warm under the canopy. In Russian, she said to the driver, "What's the benzine situation?"

"To go where?" The driver wore a Red Army cap with earflaps, and a huge red star sewn on the front. Otherwise he was dressed in the regular khaki of a Czarist soldier: trenchcoat, gloves, scarf wound round the lower part of his face against the cold, and goggles.

"Fastov, was it?" Mrs. Cornelius turned to me.

"Fastov," I said.

"We can get there." The driver was amused. "And probably back."

"Perfect."

The Chekist stood outside the hotel. His hands were deep in his pockets. He looked smug. I remembered. "You have my papers, Comrade."

As one robbed of his last consolation, he gave them to me. He must have been fondling them. Plainly he disapproved of Mrs. Cornelius, but he had no power over her. Now he had no power over me. He had become like a demon in a pentagram.

"Don't forget about the cable," Mrs. Cornelius told him. "And if Comrade Trotsky's in touch asking for me, tell him I've put Comrade Pyat on the train to Odessa, will you?"

"Yes, Comrade." He glared at us. The Mercedes, its engine cranked by grinning sailors, began to shake and mutter. Two of the sailors jumped into the front seats beside the driver. A third stood on the running board, his rifle on his shoulder. The driver engaged the engine, and we were off in style, flying the red hammer-and-sickle flag: An official Bolshevik car! More than once, as we left Kiev behind, we were cheered by the conquering Reds. It was an irony I think Mrs. Cornelius appreciated. She would often wave back, but more like a queen than a comrade. It was then that I experienced one of my first "releases." There are a number of them. I value them greatly. They are all specific to this century (i.e., I do not include the release of sexual fulfillment): the Release of Flying; the Release of Steam-liner Sailing; the Release of Rapid Train-Travel; the Release of Motoring. In that monstrous German automobile, guarded by elite members of the Revolutionary Army, with a beautiful foreign woman at my side (her rose perfume, her furs, her wonderful complexion, her stylish self-assurance), I knew the Release of Motoring. I resolved to obtain such a car as soon as possible. She, too, was enjoying the ride. She chuckled. "Wot a pair o' survivors we are, you an' me, Ivan. That's ther fing I like most abaht yer, I fink."

I was still dazed by what had taken place. It was she, after all, who had rescued me. Without her, I should be dead. She nudged me in the side. "Never say die, eh?"

Suddenly I was laughing as she, alone, has ever been able to make me laugh. I laughed like a child.

Between avenues of lime trees, we traveled toward Fastov. I remembered my gypsy, Zoyea. I imagined myself driving her in this car. It was not disloyalty to my rescuer to enjoy this fantasy. Mrs. Cornelius had no sexual claims on me. I had none on her. She is the best friend I ever had. And all because I had visited a dentist in Odessa and been able to speak English! All my luck since then was to stem from her. She became my mother, sister, goddess, guardian angel. And yet most of the time she hardly noticed me. I amused her. She had as much affection for me as a woman might have for a favorite cat. No more and no less. And, like a favorite cat, I survived to give her some comfort, I hope, in her old age. She wore very well. It was only, really, in the fifties that she began to decline and run to fat, though she had always been built on proper feminine proportions. I hate these skinny girls who try to look like boys. No wonder everyone today is a homosexual. We had thin girls in the twenties, but Mrs. Cornelius was always feminine. I cannot say I have been as completely certain of my own sexuality as she, but for that, I suppose, I must blame Prince Nicholai Feodorovitch Petroff and perhaps even my cousin Shura. Unwittingly, Shura showed me that women are not to be trusted: they try too hard to please too many people. It is a man's world.

The sailors were surprisingly good-natured about the trip. I think they enjoyed the motor car. They had seen a great deal of the world. They had known what it was to risk their lives. They were, in their way, men of good will. They have not changed much, our Russsian sailors. When I go to the docks for my vodka, as I still try to do, I meet them and speak to them. They are just as self-confidently tolerant and tough. They were fond of Mrs. Cornelius. They flattered her with all sorts of purring Russian endearments, as they would flatter their sweethearts. She responded by blowing them kisses and sharing her food and cigarettes with them.

Scores of dead horses were piled alongside the Fastov road. They were stiffening. Some were still warm; you could smell them. There were human corpses as well, sprawled in the winter sun; young peasant bodies left behind as Petlyura had tried to leave me behind, to cover his escape. Petlyura had been another sentimentalist who betrayed all he claimed to stand for. As usual he had accused as traitors those he had misled; sacrificing them to his enemies when they had come to doubt his lies. They probably deserved their fate. Some still held their booty: a pair of women's shoes, a length of cloth, an ornamental sword. But most had already been stripped by the followers of Marx and Lenin. We passed a black line of dead Orthodox priests. The line had fallen neatly against a snowdrift. Behind the drift was an almost identical line of birches. It was as if shadows had been reversed, for the sun was on our side of the trees. There was blood, too, and that was black. The priests had been dead for some while. Their crucifixes had been cut from them, of course, as well as their rings, but otherwise their clothing was neatly arranged. Some pious woman had come upon them in the morning and attempted to give them a semblance of dignity. I remembered the church and the singing. The sweet girls' voices. I think Catholic Petlyurists had shot the priests.

Mrs. Cornelius avoided the sight. "Between you an' me, Ivan," she confided, "I wasn't expectin' nuffink like this. It's wot comes o' bein' English, I s'pose. It wouldn't 'appen over there. You wanna get ter London, mate."

"I had considered it."

"Yer might find me there a'ead o' yer." She gave the sailor on the running board a cigarette she had already lit. She winked and laughed with him. "It woz a soft spot fer sailormen got me inter me present predic, really, wannit?"

"You've not been back to Odessa?"

"Nar! I 'alf 'oped, see, ter make ther Finlan' train an' go that way, like we wos talkin' abart. But fings got orl wonky some'ow. An' Leo can be a jealous pig. In spite o' the fac' 'e's not exactly single."

"Why not come with me to Odessa? The French are in control there."

"An' a lot o' bloody Bolshies, mark my words. I've 'eard."

"Are you frightened they'll do something to you?"

"Nar! They got no reel respec' fer women, any of 'em. That's me strengf, yeah? Know wot I mean?"

"I think so."

"They don't reckon women count. Unless they're in ther Party, that is. I'm just a fancy-bit ter them. I'll be orl right. If Leo 'eard I'd got on that bloody train wiv you, 'e'd jest bring it back, wouldn't 'e?"

"I suppose he would." I rather regretted the principles which had stopped me (and always will) from leaguing myself with the Communists. They certainly knew how to gain and hold power better than any of their rivals. They saw and accepted no ambiguities. Many non-Bolsheviks eventually came round to Lenin. It was better to have Bolshevik order than no order at all.

As we entered the rather unattractive town of Fastov, I saw a red flag flying from the dome of the church. A synagogue was burning. There were Red Cossacks everywhere and a considerable amount of filth and confusion. Overhead, a biplane dropped, observed us, then flew away toward the West. As if waiting to board a train, guns and horses crowded the street leading to the station. The long Odessa train had been shunted off the main line into a siding. People crowded around it. There were Red Guards, Chekists, women with babies which they displayed like talismans, Jews who argued vehemently with officials, men in uniform from which all insignia had been ripped: the wadding showed through their greatcoats, so urgently had those symbols been removed. Youths gave the Bolshevik salute, old men wandered about in the deep snow, looking for things which had been dropped, beautiful girls fluttered their eyelashes and tried to flirt with the leather-jackets. Cossacks, with red stars on their caps, were lounging over their ponies making filthy remarks to all and sundry (there is nothing worse than a Cossack who has gone to the bad), while sailors marshaled whole lines of workers and peasants beside the train and into the first-class compartments which filled up rapidly and had begun to smell of urine. The richer people were being forced to enter the fourth-class compartments, or even the animal wagons at the rear.

The car bumped along a track and came to a stop. An officer in ordinary military clothes, wearing a cloak and an old Czarist blue-and-white uniform with the inevitable red stars, came up to us. He did not salute. All the usual disciplines had been abolished at that time.

Mrs. Cornelius knew the officer. She greeted him. He grinned at her. "What can I do for you?"

"It's my friend," she said. "He needs to be on the Odessa train. Party business. He's a courier for Commissar Trotsky."

"There's a carriage at the front for proletarian representatives. They plan to argue with French soldiers. Do you think they'll succeed, Comrade?" He seemed anxious for an answer from me.

"There's every chance," I told him. I privately prayed the canker of Bolshevism would never touch France. But it was like a gas used in the trenches. It touched everyone. Bolshevism would have died out completely by now if it had not been for that shot at Sarajevo.

The soldiers had rounded up a number of people in civilian clothes. I had seen some of them only recently. Then, they had been wearing Petlyurist uniforms. They were taken away behind an embankment. There was a burst or two of machine-gun fire and some laughter. The guards returned without their prisoners. I thanked God and Mrs. Cornelius for my escape. By oversleeping, I had missed the train and probably that firing squad.

Mrs. Cornelius, with a gesture which reminded me of my mother, at once began to joke with the sailors, asking them which girl they liked the look of most. "Anything would do me at the moment," one said. "I'll take a horse if the Cossack leaves it alone for a minute."

I whispered in English to Mrs. Cornelius. "Why do they shoot them so mercilessly? It will only bring more death."

Because she was frowning I thought I had offended her. Then the frown became a wink. She said seriously, "They're bloody shit-scared, Ivan. Leo an' the ovvers, more than these bleedin' fugs 'oo don't care 'oo they kill. It's like tryin' ter stay on top of a bloody eruptin' volcano, innit? They carn't get ther stopper back in. Shoutin' at it don't exactly 'elp! So they're tryin' dynamite, right?" She screamed with laughter all of a sudden. "Pore buggers!"

"A volcano expends its energy with less loss of life," I said.

"Not in bloody Bali." Mrs. Cornelius was smug. "They orl run up ther bloody 'ill an lie darn in front o' the bloody lava. If it gets enough o' 'em, they reckon, it'll stop." She drew a handkerchief from a muff on the seat beside her and blew her nose. "I read that," she said with some pride, "in ther *Penny Pictorial*. Yer don't see ther *Penny Pictorial* rahnd 'ere, I s'pose?"

"I have never seen it."

"Me neither. I could do wiv a nice read. It was a lot less borin' fer me before all this broke aht, yer know. 'Ow long's it bin? Two years? Well, just over a year since the Old Man—'e don't like me, neither—nearly bungled 'is larst chance. 'E won't give an ounce o' credit to Antonov, will 'e?"

I scarcely understood her. She was so immersed in the internal gossip and politics of the Bolsheviks she assumed everyone took her meaning.

"Never met such a bunch o' self-important buggers. They orl ought ter be given little kingdoms of their own. No wonder I carn't keep me eyes off ther bloody sailors!" She sighed. "Well, it woz fun while it lasted. While they 'ad nuffink ter do but talk. I'll be glad ter be art of it, an' no mistake. Yer goin' ter Blighty?"

"I hope so."

"I'll give yer me address in Whitechapel. Somebody'll know if I'm back an' wot I'm up ter. But, I tell yer, Ivan, I'll be up West first charncet I get."

With these cryptic words she stretched across me, all soft fur and French perfume, and opened the door of the car. As I began to climb out, she fumbled with gloved hands in a reticule, removed a pamphlet printed on coarse paper, and with a pencil slowly wrote down a single line. She gave me the pamphlet. "Don't mind if I wave bye-bye from 'ere, do yer? I'm not goin' in that bloody snow if I can 'elp it."

Two sailors shouldered their rifles and took my bags from the box at the back of the car. Between them I walked through dirty slush to the carriage nearest the locomotive. A variety of desperadoes, male and female, regarded me through misted windows. The sailors dumped my bags on the metal steps. Stumbling through the door I found I was in a sleeper. The compartments, however, were fairly full and there would be no way in which I would be able to stretch out. The majority of the people were dressed as peasants and industrial workers. There were one or two "intellectuals" in dark overcoats similar to my own. My natural inclination was to join these. I had stored my luggage (including a small hamper from Mrs. Cornelius) before I realized I had made a serious mistake. I would not be able to answer their questions or understand their references. They had made space for me. They were calling me comrade. I shook several hands and then went back to the carriage door to wave to Mrs. Cornelius. Fox-fur arms saluted me. The car was already turning. One of the sailors now sat next to her, grinning at his friends and at me. I heard a faint "Keep yer pecker up, Ivan!"—and she was gone. I was left with the cursing Cossacks, the pallid Chekists, the weary sailors. I returned to the relative security of the compartment and was offered a flask of vodka. I accepted it and sipped. It was raw moonshine; the kind they brewed in Shulyavka, the foulest slum in Kiev. I expected to go blind instantly and it affected my vocal chords as the arrack had done in Odessa. The man who had offered it, a round-faced Ukrainian with a bushy red beard and thick spectacles, laughed and said, "You're used to better, eh?"

I managed to say I was not a great drinker. This gave him further amusement. "Then you can't be a Katsup. What are you? A Moslem?"

I considered claiming I was from Georgia or Armenia, but the problem there was that someone else in the carriage might know those areas. I shook my head and said I was from Kiev. I had spent some time in Petrograd and elsewhere.

"I'm Potoaki," he told me. It was a name with Polish resonances, but that was not strange in Ukraine. "You?"

"Pyat." It was what Mrs. Cornelius had christened me. It simply meant "five" in Russian. I thought it gave me exactly the right air. I had decided how to play my game.

He said "Most of us have only two" and introduced me to the three men and the woman in our compartment. I remember only the name of the woman. She was Marusia Kirillovna and she was dark and delicate and grim. My mother must have looked like her. She had the same dark eyes, the same expression, half open, half shut, "Good afternoon, Comrade," she said. She was pulling on tight leather gloves and there was a holstered automatic Mauser in her lap. She sat nearest the window. Her book was poetry by Mandelstam and of recent issue, judging by the bad production. The others were good-natured idiots, but Marusia Kirillovna seemed a woman of reliable instinct. I determined to say nothing to her unless asked a direct question. Russia was throwing up better women than men at that time. All the worthwhile men had been killed. And they were more ruthless, some of those women. They judged themselves harshly. Their self control became fanatical: dangerous to anyone who did not display the same quality. That was one of the reasons I remained uncommunicative. The only way to impress such women is to let their imagination work on your behalf. They are always inclined to see virtue in silence. They assume that a man with nothing to say is more intelligent. I have had long relationships, since my Russian years, which were only maintained because I had the sense to keep my mouth shut. I could have been Sophocles. It would not have mattered. Two or three sentences, and they would know I was "a sham." They are the kind of women who shun mirrors as vanity, yet forever seek mirrors in their lovers. Sure enough, by the time the train was on its way, leaving corpses and cheering Cossacks in its wake, she had already begun to treat me with exaggerated respect. I pulled my hat down over my eyes, pretending to sleep.

Dante driven into exile inspired Liszt to create those painful Bol-shoi voices, those Russian girls singing in Latin. What do the English know of exile? They cannot bear it. Everywhere they go they create another Surrey. New Zealand mutton and mint sauce. And throb-bing, terrible Australia, with its two-legged lizards, even that they have attempted to turn into some spiritual Torquay. The Romans left roads and villas. The English leave cold cups of tea and stale crumpets and "guest houses" littering the world from China to Rio de Janeiro. They cannot abide emotion. They cannot face death, any more than can the Americans. So they smooth it away with polite voices and coffee-mornings. And because death is so unpleasant, be-cause they cannot look Terror in the eye and smile back at him, they let their Law decline, their Empires fade—and they, too, have lost their honor. Phoenicia went sailing. What can save the world? Not the Jewish-Moslem God. We have had our taste of the power of the rabbi and the Khan. Our Cossacks dealt with them and will deal with them again if need be. Only the Son can save us. Christ is a Greek. The Greeks knew that. They laughed at the Jews when they spoke of these strange new ideas. The Greeks took those ideas to Palestine. They were welcome again in Byzantium. Defend Greece.

How did the English defend Cyprus? They let Turkish peasants foul it. Those sons of Islam knew nothing. They could not look after the houses they stole. They could not look after the olive groves or the vineyards. The Greeks lost everything. Islam is rising. Zion is rising. And from the East the Khans are galloping again, with skulls for banners, but now it is the skull of Mao who grins down at us from the lance poles. Must Russia defend the West alone? Still?

As night fell and the train became colder I was forced to share the chicken and salami from my very obvious hamper. They were all grateful. Even the woman ate with unfeminine greed. The train was moving very slowly. Since we had not yet passed Vinnitsa, it would be a long time before we reached Odessa. Once or twice we heard firing, or saw flashes of rifles and artillery in the distance, but nobody was able to speculate with any authority as to the identity of the antagonists. Marusia Kirillovna suggested it was probably just Haidamaki fighting amongst themselves. I think she could have been right. There were thousands of petty warlords seeking to hold smaller and smaller territories as the major participants moved closer together for the decisive battles of our Civil War. Sometimes shots were fired from the train. We had a Red Army escort which would disembark when it reached a territory occupied by bandits who (like Vietnamese today) found it politic to declare themselves Bolsheviks. Thus they received arms and money to achieve their own petty ends.

Potoaki became bored. He kept leaving the carriage, presumably to use the lavatory (although there was one in the adjoining cubicle) and returning, stamping his feet and clapping his gloved hands together. The woman looked at him with considerable intolerance. "Trying to make the train go faster, Comrade?"

"I'm supposed to be at the docks by tomorrow morning," he explained. "There's a French ship arriving."

"What will you do?" another occupant took Marusia Kirillovna's lead. "Speak to each French sailor as he comes ashore? Explain he's hampering the course of world revolution?"

"They're unloading supplies." Potoaki sat down beside me again and brought out his bottle of vodka. "It will be up to me to find out the kind of guns we'll be confronting." With a self-important movement of his hand he finished his vodka.

"I hope you don't broadcast that particular piece of information so efficiently," she said. She stood up, arranged her dark skirt, then carefully reseated herself. "Has anyone the time?"

I took out my watch. It had stopped. I replaced it in my pocket. "I am sorry."

"We must be nearing Hrihorieff's territory." Potoaki bent across the dark-faced man who sat reading a newspaper by the window. He wiped away condensation. There was nothing but ice inside and out. He rubbed at his waistcoat. "That salami of yours must have been cat and rat." He belched. "It can't have been dog. Dog never disagrees with me." He laughed. We were all becoming irritated. He could sense it. He apologized, farted, and left the smell behind him as he stepped again into the corridor. We kept the door open, in spite of the cold, until the air was clearer. Nobody mentioned the source of the smell. The train stopped completely. I thought I heard shouts from the locomotive. Booted feet ran past our carriage. There was a clatter. The feet ran back. Our train began to build up steam and again we were moving. Potoaki came in and told us there had been trees on the line. Soldiers had cleared the track. "They're used to it. I've never seen such efficiency." He hesitated. "I'd hoped for a smoother ride. You'd think they'd let refugees through."

The dark man with the newspaper was puzzled. "We're not refugees."

"They don't know that, do they? What bastards these people are. Worse than the Poles."

"You're from Galicia?" asked the woman.

"I spent years in Moscow. And two years in Siberia."

"Where in Siberia?" asked the man opposite him.

"Near Kondinsk. Then I was a few months in the army."

"I know Kondinsk," said the man who had asked the question. He looked at me. "Are you a 'Siberian,' too?"

"Happily," I said, "no."

"It's an experience," said Potoaki. "It gives you a better idea of what you're fighting for. You live like the peasants. All our people should do it voluntarily. It keeps your feet on the ground."

"Or under it," said the dark man. Only I and Marusia Kirillovna did not laugh at this.

"You get your milk in slices up there." Potoaki became nostalgic.

"You had milk?"

"The peasants did. They were often very kind. You have to saw it. Have you watched them sawing their milk?"

The man opposite nodded, but now he was looking skeptically at Potoaki, as if he did not believe the man had been a political prisoner at all. There was a great deal of elitism involved. Whatever your intelligence, the length of your Siberian sentence gave extra weight to any argument you might make. They were like savages. And all obviously originally well educated.

The train was going faster. Soon it was moving as rapidly as any prewar Express. This cheered us. "We could be in Odessa by morning," said Potoaki. He relaxed.

His fellow Siberian said quietly, "I never feel lonely now. Not after so much solitude. Every spring I am utterly reborn. A new person. But with the same political convictions, of course. That, however, is the mind. The mind remains. But the spirit is reborn every spring."

He was becoming as much a bore as Potoaki. The man by the window uttered a choking, tubercular cough. The coughing became worse. He began to snort and wheeze.

"It's asthma, I think," said the woman. She made to open the window. We all protested.

"Get him into the corridor." Potoaki helped the man to his feet. Blood was on his lips. He tried to suppress the coughing and at the same time gasped for air. "What we need is a doctor."

From boredom and to show I was a good comrade, I got up and moved along the carriage, asking if a doctor were present. Naturally, there was not. Any person with a real profession would have refused to be in the "political" carriage. They would have had proper work to do. The coughing subsided as I returned. Ice was falling away from one of the forward windows, melted by gusting steam. I saw a few bare trees and small, snow-covered hills. We passed what I took to be gypsy fires. I felt much better now we had picked up speed.

I remained in the corridor for the next hour or two, smoking and thinking. I had been lucky. None of the Bolsheviks had questioned me. All assumed I must be on important business because I had arrived in an official car. Dawn came, miserable and cunning. The train's pace did not slacken. We were at least halfway to Odessa. The woman emerged from the compartment. She was stiff. She stretched her legs and arms like a dancer. Her pistol was on her hip. I realized, with a hint of amusement, that both skirt and black blouse were of heavy silk. She had not had a deprived childhood. She was used to the best. She nodded to me and asked for a cigarette which I willingly gave her. I had several hundred with me. They were likely to prove invaluable. We smoked. She rubbed at her neck. She seemed paler. I wondered if she were Jewish. There was something about her mouth. She yawned, looking out onto the grey snow. The sky was heavy and melancholy. There was yellow-grey mist hanging between it and the land. I have never really seen anything like it since. It seemed to depress her. I had a stupid impulse to put my arm around her shoulders (though she was almost as tall as I). I motioned. She looked into my face. She seemed startled. She said rapidly, "You're tired. You should rest."

"Aha," I said. This was significant, even to me.

"You must have a great deal on your mind. Too much thinking is exhausting, eh?"

"Oh, indeed, Marusia Kirillovna."

She hesitated. "I'm disturbing you?"

"Not at all." I put my hand out to her without touching her. "I'm bored."

This relieved her. "I can't stand being still. It's what makes a revolutionary, I suppose. Impatience."

As one whose main virtue is patience, I could say nothing. Perhaps her generalization was correct and that was why I was not a revolutionary. I have no patience with fools; but you will not find me complaining after five minutes if a bus does not come along.

She continued. "One desires to create Utopia overnight. It's hard to understand, isn't it, why people resist? They haven't the imagination, I suppose. Or the vision. We have to supply that. It's our function. We all have a role."

I nodded. The train slowed, then gained speed. It drummed down a gradient, turning in a long curve, and everything was grey, including the locomotive, part of which I could now see. Our skins were grey. The windows were grey. The smoke from our grey cigarettes blended together to form a single grey cloud near the ceiling.

"But what is duty, I wonder?" asked Marusia Kirillovna.

There came a noise from outside the train. I looked up at the embankment. I saw men in heavy coats squatting behind machine guns. Others were mounted. They fired at us with carbines.

The glass shattered. I fell to the floor, bearing Marusia Kirillovna with me. The train began to shriek and shudder. Cold air filled the squealing corridor. The train jolted as if mortally wounded, skidding down the gradient for a few more yards. It twitched and became lifeless, save for the sound of steam escaping, like the last breaths of a corpse.

Marusia Kirillovna's blood stained my shirt and jacket. It warmed my hands. Her face was all blood. The only thing I could recognize was one sad and disapproving eye. Even as I crawled back toward the compartment I thought she had died exactly as her romantic nature might have demanded. Few of us are given the opportunity.

The Bolsheviks in my compartment were searching in their luggage for the pistols they all seemed to carry. I was astonished to see so much metal in those limp hands. I pulled my own bags down from the rack and, pushing them ahead of me, scrambled through the connecting door into the next carriage. I had no wish to be identified with the Reds.

I found myself in a press of peasants who screamed uncontrollably or sat with their hands covering their heads. The glass here had also been shattered. Several people were wounded while others were quite dead, sitting bolt upright between fellow passengers who could not or did not wish to move. It was a peculiar moment. The peasants thought I was an official. They began asking me what had happened. I said I intended to find out. They must let me through. They pushed one another back, some even removing their caps, to allow me to pass. There were more machine guns firing. It was from our side. Another volley. There were shouts from the embankment and from our own soldiers. The firing stopped. They seemed to be parleying.

I reached the end of the second carriage and decided to wait where I was. The lavatory was occupied. I balanced my bags on top of some sacks and moved a little distance away, as if I were merely waiting to use the lavatory. Through the broken glass I saw stocky figures stumbling down the embankment. They made dark scars in the snow. They were laughing and using words like "comrade" and "soviet." I began to feel a little less anxious. These were Bolsheviks who had fired on us by accident. They were a long way from Bolshevik lines and wore no red stars. Indeed, they had no identifiable uniforms at all. I guessed they were irregulars.

THIRTEEN

They were using a mixture of Russian and Ukrainian which was easy enough to understand. At least half of what they shouted was slogans. The attackers had begun to argue with the defenders. They needed supplies. The Red Army soldiers pointed out that the train only carried passengers. I heard one of the newcomers laugh. "They'll have supplies. What are they? Katsupi on their way to France?"

"There are important comrades on board. They have work in Odessa."

"We have work, too. Give us the Jews and a Katsup or two. We need food. Do you know how long we've been out here?"

"Who are you with?"

"Hrihorieff."

"He's turned against us."

"He's turned back again."

"How do we know?"

There was silence. Then murmuring. Then some oaths. A few moments later sailors came alongside the train thumping with their rifle butts on the doors. "Everybody out for an inspection, citizens."

They stopped when they got to the "Party carriage." I began to make my way to it, but now the peasants were even more confused, trying to get their bundles together. I was pushed back. I managed to grab one suitcase. The other was left behind. I decided to return to my compartment by way of the ground. I had no galoshes. I plunged through melting snow. It was freezing. My shoes and trousers were soaked by the time I reached the carriage. I was climbing up when a soldier shouted, "Stay where you are!"

I looked at him, smiling. "I'm merely going to my carriage, Comrade. I've been trying to help the people back there who were shot."

The soldier, a heavy-faced Russian, paused. He thought for a moment. I continued to climb. He said, "Why do you have a suitcase with you?"

"I picked it up instinctively. My comrades will vouch for me."

I opened the carriage door. The guard drew back the bolt on his rifle. "Stay there for a moment. I'll have to check this."

"You're being foolish."

"I must be careful."

I was glad I had the suitcase with my spare papers in it. At least they would show me as nothing more than an innocent engineer, my "cover," if they liked, for Odessa. There were more people out in the snow now than there had been at Fastov. I heard a peasant ask an insurgent where we were. Near Dmitrovka, he said. It was a town some fifty versts from Alexandriya. It meant we had not been on the direct express route at all, although we were certainly heading for Odessa.

I was relieved that we had not yet reached territory controlled by the notorious "Batko" Makhno. Batko meant "Little Father" or "Elder," but with a more democratically affectionate ring. Makhno was supposed to be fighting on the Bolshevik side but was notorious for his treachery. He had almost defeated the Nationalists single-handedly at Ekaterinoslav in November.

Hrihorieff's men were a small unit left by the line to stop any passing train. People began to argue that the loco had been flying red flags. The Haidamaki claimed they had been confused. Nationalists were not above playing tricks.

Their swarthy leader appeared. He was a barrel-bodied brute with heavy black eyebrows. He was dressed in a dark, red-belted caftan, with bullet pouches, a sheepskin shapka, French army trousers, riding boots. He carried two Mauser pistols, a variety of knives and, of course, a Cossack saber. He sported a vicious horsewhip. Like all Cossacks, he knew the value of that whip in inducing terror. It could kill. The villain was enjoying his power. I began to think I should have been better off with the Chekist.

He stopped, as I had expected, when he got to me. He looked with some amusement at my good-quality clothes. They were wet to the knees and I was still covered in Marusia Kirillovna's blood. "What's in the suitcase?" He spoke superciliously. "Gold?"

"Of course not. I'm on Party business."

"From Moscow?"

"From Kiev."

"They're all yids in Moscow now." He fingered his whip reminiscently.

I nodded.

"And in Kiev. That's what I don't like about this. We're actually helping the yids." He looked away from me in disgust and turned as if for support to the frightened peasants. "Where are you going?"

"Odessa," I began.

He turned back. "I was talking to these. Where are you going?"

They chorused the names of various towns and cities. He scratched his heavy eyebrows. "That's enough." He pointed with his whip at some obvious Jews, including two who wore skullcaps, and told them to stand forward. They came shuffling through the crowd. They looked hopeless.

"Everyone else back in the carriage," he said.

I started to climb the steps again but it was "Not you" and "Back here." I became impatient. "This won't do, Comrade."

"You're a bloody Bolshevik yid."

I was shocked by the double insult. "My name's Pyatnitski. I'm an engineer."

"What's your real name?"

"I have a passport," I told him. I put my suitcase on its side on the step and opened it. I removed my spare set of papers. I offered them to him. It was the look of rage he gave me as he took them which made me realize he could not read. But he held them to his nose, going through them slowly. He put them in his sleeve, having studied the photograph very carefully. "Pyatnitski. That's a Russian name."

"I can't help my name, Comrade. I'm working for Ukrainian interests."

"Nationalists?"

"I don't care what they're called. I'm trying to free Ukraine from all foreign interests."

"Including yids?"

"Naturally."

"So you're a traitor, too."

"I'm not Jewish."

"Then you're the only Bolshevik who isn't."

"May I return to my carriage?"

"Why aren't they outside, too?" He glanced at the windows.

"We're Party people."

"Yids going home to Odessa." He struck at a pane of glass with his whip. It cracked. He laughed. "Come on, Comrades. All out. In the snow with the proletariat."

They would not come. Eventually some of the bandits had to board the carriage and drive everyone down. They stood in groups like angry chickens. They had put their revolvers back in their pockets or in their luggage. Many were protesting. Not a few displayed special cards and passes. They made more noise than the whole of the rest of the train. "Shut up!" shouted our persecutor. "What money have you got?"

"Money?" It was, I think, Potoaki speaking. "Hardly any."

"Bloody Red yids. Gold!"

"Pogromchik!" said a thin-faced woman in a head scarf. "You've killed half the people in there. Corpses all over the place. You killed a girl!"

"We're used to killing, lady. It doesn't mean a great deal to us."

"Trotsky will learn of this," said someone else.

"Then Trotsky will find out how we treat yids in Ukraine. We're not working for yids, Red, White, Green or Yellow. We've had enough of them."

"Anti-semitic, ignorant capitalist . . ."

"I'll admit to all of that, Comrade. Hrihorieff is fighting with your masters because it suits him. To get rid of the landowners. You think you're using us. We're using you." He lashed out with his whip. Its thongs whistled over the woman's head. She ducked and sobbed.

"You bastard."

"We want gold and supplies. We were promised them by Antonov. Where are they?"

"They're on the next train," I said. "A special train."

"How do you know?"

"We discussed your supplies before I left. We knew it was urgent."

"Coming down this line?"

"Following us."

"That's right." Someone had guessed what I was doing. "It shouldn't be more than half an hour behind."

"Good," said the Cossack. "We'll wait for it."

"There might be a crash," I pointed out.

"Fine. We'll be sure it stops then, won't we?"

"You'll foul up the alliance," said Potoaki. "You'll lose all our support."

"We've been doing fairly well without it. We need a few immediate supplies, a bit of ammunition. You might see us in Moscow before the spring's out." He was glutted with provincial pride because of a few local victories. He was like those Vikings who attacked a town on the Seine and came home claiming they had sacked Rome. He made a noise in his nose and looked me up and down. "You're an engineer. What sort?"

"Most sorts."

"Know about motor engines?"

"Of course."

"You can fix one?"

I decided I had to ingratiate myself with this idiot or stand the risk of being shot. "All things being equal."

"What?"

"If no new parts are needed. I can see what's wrong. If something's missing I might be able to improvise. But if you've lost something crucial . . ."

"We've got a truck," he said. "It stopped. Will you look at it?"

"In the common cause?"

He shrugged. "Will you look at it?"

"If you promise I get back on the train when I've done so."

"All right."

I did not know if he would wait for the fictional supply train or whether he would be afraid to face it. I returned my bag to my compartment. On a page of the notebook I carried I wrote Uncle Semya's address. I put it in the suitcase. The other case had only clothes. This one was the most important, because it contained my plans, my designs, my notes.

I joined the scowling Cossack. His men were already looting the train, watched by helpless Red sailors. Not only Jews were suffering, although these were getting the harshest treatment. A Hasid with a bloody crotch was spread-eagled, dead, halfway up the embankment.

I followed the Cossack as he plunged toward the crest. Having slipped a couple of times, I was now covered in snow. I was shivering and uncomfortable. We reached the top. We looked down on a thin earth road. There were some ponies standing there, attended by a young boy in a tattered sheepskin. Their breath looked whiter than the snow and there seemed to be a tranquillity here. Farther along the road were three carts, harnessed to horses, and a motor van. From the van came more vapor. German insignia had been partially scraped from its sides. It flew a red flag. The hood was open. Two Cossacks were arguing about what they could see inside. They spoke in dialect. As we approached, they fell silent. One of them removed his cap, then put it shamefacedly back on. Their leader said, "This is a mechanic from Moscow. He'll look at it."

I could see immediately that the radiator hose had come loose. All it needed was tying back on with a leather thong. I decided to try to impress them. My life depended on it. "Who drives?" A sickly fellow, the one who had removed his cap, raised his hand. "You start the engine," I said to his companion. The crank-lever was already in position. He began to turn it like a peasant winding a bucket from a well. At last the engine fired and immediately began overheating. I enjoyed its warmth in that bitter air. I walked round and round in front of the truck, as if thinking deeply. I told them to stop the engine. I told them to stand back. They did this with alacrity. I took the hose in my gloved hands and replaced it. I asked for a thong. One was found. I bound the hose up, unscrewed the radiator cap and told them to put snow into a bucket and warm it on the engine.

"Snow!" said their leader. "The thing runs on benzine."

Even I was surprised by this ignorance. "Do as I say."

The two men found a large water container and began to pick snow up in their hands, cramming it in. When it had melted I told them to begin pouring it into the radiator. "Not too quickly."

Eventually the radiator was brimming over. I told them to start the engine again. As the truck spluttered and shook the leader yelled at me, "It hasn't worked. What else is wrong?"

Then the motor was turning. The Cossack who had cranked it jumped back. By the smell of the fumes, it was hard to know what kind of fuel they were using. The black smoke suggested it might have been unrefined oil. The truck began to roll toward me. The driver yelled and swung the steering wheel. Their driving was only slightly better than their knowledge of the internal-combustion engine. A brake was applied. I picked myself out of the snowdrift. From behind the embankment I heard sounds and saw steam. "The train's leaving."

"You've just saved your life." The leader grinned. He was pleased to see the truck running. "Thank God, if you like. What's a trip to Odessa worth now? You've just been saved a trip to Hell. I don't know what you thought you were: yid, Katsup or Bolshie. But you're now an official engineer with the host of Hetman Hrihorieff, serving under Sotnik Grishenko. Aren't you proud?"

The bandits were coming back, grinning, waving and displaying their dishonorable booty. The stuff was thrown into the truck. I was made to climb aboard with the rest of the loot. I found myself in a tangle of stolen goods, machine guns, ammunition, salted pork and two small girls who giggled when they saw me and offered me some herring. I accepted. It might be the last food I would get. The girls murmured at me in their thick accents. They were survivors from a village fought over by Reds and Nationalists. The truck moved off. Sotnik (Captain) Grishenko rode up close behind us. He had a look of self-satisfaction on his hard features. "Fix the canopy, if you like. You'll be warmer. Don't eat too much. That's food for a lot of soldiers."

"Where the hell are we going?" There was no point in my remaining polite.

"Don't worry, yid, you're in safe hands."

I shouted back at him, "I'm not Jewish. I'm traveling on Party business!"

"Then you're on Jewish business, aren't you?" He was pleased at his wit. He whipped his horse into a trot and was gone. I looked out at the bleak, uninhabitable hills. The line of yellow mist had joined the land. I tried to see smoke, either from the train or from a farmhouse where I might seek refuge. But there was nothing.

All I had worked for was in a suitcase in a carriage full of Bolsheviks who would steal it without a scruple. My mother and Esmé might be waiting at the station and learn of my fate. There was nothing I could do except hope we passed through a town. I would try to escape and send a telegram to Odessa. I shifted myself into a more comfortable position against a machine-gun tripod. In the end I was forced to rest my elbow on a side of pork. It became colder. I lowered the canopy, but let a corner flap. I would be able to see if we reached a good-sized settlement.

I was in the position of an enslaved magician. While I was able to perform simple tricks for these barbarians, they would keep me alive. I had been horrified by the bandit's assumption that I was Jewish because Cossacks felt no conscience at all about killing Jews. Accuse a Slav of being a Jew and you take his breath from his body, the saliva from his mouth, the soul from his eyes. I do not fear death. I have God and I have my honor. My pride has gone. They laugh at me in the market. They call me names, even Jew. They steal from my shop and put their greasy hands on my clothes, and they sneer and ask stupid questions. Mrs. Cornelius screamed at them and made them leave. The young girls are so sweet. They buy the white nightdresses and the little blouses and the silk knickers and they are so beautiful. They should sing the "Dante" of Liszt to the music of harps. Lament for exiles; lament for Dante in his exile and his greatness. Lament for Chopin, who could never come to terms with his own Slavic spirit, and who also became an exile. I should like to die in Kiev, looking at lilacs and chestnut trees. The Bolsheviks have probably cut them all down to make their motorways. It is all flats. It is like the flats around here. That is your socialism. The rationalists destroy our world. Where we see beauty and the boundless wonders of science, they see only tidy shapes; their flats. Give me the old Russian rutted track across the broad steppe. Give me that again and I shall forget God's gifts of Science and Prescience. The people do not want Prometheus. Prometheus is burdened by knowledge.

The road did not improve. The truck had no real suspension. It veered frequently. The driver used vodka as a substitute for experience. He needed courage, considering the speed at which he was driving and the condition of the road. Horses and carts vanished behind us. I would have had a better than average chance of escape if I jumped clear then. But I would have frozen to death. I had no proper clothing. I had no map or knowledge of the area. I was not even sure which province this was. In spite of the noise from the truck, the discomfort and the fighting of the two little girls, toward evening a sense of peace came. The truck began to slow. I looked through the flap. To my elation I saw we passed through a fair-sized village. I eased myself toward the canopy and was about to squeeze out when the truck stopped. I was thrown among pork and machine guns. The little girls squealed and giggled. Voices came from the twilit street. I drew back the canopy and jumped out. I faced two men wearing blue jackets with gold frogging. For a moment I thought they were officials and was relieved. Then I realized they also wore bandoleers. One had a sailor's cap. The other had a fur hat with earflaps. They were heavily bearded, with a slight Oriental appearance. They were bandits.

"Fraternal greetings, Comrades." I spread my arms wide, as if to embrace them. "Pyatnitski. Engineer and mechanic."

In Russian one of them said dully, "What?" I repeated myself, word for word. A man in a clean, grey greatcoat and regulation cap came striding up. He said cheerfully, "They don't know any Russian except military stuff. They can take orders, poor bastards, but they can't follow a joke. They're from Volhynia. They'll understand Polish."

I thought it best not to mention my Polish. Knowledge is often of most use when kept to oneself.

"Where are we?" I asked.

He was amused. "Purgatory. We've taken over the town as our base. Who are you with?" He was clean-shaven and spoke with an educated accent. He signed for the truck to pull over toward a church being used as a storehouse.

"I was going to Odessa. Grishenko asked me to fix the truck, so I obliged. Is there anywhere I can send a telegram?"

"Someone's repairing the wires. They'll be working by morning. At least as far as Ekaterinoslav."

It would be possible to catch a train from Ekaterinoslav. Sotnik Grishenko and his men came plodding up on weary ponies. "Trust you to be hobnobbing with Jews, Yermeloff!" He dismounted and yawned.

Yermeloff laughed. "He said his name's Pyatnitski."

"He's got papers to prove it, too." These were drawn from the dirty sleeve. "See?"

Yermeloff could read. In the bad light he looked at them and shrugged. "They're good papers. Are you on your way out of Russia?"

"Certainly not." I reached for my passport. Yermeloff hesitated, glanced at Grishenko, then gave it to me. I put it in my pocket. "I'm working for the Party."

"You're from Moscow?"

"No. I'm from Kiev. I'm as good a Ukrainian as anyone. I want Ukraine to have her old pride back."

Grishenko snorted. "Well, Katsupi and yids stick together. Good luck with him, Yermeloff. Bu don't let him escape, eh? We've uses for him. He muttered a spell over our truck and she's as good as new." He crossed to the church and, leading the two little girls by their hands, entered the doors, like a father on his way to worship.

Yermeloff said, "You needn't be afraid. I have Jewish comrades."

"I have Cossack blood," I told him. "It is my misfortune if I look Jewish to you. Is everyone who is not fair-haired, pink-skinned, a Jew? Is your leader a Jew?"

"Everyone's a Jew to Grishenko. It makes killing them easier. You don't really talk like a Jew. I apologize."

This well-educated man might be useful as an ally. I accepted his apology in the hope of encouraging his protection. The trouble with brutes is that they are suspicious of Reason yet become aggressive if you shout at them. God knows what their lives are like as children.

We had arrived at a house on one side of the broad, muddy, unmade streets, some distance from the church. It was a small house, built around a courtyard in which two ponies and a goat were teth-ered. "Are you really an engineer?" Yermeloff asked. "Or were you just lucky?" His cool eyes looked into mine with an expression of the mildest curiosity. He laughed. "I was a lieutenant in the Czarist army. I'm a captain with our Ataman. Would the Bolsheviks make me a general, do you think?"

We entered the doorway. A black-clad woman of indeterminate age shuffled ahead of us along a dirty passage. The walls had patches on them where icons and pictures had been. "That's our hostess." Sotnik Yermeloff called out to her, "Is there any tea left, Pani?" She went into her room. Bolts were pulled. He was philosophical. "She pretends to be deaf. You'd be surprised how many deaf people there are in this district. Everywhere else we've stayed, too. At least three quarters of the population. They go deaf at about nine years old. Before that, they're dumb."

We came to a square room with a stove in it. The stove had been decorated with primitive paintings. Most of these had peeled away or been blackened by soot and time. Three other officers, all in different uniforms, sat at benches around the stove. They shared a large piece of meat which they passed from hand to hand. There was black bread. Some vodka.

"Do you mind if this comrade joins us?" Yermeloff went close to the stove. They looked at me. One of them, with a dark half-beard and scarred forehead, chuckled. "Not at all. Have some bread. Have some pork." I had already had the herring and I did not look forward to mingling spittle with these ruffians. They probably had at least three kinds of venereal disease. I contented myself with a large piece of rough bread and a can of thick, acrid tea which had been left on the stove. I was offered no vodka. I had become very tired. I had had

little sleep for nights and no opportunity of a reviving sniff of cocaine. I said I wished to urinate; was there a place? "In the yard with
the horses. The real privy got damaged last night. We tried to pull
Yuri out because he'd been in too long. But we pulled through the
wrong hole." I left these jolly fellows and returned to the yard. It was
so cold that any desire to answer the call of nature was instantly
dismissed. With the house-door shut behind me, I stood looking at the
ponies. The goat was now in the corner, being milked by a crazed-
looking girl.

I reached surreptitiously for my cocaine, found a small "single-
dose" packet I had hidden, dragged out my handkerchief and pretended to blow my nose. It is not the best method of taking cocaine,
but it was the only one available. I emptied the packet into the handkerchief. It was a large amount. I had come to overuse the drug
while working on the Violet Ray. Even this dose had only a minimal
effect. I still felt slow and drowsy. But my head had cleared a little.

Nobody knew what was going on in Ukraine in those days: armies
came and went, won and lost battles, looted towns, were termed
glorious allies, barbaric enemies, treacherous comrades often within
the same hour: bandits, Cossacks, Anarchists, Bolsheviks, Nationalists. The words were meaningless. The loyalties of the various
armies were, as we say in chemistry, highly volatile. I could not know
if Hrihorieff (he had already fought with Skoropadskya and Petlyura) was with the Bolsheviks or not. He could be pretending to be
with them; he could be pretending to be against them. He could be
pretending to parley to gain time for his men out on raids. It was the
essence, I suppose, of guerrilla war. Our land had become worse than
the American prairies at the time of Custer. It was even more savage
and with no single government in control.

The oil lamp in the room was burning low as I came back. All the
soldiers with the exception of Captain Yermeloff had huddled down
into rags and stolen skirts and were going to sleep. Yermeloff unbuttoned his greatcoat. He tried to roll a cigarette out of newspaper and
tea leaves. I slipped two of my papyrussa from my pocket and offered
him one. He was grateful. We lit the cigarettes. It is a twentieth-
century ritual, this exchanging and lighting of cigarettes. It requires
proper analysis by those who study human behavior. We sat down
together against the wall nearest the door. Yermeloff put the lamp between us. It was cold. The other soldiers had taken the best positions
near the stove. "Where's your main host?" I asked.

"Hrihorieff? His headquarters. Alexandriya. We're a foraging force."

"My father was a Zaporozhian Cossack," I said. "'So I have blood ties with the Ataman.'"

"You're probably right. You're both as likely to be Zaporozhians as not." Yermeloff was amiable. "He's got about fifty titles, at the present count. More than Krassnoff." He enjoyed the cigarette slowly. He let it go out and then relit it from the waning lamp. "It's strange how five years ago we were merely farmers or workers or even schoolboys. Infantrymen, cavalrymen. Now we're all Cossacks. There must be enough of us to drive every Turk and Tartar over the edge of the world. But instead Christian kills Christian and socialists ram bayonets into the groins of socialists." He scratched his head and laughed.

"You're not a Cossack?"

"I was with a Cossack brigade." He shrugged. "I can ride a horse. It's enough. We're fighting cavalry actions all over the place. Doesn't it seem strange? Has some atavist engineered the whole thing for his private amusement? We've gone back in time a hundred years at least. Look." From the belt beneath his coat he drew two large and very beautiful flintlock pistols. I had seen old prints of Cossacks wearing them. They were black with elaborate silver decoration. Typically Caucasian, the weapons had buttons where triggers would normally be. There were flints in the locks. They looked as if they worked. "I got these out of a museum while everyone else was busy looking for gold and meat. I've shot two men wth them now. One was wounded. One fell over and cracked his head. But he was killed. You use ball bearings of the appropriate caliber. And I take them seriously. They're loaded now. Think how many poor Jews' arses they've been fired up!" He balanced one in his gloved hand. "And they're worth a small fortune as antiques."

"They're not very practical, are they?"

"They kill." He spoke in a baffled voice. "And if I wanted to make a run for it—I don't know, to Berlin or somewhere—I could live for a month by selling them for the silver alone. I've seen two lots of men fighting, in the past week, with sabers and whips, just as in the days of Taras Bulba. Is it happening all over the world? Is it the Dark Ages?" He seemed anxious to hear my considered opinion.

"It looks that way," I said. "But the Entente forces still have aeroplanes and tanks. Even the Bolsheviks have a Spad. I saw it outside Kiev. Flying well."

"For how long?"

"You really think it's the end of civilization?"

"If I didn't I wouldn't be here. I want to learn how to survive. I want to become a successful savage. Can you see my point?"

"It's defeatist."

"So was deserting from the Galician Front."

"You deserted?"

"With everyone else. I'm not an individualist, Comrade. I'm a Zaporozhian Cossack, like you. I've thrown away my Tolstoi and my Dostoieffski. Now I sing dirty songs and make jokes about yids and I get drunk on bad vodka. I piss in a line with thirty other drunks all farting and swearing and boasting of the human beings they've killed, the girls they've raped, the horses they've stolen. I accepted civilization as a gift. I never thought twice about it. Now I'm morally obliged to accept barbarism. I don't intend to think about it. That's the end of that." He got up and found a cup in which some grubby vodka still swilled. I refused it, so he drained it. "How did Grishenko get you?"

"He held up a train. I was on it. I agreed to fix his truck. He let the train go and I was stuck. He promised to let me back on the train."

"He would. He's a bastard. Nobody likes him or trusts him. They say he's a Jewish spy, a Bolshevik spy, a White spy. He's careless, you see, about who he robs. But he'll succeed. This is his world. I model myself on him. We're friends. He gave you to me as a sort of present. He knows I can read."

"He likes you?"

"I wouldn't say that. But everyone needs a friend and I'm Grishenko's friend."

"And what do you think of him?"

"He's a beast. He has no morals. He has hatred instead of a brain. He has malice in place of a heart. I want to be like him. We're both Sotniki at the moment, but he'll rise. Hrihorieff's already noticing him. The Ataman pretends to disapprove of him when the Bolshevik liaison people are about. But he doesn't care. Grishenko's a wolf. Hrihorieff's building up a pack of them. Like Ivan's oprishniki: a circle of iron, of snarling teeth. He's bright enough to use current political catch phrases, but he aims to become Czar. When he does, I'll be a wolf, too. The oprishniki were the only ones ever safe from Ivan the Terrible's blood lust."

He seemed mad. "You could emigrate," I said.

He shook his head. "The world's the same all over. Russia was just the start. The War's done it. Germany's going. There are soviets in England. All the most civilized nations are breaking apart. It's like an earthquake. It can't be stopped. Maybe it's natural. Maybe it's something to do with the sun or the moon. What do you think?"

"It's not possible," I said with self-mocking earnestness, "to reach an analysis with such subjective data. But you're not the first Russian to develop a philosophy based on despair. And you might not be the first to have been wrong."

"I can, as I say, only go by the evidence. Do you read modern poetry?"

"It isn't to my taste."

"Our poets predicted an age of blood and fire. The Apocalypse. Didn't they identify themselves with the end of the world?"

I was not sure. There had been so many -isms and -ists in Petrograd I remain confused to this day. They are all forgotten, those Acmeists and Constructivists. They went mad or killed themselves or were killed by Stalin. As I said recently, I am personally nothing but a "Lisztist." Naturally none of those ignoramuses in the pub followed a word. I begin to believe now that Yermeloff was right. The process has merely been slower, less dramatic and less interesting than he thought.

"Will they let me send a cable to my mother in Odessa?" I asked.

"We're a bit nervous of the telegraph, we savages." He bent to the lamp again, to relight his cigarette. "The message has to be of 'military importance.'"

"The Ataman's still loyal to the Bolsheviks?"

"Technically, yes."

"Then I'll introduce myself as a comrade. I'll say the matter's political."

"He's cunning."

"How old is he?"

"About my age," said Yermeloff.

"Forty?"

"Thirty-five. Have I only aged five years? I must be adapting better than I supposed." He took no offense at my blunder. "I could get through it, yet, eh? I might even witness the reinvention of the wheel."

"Is Hrihorieff like Grishenko?"

"He's much cleverer."

"Why does Grishenko think everyone's a Jew?"

"That's simple. He enjoys the sufferings of others. And nobody enjoys suffering more than a Jew. So Grishenko makes a whole damned circus of it. It's a sort of conspiracy between both parties, I think."

"He believed me a Jew. He didn't kill me."

"He's not sure. He calls everyone a yid who looks a bit wrong to him. If they start to whine and grovel, he knows he's right. It's not complicated logic, is it? There's no secret to it. He's a savage dog. He can smell fear. If one wants to keep his good opinion, by the way, it's as well to display as much savagery as he does."

"I can't accept your cynicism." My head ached.

"We all have ways of surviving. We have to find strong masters in a world like this one."

"Why not aim to be your own master?"

"It's the second rank which survives. I studied history. As a cadet. I was in the army most of my life."

I had guessed. He had the stance and way of relaxing of a regular soldier; a way of economizing on his own energy and that of others. God knows what passions really slept in him. But he would not allow them to wake up. It was his training. He was doing his job as best he could. Having no cause, no Czar, no God, he desperately rationalized the situation by looking about for the most likely Czar. That, at least, was my belief.

It now strikes me how narrowly we missed achieving the founding of a new dynasty in Russia. I imagine we should have had a Czar Grigori of one family or another. Rasputin, perhaps, or Hrihorieff. Or a new Peter, in Krassnoff. I suppose none of them allowed themselves to admit the fullness of their ambition. But they would have let their supporters proclaim them Czar. Rasputin: Theocrat of All Russia. What might he have achieved? An Enlightenment? Or an Age of Terror to match Lenin's? Was he Lorenzo the Magnificent or Savonarola? Did we need both in one? Evidently we did. The theological student from Georgia, Stalin, became Priest-King in the end. He widened and extended the Russian Empire. Kerenski balked at using the whip. He screamed like an hysterical mother at her children, begging us to be good. Stalin proclaimed that Russia should be orderly, and it was orderly. We have had ages of greyness and we have had ages of silver in Russia. In the distant past we have had fleeting ages of gold. We long for those golden ages. But when they come, they are like the gold of an Arctic autumn, seen for a single day. Then Winter falls.

I asked Yermeloff, as he went to sleep, why Grishenko had not waited for the second train of which I had spoken.

"If it was a Bolshevik train, he would have had to wipe everyone out: all witnesses—passengers, soldiers, drivers. The lot. It wasn't economic. He got the best he could. Loot from the Jews and a mechanic to fix our transport. You were quite a coup. I'm honored to own you."

"What fuel was in that truck?"

"Moonshine," said Yermeloff, "in all likelihood." He turned his back and began to breathe deeply.

I did not sleep. I went out into the yard again. I wished I could ride. I considered stealing the truck. But it would be hard to start and it might be low on fuel. I did not dare risk Grishenko's anger. I would wait until we got to Alexandriya and look for Bolshevik "comrades." Politicians were easier to deal with than wolves, and Yermeloff was merely a comfort to me, not an ally. He served his own private Czar: the Emperor of Destruction, the God of Despair. It was almost traditional: to ally oneself with the Devil in the belief that God had given up the world.

FOURTEEN

Music is meant to soothe us.
Even the Cossacks understood that. They had their drinking songs;
their mournful ballads of death and love; and their lullabies. A
Cossack, his rifle on his back, his sword at his side, singing a lullaby
to a child, is one of the most beautiful sights and sounds in this world.
I saw this when we camped on the way to Alexandriya. I had been
dumped into the booty truck and, ahead of the entire squadron, driven
through the grim February snow. With Kiev captured, Antonov was
now heading south, Yermeloff said. We were all supposed to be
fighting for socialism.

In this Age of the Ego, I was to learn, "socialism" can be anything
one wants it to be. These bandits were all Catholics. Catholicism is
the last rung in the ladder to Communism. Socialism or freemasonry,
call it what you will, it is all tainted with the same false pride. Only
the Greek Orthodox religion is free of the taint. In our religion,
Christ rules. There is no such thing as an independent conscience. It
is the only religion which can save us from Carthage. I thought God's
gifts to me were enough. But they were taken away because I accepted them, without Faith. That is why the world now has its Pollo
alla Kiev, its Boeuf Stroganoff, its Strawberries Romanoff: because
the generals, the politicians, the lawyers, betrayed God's Faith. They
had to become waiters, porters and chefs all over the world. It is why

I am selling secondhand clothes in the Portobello Road, to Germans who push me off the pavement to get at some mock-silver Indian bracelet to take home to Munich; to French girls who laugh at me and talk amongst themselves, not knowing I understand every filthy word; to Americans with their terror-stricken condescension.

I had not expected to find such a large camp at Alexandriya. The town itself was of average size. But this was Hrihorieff's home base; his wife and family were here. He had a far larger army than anyone had suggested to me in Kiev. There he had been described as little more than a petty leftist warlord. He had the loyalty of thousands of Cossacks. They swarmed around him. They accepted him, in all loyalty, as their Ataman. He was as powerful as Krassnoff of the Don, who wrote that important book revealing much about Jews, Catholics, Freemasons and their betrayal of Russia. It was published in German in the twenties in four volumes: *From the Two-Headed Eagle to the Red Flag*. It is more truthful than anything written since. That was why the commissars hanged him when they got to Germany. He should have changed his name. I see him taken out into black trees and executed for telling the truth.

Hrihorieff had none of the dignity or literacy of Krassnoff. His bombastic proclamations were pasted up on every available space in Alexandriya and its environs. His camp lay outside the town, beyond the railway yards. Here armored carriages, goods wagons, passenger cars, mobile guns and all the rest of his loot was heaped. They had army tents, shanties, every sort of temporary housing; a massive water cart was constantly filled with vodka, from which any soldier could drink. Not only Cossacks, but regular infantrymen, artillerymen and Haidamaki had joined Hrihorieff. They were all drunk. "Changeable," Yermeloff warned me. He helped me out of the truck and then lifted the little girls down. He called to a woman washing her laundry outside a stationary railway carriage. He told her to look after the girls and feed them.

Now I was Yermeloff's mascot. He tied a red band around my sleeve and told me I was a liaison man with "our friends the SRs." Most of the Cossacks supported the leftist Social Revolutionary group known as Barotbists. These had a great deal of power in Kharkov at that time. (*Barotba* means Struggle, the name of their newspaper.) Hrihorieff issued many of his proclamations on behalf of these near-Bolsheviks. He might not have believed in their cause, but he was wise to accept it. The Cossack will serve his Ataman only if the Ataman serves him. Some of them would even spit when the word "Bolshevik" was mentioned. I noticed a few "leather-jackets" in the town. Apparently Antonov had already sent his officers to parley with Hrihorieff. I asked Yermeloff if I could visit the telegraph post. He shook his head. "You are in my charge. It's my duty to keep an eye on you. Grishenko said so."

"You're of the same rank. Why listen?"

We passed a broken Nieuport and an Albatros. Someone had tried, stupidly, to combine the parts. Neither plane would ever fly. Yermeloff ignored my question. Like a master with his dog, he let me stand by the aeroplanes, as if waiting to sniff at something interesting. He said, "You musn't approach the commissars. Grishenko wants to keep you for us. We need mechanics, you see."

"Hrihorieff will have him shot. I'm a resource being diverted for Grishenko's own use." I was outraged. I had really become a slave; a pawn.

"Hrihorieff might pretend to have Grishenko shot. But Grishenko would not die." Yermeloff was amused. "I, however, would be shot if I let you go. You see the game Grishenko's playing? You are now my responsibility."

"It's a children's game!"

"All war's that. Have you any titles, by the way?"

"I have a Doctorate from the University of Kiev. Petlyura made me a major against my will."

"Major will be good. You're now Major Pyatnitski of our Engineering Corps. Work well with us. You'll get quick promotion." He helped me pick my way through a group of drunken, coughing partisans who lounged outside a hut. By the smell, the place was used as a latrine. "You outrank me already, you see!"

I was still tired. I was out of my depth. I had to stay with Yermeloff. He was my sole link with sanity in this unholy chaos. I resented him, nonetheless. He mocked me. The camp stretched for miles along the railway tracks. Occasionally long trains steamed in. They dispensed soldiers, guns, booty. Cossacks stumbled between moving locomotives, scarcely aware of them. I saw several men come close to being crushed under the wheels.

We entered a tent with two camp beds of standard army design. Yermeloff scratched himself and frowned. "We'll have to find you a palliasse."

"You share this tent?"

"With my friend Grishenko."

So I was to sleep with Yermeloff and his master. I was to be the slave of a slave. Yermeloff opened an ammunition box. It had not been locked. Anyone could have stolen from it. He took out a bottle of good vodka: a brand I recognized from my Odessa days. I accepted his offer and drank deep from the neck. Alcohol warms and blurs. Cocaine brings coldness and clarity. It was alcohol I needed. Yermeloff told me to wait. He closed the tent flap behind him as he left, but I watched through a parting. He headed back toward the railway yards, laughing and joking with the soldiers, walking with a brutal swagger which made me suspect his "gentle" manner might actually be the façade. I sat down on one of the beds. I tried to make sense of things. It was impossible. I had been captured by Cossacks. I was only alive because Grishenko thought I could help his prestige, his ambition, while Yermeloff wanted an audience for his sentimental drivel. I could be shot with impunity. I could be tortured. I took another drink and began to laugh. Here was a test of my wits. I would use the alcohol in order to sleep; then tomorrow I would make the best use of some cocaine. I had decided to follow Yarmeloff's lead. Until I could get to safety, I would be as hardened a partisan as the next man. I would elevate myself, not as Yermeloff intended to do, but through my intellect. I would make myself indispensable to these savages. I recalled stories by Conan Doyle and Haggard, where white men fell amongst natives and baffled them with simple scientific tricks. Not Grishenko or even Hrihorieff but *The Lost World* and *King Solomon's Mines* would be my models.

Yermeloff returned. He took the vodka from my hand. "That stuff's hard to come by. I had to trade a woman for three bottles." He stood aside as two filthy partisans with rime and spittle in their beards placed a straw mattress and a blanket on the ground. Dumped on top of these was a ragged greatcoat, a sheepskin hat with parts of the sheep still clinging to it, a pair of clumsy felt boots and some moth-eaten fur gloves. "Much prized." Yermeloff corked the vodka. "Put them on."

"My own coat—"

"We Cossacks are touchy about people who are too proud to dress like everyone else." He spoke insouciantly, but with such a significant little gesture of the bottle that I followed his advice. My good coat was removed; the rags were donned. Lice were already crawling on my body. The felt boots were big enough to fit over my shoes. I almost immediately became warmer. "Let your beard grow if you can," said Yermeloff. I was resentful of this. I had tried to grow a beard. The result had made me look like a cankerous spaniel. It would be two or three years before a proper growth would come. By then, of course, beards were out of fashion, in reaction to those elders who had proven themselves so useless in allowing the War to begin. A small mustache would give character to my face by 1925.

Yermeloff stood back, looking me over. "Wear the hat set high and to one side." He pushed it into position himself. "Don't you know the expression: 'Beware of men who wear their caps over their eyes'? A cap pushed up shows you to be a brave, open Russian, a daring Cossack needing no protection from anything. You say your father was a Zaporozhian. Didn't he teach you this?"

"He's dead." How things had reversed. I brought myself a certain glory from what had been, until now, my shame. "He was a Socialist Revolutionary. An assassin. He was shot in 1906 for his part in the uprising."

Yermeloff was pleased. "You really are what you say! You're a puzzle, young major. A boy genius, a hardened socialist, and half a Zaporozhian Cossack. What was your mother?"

"Her family was Polish."

This seemed significant. He nodded his head but remained silent. I sat down again on the edge of the bed. He uncorked the bottle. "Take a small swig this time. I'm mean about vodka of this quality."

"You shouldn't leave it untended. It could be stolen."

"Cossacks don't steal from each other." He was sardonically serious. "Zaporozhians have their pride." He unbuttoned his coat, wiping at his neck with a piece of rag. "Would you dare steal from one?"

"I'm not a thief."

"We're not thieves. We forage, particularly in ghettos. We make appropriations, particularly from unguarded trains."

"I was taught to respect Cossack honor. You need not remind me of, nor should you mock at, true Zaporozhian ethics. Those men out there are scum."

"The Cossack hosts began as scum. When Moscow sought their help against the Tartars she made them into wholesomely romantic figures. They do the same to this day to trappers and cowboys in America."

This was ridiculous. But it was best to say nothing. Yermeloff took out one of his black-and-silver flintlocks. He sighted along the barrel.

"These are useless if you try to handle them like modern firearms. According to logic, it would be impossible to hit anything with one. That's why these are mine. As some men can master a particular horse, I can master these. They are the symbol of my survival!"

I was unimpressed. Later, Paris and Berlin would be like nineteenth-century arsenals. Every "Ataman" would be selling his booty as family heirlooms.

The tent flap opened. Grishenko swaggered in. He had a coarse-featured girl with him. He said nothing, but Yermeloff buttoned up his coat and signed to me. We left. Grishenko chuckled and spoke to the girl in Ukrainian. Her answering giggle was ghastly. I would not have expected this sound from so experienced a whore.

Yermeloff looked at the sky. It was grey as the snow. He cursed. "I left the vodka. Grishenko's bound to drink the lot."

"I thought Cossacks never stole from each other."

Yermeloff walked ahead. Again he was the bullyboy. He said in a harsh voice, "Grishenko's my friend. What I have is his."

"And what he has?"

Yermeloff stopped, then he laughed. "His." He came back to put an arm round my shoulder. I remembered Mrs. Cornelius and her fox pelts. I longed to see her Mercedes. I longed for Odessa and my mother and Esmé. Yermeloff led me toward the water tanker. "We'll try some of the ordinary." Bandits took no notice of me. I had reduced my outer appearance to the level of their own. A tin cup was passed from the crowd around the wagon. The vodka was no worse than that I had had on the train. Potoaki would by now be in Odessa, enjoying the benefits of the Rule of Law while plotting its destruction. The Revolution had been a work of modern art; convulsive, undisciplined, emotional and formless. Lenin and Denikin were trying to repaint it to their own tastes. Trotsky had been the catalyst for this whole war and how he enjoyed himself, standing on the roofs of trains, making speeches to soldiers from motor cars, stalking ahead of his generals. What a fool that Jew looked to anyone with half an eye. A goose in the heron pond. He was ridiculous in his glasses, his beard, his uniform. An irritating, self-opinionated buffoon. I could not see why Mrs. Cornelius found him attractive, unless it was his power. He was a bungler. Almost every disaster after 1918 can be blamed on him. They called him the greatest general since Joshua; it is an insult to Joshua. Lenin loved him. They were two of a kind. Antonov was an intellectual but he knew how to fight. Mrs. Cornelius should have taken up with him. But perhaps Antonov was too strong. She liked men, in those days, she could manipulate. She had a weakness for a fool. She liked them safely married. I do not think Antonov was married. I know nothing about him. Stalin probably had him killed in one of those trials. I avoided Russians between the wars. I would sometimes even claim to be Polish or Czech. I could not stand the sympathy of those who took up with émigrés; they made me self-conscious. I want to be myself; not the representative of a culture.

We approached a railway siding where a proclamation had been pinned to a telegraph post. The vodka was affecting my stomach. I mentioned this to Yermeloff. "You're hungry," he said. "We'll get some food here."

A carriage once belonging to a first-class train was being used as a canteen. From the galley came hideous smells. I felt far worse. Yermeloff swung up the steps. Not wishing to be left alone and yet terrified of what I should have to eat, I followed him. We seated ourselves amongst a group of Cossack officers who ate soup and complained about it. A boy brought us two bowls and a piece of bread each. The soup was dark yellow, containing pieces of pale meat. I tried to gather my courage. Yermeloff joined some of the others in laughing at me. "He's new. An engineer. Major Pyatnitski." I grinned with dry lips. This caused them further amusement. I drank a little of the broth and felt no worse for it. The taste was loathsome. I nibbled the meat. It was oddly tender. I swallowed and hastily ate some bread. It was hard. It had the texture and flavor of cheap soap.

"Where are you from, Comrade?" This from a burly Cossack wearing beard and mustache in the old Czarist style. He was handsomely uniformed, though with the inevitable red cockade in his cap and an armband on his sleeve.

"From Kiev."

"They make young majors there."

"Without much effort," I told him. "I was a civilian engineer."

"Who did you work for?" The question was not emphatic but I was unsure of its meaning. I looked to Yermeloff who rescued me with: "His father was an SR."

"Oho," said the Cossack, "so nepotism exists even in revolutionary circles. Where's your dad now?"

"He was killed in '06. My mother's in Odessa."

He looked at me sympathetically. "Don't fret, little major. We're on the way. Those niggers won't get their hands on our women."

French Zouaves were rumored to be running amok, having formed an alliance with Odessa's Jews. Asia and Africa, they said, were shitting on Russian soil. "Nikolaev first, or Kherson, to get fresh supplies. Then we'll be in Odessa. We're the biggest army in Ukraine. They won't stop us."

I thought of my Esmé, my angel, in the grip of some grinning, befezzed Negro. My stomach went sour. For some reason I was able to finish both soup and bread more easily. I felt as Yermeloff had predicted, much better for the heat. Yermeloff spoke to the man who had addressed me. "Did you read the proclamation, Stoichko? What did it say?"

"The usual. How well we're doing. How good we are. How we bring honor to Ataman and aid to Barotbist. How we've recruited Bolshevik help in sweeping Chaos from the land."

"Nothing else?"

"The Fourth and Fifteenth are to entrain for the 'new front' at six-thirty tomorrow morning."

"Where are we going?"

Stoichko cleared his throat. He picked up a piece of bread I had abandoned. "South. There are forty rumors as usual." He munched. "How's that bastard Grishenko?"

"Relieving the pressures of manhood in the tent." Yermeloff wiped his lips. The others became silent.

I looked out of the grimy window. Two priests walked past, chatting together. They might have been in a tranquil country street. I was heartened to see them. They were of the Greek faith. Later I would notice them blessing some red flag or other. There are priests and priests, just as there are Cossacks and Cossacks. But a bad priest, in my own view, is bad indeed: he will use God's word to utter the commands of the Devil. How cheerfully those priests accepted Bolshevism. The few who did not were liquidated or attacked by their fellows.

Stoichko, still with a full mouth, said to Yermeloff, "Want to bunk in with us? We've some spare gear."

Yermeloff shook his head, took off his cap and scratched. He also was running with lice. Lice are not so bad. Often they are the only company one can trust. They frighten people not used to them. But they are only uncomfortable in large numbers. You keep them down by catching and killing them. This relieves the boredom of a soldier's or a prisoner's life. Some members of a military band I knew would draw racetracks on drumskins and race their crabs, as some race mice or frogs. Large amounts of money would change hands. The owners would claim to be able to recognize favorite runners. I do not believe that. To me, one louse is much like another. Cleanliness, according to the English, is next to Godliness. But there are sects in Russia who think exactly the opposite. There are very rich sects who cut off their private parts to be closer to God. The money they make goes to their families. I find that disgusting. But it is understandable.

Yermeloff cracked a louse or two as he considered Stoichko's offer. Then he declined. "Grishenko's never long."

"No girl could live," said one of the others, "if he was. I had a little Jewess after him. I thought she was moaning with pleasure. Then I realized her arm was broken. He's a bastard. She was willing. Willing enough, at any rate. You don't need to use force." He was proud of his professionalism as a rapist. "One wave of a bayonet works wonders. Poor little thing. I told Yashka to be careful with her when it was his turn. I felt a fool."

In spite of my interest in their conversation, I got up. I asked where the latrine was. Yermeloff looked at my face. "That vodka must be bad. You'd better get out. I'll join you in a minute."

"But where?"

"You won't have time to find it. Just go. These comrades will be upset if you vomit all over them."

Amidst more laughter I stumbled to the exit. The entire dining car had been ruined. More than one person had been sick here before. The thought of the soup was too much. I reached the observation platform, then up came vodka, soup and bread. I was shivering. I pulled the old coat about me. I looked back. Yermeloff could not see me. Ahead, in the dusk, was the town. There were Bolsheviks and presumably fairly civilized officers there. My legs were weak, but I began to run until I was safely invisible, with two or three lines of coaches between me and Yermeloff. I pushed through a broken fence, went past a gabled house where a stuffed eagle looked at me from a ground-floor window, and into a side street. Alexandriya was sacrosanct. Only Hrihorieff and his senior staff used it. There were few signs of riffraff from the camp. I wondered if Yermeloff would come after me to shoot me. Two motor vans went by. Their engines were running perfectly. Had Yermeloff deliberately let me go? I thought I heard my name called from the yards. There was so much babble I was probably mistaken. Had Yermeloff baited a trap? Were

he and Grishenko playing a macabre trick? I felt he had been deliberately careless. Possibly Grishenko had lost interest in me and
Yermeloff knew it. Consequently he did not care if I left.

I followed the street. There were wooden blocks paving the main
road. Those blocks, cleared of snow, were like heavenly clouds. I was
in civilization. I stopped a Cossack who was relatively smart. I told
him I was Major Pyatnitski. He pretended the name was familiar as
I had hoped. "Has Ataman Hrihorieff returned yet?" I asked.

"I do not think so, Comrade Major."

I pretended impatience. "Where's the telegraph post? General
Headquarters?" I followed his eyes. He looked toward a building
flying a large red flag.

"I think so."

"Very well." I did not salute. I let my coat fly open, although I was
freezing. It displayed my "classless" suit and revealed me, I hoped, as
a commissar. The combination of clothing was perfect: I was an
intellectual, yet a man of the people. I paused to feel into the lining of
my jacket for another "single dose." I used my handkerchief again to
inhale the cocaine. Much strengthened, I continued on my way. With
a nod to the infantryman on guard, I went through a wicket gate,
strode up a path to be greeted by a podporuchik (lieutenant) in full
green-and-gold Cossack regalia. "I'm Major Pyatnitski." I spoke
firmly. My intention was merely to get to the telegraph and send a
message, allegedly of political import, to Uncle Semya. "I'm the engineering officer. Ataman Hrihorieff told me to report here."

The podporuchik was hardly older than I. He listened carefully,
then escorted me into a hallway crowded with ordinary domestic
furniture, including a stuffed bear. Alexandriya was a town fond of
stuffed animals. There were one or two deer heads on the wall. The
place had evidently been a small hotel. We entered an office where
young ladies, like young ladies in any office in the world, were at
work with typewriters and ledgers. One used an abacus to help her
compute figures which she transcribed rapidly onto a large sheet of
paper. She reminded me of Esmé. Hrihorieff was no simple bandit.
Here was an efficient military headquarters. We passed through that
hard-working throng, through a waist-high wooden barrier, up to a
tall desk. An officer in a torn jacket from which epaulets had been
removed looked at me through tired, mild eyes. He fiddled at his
heavily waxed mustache. He moved some papers in his fingers. He
was about fifty. "Comrade?" He spoke awkwardly, taking note of my

suit. "You are from Kherson? Are the supplies here already?" He consulted a typed list.

"I'm not a supply officer. I'm Major Pyatnitski." My youth and rank had a peculiar effect. He thought it was an impossible combination. But this was now a world of impossibilities. If I was so young and yet a major, I must therefore be an important political person. The cocaine quieted my stomach pangs, as well as my nerves, though my bowels were constricting uncomfortably. "I have to send a telegram to Odessa."

He put weary arms on his desk in despair. "Have we taken Odessa?"

"Not yet. But we have agents there."

"A telegram would have to go via Ekaterinoslav."

"I don't care how it gets there, Comrade." I spoke quietly. "It will naturally be in code, as a personal message."

He was baffled. "Perhaps we should have the advice of the political officers."

"I am a political officer."

"I have no authority."

That was the cry which resounded through Russia. It echoes on to this day. Once authority came from God, via the Czar, to his officials. They knew where they were. Their authority was God's. Now, in the name of Communism, they slither away from authority. I should have thought a Communist's first duty was to accept his own responsibility and that of his fellows. Perhaps I am too stupid to understand the complicated reasoning of Marx.

"Where are the political officers?" I asked. It was a dangerous game, but it was the only one to play now. "This is of utmost urgency."

"Upstairs, Comrade." He pointed as if to heaven. "Didn't you know?"

"I've only just arrived."

"There has been no train."

"I came, my friend, in a truck. I was abducted by an undisciplined bandit who should be punished as soon as possible."

"I do not understand, Comrade. Who was this?"

"Sotnik Grishenko."

This meant something to him. He frowned. He wrote the name down. He circled it. He dipped his pen in his ink and underlined the circling. He pursed his lips. "Grishenko can be overenthusiastic."

"He abducted me from a train taking me to Odessa. Now do you follow me?"

These military clichés rang from my lips like little bells. They pealed for me. I did not have to think. Everyone spoke like that if they had any education. Only the illiterate and stupid used original phrases in Hrihorieff's army. Those in command did nothing but ape the officers they had killed and robbed in their various mutinies and desertions. I had learned this instinctively. Such instincts are of considerable use, but they can complicate one's life.

"You'll deal with Grishenko?"

"I'll report it to the appropriate division commander, Comrade Major."

"Many other comrades were inconvenienced. Some were killed. I was captured. Is that serious enough?"

"It is very serious."

"Grishenko should be severely reprimanded." I would have my vengeance. "Reduced to the ranks."

"He's a useful field officer," began the man at my side. I rounded on him. "Useful? At shooting comrades?"

All the women were looking up. Some were pretty. They were like innocent nuns working quietly, unthinkingly, in Hell. We returned through this pleasant warmth of femininity to climb wooden stairs carpeted with red pile. On the landing a group of men was talking in intense, grumbling tones. They stopped as we appeared.

"Pyatnitski," I said. "From Kiev."

None of these were partisans. Some were dressed as I was. Others wore smart, featureless uniforms of the kind affected by Trotsky and Antonov. They had the fresh-minted Bolshevik insignia: metal stars on their caps, carefully sewn felt stars on their sleeves. The Reds were manufacturing such things on a large scale. Half the people in Bolshevik-occupied Russia were employed running up fresh red flags and pressing out brand-new metal stars.

They greeted me. Some put their hands forward to be shaken. "I was on my way to Odessa. Party business. I was kidnapped, quite literally, by one of those bandits from the railway yards."

"Keep calm, Comrade." A small, prematurely wizened, creature with soft lips and white hands: "I'm Brodmann. It's a problem already familiar to us. Let's go in here." He put his hand on my back and took me into a room full of hard, straight-backed chairs. There was a map of Southern Ukraine on the wall. Someone else closed the door quietly behind us. They seemed to relax. They were more frightened than I. Broadmann said, "We are political people. Bolsheviks and Barotbists. There's been a suggestion Hrihorieff should be liquidated. That's out of the question for the moment. He's the best commander here. I say nothing, of course, against Comrade Antonov. He has also done brilliantly. Hrihorieff commands a huge army. He's sympathetic to our cause. But he's impossible to discipline. He has no real ideological education. That's why it's so important to keep him sweet while we educate his troops. When that's done our problems will be much simpler." He went on in this manner for at least twenty minutes. Anyone who wants a larger bucket of the same drivel need only read one of those novels which win the Stalin Prize with the regularity of a steel press. I picked out all the useful information and then said, "Is there no way for me to get to Odessa?"

"You were on the last train." A tall, thin man in a leather overcoat spoke from near the window. He had been observing a convoy of trucks and artillery. "You were very unlucky. The French have forbidden further trains."

"Can I send a telegram?"

His moody, lugubrious features showed a degree of amusement. "Hrihorieff controls the telegraph as his personal means of communication. One of our people is supposed to be keeping an eye on him but he's completely under Hrihorieff's spell. He'll do nothing without direct orders from the Ataman. We're only allowed to use the telegraph to communicate with Hrihorieff, or sometimes Antonov."

"And where is Antonov?"

"Trying to catch up with Hrihorieff. The bastard moves fast. It's why he's gathering so much support."

I was furious. This was socialism in action: death, destruction and slow strangulation in red tape. None of my risks had been worth a kopeck. I should have remained with Yermeloff. My best plan was to board a train to Kiev where at least I would be on home ground. Mrs. Cornelius might be able to help me. "Is there a train to Kiev?"

"Probably," said the thin man. He drew on his cigarette as a starving baby draws on a teat. "They never give us any information."

"And Grishenko? Can he be punished?"

"It depends how Hrihorieff feels. As his confidence grows he ignores us more." Brodmann offered me a chair. Fastidiously he helped me off with my coat. He placed it in a corner of the room. I must have looked odd in my blood-stained suit and felt boots. I sat down. I had a view from the window of the passing convoy. It was impressive.

"Have you made an official complaint?" asked the thin man.

"If the officer downstairs took any notice."

"He's efficient. One can't say that for most of the others. The complaint will go to the appropriate DivCom."

I was satisfied that at least Grishenko would be severely embarrassed. It was less than he deserved for cutting me off from my family, calling me foul names and forcing me into the company of coarse oafs, of cynics like Yermeloff. My new comrades asked me what I had been doing in Kiev. I said I had been sabotaging Petlyura's defenses. This impressed them. I explained how Grishenko had made me fix his broken truck. I was a trained engineer. I had crucial work at the Odessa docks. I felt my importance growing as I spoke. The gaps in my knowledge of party etiquette were thus glossed over. I was not only a "political man"; I was an "activist." Therefore I ranked very highly in their fanatical hierarchy. I drew on acquaintanceships from Odessa days, from my months in Petrograd. I spoke casually of trains wrecked and guns put out of action. Two or three of those in the room said my name was familiar. My abduction, instead of being a familiar affair, came to be seen in a serious light. My eloquence, my anger, also helped me. I think I could have formed my own socialist group there and then. Thousands would have followed me.

It was easy to become a leader in those days. Most Russians found it impossible to think in terms of self-sufficiency. We must stick together, they said, against the common enemy. The only common enemy I ever found was iconoclasm and egotism. But Trotsky did not want Russia saved. He wanted to be a god. As a god, he would stand on the roof of his Red Train and issue a proclamation: "Let there be peace." Trotsky desperately wished to be acknowledged our Savior, like an Old Testament prophet. Robbed of this, he turned against Stalin. I wonder how he faced God after Stalin kicked him out and he wound up in a Mexican bordello with a pickax in his back. I can imagine the scene. Did God stand on the roof of a train and say to Trotsky: "You are forgiven"? I doubt it. That pickax is probably proving useful in Hell.

My new friends took me down to the back of the hotel. Here was a small dining room. The thin man left us. We sat at bare tables and good simple food was brought to us (Party people always have the best in Russia). I ate little. I still felt the effects of my sickness. There was coffee. I drank several cups. This settled my stomach. The thin man came back. They had been discussing the problem of billeting me. Only a few places were available. Most of the political people slept in Wagons-Lits at the sidings. I, of course, had no wish to return there. I explained why.

"I've spoken to our friend at the telegraph post," said the thin man. "He has had a thousand messages from Hrihorieff. They all conflict, as usual. I sent a complaint about that officer who kidnapped you. It was received and acknowledged. The officer is to be shot. I saw the order."

Though the brute deserved it, I did not want any man's blood on my hands. "Could he not merely lose rank?" I asked. "Or be whipped?"

"Hrihorieff only has one punishment. Death. You're generous, Comrade. But we might not get another chance to teach those pogromchiks a lesson."

It was decided I should share Brodmann's room. Brodmann's partner would go to the yards. As I left with the small revolutionist I asked the thin man, "When will the punishment occur?"

"Immediately. An arrest. An accusation. A firing squad. I gather he's not a popular officer."

"That's true." I only hoped Yermeloff would not blame me and seek me out.

"Then we should not have much trouble." He stopped himself in midgesture as if realizing he had committed a social blunder. "Did you want to witness it?"

"No, no."

"He must be shot. Hrihorieff could return, change his mind and have us shot instead. It's happened." His lips moved in a smile.

I walked with Brodmann through the roaring darkness of a town troubled by excited military preparations. Trucks towing guns honked, teams of artillery horses whinnied. Troops of cavalry and infantry quarreled and cursed and went their ways. Men in full kit ran rapidly across the street into their division headquarters. We passed through all this to the far side of Alexandriya and reached a street of prosperous cottages. Here, so far from the sidings, it was relatively peaceful. We came to a walled garden with a gate in it. Brodmann admitted us with a large key. It was an old-fashioned latch. It had been polished. We strolled along a stone path. This part of the town was almost idyllic, with trees and fences and widely separated little gabled houses. "Our landlord," said Brodmann, "is a retired doctor.

He hates us. He calls us vampires. Of course, 'Jew' is his favorite form of insult. I advise you not to let yourself be drawn into an argument with him. He's harmless."

"Jews! Vampires! You killed the Emperor!" A high-pitched voice shrilled from what I guessed was the parlor.

Brodmann and I crept up the stairs. The doctor did not emerge. I think he was frightened of us. A mouse content to squeak from the safety of his hole.

The room was fairly clean. The beds were unmade, the linen was somewhat grubby. But it was better than Yermeloff had offered me before Grishenko had evicted us. Grishenko would soon regret that action. He was probably already dead. There was little furniture, save an old screen, an ordinary military lamp for light, a pile of pamphlets and handbills evidently not the property of our landlord, a couple of cane-seated chairs and two wooden-framed beds of the sort peasants or servants slept in before the Revolution. Brodmann drew down the blind. He went behind the screen and undressed to his red vest and his long underpants before putting on a thick flannel night-gown. "He's sold or given away everything. He's afraid of looters. He probably has a few bits and pieces hidden in the garden. I don't think he made much from his doctoring. Not in this village. He knew Hrihorieff when the Ataman was a child. Nobody in Alexandriya seems to dislike the Ataman much. The doctor says there's nothing wrong with him, that he's protecting the interests of the Czar. He might as well believe that, eh?" Brodmann continued in this vein. He was one of those politicians who loves to sound "realistic." His cheap cynicism no longer bothered me as I went behind the screen, un-dressed, and got into bed. I wore only my blood-stained shirt, from which I had removed the collar and cuffs. It was very cold. I was restless from the cocaine, but Brodmann's drone helped me sleep peacefully and well.

I became alert early in the morning. Noises from below had awak-ened me. There were heavy boots on the stairs. I was terrified. The doctor's squeaks came along the landing. I cleared my throat, but could not speak. I peered through the half-light as the door opened slowly. I at once recognized the silhouette of Grishenko the Cossack. He had escaped death. Anger poured from him like heat from fresh-cast metal. I knew that this was not a nightmare. I could see the whip at his belt.

I remember only his outline; my sense of his brutality. None of his features are clear to me. I remember his powerful hands. I knew, of course, that he had come to kill me. He held two guns. I was shivering as I sat up.

I waited for the pain of the shots.

But the guns were reversed. He was giving them to me. Like an accusing ghost. Did he want me to kill him? I put my two trembling hands toward the offerings: Yermeloff's pistols with their rounded pommels. I clasped them awkwardly. There was bile in my throat. I did not put my fingers on the trigger buttons. The guns weighted my wrists. They were too heavy. Grishenko was challenging me, I thought. I did not speak.

His voice was a throbbing, furious whisper. "They're from Yermeloff. A gift."

Brodmann moaned in his bed. Grishenko glared at him absently. Then he appeared to dismiss him as he returned his attention to me. "He said to bring them. Now they are yours."

I did not understand.

Grishenko had a tear in his left eye. He pulled one of his long daggers from its red velvet sheath. He leaned over me. "We are free. We have our own laws." He put the knife under my chin. "Up."

"Why?" I began to cough and then stopped, fearing that I would impale myself on the sharp tip. The knife point touched my jugular. I felt the vein pulsing against steel.

"Up, yid."

I recalled Yermeloff's warning. Grishenko was a savage dog who would only attack if you showed fear. I pulled at the triggers. The guns were not cocked. They would not fire. Grishenko put his face closer to mine. His breath burned me. "Up."

I had no choice. I dropped the pistols to the bed. I stood in my shirt. My legs and genitals froze. I was dizzy. He placed his free hand against my chest and pushed me against the wall.

Brodmann began to whine slogans from where he sat in his nightshirt. He babbled about "rights" and my "importance." The Cossack said absently to him, "I'll kill you. Be quiet."

I think my neck had begun to bleed.

Grishenko gripped my shoulder. It felt as if it was going to break. The knife slid slowly down my stained shirt and the shirt parted. The blade touched my groin. "He said you would know what the guns meant to him. He was a holy one. I loved him. I protected him. I thought you would cheer him up. He was not a happy man." The point was drawn down one leg and then another. I hardly felt it, yet blood trickled. I did not beg. My honor was in me. I did not beg as the others begged. When he told me to face the wall, I obeyed. "He wanted you to live. To survive, he said. I did not understand. But Yermeloff was closer to God than I am. Do you accept his gift?"

"Yes," I said. I think I thanked him.

"Yermeloff was shot last night. Because he let you go. Not because your Bolsheviks ordered it. He told me to give you the guns. So I have brought then."

I could not see what he was doing. The knife was at my heart but he was removing something else from his belt. "He made me promise not to kill you."

"You . . . "

"Shut up. I promised. But I said I must make sure you would remember him. I don't think you'll keep his guns."

I heard Grishenko's awful whip whistling through the dull, grey air. We screamed together. I can feel the pain. It was the worst pain I have known. It was the most unexpected. It was inflicted with such skill, such controlled passion, that no bone was broken. But I still bear the marks of the little lead weights in my buttocks.

"Now you'll remember Yermeloff, yid."

He pushed me onto the bed so that my face struck the pommels of the guns. I was weeping. He was still in the room, staring at me, slowly putting his whip back in his belt, his knife back in its sheath. Then he turned and went out. He closed the door quietly behind him. The monster had gone. That monster, who had killed his friend to save his own skin.

I still have the pistols. I have been offered a thousand pounds for them.

FIFTEEN

History is never the same; but events repeat themselves. Gradually, through this repetition, you learn that people are very similar everywhere you go. They have always been inclined to leap to conclusions about me. I have rarely been guilty of anything. Is it my fault they transfer their own hopes and fears onto me? I am a scientist with a scientist's mind. Few understand this. I have been humiliated. Grishenko humiliated me. Brodmann spoke of "outrages" and "lack of discipline" and used his Marxist rubbish to condemn Grishenko's attack, but I could not bring myself to take the matter further. I am a forgiving soul. I had been fond of Yermeloff. To some extent I could understand Grishenko's grief. Nonetheless, it was all but impossible for me to sit on anything hard for many weeks to come. Later, I would give the pistols into the safekeeping of Mrs. Cornelius and would not see them again until 1940. Now, they had become a comfort.

Brodmann had forced the doctor to attend me. I had won some sympathy, though still a "viper" and "Jew," a murderer of the Czar. Alone, I could have agreed with everything he said about the Reds, but Brodmann had hovered. Perhaps he had been afraid the poor little doctor would assassinate me. We were due to link up with Hrihorieff. There was a train we must catch. As we left for the station, I felt only the song of the pain, as we say. It would not be for another day before I experienced the stiffness and throbbing agony, far harder to bear and more irritating.

I saw Grishenko once more while I was boarding the train. He grinned at me. I blushed like a girl. Nobody else noticed my reaction. Brodmann was too furious, pointing out Grishenko as my assailant. In all his looted finery, Grishenko rode away on his pony, lashing at its neck and shoulders with that whip. The round pommels of my pistols rested against each of my hips. They fitted easily into the pockets of my louse-ridden greatcoat. I also had my papers, my diploma.

We received special attention. We had even better accommodations than on the Kiev train. The seats, thank God, were soft. Brodmann sat opposite me, by the window. He kept grumbling and muttering and staring out at the muddy snow, looking for Grishenko. I laughed and told him it was nothing.

"It is typical!" Brodmann would have me know. "Justice is merely their word for vendetta. And this is the material we must work with!"

Strangely, I felt elevated that morning. I felt superior. I chuckled. "Worse has happened to me, Brodmann. You should be in my trade."

"I hate violence." His soft, wizened face clouded.

"Then you're in the wrong vocation." Our thin friend entered, pulled off his long coat, folded it neatly, and placed it in the overhead rack.

"I was a pacifist. The Bolsheviks promised peace. I worked for them at the Front. I published newspapers, pamphlets." Brodmann sat back as the train began to move. "Does anyone know where we're really going?"

"Hrihorieff said he wants us at his field headquarters. He has some idea of taking Kherson or Nikolaev. Maybe he's there already."

"They're far too well defended. Greeks and French in one, Germans in the other."

"The Germans aren't happy about fighting for the Allies and the Whites. They might come over to us."

"But not to Hrihorieff. He's shown what he thinks of Germans. They wouldn't trust him."

The train moved into a wide, horizonless steppe-land. Filth gave way to the purity of late snow. It would begin to melt quite soon. The conflict might be settled by spring. Hrihorieff's and the Bolshevik's advances were rapid. Soon there would probably be a decisive battle. My only fear was that it would occur in Odessa before I could get

Mother and Esmé to safety. Hrihorieff's progress seemed relentless and inevitable. If Makhno joined us, Whites and Allies might well be wiped out. I was praying for dissension amongst the different leftist groups. There is nothing like socialism to divide men up into smaller units. Those flags were the color of the roses I gave to Mrs. Cornelius: the deepest, blood-red luster. The color of my own blood. Pricked on thorns, my blood mingled with the petals: she was my sister, my mother, my friend. Roses. I would not look back. I have no nostalgia. I have been cheated. This is the world. God's purpose will be revealed in Heaven. I had no Faith. All God's gifts were taken from me. I am selling the same fur coats (though cleaner) I was in those days forced to wear. The young men strut up and down like comic-opera Chekists. There is one who wears the badge of Anarchy. What can he know of Anarchy? He speaks a little Russian. I say to him: "What is this?" The badge. He says A is for Anarchy. I say why not wear a badge from A to Z to make the Z for Zionism, it is the same thing. He finds me amusing. He is a fool. All these murders and kidnappings. The Anarchists were fools and still are fools. They rejected power and yet accepted responsibility for their terrorism. What did they gain? What did the world gain? Anarchy? No government? It gained more, worse government. Chaos. The universe expands. The universe grows cold. Soon there will be snow everywhere.

The train stopped after about two hours. We were on the empty steppe. An apparently orderly military camp was set up on a nearby ridge. Soldiers began to trudge across to us. They carried large cans of soup. These were distributed the length of the train. We had made a scheduled food stop. Bandit or not, Hrihorieff knew enough to keep his lines of communication clear. His logistics were excellent. He controlled a wide radius of track. The track and the telegraphs gave him the power of rapid transport and the ability to modify orders quickly. The Whites further South had far less rolling stock or track available to them. They were fundamentally more suspicious of technical innovation. Here the Reds, to their credit, had the advantage. They had fewer aeroplanes, but they were prepared to use them. The Whites put their faith in cavalry charges. They were brave romantics. It was calculating Jews who looked into the future. But they did not see everything.

They say I know nothing of religion. But I have come to religion. My heart and my brain brought me to the noble faith of Russia which resisted Africa and Asia, took root here, in London, in New York, in

Paris, everywhere. Is that a dead faith? The true faith of Constantine, who made Rome Christian, who founded Byzantium? There is no purer faith. It is the faith of the Greeks who invented the Christian religion. The Jews borrowed it and handed it back to them as if it were new. Jews have always traded so.

Can nobody see but me? Spies fill these streets. It is like a nightmare. I am the sole person who realizes what is going on. Nazis and National Front have only acne and envy in common. Communists and foreigners steal our souls, our blood, our minds. But these are not Martians. This is not *The War of the Worlds*. Oh, Byzantium! Come to us with your horses and your swords to save us.

The train started up again. The soup had been a halfway decent shtshyi, with good meat. Brodmann had gone to sleep. The others read or scribbled in notebooks. That was how they fought our Civil War. Yet every man in that carriage probably had more blood on his hands than a dozen Cossacks. Sometimes cavalry trotted alongside the train. The riders gave Red salutes and waved. If we moved slowly they would exchange shouts with the troops. We were carrying guns and soldiers. Every coach was armored. Sometimes, as in our own, they had been fitted with a hodgepodge of sheet metal riveted at random. The windows were largely unprotected. In the event of an attack we were supposed to throw ourselves to the floor and hope for the best. But there were no attacks. Hrihorieff and the Bolsheviks between them had brought a kind of peace to the area. It would not be long before they fell out amongst themselves. In common with the Whites, they all had a hatred of the Nationalists. But the Devil was amongst us. Never had Russia been so divided. Only now are the wounds healing, but Islam and Zion still threaten the Slavic race.

I was to see Hrihorieff the next day. Following his usual habit he had taken over a good-sized town. Mounted on a white Arab, like Skoropadskya's, he was reviewing his troops: motley, swaggering Cossacks in a thousand varieties of clothing, all armed with good carbines. Their ponies, as always, were lovingly groomed. The Zaporozhian Ataman was fairly short, his head was shaven, he had grey, Mongolian features, but he was no play actor. He handled his horse well. His uniform was "pure" Cossack, without any stupid antique adornments. He drew his strength from his troops as Constantine did when he returned from England to claim the Roman Empire. He was a true soldier. He had served bravely in the War. He laughed, he gesticulated, but his horse was always firmly controlled, never allowed to skip or rear. Thus he displayed the intelligence and the will lying beneath the braggadocio. This was why the Cossacks allowed him to be their master, to lead them on their daring attacks on great Ukrainian cities. I understood why Yermeloff had planned to become indispensable to the Ataman, why Grishenko was so useful. If Lenin or Trotsky had possessed half Hrihorieff's manliness we should never have suffered the disasters and consequences of World Communism. There is none, in all that frightful crew, I would have served more willingly than Hrihorieff, yet I continued to be nervous of his followers. Pretending to disapprove of the pogromchik bandits, he nonetheless used them for his own ends, as Queen Elizabeth had used her pirates. Trotsky would cheerfully have killed most of his allies by 1921. He invited them for peace talks or political meetings and had them shot. Trotsky learned bandit ruthlessness but not bandit courage. I am a child in such matters.

The train stayed another day in a siding, then took us away from Hrihorieff's garrison to a nearby Bolshevik camp. This contained more uniforms but it was only slightly less orderly than the partisan camps. Many Red Cavalry Cossacks were drunk, though Chekists tried to control them. These commissars had far more authority than any ordinary officer. They were greatly feared, as Lenin wanted them to be. I was doubly glad I was an "activist," with comrades who still talked of ways and means of getting me to Odessa. We were thirty or forty versts closer, I think. I was not good at judging distance or the passage of time. Nikolaev, if that were our destination, was relatively near to Odessa, east along the coast. Kherson was even further east, on the Dnieper, as Nikolaev was on the Bug. The two towns were strategically important. They were served by main railway lines and rivers leading directly to the sea. Large ships docked at both. With these cities taken an army approaching from Alexandriya would be able to attack Odessa with its large well-equipped Allied and White garrison. This was the substance of most debates over the coming days. Allied "interventionist" forces defended Kherson and a reluctant German garrison occupied Nikolaev. Though supported by French or English warships, the cities were vulnerable. However there was considerable dispute between Hrihorieff and the Bolsheviks about strategy. I suspect Antonov wanted any victories for himself. Brodmann claimed to be winning partisans over to the Bolshevik cause daily. They were now, he said, describing themselves as "Bolsheviks" instead of "Barotbists." I was unimpressed. They seized on slogans and parties for comfort because they could no longer fight for God. At least the Whites knew what was of value to them. With better leaders, they would have given us back God and our Czar. The Roman Empire never fell. It lives on in spirit. God will return to Russia. There is a religious revival. Byzantium remains in the soil, in the hearts of the people.

The train moved a few versts a day. Grubby snow melted and revealed a ruined land; as bandages are peeled away from an un-healed body.

What surfaced, like detritus from wrecked and violated ships, was disgusting: we saw half-eaten human corpses, not savaged by beasts, but by men and women. Peasants were now being shot for canni-balism, for selling human flesh as animal meat. We saw burnt-out cottages and farms; the shells of honorable old mansions; the broken skeletons of plows and carriages; the bodies of untended cattle and sheep, hides and fleeces rotting on stinking bones. It was our shame. We had hidden it in winter, as we always do. But when buds were on those trees not smashed by shells, when shoots sprang from earth not desecrated with oil and fire and human filth, our crimes were re-vealed. No enemy had committed these atrocities, unless it was Karl Marx. This had been done in the name of the Ukrainian nation; in the name of Russia; in the name of Unity; in the name of Humanity; in the name of Brotherly Love.

Spring came, but not peace. In Russian the word for World is Peace; the word for Peace is Us; they are all derivations of the same thing—the word for Us is Earth. That is why we speak of "our earth, our world, our peace, ourselves"; why we make that identification foreigners rarely understand. To violate our earth is to violate every-thing. We are not mystics. It is only our language which is mystical. Because of its resonances. It gives us our great literature, our poetry, our songs, our music. It makes associations a German, for instance, cannot begin to perceive unless he speaks Russian lovingly and flu-ently. The steppe dweller becomes touchy and despairing if his land is attacked by unnatural things. The Cossacks fought not for Bol-shevism, not for Whites or Greens or Blacks; they fought, purely and simply, against the roads, the railways, the cities. Their idyllic Russia was a Russia of wide skies and small villages, of horses and cattle. If they could have accepted the twentieth century, the world would have been sweet for them. They would have been able to create more freedom than any they had previously known. But they attacked a town to raze it, to loot it, to take their booty home. Even Hrihorieff, even Makhno, both of them strategists of great cunning and not illiterate men, could not understand that the cities were fundamental to their world. This ignorance was the chief cause of their downfall. Control of the cities was the key to the freedom they sought. They discussed this, but they did not feel it. A Cossack must feel something in his bones before he can accept it. It was the Jew, the world over, who controlled the cities; he is its first real, instinctive modern city dweller. Even those in the shtetls hated the steppe.

Our Ukrainian war was the first great war between Urban and Country dwellers. To survive today, one must align oneself with the city. Those who leave are at best sentimentalists, at worst deserters. Ukraine was a land of wealthy industrial cities drawing on our mineral resources; of wealthy kulaks drawing on our infinite wheatlands. More than anywhere else in Russia, Ukraine displayed both the dilemma and the solution. That is why we have suffered so much up to the present day. I do not speak from self-pity. There is little of that in my nature. I speak objectively. The problem could have been defined. It could have been remedied. Ukraine could have become the world's first modern civilization. Trotsky and the Nationalists between them put an end to that. Two negative forces collided. Ego: they all thought they knew best. Chaos and Old Night were released upon the world.

Brodmann and I became friends, of sorts. He admired me and would often ask for practical advice. I did what I could to modify his excesses. I invented examples drawn from my fictitious Red activist life. As a result, my reputation grew. My engineering skills were often called upon as we moved from camp to camp. I was still a prisoner. Of course, they did not know it. Dozens of times I pointed out I would be more useful to them in Odessa. I was now ignored. They began to plan in earnest the assassination of Hrihorieff. They had received direct orders from their Moscow superiors. The Ataman was acting out of hand, refusing to take orders, winning over Bolshevik liaison men to his own point of view, seducing some of their best people. I was asked to make an infernal machine to blow up the Cossack chieftain. My conscience would not let me. I claimed materials were hard to come by. Of course they offered to requisition everything I needed. I said it was a dangerous business. Whoever used the bomb might also be blown up. They would employ someone not particularly "useful to the Party." I mentioned the possibility of people other than Hrihorieff dying. I was told that those who had gathered about him were as much responsible as the Ataman himself. I heard the whole litany; the now-familiar Bolshevik rationalization of cold-blooded murder. This, too, would establish itself in the consciousness of all kinds of socialists, including the National Socialists, who hampered their own cause by adopting the tactics of those they opposed. They also inherited the Bolshevik talent for efficient-sounding neologisms. Lenin and Trotsky and Stalin have a great deal to answer for. Stalin regarded himself as a philologist. I was not surprised to learn that. It was easy for him. He had invented the very language he pretended to examine. Zamyatin, with his eloquence and insight, pointed this out in his book *Mi* (*We* in English). He had all his ideas stolen by Huxley and Orwell, those poor imitators of H. G. Wells. The Anarchists on the other hand were always bad at inventing new words, though most of their best slogans were taken over by the Bolsheviks. This was probably the reason for anarchism's failure. It could not simplify problems. Lenin understood how effective simplification could be. *Cheka*. The word is a chilling abbreviation of words meaning Special Commission for Internal Affairs. We would be wary of such a name, but we would not immediately fear it. In Scandinavian the word for terror is something like *Skrek*. Skrek would have the same mixture of coldness and authority: a nononsense sound. And how the Chekists loved to use their name!

"Cheka!" And off would come the hats and caps. Men and women would even kneel. Russians were still scarcely aware they were no longer serfs, let alone that they were "comrades." "Cheka!" And out would come the pathetic little hoards, or the papers, or the pleas for mercy. And the machine guns would go *cheka-cheka-cheka* just to prove what mercy meant: a quick death rather than a slow one. Of course the Chekists turned on one another in the end. Down they went, in cellars, in ditches, in camps, until the name was so foul it had to be changed and Beria began his rule, whispering words of fear in Stalin's ear. They say he laughed when he saw Stalin was really dead. He strutted about as if he had achieved that death himself. He thought he had triumphed entirely. We should have had a Jewish Czar sitting on the Russian throne. Luckily Beria met the fate of Rasputin, an amateur at manipulation compared to his famous successor. Stalin was ready to begin an action against the Jews. That was why Beria poisoned him. But these facts are obscured. What did Stalin do, for instance, with Hitler's body? To that uncertain, Georgian mind it was his by right of vendetta. Or was Stalin the first true robot; this "Man of Steel"? Is that the joke Beria played upon the world? In Russia they still call KGB "Cheka"—it has become a slang word.

Brodmann confided to me, at last, that he wanted no part of the assassination plan. I told him I agreed. As a professional saboteur, the killing of Hrihorieff was beneath me. "My violence is done to machines and communications," I said. We shared a Wagon-Lit. It had been parked in a siding somewhere to the north of Nikolaev. We got few reports. Hrihorieff seemed undecided which town to attack first. Antonov did not want Hrihorieff to attack either. He claimed he wished to "save" the citizens from outrage. He really needed to prove himself to his masters, to claim Hrihorieff's glory. Hrihorieff, in turn, boasted of a dozen conquests a day. Half the towns taken were shtetls or gypsy camps. But his boasting had the desired effect. More and more partisans joined him as he moved toward the cities, firing threatening cables before him as an ancestor might have fired human heads, to frighten the garrisons and undermine their morale.

At some time in March we learned Hrihorieff had taken Kherson by storm. His telegrams TO ALL, ALL, ALL! came back and were posted throughout southern Ukraine. The city was occupied in the name of "The Working People of the World," but the tone of his messages was clear: Hrihorieff, Ataman of the Zaporozhian Cossacks, had done what the Bolsheviks could not do. The pogroms continued. Even Antonov, in control of Kiev, had been unable to stop the sacking of Podol by regular Red Army soldiers.

There was a multitude of rumors. We were fifty versts behind the lines and received no direction information. I was only interested in Hrihorieff as far as he concerned me. I still could not get permission to go to Odessa. Antonov had become suspicious of Bolsheviks playing "happy ships" with Hrihorieff. This naval term describes what happens when one crew falls in love with another. The Bolshevik officially in command of irregular units did whatever Hrihorieff ordered. We were not all so sure of the chieftain's ability to hold his gains. This was why Antonov wanted him liquidated.

What had happened in Kherson was this: Hrihorieff issued an ultimatum to the garrison's commander in chief. The dignified Greek replied it was his duty to defend the city to the last. He had confined leftist hostages and their families in a warehouse. The French frigates in the river opened fire on Hrihorieff's Cossacks as they swept into

Kherson. The French used incendiary shells. These set the warehouse afire. Hundreds of men, women and children were burned alive. Hrihorieff took ghastly revenge. The French escaped, but not a single Greek was spared. They were killed as they fought or as they surrendered. Hrihorieff filled a ship with their bodies and sent it down the river to Odessa: the first modern corpse ship. The effect on the morale of the French garrison in Odessa and, when the news came, Nikolaev's German garrison, was of course devastating.

Kherson had given up her matériel: tanks, guns, ammunition, food. The city was looted in true Cossack fashion. Hrihorieff continued to pretend he served "Soviet" authority. His men were seen selling their booty in our camp, in every village they stopped in; women's dresses, suits, boots, crucifixes, icons, paintings, delicacies, antiques. Half the "boorzhoos" had sought refuge in Kherson. The Cossacks had found them easy victims.

Nikolaev surrendered soon after this and Hrihorieff gained greater strength. Thousands of Cossacks, Haidamaki, partisan divisions, tanks, infantry in armored trains, began to move on Odessa. Panic filled me. Anything could happen to my mother and Esmé. I applied through Antonov's field commanders to be returned to Odessa. I received no reply.

I heard a rumor. One of our trains was leaving for the "Odessa Front." It carried Bolshevik troops. Antonov hoped to strengthen Hrihorieff's units and pretend Bolsheviks were responsible for the victory. With Brodmann and one other, I at last got myself assigned as political commissar; because I knew the city well I could contact Bolshevik comrades already spreading propaganda amongst the French, local people and Whites.

I shared the staff carriage with a dozen half-drunk Red Army officers, Brodmann and the other commissar. His name was something like Kreshchenko. When the train was on its way the officers revealed their orders. We were not going direct to Odessa. Our first job was to contact Makhno to try to gain his sympathy and help in curtailing Hrihorieff. Apparently Makhno disapproved of Hrihorieff. His support, the equal to the Ataman's, had been given reluctantly. The Red Army men said the French were weak, divided at home, confused in their orders, understanding nothing of the issues involved. Those Moscow Bolsheviks could as easily have said the same of themselves. They had no clear idea of Makhno's or Hrihorieff's political stands. Their distaste for the irregulars was evident (they were all ex-Czarists). I sympathized, but I had been forced to survive amongst the rabble. I knew at least how feelings ran. Even the Red Cossacks believed "Russian chauvinists" were not true Communists. The Cossacks, they argued, were Communists by tradition and experience. The single fact Trotsky understood was that Ukrainian partisans were hard to discipline. It had been easy enough for him to take over the remnants of the Czar's army; but he loathed the peasant fighters. He would destroy as many as he could once they had served their turn. Stalin completed his work. Every Bolshevik success involved a revival of Czarist methods. Tell me who was vindicated.

The ghosts of those murdered Greeks hang over the misty waters of the Dnieper; they rise and fall on the bloody waves of the Black Sea. The marrow was sucked from their bones. Greece, Mother of Civilization: your children dishonor your name. And what if Cassandra had been there to see, to warn them, would they have listened? The good do not listen; the innocent do not listen; only the evil listen. Their faces were smashed with rifle butts. Their clothing was torn from their bodies. They were piled like rotten meat into the boats and sent down our Russian river to our own sea. How the Turk must have chuckled when he learned with what brutality we had turned upon one another.

In Athens, the Greeks sell themselves to anyone; they destroy their honor: but can they be blamed? Greece, Mother of the World, raped by her own sons. So she becomes a cynical, painted whore? Odysseus! We built a city in your name; and we defiled it. We filled it with offal. We killed your brave men. We stabled our horses in your holy places. We raped your priestesses. We tore down your golden paintings and smashed your statues. But Greece must rise as Christ shall rise; ennobled by sacrifice, strengthened through pain. They beat me with their rods. And God comes to me. Istanbul? That is a name to wail from corrupted towers raised by self-pitying, greedy, cruel Turks; to shriek for jihad and revenge on the People of the Lamb. Айя-софия... и всем векам – пример. Юстиниана...

Their oil will flow into the sea and the world shall die. Fear Africa. No one will listen. They are fools. They are innocents. They call me a racist. I am not. Race is nothing. It is their religion I fear. Religion based on hate and envy. Carthage, with its dark and ancient eye, its red lips, its blue-black beard, growls for vengeance. Byzantium shall rise. The drums shall cease. The gongs shall not echo. The snow shall be our own and our rivers will be silver. We must be ready.

Brave, free Cossacks and the Byzantine faith. Are they to go the way of Greece? Will our Cossacks dance and drone on dull red stages and our priests sell dirty photographs in Leningrad streets? Where is peace? Where is the Lamb of God? They took Krassnoff and they hanged him from a black tree. They plotted to kill Hrihorieff. They killed Makhno's commanders. They drove others to suicide. And you tell me they are not to be feared?

Brodmann was nervous of visiting Makhno. He sat in a corner of the carriage and complained. He hated Anarchists worse than Whites. He had probably supported both in his time. He argued that History was not ready for Kropotkin's dreams. Men were too vicious and self-seeking; they had to be trained to the idea of Communism, as dogs. He was like a religious convert who turns against all he once admired because it had not proven perfect. I have met the type often. He sought to impose a grey vision on the objective world because he had lost his center, his inner life. Christian or Communist, the temperament is the same. They hated Makhno, in those days. The Bolsheviks, the Whites, the Allies. Not only was he as successful as Hrihorieff, he had been able to hold his gains better. He became a drunkard in Paris. A lost, wretched, confused consumptive whose wife and child left him, who talked and coughed and wept his way to extinction. I was to meet him there, in Paris, where so many lonely Russians live.

SIXTEEN

I decided to escape. In the night, while we were stopped and everyone slept, I took a map from the table, took a bottle of vodka and some food, and left the train. There was no snow worth mentioning. My plan was to strike out for the nearest good-sized town. Now I was *au fait* with the ways of partisans I could bluff someone in authority and get transport to Odessa. It might be possible to find a truck. I could repair it as easily as I had repaired Grishenko's. I was in something of a trance. My memory of those days is hazy. But I know I was anxious to reach my mother and Esmé. I had no other particular plan in mind, save that I might sell Yermeloff's pistols and purchase a passage on a ship bound for Yalta, which was then in Denikin's hands. Nobody was sure the French would be able or willing to defend Odessa for long.

I came to a dark village. It stank, as so many of them did, and it was silent. The houses were ramshackle. Some were crude thatched huts. It was like an extended, badly run farmyard. I had been through such places with the Cossacks. I had seen them burn. Before dawn, I settled down against a wall and slept for a little while. I awoke to find a Jew standing over me: a Hasid rabbi. In Yiddish he asked me if I were hungry. I told him I was not. I got up. I had fallen into the hands of Zion. A shtetl. Everywhere signs in Yiddish and Hebrew.

The sun shone bright and cold on this stronghold of avarice. I had been sleeping next to a synagogue. My bones ached. The marks of Grishenko's whip stung, every one, as if fresh. I told him I could not speak Yiddish. He smiled. He spoke through his beard in halting Hebrew. I told him in Russian that I could not speak Hebrew. He did not understand my Russian. I used German. It was better than Ukrainian, which was like Yiddish to me. Even this was difficult. How did they trade? How did they manage to exist? The land was poor here. It was rocky. It was not like our Russian steppe. It was like Old Testament Palestine. The rabbi beckoned to me to follow him. I shook my head.

"Emmanuel," said someone in the group. Black-clad men and women; perhaps it was Saturday. I was outraged. I remember the sensation of terror. My head began to ache. It aches now. I drew myself up. I told the rabbi I represented the Soviet Authority. He nodded and smiled. He was trying to trap me, I suppose. They probably thought I had money. I reached into my pocket and found my pistols. I did have some Petlyura money, with my papers, in my secret pocket. I was too cautious to touch it. They would know. They would set upon me. They would strip me. "You are a Jew?" said a young man in Russian.

Judas call me. Or Peter. I would not confirm it: but I was too frightened to deny it. I made a gesture with my hand.

"Why are you afraid?" He was wearing a black suit, a prayer shawl and a peasant shirt. He had a cap on his black hair. His face was the picture of innocence. This made me wary. "Cossacks? You have been pursued?"

They had come out of the synagogue. They surrounded me. I kept my head. My hands were on the pommels of the pistols. They took me to a sort of tavern. They opened it. It made Esau's in Odessa seem like a Petrograd cabaret. I told them I had relatives in Odessa; I was on my way there. They asked where my people lived. The young man had been to Odessa. I remember the sensation of humiliation as I let go of my pride. I told them Slobodka. I had to match cunning with cunning. After all, I had suffered from being called a Jew. Now at least I could turn it to my advantage. I regretted I had left the train. I took out my map. I asked someone to show me where we were.

We were in the region of Hulyai-Polye, a large village whose name was associated with Makhno as Alexandriya was associated with Hrihorieff. These places were fundamentally Cossack fortresses. We were a good hundred miles at least from Odessa. Possibly two hundred.

What wretches they were, these Jews. So poor. With that terrible, accusing humility they all affect. I had begun to shiver, in spite of myself. My self-control was slipping. I needed cocaine. Hardly any was left. It should not be wasted. Was Makhno at Hulyai-Polye? They did not think so.

"He is away," said the youth, "fighting for us."

"For you?" I almost laughed aloud. Even an Anarchist would not league himself with such creatures. They had no pride; they did not fight; they fell on their knees and they prayed and they cringed. I have seen them. They do it to frighten their enemies. They rob Christians, yet rely on Christian mercy. Christ said to forgive them. And Christ must be obeyed. It is not for the killing of Jesus I hate them. I am not simple-minded. I am not guilty. Yahweh, they say, destroy our enemies. But they will not do it for themselves. What is Israel but a landing stage for Europe? A landing stage rotting from lack of use. The Allies have forgotten. They court the Turk and African. Those Jews sit so proudly in their American planes, their British tanks. It is a sin. They beat me with their rods, but I do not whine. To whine is to die. Yermeloff taught me that. They offered me food. I would not accept. I pulled out my vodka and drank. I offered it. They refused. "Where is Makhno?" I asked.

"Fighting," said the youth. "How do you not speak Yiddish?"

"My father," I said, "was a revolutionary." The rabbi guessed my meaning and shook his head. He was ignorant. There was a damp, chilling smell of poverty attached to their priest and their tavern. To insult me so! I have never been in a poorer place. It was barren and old. It was falling apart. Did they not have enough dignity to mend their houses? At least I would have put up a fence. But their fences sagged. Their gardens were overgrown. The shuttered shops, with their Yiddish signs, were unpainted. Russian villages could look the same, but there was a reason for it: the peasant had been robbed. And who had robbed him? I shall say no more. The synagogue: that was clean. The synagogue had its share of gold and fine tapestries, no doubt.

"These are bad times," said the youth. "Here as everywhere. Which flag do you fly?"

"Flag?"

"Red or Black?"

"I fly no flag," I said. "I am my own man. I am my own man." I felt weak, as if a chill had come to my stomach. It is still there. It has always been there. Like a piece of cold metal which can never be warmed, not even with blood.

That spring, in the area about Hulyai-Polye, there was a cone of silence; perhaps it was the eye of the hurricane. The Anarchist territory was the only territory where peace reigned. The world is full of ironies. I stayed in the village, but I was cautious. When the troops came through, with bread for the Jews, they put me in a tachanki, the little machine-gun carts Makhno made famous (they gave him superior speed and fire power). They were true Russians: kindly and friendly. I do not know why they supported Makhno. They were Chernosametsiya (Black Flags) but were far more like idealized Bolshevik fighters of Soviet fiction. We stopped at another village. It was Greek. Bread and flour. We were offered tsatsiki. They took nothing. We stopped at a farming commune named after the Jewess Luxembourg. I was drunk. I was baffled. They asked me my rank. I told them I was a colonel. This made them laugh.

I was Comrade Pyat. I was Commissar Pyat. I was Colonel Pyat. They would hold up their five fingers when they called my name. They had healthy faces. I suppose they were the true servants of the Devil, for they seemed so normal. The noise was gone and the mud was gone. We sometimes crossed a railway track, that was all. I said I must go to Odessa. They said everyone was leaving Odessa. Hrihorieff had taken it. The French had deserted it. Hrihorieff and the Bolsheviks were in open dispute. The Bolshies were losing control. Hrihorieff was a pig, but a clever one. The Black Flags bided their time now. There was sunshine on my face. It was spring. The fields were as they should be. The villages were as they should be. Tranquillity was here, as it should be in the countryside. It was the first time I knew fondness for open spaces. I understood the attraction of the steppe, the fields, the villages, the little woods and rivers. The sky became blue. The Makhnovischini talked urgently to me by the fires in the evenings. They asked me to understand their own faith. They were like early Christians. I believed in God, not governments. Some of them agreed. They were too clever, Makhno's men; they almost had me convinced. Just before the detachment took the warm white road for Hulyai-Polye I pretended to become a Black Flag brother. We passed through armed camps. We reached the town. I wanted to see the Batko, the Old Man, the Little Father. I was taken to him. He was in a long room, possibly a school, with some comrades wearing the usual motley: sailor hats, Czarist jackets, bandoleers. He wore a green military coat with black frogging, a sheepskin hat on the back of his head. He was small and he was drunk. He had an open Slavic face, a broad forehead. He spoke in a soft, friendly voice, like a Mafioso's. He spoke pure Russian, full of power. He offered me vodka. I accepted. I had been drinking all day, every day. He asked me if I were SD or SR, if I supported this group or that. I told him I supported the Nabat. A man in a black overcoat, with a black, wide-brimmed hat and a small, black mustache, came over to me. "But you're a Bolshevik."

"Nonsense. An Anarchist."

"You're Pyat?"

"Yes."

"We've heard of you. A saboteur from Odessa. SR."

"Who told you?"

"Brodmann."

"He came here?"

Makhno's laughter, too, was soft. "He's still here, somewhere. Isn't he?"

"We handed him back," said the man with the mustache.

A woman entered. She was small, stocky, like Makhno. Perhaps she was his sister. At any rate, he greeted her as one would greet a relative. She told him his brother wanted him to come to eat. He was compliant. He slapped me on the shoulder and called me "Comrade." He limped from the room. That was the Anarchist, Nestor Makhno, in his heyday. He was the best of all who fought in our war, which will tell you something. Even then he drank, but he was cheerful. He had raped. He told me in Paris, after Semyon Karetnik and Fedor Shschusa and his other lieutenants had been betrayed by the Cheka or killed in battle. Makhno was glad of any listener, then.

I was taken to a small barn and put in with a couple of bewildered, unkempt individuals too gloomy at first to do more than introduce themselves. They lounged about in the straw, throwing sticks at the walls. They were also drunk. Everyone was drunk here. They were Abramavitch and Kasaroff. There was an Abramavitch convicted of sabotage in the twenties. He might have been the same one. They were Bolsheviks. Arrested for trying to organize a "RevKom" in a neighboring village. Revolutionary Committees were banned by Makhno. These were like others of their type, full of whining self-pity and self-congratulation, experts on The People, embittered with Moscow for "letting us down," angry with Makhno who was, they said, politically ignorant. Abramavitch had dark, Jewish features. He was quite young and had a scar on his lip which empahsized his sardonic, despairing manner. Kasaroff was older, with heavy, Great Russian features which had once been handsome. There is a type which will look like Nijinsky one year and like Brezhnev the next. He was that: fat with stolen bread and drink. I kept my own company on the other side of the barn.

I merely asked the date. It was 1 May. They found this amusing. I had been a prisoner of Bolsheviks, Jews and Anarchists for two months. From then on, I became more sober. It had been a strange holiday.

I was only with the Bolshevik prisoners for two days. They knew nothing about Odessa. I was taken from the barn by grinning Makhnovischini and told to go to a house they pointed to down the street. I had no escort. I still had pistols, papers, a few bank notes in my pocket. I must have been utterly filthy. I had not changed clothes or shaved or properly washed for at least six weeks. I was nineteen years old. They laughed at me and saluted. To all who passed me I was "Colonel Pyat." It was my salvation, my youth. The house was wooden, with typical Ukrainian gables, painted in a variety of light colors, with a veranda and a heavy, double door. I opened the door. A soldier told me to go through the passage to the back. I walked along the passage. I assumed Makhno had sent for me. There was the sound of water. It was warm and quiet in the house. I heard a girl laugh. I knocked on the door. I was told to enter.

Esmé was naked. She was in the tin bath looking up at me and grinning. She held out soap-covered pink arms, exposing her breasts. Her golden hair was darkened by water. Her body smelled of clean skin and soap. She was shameless. I turned away. A girl in a grey dress was scrubbing Esmé's neck. "He's embarrassed." It had been a trick.

I sat down on a chair, near a screen. My back was to her. "How did you get here? Are the Anarchists in Odessa?"

"The Whites have Odessa," she told me.

The grey girl began to whistle a folk tune.

"I never got there." Esmé stood up in the water. I heard her. I saw her shadow. The sun came through a window in the door. "We stopped at a station for food. I was taken by the soldiers. I was raped.

I've been raped so often I've got calluses on my cunt." The grey girl spluttered and giggled. They had planned this, surely, to make me upset. But why should Esmé feel aggressive toward me?

"Mother?"

"Got off the train. Still in Kiev. With Captain Brown." Esmé's voice was softer. I felt her come close. I stood up and went to the door. She wore a sheepskin. She smiled at me. "Max?"

I do not know why I began to weep. It was probably a mixture of exhaustion and vodka. I had wasted so much of myself trying to get to Odessa. I hated her as I wept. She stroked my face and I still hated her. I had suffered for her and Mother. Neither had been there at all. I had lied, endured terror, endured pain. I could have stayed safely in Kiev with Mrs. Cornelius to look after me; with my mother. It was not Esmé's fault, of course, but I blamed her then. "She never meant to go to Odessa," said Esmé. "She heard it was the last train. She said you wouldn't come. She said she'd be all right."

"And you were raped?"

"I'm not raped now. I have a respectable job with the education team. We take a train with food and books and clothes to the villages. The station's about five miles away. I just came in. I heard about you. I asked to see you."

"You've changed," I said.

She was amused. "Look at me, Max. Do you want the bath water? It's still hot."

Esmé had been my virgin sister; without vice or passion. My oldest admirer. My friend. My rose. And she spoke foul words and had no shame. She told me to bathe. I was still drunk and dazed. I let the women take off my clothes. I did not mind if they saw my stigmata. I have suffered much from Cossacks with their whips and little knives! And I let them wash me. Esmé was soft. She murmured to me as she soaped my head. They put something in the water. It stung. It killed the lice.

They washed me with their hands, one in grey, the other naked but for a worn sheepskin. "I thought it was you," she said. She had been fucked so often she had calluses on her cunt. I shivered. I was still weeping. I became very cold. I shivered. I was swaddled. Esmé took me to a dormitory where there were two rows of empty beds. I had a fever, she said. A mild form of typhus. I don't know. Where have you been? Everywhere, I told her. With the Bolsheviks? With that Brodmann and his gang who came? I was away. No, I said, I was only with them because I was searching for you. I thought you were in Odessa. Are you an Anarchist, Esmé? She said she did not have to be. She was a nurse. She worked on the education train. There were two doctors, both Jews, who also helped. Seamstresses. It was a community, she said, in which some sort of order flourished. Though it was protected by Makhno's bayonets. Soon these would go. Why? Because the Whites were advancing. The Don Cossacks were on their way and Makhno had let too many units help the Reds. But it would be a while yet, she thought. Who raped you? I asked her. Many, she said. Who? It was true, she said, a Cossack whipped you. The beast. Did Brodmann rape you? I asked. That swine! She said no. Makhno? He saved my life, she said. It was not much of a rape. It was a token. His wife knows what he does. She tries to stop him. He feels bad afterward. He's drunk. His men expect it of him. Not here, but out there. The ones here know him and his two brothers. He should not have raped you, Esmé. It was a token. You should have been there when the first one happened. I trembled. I felt sick, but all there was in my stomach was vodka. It returned as bile. Esmé! Esmé! I can nurse you for today, she said. It was good I came here. Who else? Raped me? She laughed. Lots. It's silly. It's over. I'm doing my job again. I have a boy. He wants to marry me. It was quiet in the dormitory. There was no one there. I was confused. She stroked my whole body. My new, clean body. She held my cock. She stroked it. I began to relax. I love you, Esmé. I love you, Max. She stroked my cock. She stroked my nipples. She stroked my face. She put ointment on Grishenko's marks. She told me I would be better. She loved me. Esmé. Raped by Jews and Bolsheviks, yet still you were full of pity. We could have been married as Mother wanted. Lived in that village. Where are you? You said I had a fever. I did not know you left while I slept.

A week later she returned. Now the dormitory was filled with dozens of wounded men. She was tired. She was slatternly. She was a slut. She helped the others more than she helped me. I was her own brother. She nursed the very men who raped her. I was sweating. Without vodka, which had controlled it, the fever increased. Those Jews had poisoned me. They put a piece of iron in my stomach. I had been ill for months. I was dying. She soothed the others, just as if they were me. Mrs. Cornelius would not have done that. She would have left me alone. They had poisoned me. I had been right to mistrust them. I had been a fool. The men made too much noise. They stank of gangrene, of blood and cordite. They were hideous.

I was taken with them, in carts, to a train. I saw Esmé in the crowd. I think she was looking for me, but could not see me because of the other bodies. Then she was gone.

SEVENTEEN

Ithink the girl in grey had mended my clothes. They were clean. Everything was in order. I had a different coat. My pistols and papers were still there. Yermeloff's gifts were in deep "gun pockets" in a dark-blue caftan. The chill was still in me. There was firing. We were taken from the train and put in ordinary peasant wagons. Makhno had disappeared. Riding a horse, someone said. Makhno rarely used a horse, because of a wounded ankle which made it hard to mount. The others went with him. Hulyai-Polye had been taken. I do not know which side was victor, White or Red. Perhaps both. They came and went.

Little teeth suck the marrow from my bones. Esmé: How coarsened by despair you must have become as your life and idealism faded into the grey scum of Bolshevism. Mother: Did the Teuton kill you where I flew my first machine? Did the Teuton kill you, for I'll swear I heard you scream? Your world flared in 1941. And then it died. The conquerors made you happy. Was it because you fought Satan all your life so whenever you saw Him marching along Kreshchatik you welcomed Him as a familiar adversary? I did not mean to lose you. Love was never in your eyes. But you were happy.

Western Europe is too easy, too warm, too soft. The hardness of our climate gives us everything—our isolation, our inner life, our language, our genius. We are lost in the crowds and the heat. Let me go back. They dispossessed us; they drove us away. Now we live in crannies. We are humiliated and mocked. We might have survived. But God deserted us. He deserted Denikin. Makhno and Hrihorieff might, like Villa and Zapata, have fought for liberals allowing freedom of religion and pushed the Bolsheviks into the Baltic, to become the émigrés. But the Whites were too proud, the Nationalists were too small-minded, and the Allies never will understand what goes on in Russia. A Russian has himself. He retreats there as the Englishman retreats into rationalism. Borrowed, foreign rationalism has always been the bane, the destruction, of the Russian soul. Faith in God and His authority provides the only true freedom: the freedom to live an inner life.

It was Makhno who avenged me. He went to Alexandriya for a parley with Hrihorieff. Makhno denounced the Ataman's pogroms. Hrihorieff laughed. He was disbelieving. Was it so important? One of Makhno's lieutenants (Keretnik, I think) drew his Colt and shot the Ataman. Makhno finished him off. The other Anarchists killed Hrihorieff's bodyguard. Makhno shot Grishenko between the eyes and down he went, whip and all, into the July dust of Alexandriya. Makhno, with his eloquence, won over Hrihorieff's men in an instant. It was an old-fashioned act of bandit audacity. It impressed the remnants of the Zaporozhians, many of whom were now ragged and barefoot, for Hrihorieff had never consolidated his gains. They agreed to follow the Batko. But they were doomed. That Jew-loving Anarchist dismissed them in the end. He fled into Rumania and went to Paris, haunted by the knowledge that he had deserted Russia. He was no Nationalist, at least. He and his wife and daughter loved the whole of Russia. They spoke Russian. I met them again in Paris. It was hard for his wife. I think his daughter went back. He lived off the other émigrés. He drank the cheap French wine which makes sickly sentimentalists of everyone.

The carts rolled into the summer and there were poppies and fields of wheat and the stink of gunpowder and the hum of bullets. I had almost recovered but decided it was unwise to leave the wounded. Who would bother the near-dead? We reached a village, half burned already, and we were left in a Catholic church which had been stripped. We lay amongst refuse not even valuable to peasants, on the stains of horse droppings; the droppings themselves were worth something. We watched thin rats who, in turn, watched us, wondering who would die first, who would eat whom. The peasants would not release us. Our comrades never returned. The doors were locked and the windows were high. The peasants were too cowardly to kill us.

My cocaine had been stolen, I think by Esmé. It would have given me strength. It would have helped me. In turn I could have helped the others. We called out for mercy. Our weak voices echoed in the empty church. The priest was dead; hanged by some militia or other. The peasants hated us. They listened to our voices. They were probably inspired as others might be by the *Dnes Spaseniye Miru.* This day salvation has come to the world. *Dnes spaseniye miru byst. Poyem voskresshemu iz groba.* Let us sing to the One who rose from the dead—*I nachalniku zhizni nasheya: I nachalniku zhizni nasheya:* Having destroyed death by death, *Razrushiv bo smertiyu smert,* He has given us victory and great mercy. *Pobedu dade nam, i veliyu milost.* Our spirit. Our spirit. They were slipping away from us, our souls. And not one of us could be sure either God or His Heaven still existed. We sank into that easy euphoria which comes between being alive and being dead.

There was the firing of machine guns and artillery. It might be salvation. The starving wounded stirred amongst the corpses. I still had my pistols, but no powder. We heard artillery limbers go through the town. Horses. We heard shouts. The church began to shake. I heard the blessed noise of engines. An argument outside the door. A shot. I cried for joy as a White officer stood in the doorway. He held a smoking revolver at his side. He held a handkerchief to his face. He wore the pale-grey infantry jerkin, with red-and-gold epaulets. He wore a cap with the old Czarist badge. He wore blue britches tucked into black boots. There were medal ribbons on his jacket. There was a sword at his side. He had a well-trimmed beard and though his face was filthy and his uniform patched with powder smoke he represented something I had never expected to see again. He called out to the soldiers in their helmets and khaki. They ran into the church with their rifles. They began to cough. Some of the wounded had been dead for several days. I crawled forward and raised myself to my feet. I was smiling. But I had been deceived once more.

The White officer said, "Get those who can walk out. Shoot the rest where they are. It will be a mercy." An NCO ordered the men to advance. I was pushed into the sunshine. It was a small unit of infantry. There were some horsemen with the long whips and wide red stripes of regular Don Cossack cavalry. Both riders and horses looked weary. There were two khaki tanks: massive things, with gun turrets and side-firing Lewises. There were three good-sized artillery pieces and about ten machine guns. There was a large, open car. I tried to speak to the officer, but he was striding over to the tanks which were opening their hatches. Behind the tanks, as if worshiping new gods, peasants were on their knees in a line, holding their caps before them. I was pushed on. I protested. "I am a loyal subject of the Czar."

"Tell him yourself," said one of the soldiers, shoving his helmet onto the back of his head. "You're going where he went."

I was too weak. I waved again at the officer. They were going to rob me. It was of great urgency to me that they did not take my remaining property. My life seemed unimportant. "Captain! Captain!"

Four of the wounded men were thrown against the wall and began to slide down it even before the bullets drew their blood. It was a waste of everything. The men would have died in a few hours.

A tall, slender officer, wearing khaki shirt and shorts, with a large nose and long jaw, his cap reversed, goggles on his forehead, moved rapidly in our direction. He was shouting in English. The soldiers were taking me to the wall with three more partisans. "Stop! You bloody-handed bastards. Can't you see he's a gentleman!" They hesitated, looking toward the White captain, who had turned. The sun was making me squint. The captain shrugged and said in Russian, "We'll find out who he is." He spoke French to a short, broad-faced lieutenant who translated this into bad English. "They say to question."

The tank commander was Australian, as were both his crews. He wore an expression of permanent disgust on his long face. He complained he wanted to get back to Odessa and from there take a ship straight to Melbourne. He rubbed at his nose all the time, as if it itched. I spoke to him in English as he leaned, sighing, against his tank. "I am most grateful to you, sir."

I was startled by his reaction. I did not know him. He grinned at his men. They had clambered out of their machines and were lounging on the warm metal, drinking from their canteens.

"Someone who speaks real bloody English!"

The shots continued from inside the church and from the corner of the street where the walking wounded were being executed. "Jesus!" said the tank commander. "What else can you say?"

"I am familiar with your language," I told him. "Blimey O'Reilly, not half!" This to show I could speak the common dialect, as well as what Mrs. Cornelius insisted on calling book-talk. "I learned in Kiev. I am a Doctor of Science from the University there and a qualified engineer. I have the rank of major."

"In whose army?"

"Loyalist, I assure you." I began to explain, but then I had fainted. I awakened in twilight. An Australian soldier was waving a mug of sweet soup under my nose. I was not interested in food. It made me feel strange.

"You got to eat, mate." He was like a Russian babushka. For him, I sipped the soup. Some of it remained in my stomach. "They're bastards, these peasants," he said. He was about the same age as I. "I hate them worse than the Reds, don't you?"

"They have suffered," I said.

"They certainly have." He shook his head. "Our Russkies are doing horrible things to them now. They're all bloody savages. It don't matter what bloody uniform they're wearin'." He sighed. He did not understand. He did not want to be on Russian soil. Like his commander, he longed for the bush of his native Outback. "We're going to give you a lift. We need an interpreter and we could do with an engineer. We've lost two of our chaps from typhus already. Know anything about tanks?"

"A little."

"Carbs?"

"I should think so."

"Spiffing. Now, then, you have some shut-eye. Some brekker in the morning and you'll be fit enough to look at Bessie." Almost all tanks, I was to learn, were called Bessie by Australians. He spoke with kind assurance, as one chanting a spell whose efficacy has been thoroughly proven.

I slept in a sack beside a tank. The Russians were piling what little booty they had been able to find on the ground, under the eye of the captain, Kulomsin. He was thought lenient by his men. They called themselves, of course, Volunteers. Few of them were actually that. The Australians were contemptuous of them; ashamed of their association. The French-speaking liaison officer was a Serb. I guessed he was some sort of failed adventurer who had taken up with the Whites in order to save his skin. I breakfasted on bread and more soup, which they thinned with water. They kept their own stores and refused to share them with the Volunteers. They gave me a cigarette. It was milder than I had been used to. It was real Virginia tobacco. I cleaned their carburetor for them and reconnected it. They tested the engine. It ran well enough, but it had been badly overtaxed; driven too hard and too soon. I would have no more trouble servicing it, however, than if it had been a tractor. We were leaving the village. The Whites burned it. For harboring Reds, they said. I did not see it. I was excited by my first experience of the choking interior of a tank. Those machines were even more cramped than the modern kind, which are Rolls-Royce limousines in comparison. We moved slowly ahead. The Australians hardly spoke at all amongst themselves. I asked where we were going. They were joining up with other units, they said, for "some real fighting." By this, I gathered, they meant an attack on a city.

The tank was hot and stuffy. I did not care. In it I felt secure for the first time in over two years. Every so often we stopped. Maps were inspected. I translated between Captain Wallace, the Australian commander, in his tank, and the Russian officer, who had a staff car. My heart was singing. We were on our way to Odessa! The Serb glowered at me. His function had gone. When I last saw him, through one of the observation slits at the side of the tank, he wore an expression of morbid despair. I was called upon to tune the other machine's engine as best I could. I was worth, said the Australians, my weight in gold.

All the gold would soon be gone from Russia. You see it in the Kensington antique shops still, just near the Soviet Embassy.

It was August, I learned. It grew hotter and hotter. Whenever possible, the hatches would be left open. We would take turns in the turret, trying to cool ourselves. My face and hands became quite brown. I was happy and very content by the time we entered a range of low wooded hills; it might have been Dorset, said Captain Wallace. We halted. Wallace conferred with Kulomsin. Kulomsin indicated a small, dusty road, wide enough to take a carefully steered tank. He would go ahead in the car.

I had just taken my turn in the turret when we emerged from the wood and began to roll across an overgrown lawn leading down to an old ornamental lake with ruined balustrades. There was an artificial island in the middle. On it were willows and the gutted remains of a Japanese gazebo. Far across the murky waters I saw a large, neoclassical mansion. It was pitted by recent artillery bombardment. It's southerly side was half caved in from what I took to have been a recent fire. Doubtless peasants, Bolsheviks, Nationalists, Socialist Revolutionaries, Anarchists, bandits of all descriptions, had had their way with house and estate. But it retained a good deal of its antique dignity. The Volunteer Army colors were flying from the roof now. The owner, doubtless dead or fled, would have been reassured to see the flag, if not the rather battle-weary White troops who moved around the grounds, setting up a camp.

The tank followed the curve of the water until we reached a kind of paddock where several more tanks were already at rest. To my absolute joy I saw, near a jetty on the far shore of the lake, two sea-planes. They had been hastily painted with Volunteer insignia and obviously had belonged to the Germans. There was a large machine and a very small single-seater. The first was a double biplane with huge sets of wings fore and aft: an Oertz Flugschooner. The other was a Hansa-Brandenburg W20, meant to be flown from U-boats but never actually used for that purpose. It could be collapsed and stored very quickly and was just as easily reassembled. It was an ideal plane for this sort of campaigning where water, of course, was not always available. Hansa-Brandenburgs were wonderful aircraft. The Oertz on the other hand had a bad reputation. It was difficult to bring in on even the calmest waters. I could not take my eyes away from either plane until the tank cut its engine. We began to disembark, the Australians exchanging loud, friendly greetings and complaining about their Russian allies. Eventually, Captain Wallace came up to me. He would introduce me to our Russian CO. We walked around the lake to the mansion. There was a smell of decay I found pleasant. The Volunteer units had made the house their General Headquarters.

I knew more than a little regret for the idyllic past, when the house and estate had represented the acme of civilization in South Russia. However, I was glad enough to enjoy what it still represented. I imagined how it must have looked in the days of Turgenev who wrote so beautifully about such places you might have imagined yourself in France. The hall was wide and cool. A spiral staircase led off it. As usual all pictures and anything of the slightest value had been carried off. There were a few camp chairs and collapsible desks for the staff, maps on the wall; an atmosphere of lassitude created, I suspect, by the heat. The majority of the soldiers were Russians in the smart uniforms of Czarist times. There were also French, Greek and British officers among them. We were, I learned, less than twenty versts from Odessa and were quite near the coast. I could almost smell the beloved scent of flowers and salt water.

As I entered a large room, I thought I recognized one of the Russians. He was of average height, with a monocle and a small mustache, wearing a dark leather jacket open to reveal a light-blue army shirt. The uniform, with its red, yellow and black flashes, was that of the Russian Engineers. He was a Second Lieutenant. He was someone I had met in Petersburg when he had been home on leave. I saluted Major Perezharoff, the Russian ranking officer, who sat moodily on his desk smoking. Captain Wallace introduced me to him as "Major Pyatnitski, Intelligence." Major Perezharoff regarded me with a scowl. He had a dark, unhappy Crimean face. He spoke in the purest French, asking me how things were in Nikolaev. I explained I had been serving with the tanks. He nodded. "You speak English. That's something." He sighed. "And you were spying on the Reds?" He glanced distastefully at my clothes. "We have no spare uniforms."

"I was captured. And rescued by Captain Wallace."

"Where were you last?"

"Hulyai-Polye. Before that Alexandriya. Before that Kiev."

"Do you know what Antonov's up to?"

"The different factions are at loggerheads, unable to agree amongst themselves. Their movements, I regret, are now a mystery to me."

"Well, their morale's no better than ours. I'm glad." He turned away from me. I saluted the Second Lieutenant and brought my heels together, unable to match the precision of the true Russian soldier. "I believe we are acquainted. Are you not Alexei Leonovitch Petroff, cousin to my old friend Prince Nicholai Feodorovitch Petroff? We met at the Mikhishevski's some years ago. In Peter. You knew me than as Dimitri Mitrofanovitch Kryscheff."

"Ah, yes." He blinked and removed the monocle from his eye. He had become more expert with it now. "We talked about Rasputin." He uttered a rather unpleasant laugh.

"Kolya and I were very close. I was studying science."

He looked at me with a familiar insolence. I had not really experienced anything like it since Petersburg. I remembered how irritating he had been. But we were now, after all, equals. Indeed, I outranked him. "Do you know how Kolya is? Where he is? I know he went into politics."

"Kolya?" The laugh was challenging, as if he laughed at a conqueror. He was puzzling. He said, "Who knows? Cheka?"

"He's in prison?"

Petroff laughed again. "Unlikely. They don't keep too many prisoners for long, do they? Particularly Kerenskyite princes."

I knew a terrible sadness. He spoke almost accusingly. I wondered if he associated me with Kolya's political comrades.

"You have English, I hear?"

"Yes." I was mourning Kolya. He had been the best friend I had known. "I'm in Intelligence. I was acting as interpreter with the Australians."

"I could do with an interpreter. It always takes half an hour to translate a report. We'll lose Odessa at this rate. Why don't you come up with me, as my observer?" The engineer's uniform had deceived me. I remembered his conversation, then, in that Petersburg drawing room. He was, of course, a pilot officer. His was one of the planes on the lake. It could be my first trip in a machine not of my own making. I was curious to experience the differences.

"In the Oertz?" I said.

"It's the only two-seater. Done any observing before?"

"Not really."

"It's fun." He laughed again, still sardonically, still as if I had somehow cheated him at a sport. "What do you say, Kryscheff?"

"If your seniors agree . . ."

"I have none. I'm a flyer. Like the tank people, I'm my own man. They need us too much to make us go through all that palaver. I'm going soon. There's something I have to do in Odessa. You know the Church of the Vanquisher?"

"It's a strange name for a church." I tried to join in whatever his joke was. But Kolya's memory was too strong.

"Isn't it? There's a map in the plane. You can make notes of positions." There was a despairing quality about him. All his ideals had gone. He wanted to be revenged on something but could find nothing to blame. I should have been more nervous of him, but I wanted to forget about Kolya and I desperately wanted to take the aeroplane trip.

Petroff saluted Major Perezharoff. "Sir, this officer will be of considerable use to me as an observer. He can also relay reports directly to the English liaison people. I should like to take him up with me."

Perezharoff shrugged. "He'll be out of our way."

Having said farewell to Captain Wallace I left the mansion. I wandered with a suddenly silent Petroff down to the lake. A small wooden jetty had been repaired and led out to where the seaplanes were moored. "Do you know the Oertz?" he asked.

"I know the Germans rejected them for war work."

"Not at the end. That's how we got it. They're devils to handle, but they've their own beauty. The little Hansa is a gem. You'd hardly know you were taking off or touching down. Like a dragonfly. But she's a one-seater."

"You use both?"

"I'm the only airman left. You've had some plane experience, didn't Kolya say?"

"Mine were experimental."

"Yes." He was thoughtful. "Kiev, of course."

"I owe Kolya much."

"You were a special friend? He was a true Bohemian. But he knew his duty."

"Politics?" I shrugged. I was missing a clue to the nature of this exchange. We reached the end of the jetty.

"Hot as hell, eh?" Petroff removed his cap. "It's cooler up there." He seemed to yearn for the sky. The sun caught his monocle. It blazed like a dragon's eye. "You survived, however. You're a bit of a fraud, aren't you? So you went into Intelligence."

I ignored the insult. "It was my only possible contribution."

"Spying."

"Sabotage, too. As an engineer, I had to make the best use of my talents. In the struggle."

"You were always against the Reds?"

I wondered why he was interrogating me so intensely. "Profoundly opposed."

"You disagreed with Kolya?"

"On that alone."

"I supported him. I was with Kerenski, you know. We're all guilty."

"Kerenski's revolution cost me my academic career."

He looked down at rainbow oil on the water. "We're all guilty. But you and I have survived Kolya."

"Guilty? For what?"

"For not listening to our hearts. Everyone possesses precognition, don't you think? It's just that we refuse to accept what we see."

"The future?"

"In a tea cup or on our palms. In the cards, or in a cloud."

"I am not superstitious. I regret I'm an unmitigated rationalist."

"Ha! And you're alive, while Kolya's dead." He called over to a group of mechanics who lay on the grass at the water's edge. "We'll be wanting the Oertz started up." Then his attention seemed drawn to some distant willows.

"We're going now?" I asked.

He grimaced. "Why not?" He was abstracted. I thought he was unstable. "There's something I want to do. For the future." I assumed he was thinking about death and meant to write a will.

"You want to give it to me?"

"What? If you like." He rubbed under his left eye with a gloved finger. He grinned. "If you like. You can't see the future, then? And you a scientist!"

He had picked up some fragments of fashionable mysticism at the Mikhishevski ménage, perhaps from his sister Lolly, that "Natasha" of happier days. "Come."

I returned with him to the mansion and a small ground-floor room evidently shared by several people and which had formerly been a pantry. It still smelled of bread and mice. From under his mattress he drew an unopened bottle of French cognac. "You like this?"

"I did once."

"Good. We'll drink it. For Kolya."

"I cannot refuse."

We sat on the ledge of the little window. There was an untidy kitchen garden outside. Two privates were trying to make something of it. They were working expertly, like peasants. Petroff uncorked the bottle and handed it to me. I drank sparingly, with relish. He took it from me impatiently and tilted his head back to drink nearly half the old brandy in a single swallow. War had evidently coarsened his palate. He gave me the bottle. I drank deep but there was still a fair amount left. He laughed that irritating laugh of his. I remembered it from Petersburg: universal irony tinged with tension and resentment. He finished the stuff off, but for a few drops. "It's how airmen drink. We need it. Did you hear about those silly bastards who dragged their own planes on sleds for hundreds of versts to get to fight for Denikin? They were keen, eh?"

"The drink doesn't impair your control over the plane?"

"It improves it. I'm the last member of the entire squadron."

"I know what it is," I was by now a trifle drunk, "to crash."

"You do?" He smiled.

"I designed several experimental planes. One went out of control while I was testing it. In Kiev."

He drained the bottle. "That's to the Wright brothers. Damn them to hell. And all inventors. Faust deserved no redemption."

"Shouldn't you rest?" I suggested. I could make neither head nor tail of his references.

"Very soon, Doctor." He searched under his mattress. "I'm sorry. That was the final bottle. Let's go aloft now."

Less nervous than if I had been sober, I followed him back to the lake where the Oertz was ready. Her propeller was spinning and she was pointing out at the long stretch of water. Mechanics, grateful for the breeze, held her by her tailplane and huge rear wings, as Cossacks might hold ropes on a fierce, unbroken stallion. The smell of oil was sweet. "You go forward," said Petroff. "Get in the front cockpit. You'll find a harness. Strap in. There's goggles and stuff, too. All you'll need." He was tucking a bulky object, wrapped in a piece of calico, into his jacket. I wondered if it were a bomb. I was rather uncertain of my chances of reaching the cockpit. The fuselage was only wood and fabric. But I climbed through the struts on the rocking aircraft until I managed to lower myself into the small observer's cockpit with its bucket seat and spring brackets where, in the other cockpit, the controls would be. There were binoculars fastened to the inside edge, a pistol in a holster, a map case and a clipboard, some pencils and a pair of goggles whose rubber was frayed and hardened. Still in my caftan, with my own Cossack pistols pressing to my hips, I settled myself and buckled on my harness, putting the goggles over my eyes. Petroff was behind me, now, signaling. The engine and propeller were, of course, making too much noise for him to bother trying to talk.

The machine suddenly moved forward at a rapid, almost maniacal, speed. It was like a bucking horse, an erratic sleigh ride, at once exhilarating and alarming. Foul spray flew into my face. I almost drowned in it. The lake was stagnant.

The plane began to vibrate, to slew in the water, tipping to starboard. Then I saw ailerons move on the wings and we were rising over the green lake and the willows, banking steeply, and the brandy suddenly warmed my whole body, my mind and my soul. We were up, flying over the woods, the damaged house, the neglected fields; flying toward hills and the blue sea, a haze between sky and land. I saw the limans, with their abandoned resorts, glittering and shallow; columns of marching men; riders; motor vehicles; gun tenders and artillery. This was the Release of Flying. There is no greater pleasure. Why did people bother climbing mountains when they could gain so much more from this? The air was roaring and yet at peace; it is a combination of adventure and tranquillity no jet setter will ever capture. A grey mist became the city. Odessa from the air, with her factories and her churches, her ports and railways, looked exactly as she had looked when Shura first took me there: exotic in her aura and golden in the sun; but so great was my experience of Escape that I did not care if I saw the city again for months. I was conscientious. I began to do my job. There were large groups of people on the docksides, filling the wide quays. There were few ships on the turquoise sea. There were pieces of large artillery. In the outer suburbs were guns, cavalry, infantry, but apparently few. The Reds were ill-prepared to meet Denikin. There came banging from below. For a moment the engine stopped and all I heard were the guns and the yelp of Petroff's laughter. He dropped the nose. I felt groggy. We were being fired upon. The engine started again. Flak burst around us. Shrapnel tore at our canvas. It did no real damage.

Down into smoke and yelling murder went Petroff, flying low across office buildings, hotels, flats, while I scribbled on my maps. We went over the St. Nicholas steps where I had gone on my first day with Shura. We flew round and round the dome with its huge ornamental crucifix, the cliffs on one side with their gardens and trees, the fashionable Nicholas Boulevard, the sea and its ships on the other; round and round, like a toy on a stick. This was stupid and risky. Petroff was still laughing. The guns from the docks continued to fire at us. Was he daring them to shoot us down? There were clouds of smoke everywhere. Petroff fumbled open his flying jacket and took out the object he had placed there. He held it in his gloved left hand. The calico fell away from us like a dead bird. It was not a bomb he held but a large hourglass on a marble stand. I think it was Fabergé. The marble was white with pronounced blue veins. The glass glittered. The sand was silver. Petroff stretched out his hand, then banked even more steeply toward the dome. I felt as if I were going to vomit. Guns continued to bang. I could hear them through the engine notes, as if far away.

His plane almost hit the cross. Petroff flung the hourglass down upon the golden roof of the church. He was laughing. I could see his teeth. His goggles made black cavities in his skull. He was white. His nostrils flared. Through my binoculars I saw the object strike the dome and smash; I saw marble break to fragments. Sand scattered like money. Then we were flying down on the dockyard guns. Maniacally I began to make notes on my map. There was a sudden lurch. I looked back. Petroff had been hit by shrapnel. It had ripped his coat and exposed a bloody mass of flesh. He continued to grin. Because of his goggles, I could not read his true expression. He saluted me with his wounded arm; then the plane climbed into Odessa's blue-green sky and we were at peace. The engine cut out completely. We were drifting. Petroff called to me. I think he was delirious because he referred to me as "Colonel" and spoke of "the Vanquisher." His laughter became uncontrollable. He shouted "Good-by" and then refired the engine. Laughter and engine note became one thing to my ears. We had started a power dive toward the sea. I realised he intended to kill me. Something tore away from the plane. It was part of the upper forward wing, I think. Then we were spinning in silence. The engine made laughing noises. In my terror I tried to reason with Petroff. He was quite insane. His hatred of me, or of what he thought I represented, had overwhelmed his reason. I still cannot understand it. He was dead, or at least unconscious, hanging in his straps. I could not reach the controls. I released myself from my own harness and curled up. We hit the water and went through it as if we were still going through air. I began to drown. I thought my ribs were broken. I pushed myself toward the surface. Petroff and the Oertz continued to drop away below me. I could not swim properly. On a current which carried me in, I floundered, astonished, to the beach. I stood up and waded between slimy rocks. The beach sloped steeply and became grass. I had already seen a few houses. I was gasping. My ribs seemed undamaged. There was no sign of Petroff or the plane. That beautiful machine was gone forever. I do not think that they manufactured any more. My feet would not grip. I had to keep bending down to steady myself with my hands, yet I felt quite revived as, fully clothed, my pistols weighting my steps, I climbed up the beach and saw, on the faded promenade, a deserted bandstand. I had come ashore in Arcadia.

EIGHTEEN

City of sleeping goats; city of crime; city of bleating crows; the wide-boys lie sprawled in the alleys; the little birds sing untruthful songs. The synagogues are burning.

Steel Czar marching from the Southeast; from the sloping city of goats; ancient ruins. Steel pressed them back to the ruins. To old, alien seas, washing rock that was rotten. Adrift from their homeland. Down into dishonor; bereft of God. Where could they go? These noble people had fought too long for their land; too long for memory. Why did they fight? Why do they not fight now, those Russians? The stars were destroyed. To hell with the yashmaks. The stars marched into that vast, dark sun. The sun set over Russia; and Chaos and Old Night reigned dreadfully. We were just learning subtlety. From the mountains, from the sloping city of goats and ruins came the black, Georgian Czar, Stalin, wailing for a Russia his master had destroyed: praising the Devil but longing for God. Praying for the vibrancy, the silence, the secrets of old times; and yelling at pious eyes, at old beards, their stinking superstitions, their khans and their pharisees; and shooting in the back of the head any who reminded him, in word or deed, of what he had lost. Mad, steel man; spoiled priest, you brought a religion of vengeance and despair to Russia. Two heads, two souls, two wings. Doomed king of the crushing hammer, the reaping sickle. Disguised and deadly, those tools. I have seen the peasants with those weapons in their hands. They are the weapons of the brute. I have seen them advancing on the Jews. They were robbed of their innards and made a virtue of despair. They put a piece of metal in my belly. They bled me. They drank my blood. They polluted it. And the metal is a cold fetus, and I shall not let him come to life. Not until I die shall the world know what I carry; my little, dancing agreeable, grinning tin doll. It threatens my whole being. I will not let him grow. I shall not let him jig. I shall not let him bow. In turn he will not let me bend. Is this pride? Conscience? I have no conscience, save my duty to God. I have no duty to Man. Only to Science. I follow no flags. I am myself. Why do they make of me more or less? What can I not possess? God is my Father. My Father betrayed me. Christ is Risen. Why do they punish the people of the Lamb? The Greeks came in to the city of Odysseus. The French, the Australians, the British and the Italians. In those days they had recalled the nature of the Turk. They were still fighting him. And Islam was being crushed. Britain fell in love with Islam and let her rise again. Britain and her romantic stupidity, her Jewish prime ministers, her bankers and her brothel masters. She lied to me. She was not raped. Educational trains. Happy kulak husband. Dead husband. Oh, Ukraine, heartland of our Empire, bastion against Islam. Did you die with so much dishonor, turning on your own flesh, rending your own children, attacking all who loved you? The hyena laughs over your churches. The Greek went away from Odessa. He had been hiding in Moldovanka. The old houses were in the places they had been in before the war, but they smelled of moisture and mold. Nobody had bothered to come out as far as Arcadia, except a few Jews. It was a Jew who took me to a house which could not possibly have been his. It was too fine. It was in good taste. He walked easily and his sadness was open; his touch was friendly. He was quite young. He had a job writing for a newspaper in Odessa, but now he had lost it. He said the newspaper came and went, with different conquerors. "And you are safe?" I said.

"I am safe enough," he said, "but I am fascinated by terror, aren't you?" It could be the end of me. I lay in a little white bed. The sheets were damp.

"No," I said, "I have had my fill of it."

"You have been in there?" He pointed toward Kiev.

"I have."

"That's what I shall have to do."

"They'll kill you. You're a Jew."

"Jews survive."

"Some do," I said. I had to be polite to him because he had helped me. Besides, I always had a soft spot for the cosmopolitan Odessa Jew who is a different type altogether. A Jew of the better kind, as we used to say.

He laughed as if I had made a joke. He laughed appreciatively, unlike Petroff; but I was thinking the whole world was convulsed. It was possessed. I became wary. And I had fallen in love with him, this Southerner, this soft-mouthed sardonic Jew. I wanted him. I admit it. I am ashamed. I admit I trembled as he brought me broth. "It's made of seaweed," he said, "but it's good for you. Not that you've been starving. Are all the stories wrong?"

"I was with a tank unit."

He had dried my clothes. He had polished my guns. The silver was bright. They lay on the seat of the chair, with the military caftan behind them. He had found a shapka to match.

"You were in that plane," he said.

"An observer."

"So they're attacking."

"Well . . ." I wanted to kiss his long hands. He fed me the soup with a dull, wooden spoon. "Well . . ."

"You're not allowed to say, of course. There goes my job. As I guessed."

"You'll get out?"

"No need. I'll join the next newspaper. They have dozens of newspapers and dozens of political creeds, but good journalists are in short supply."

"I have seen how they can destroy. Anyone."

"I'm facile." He shrugged. "It's those with strong needs who die, you see."

"You said you were going inland."

"Later. When things are more settled. Will they still kill me, then?"

"Possibly."

"I can't understand it, can you?"

"I understand them," I said. "It is all the fault of the Poles."

"My sentiments exactly." He opened a small, green book. He showed me a line of poetry. I do not recall it.

What was my fascination for that intellectual Jew? Christ on the Mount? No, that is blasphemy. I loved him. I cannot feel disgust. I owed him nothing. I was an audience for him, I suppose. He was living alone in a house he had never been able to afford. He would soon be kicked out of it. He knew. I asked him if the trams were still running.

"You know Odessa?"

"I spent some of my youth here. I was happy."

"There's a tram that runs sometimes. A horse one. A steam one. An electric one. Depending on what fuel's available. It's a long walk and you're hurt. You could wait near the fountain, but I can't offer much hope."

"I have relatives there."

He shrugged. I did not want to leave him. He was gentle. I trusted him. Was he pretending to be Jewish, the way Tertz does? An affectation? I waited for him to touch me. He never touched me. I went with him to the tram stop. My clothes were dry, from the sun. My pistols were clean. The whole resort was tranquil and decayed. Since then I have had a liking for deserted seaside towns. I used to go to them in the winter, with Mrs. Cornelius, but, in those circumstances, she was never the best companion. She liked, she said, a bit of fun when she went to the seaside. Russians long for solitude. It is our only commodity now. Even that is being taken from us. They are trying to turn Russia into America: America, with its sentimental social conventions, destroying its culture, its language, its intellectual strength. America before the war was a very different place. It was harder.

I became strong in the company of that journalist, on the outskirts of the city of black, sleeping goats. The tram came. It was half full of SR volunteers. They had the same uniforms as the Whites. I fitted in easily. They paid no attention to me or my companion who had decided, he said, to "see the action." Halfway to Odessa the electricity was cut off. There were no horses for the tram. The soldiers decided to stay where they were. We walked into the twilight. The city grew larger. There were a few fires. It stank. My Odessa had become a cesspit. Vandals had used it carelessly. The Reds had gone. The Whites had not yet arrived. I went with my friend to Uncle Semya's house. It had been gutted. My room was a jagged hole. I asked at the only shop still open in the square. It sold "mixed meat." All the trees had been cut down. The railings had gone for scrap. They said that Uncle Semya had "sold up." He had not been there when the house was burned. Someone had heard he had been caught profiteering and had gone to prison. This had already become a euphemism. He had been robbed and shot. And Shura? Conscripted. Dead. And Wanda? They did not remember Wanda. And Aunt Genia? They thought she might have gone to the Crimea. Quite a lot of people had left for the Crimea. The proprietors of the shop were planning to go themselves if they could get passage money and permission. They said they were not eligible for evacuation. They would have to pay a "private fare." My friend was weeping as we came out. He had overtired himself, I suppose.

"You're a hard one to read," I said.

"Oh, yes. I am. Do you want to come with me while I find out which paper I am working for now?"

I shook my head. He left. I was glad that he went. Such a relationship would have been impossible. He walked toward the Goods Station. Soldiers were coming in now. Horses and motor vehicles pulled gun limbers toward the docks. I went to look for Esau's in Slobodka. It was rubble. I went to find the ironmongery shop where Katya lived. It was looted. There were broken shutters all over Moldovanka and hardly any people on the streets. Those few were, by the way they slouched, to be feared. I went to the St. Nicholas Boulevard, by the church, and looked out over the harbor. There were no fashionable people here now. A French cruiser was coming in. They must have waited until they learned Odessa was in friendly hands. I found a fragment of blue-veined marble and put it in my pocket. Why had Petroff wanted to kill me? Had Kolya said something which his cousin had misinterpreted?

There were still crowds on the quays. There were limousines and carriages. All that remained of Russia's decent people were here, hoping to leave. I saw them fighting. I decided I must return to Kiev, bring my mother back by force if necessary and get her to Yalta. In those days Yalta was considered permanently safe.

Diseased children gathered around me. I think they were threatening me, but they were too weak to do much. I laughed at them and gave them my Petlyura money. Let them spend that, if they could. They began to tug at me. I was too tired to play. I was busy. I had to think. I drew a black-and-silver pistol and they ran away. I returned the pistol to its pocket. A group of soldiers was coming toward me. They asked for my papers. I told them I was Major Pyatnitski and that I was working for Military Intelligence, I would rather not be seen talking to them. They believed me and went on. There was some firing from the harbor but it hardly lasted a moment.

I decided I must go to the station. People would be traveling back to Kiev soon. It would be as well to get in the queue as early as possible. But the station, which had emergency oil lamps burning, was so full I knew I would not have the strength to cope with it. I realized, too, that I had no real money. I tried to find some tanks, to seek the hospitality of my Australian friends. The tanks were probably still on the outskirts. I could hear artillery fire from the northern suburbs.

As usual, flags and proclamations were the first priority. They were spreading over the city as if to hide the damage. Military cars went by. Everything seemed very busy. The Volunteers and their Allied friends were in control and were feeling, as new conquerors always did, efficient. The "representatives of the true government of Russia" were issuing orders not so different from those I had read before. There was a curfew for "all civilian personnel." I was glad of my caftan and shapka. I tried to walk with more of a military gait. I entered a small café in Lanzeronovskaya, near Theater Square. There was to be a performance that night, judging by the comings and goings. It was, someone said, a sign of the Odessa spirit. "We live through anything—and enjoy ourselves through anything," said a waiter. He called me comrade by accident and apologized. It was difficult, he said, to remember who was who, these days. Had I come with the "new troops"? I had, I said. He asked me if I knew what had happened to the aeroplane which had been seen flying round St. Nicholas earlier that day. Was it hit?

"It was hit," I said. "I know, because I was in it."

Naturally, I became their hero. I was bought whatever there was to buy. Vodka, bread, sausage. People of noble birth shook my hand. Bankers saluted me. There was music. I was getting some small satisfaction from my adventure. I was asked my advice on every topic and gladly gave it, since it was in the main very good advice. When I said I needed to get back to Kiev to find my mother, I was offered almost every form of transport. I made an arrangement to see some prince or other on the following day at his hotel. I lost the card. In a carriage owned by an industrialist from Kherson I drove through the dark and foul-smelling streets to a small, undistinguished hotel. It had been, he said, the best he could find. We knocked on metal shutters and were cautiously admitted. The industrialist was drunk. He introduced me as his brother to a sour-faced Georgian woman. She said that I would be extra. The industrialist laughed and said, "Panye, I was prepared to pay for a suite at the Bristol, so I do not think it will mean much if I have to bribe you for an extra blanket and a mattress for my brother." We were, he said, as we went upstairs, all brothers now.

I slept on his floor. He was still snuffling and murmuring when I left. I was hungry. I had no money of any value. I had no gold. I would have to sell the pistols. I went to the old market. There were finer pistols for sale at a few rubles. I walked until I reached Preobraz-henskaya and stopped at the doorway. The dentist's name plate, H. CORNELIUS, was still there. I began to vomit in the gutter where the cabs had once plied for hire. I have never been so ill in that way. There was a weight on my head, perspective distorted, lights flickered, a searing pain in my buttocks and thighs, a chill in my stomach like a piece of iron. I was cursed as a drunk by passers-by. A woman in a fashionable dress screamed. I thought she was Mrs. Cornelius. I reached out. A gendarme, who might have been released from prison that morning, came along and escorted me to a side street. He had every respect for the military, he said, but I should choose less public places to make a spectacle of myself.

I was shaking. I sat on a step in the doorway of an abandoned shop and watched the cars and horses come and go. The city had achieved a peculiar radiance, like a half-resurrected terminal patient: they seem to gain health just before they die. I think it is because they begin to relax and become reconciled to making the most of what is left. When I was strong enough, I walked to the harbor, but the Nicholas area had been for some reason cordoned off. I heard more shooting. I found a church. It was as crowded as the railway station. I squeezed in and let the other bodies hold me upright. I did not, then, know the words of the prayers or the responses, so I mumbled. The crucifix was displayed. The priests chanted. Censers were waved. White and gold. White and gold. But God was gone from Odessa and a black sun was setting over Russia.

I wanted some milk. This made me smile.

I had discovered that cocaine was impossible to obtain; or that it could be obtained in exchange for solid gold, nothing else. If there had been anything to steal in Odessa I would have stolen it. That evening, I went to the café where I had met my prince and my industrialist. The café was shut up. It had been, said a chalked notice, harboring profiteers. There was a reminder that Odessa was under military law and that looting and profiteering would receive the death sentence. I was very hungry. I visited several newspaper offices, looking for my friend, whose name I had forgotten. Some of the journalists knew him but thought he had left Odessa or was "in hiding" at his house. Had I tried there?

There were no trams running to Arcadia. I did not have any money for the fare. I prayed for the tanks or for someone who would recognize me. I was sure Mrs. Cornelius would rescue me. Eventually I found myself outside a military headquarters in Pushkinskaya, not far from the Alexander Park, which was now a wasteland. I entered, introduced myself in my usual fashion, and said that I had become separated from my unit. I said I had been with the tanks. I was told that I might be able to get a train to Nikolaev. The tanks were on their way to that city. They were needed to help put down an uprising. I asked if I could send a cable to Kiev. They said that unless I had a priority order I would have to wait. They were kind enough. They offered me a chair. I told them I had been the observer in the aircraft. They were sympathetic to learn of the crash. "The ridiculous thing is, we had more information than we could handle." It grew colder. It was almost September. I sat in the military post with some tea and a piece of biscuit and chatted with the soldiers on duty. I was all but starving to death. I had become quite used to it and almost enjoyed the sensation of euphoria and self-possession which comes with it. We made jokes together as I wasted away.

Stalin came out of the city of ancient tiers to impose his will on what little was left of our Enlightenment. Revenging atavist, furious failed priest. He descended upon the city built at the command of the woman Voltaire advised: Catherine the Great. Odessa was founded on 22 August 1794, in the first era of modern revolutions: the Age of Reason. A city of order and civilization, classical and European, the city of Pushkin and Lermontov. The Bolsheviks have left their statues alone. They have put up new ones. They have named ships after them. Russia has become a Disneyland of Human Dignity. There is a deep insult, if you like. They name ships after writers who would have cried out against everything the Bolsheviks have done to our Russia. The Steel Czar rode through our streets and he spoke quietly so that none should know how many he killed. The Germans rode through our streets. Odessa, built on Tartar foundations, built on Phoenician foundations, fell into dishonor. Carthage came in on a red tide.

They will not admit that Russian humanity is their best publicity.

Even the beggars on the trains, the dirty station sellers, the gypsies, the poor, the murderers, the drunkards, are part of our ancient dignity. But what do they show the world? Science fiction. Tractors. Sputnik.

I wrote a letter to my mother and told her I would return to Kiev soon or would send for her. I told her to bring Captain Brown, if she wanted an escort; that I would pay. I asked one of the soldiers to see that the letter was put in the mail bag for Kiev. He accepted it and issued a receipt. I had done all that I could, for the meantime, in that area. My mother, at least, had seemed happy. I hoped that she was still happy.

By morning the telegram had gone to Nikolaev, to the tanks. A reply stated that Captain Wallace sent his compliments. He was no longer in need of a Russian intelligence officer. He added that he was glad I had survived and he wished me luck. Two captains came out of their room and invited me in. They, too, they said, were with Intelligence. They said there was no record of me and apologized. A picture of the late Czar was hanging on the wall. It was like old times. I became calm.

"I worked in Kiev," I said, "and for a while was a liaison officer with Hetman Skoropadskya's forces. Then I was employed on behalf of General Krassnoff's Don Cossacks. I was gathering information at Bolshevik headquarters. I was responsible for anti-Petlyurist sabotage in Kiev." They wrote down what I told them. Times, they said, were confusing. I said I had had to destroy my military identification, but I showed them my diploma. I mentioned that I had been a friend of Prince Petroff and that I had been with the Prince's cousin who had crashed in the sea. They asked me if I had done much civilian interrogation. It was dull, routine stuff. This was their main problem at present. I told them I had done nothing worth speaking of but I was willing to work in any capacity. I was given papers, a new uniform, a side arm, a bread ration, a bunk in a room shared with only three others, and some bits and pieces of kit. I also had a pay-book, but was warned that pay was erratic and one was expected to forage a little. There were shortages of every kind of equipment. I had become an Intelligence Officer in the Volunteer forces, attached to the Eighth Army Corps. It would be my job to vet and to issue passes and other papers to those applying for them. I began work the next morning.

Within a week I had become rich enough to purchase some good cocaine. I can still remember the frisson as I took my first delicious sniffs. I was not alone. All the other officers joined me.

Odessa, it seemed to us, had begun to come fully alive again. The houses of pleasure, in a certain familiar street near the Quarantine Harbor, were in full bloom, with a host of fresh buds and petals, and roulette remained the favorite game of the sportsmen, mainly soldiers, who visited them. We would wear our dress uniforms when "on the town" and I had mine at last. It was white and gold, with green-and-black insignia, made by a local military tailor. He was very cheap. While I was in his shop he offered to modify another fine uniform for which the customer had never returned. It was, he said, exactly my measurements. It was the dress uniform of a colonel in the Don Cossacks. I inspected it and told the tailor I would accept it as it was. Both were delivered two days later to Madame Zoyea's, where I had taken up residence.

Madame Zoyea was young, plump and witty. Her coloring was the same as my gypsy's from the canyon, but she would never tell me if she were the same girl and she would never let me make love to her, for all she seemed to hold a special affection for me. Perhaps she had a disease. Although it was impossible to recapture the old days completely, I was fortunate in meeting several friends from the past, including Boris the Accountant, who had married his girl. He was working for one of the few shipping offices still operating. As a result, I came into frequent contact with him. He would do me favors and we would split the proceeds. He wanted me to help him get to Berlin and I was able to supply the necessary documents at a reduced fee. Boris told me that Shura was not dead, that he had deserted, spent some time in Moldovanka and then "gone east," he thought. Wanda had become a whore, in common with almost all girls of her class, and had been killed during a fight. The child was being raised by relatives in a small port farther up the coast. Uncle Semya and Aunt Genia had been arrested during Hrihorieff's occupation and Boris thought they must have been shot "since so many of us were." I put the past behind me and considered the future.

My fellow interrogators and I were all doing excellent business. None of us was too happy about the system of vetting people and issuing passports. Our attitude was simply that we could not blame anyone for wanting to leave. Red or White, they would at least be clear of Russia. We worked in a large room which was always full and, even as winter advanced on the city, always stuffy. We worked hard. We were conscientious enough. Our main job was to check for too much gold being taken out and to consult a list of people wanted for questioning. As Christmas approached, I began to make plans for leaving both Odessa and my job behind. I had my real work to start. It was obvious that I should be hampered at home. I would go abroad, send for my mother when the time was right, and make my reputation either as a teacher at a Western university, or as an engineer and inventor, perhaps in France or America. The cocaine had restored me to my old optimism, judgment and vigor. I was able to work during the day, calming, consoling, making arrangements for people, weeding out the undeserving from the mass of petitioners; and I was able to play at night.

Once, at the roulette in Zoyea's, I was drinking a glass of bad anisette when I thought I saw Mrs. Cornelius, in an Erté frock of gold and black, pass through the room. But I had become used to hallucinations by then. Esmé, my mother, Captain Brown, Kolya, Shura, Katya, Grishenko, Yermeloff, Makhno, even Wanda and Herr Lustgarten, seemed to appear in crowds from time to time. My money was on the black. I lost it.

I asked after an Englishwoman amongst my companions. I asked Zoyea. She shook her plump head and said that Englishwomen did not frequent such establishments. She was amused. "Very few Englishmen come here. They have an Empire which speaks English, just so they can feel at home wherever they go."

East is East, says Sir Rudyard Kipling, the poet, and West is West, and never the twain shall meet: but they met in South Russia, in my Ukraine; the borderland, the no man's land, the marches where the Heroes of Kiev fought for Christendom as no other Heroes fought before. Russian chivalry was destroyed in Ukraine in 1920. The Mother City was raped; the Mother of God was cast out. Later the Germans came. I think the X-rays are wrong. There is a piece of shrapnel in my stomach. It is an old war wound. But so much for doctors and their socialist health schemes. Why should they care for an old foreigner? They used to be kinder to us in France. I met Willi. Colette offered me a position. I knew them all. But these days everyone is ignorant. I hated Gertrude Stein. At least I knew her name. Bely and Zamyatin? Who speaks of them today, even in Russia? I used to like the early stories of Nabokov-Serin, though I could not always understand them. He had talent then. Later he went mad and looted his peers because no one outside Russia knew about them.

That was why he decided to write in English. And his Russian became coarsened. Gerhardi, aping the worst of our people, was never my cup of tea. As I stamped passports and approved documents, I thought I was cleansing Russia of decadence. Who was to guess I should still be suffering from that particular delusion?

What is race but the sum of geographical and social stimuli inducing a state of tribal shock? It can last for thousands of years. Diversify and survive. Serin became self-conscious of his own Russian being; that is where he went wrong. Fear Carthage. I am weak. My temperature is rising. There is no snow here. Stalin's and Hitler's racial experiments were too simple-minded. We must interbreed at once. But the thought of the result is terrifying. I am terrified. I do not deny it. As terrified as Man was when he conceived the idea of creating fire. Prometheus, the Greek, the Lord: Prometheus is betrayed. Christ is crucified. When shall He rise again? Byzantium must be purified. Banish guilt: it is the viper in the bosom of chivalry. Russia is betrayed and in turn betrays. Fear Islam. Fear Zion. Fear vengeance. Rome is in peril. Fear ignorant priests and stupid scientists. Fear politicians. Fear old Carthage. They come into my shop. They laugh at my voice. They hurt me. I hate them. I will not bargain. I would rather give them that antique shmatte. Let them mince in the robes of their elders and make a mockery of wisdom. They are unlettered and careless. They have no love. They think of nothing but themselves. This is the Age of the Ego. I blame artists, politicians, psychologists, teachers for encouraging them.

They are outraged by their parents as soon as they can climb onto two feet, as soon as they are human. They are imbued with cynicism. Yet let a man touch a child, be it in love and gentleness, and he is branded a pervert. There is no law to say that betraying words must be punished, that betraying ideas and received opinions are more dangerous than a poor old man who bounces a little girl on his knee and kisses her cheek and strokes her hair and reveals his need to love for just a few dangerous seconds. Imagination can be like the horns of the goat: useful until turned inward; whereupon, in the course of time, the horns pierce the brain and the goat is destroyed. Mrs. Cornelius had no imagination, but she was fond of those of us who possessed it. She protected us. It was our downfall, perhaps. She used us, some way. She was a whore, a *femme fatale*. But I say she gave too much. Mother of God! She gave too much. The strong are often called upon in this way. They can expect nothing in return, save abuse and, very occasionally, affection. That is how God blesses them. They shall sit with Him in Heaven and help to bear the sorrows of the world.

We were working at our desks in that great office, which had once belonged to a shipping company. They would move along in their lines, rich and poor, old and young, trying to look confident, or humble, almost always in reverse to their station in life, and I would take some aside into the special interrogation room, where the business transactions were mostly done, and I would reject those who had not the means to get to their destination. It was a mercy: I knew of Ellis Island and what could happen there. I knew of Whitechapel and how refugees were courted by Jewish sweatshop owners and white slavers. They would not have been worse off under the socialists. I did my best to be fair. We were not hard men. We were not cynical. We bled no one. Often we would let people through who had no business leaving.

On the day before Christmas Eve, during a difficult afternoon, I looked up at my next client. It was Brodmann, in his dark overcoat and his homburg hat and his spectacles and quivering lips. He looked older but more innocent. "Pyat," he said. I was easy with him. I had anticipated such a problem. "Brodmann." I looked at the application. "You are going to America."

"It is my hope. So you were a White all along?" He became alarmed.

"And you are still, then, a Red?" I asked.

"Of course not. They have reneged on everything." He sniggered. I lit a cigarette. I told him he had better go into the interrogation room and wait. I dealt with two young women who were planning to board a British ship bound for Yalta, then I left my desk and entered the small room. Snow was gathering against the windows and the skylight. I wished Brodmann the compliments of the season. "You're not going to Germany, then? This application is to travel by train to Riga."

"From Hamburg I can go direct to New York." He was very frightened. I began to understand the power and the wonder of being a Chekist. I restrained that ignoble lust and sat down, hoping this action would stop him shaking. "I was never in Germany," he said. "It's just my name. You know that."

"Your Red friends abandoned you."

"I was a pacifist."

"So you decided to leave the conflict?" I was joking with him quite gently but he did not seem to understand that.

"There is no more to be done. Is there?" His shaking increased. I offered him a cigarette. He refused, but he thanked me several times. "Were you always with Intelligence?" he wanted to know. "Even then?"

"My sympathies have never changed," I said.

He gave me an adoring look, as one might compliment the Devil for his cunning. This made me impatient. "I am not playing with you, Brodmann. What do you want?"

"Don't be harsh, Comrade."

"I am not your comrade." This was too much. I hate weakness. I hate the calling on common experience as comfort.

"As a fellow Jew, you would help me?"

"I am not Jewish." I stood up and pinched my cigarette out. "Is this the appropriate moment to insult me?"

"I am not insulting you, Major. I apologize. I did you no harm. But in Alexandriya I saw . . ." He became very white.

He had seen me whipped by Grishenko. I did not mind that. Why was he pursuing this? Then it dawned on me that he had seen me naked and had made a frightful assumption. I began to laugh. "Really, Brodmann, is that what you thought? There are perfectly ordinary medical reasons for my operation."

"Oh, for the love of God!" He had fallen to his knees. He groveled. I felt sick.

"It will not do, Brodmann." I was losing control of myself. He was weeping. "Brodmann, you must wait. Think things through."

"I have suffered. Show mercy."

"Mercy, yes. But not justice." I was ready to let him go. I wanted him to go. Another officer, Captain Yosetroff, came in with a middle-aged woman wearing the same perfume as Mrs. Cornelius. With some difficulty, Brodmann rose to his feet. He pointed at me. "Pyatnitski's a Chekist spy. Haven't you realized? I know him. He's a saboteur, working for the Bolsheviks."

"The poor devil's insane," I said calmly.

Yosetroff shrugged. "I'd like the room to myself for a little while, Major, if it's possible."

"Of course. You'd better come back tomorrow," I told Brodmann.

"It's Christmas Eve. The office is closed. I read the notice. I've got to be on the Riga train."

"I had forgotten." I sighed. Yosetroff frowned. He apologized to the lady who grinned and scratched her ear. He stepped forward.

"Can I help?" Yosetroff's neat, pale face blended thoroughly with his uniform so that it was almost indistinguishable. "Shall I take over?"

"No need," I said.

"He's with the Reds. How did he come to be working here?" Brodmann's hysteria threatened both our lives.

Yosetroff hesitated. There was nothing I could say. I slapped Brodmann's face with my gloved hand. I slapped it twice more. He was weeping as the guards came in at Yosetroff's command. "Do you want him taken away?" asked Yosetroff. It meant Brodmann would be imprisoned, possibly shot if his Bolshevik associations came to light. I owed him nothing. He had made his own mistakes. I nodded and left the room.

" 'Ello, Ivan!"

Mrs. Cornelius waved to me. She was dressed in high fashion and was on the arm of an evidently uncomfortable French naval officer. She had fresh papers. She waved them. She was delighted. "Thort I'd seen yer abart. Where yer bin 'iding yerself?"

"You were at Zoyea's?" I was still suffering from my encounter with Brodmann. He had been escorted discreetly out. "A few nights ago?"

"That the 'ore 'ouse wiv ther games?"

"That's the one."

"Yeah! Yore lookin' smart. D'yer know me boyfriend? 'E's in ther navy. François, 'e corls 'isself. Don't speak very good English. Say 'ow do, France."

I told the naval officer I was enchanted to meet him. I asked which ship he was with. He was Second Officer on the *Oreste*. They were leaving for Constantinople tomorrow, with troops and passengers. There had been trouble with Kemal Pasha. We spoke French, of course.

"The British are trying to take over the whole thing," he said bitterly. "They are acting in a very vulgar manner."

I was amused. The quarrels between these allies was reminiscent of the Crimea. But I remained grave. I heard Brodmann squealing "Treachery!" as he passed by outside. "And you are kindly giving Mrs. Cornelius a passage on your ship."

He shook his head. "We are already full. She will be meeting me in

Constantinople. I have spoken to the captain of a British merchant-
man. He has agreed to add a few more passengers. We had to arrange
Mrs. Cornelius' papers, of course. She was good enough to ask me to
escort her here. It is a pity we were not acquainted before."

"A great pity," I said.

Mrs. Cornelius nudged me. "Stop it, the pair o' yer. Manners! Tork
English!"

We both bowed. My CO had entered the room and was looking
thoughtfully at me. I said to Mrs. Cornelius very rapidly in English:
"I have papers. Can you get me aboard the British ship?"

She could tell I was anxious. She smiled and put a girlish, beringed
hand on my forearm. "We got married, didn't we? Yore me 'usband.
It's ther *Rio Cruz*. Yer'll need a license or some'ink." She once more
became the lady. "Delighted to meet you again, Major Pyatnitski." I
clicked my heels and kissed her hand. I saluted the Frenchman. My
CO, Major Soldatoff, signaled for me to come over. I did so with
alacrity. I had been impressing him with my military discipline for a
couple of months. He was an old Okhrana man, not naturally suspicious, but very sensitive to discrepancies of any kind. He had a
seamed, ruddy face of the Great Russian type, with a white beard and
mustache. He wore a dark uniform. I entered his office. He closed the
door. He offered me a chair and I sat down. "Brodmann?" he said.

"A Red," I said. "I met him in Kiev, I think. When I was doing
sabotage work. I told him I was on his side, of course."

"He says you're Cheka. That you were a link between Antonov
and Hrihorieff."

"I let him think that. At the time."

"I shall have to look into this, Pyatnitski. But it is routine, naturally." Obviously he was in no way seriously worried. He was almost
apologizing. "You're a good interrogation officer and we need everyone. The Reds are coming back and they're much better organized.
We're a little worried about spies."

"I understand completely, sir."

"There'll be an inquiry. An extensive one. I don't want to waste a
man guarding you. Will you promise to stick near your quarters until
the morning?"

"I am lodging," I said with embarrassment, "at Zoyea's."

"I know that. You won't need to leave, then, will you?" He was
like an uncle. "Brodmann's accusations are heard every day. I'll have
him properly questioned tonight. It could be he'll admit he knows

nothing. If that's the case, it shouldn't take long for you. You'll be back on duty by the afternoon."

"It's a holiday," I said with a smile.

"All the better. After Christmas."

I thanked him civilly and left. Walking through the snow toward Madame Zoyea's I stopped to buy a bundle of cigarettes from a ragged young girl. For some reason I gave her a gold ruble for them and thanked her in English. She replied in the same language. I was amused. "You speak it excellently," I said.

She was flattered. She was shivering worse than Brodmann had shivered. She had been attractive. In other circumstances I might have spent more time making her acquaintance. There was something about vulnerable young women which brought out the best in me. It was almost love. She told me her husband had been a White officer. The Bolsheviks had shot him. She was supporting her mother. There were many young women like her in Odessa, selling small things from trays. She had a quality of the sort Esmé had once possessed. I supposed she would lose it, if the Reds came again. The Allies were already regretting their enthusiasm for the Volunteers. They were horrified by what they took to be our moral weakness. It was, of course, only our despair. The British hate despair. They will do anything to fight it, even going so far as to let socialists hold the reigns of power in their own country. The Americans share the British hatred but have so far resisted socialism. It will come, no doubt. The French have a healthier reaction. They are merely disgusted by poverty. Disgust was at the heart of their colonial policy. It enabled them to withdraw from Indochina with rather more honor than the Americans. But, to the British, despair and moral weakness are synonymous. It took me some years to discover this fact.

At Madame Zoyea's I packed two suitcases. I had jewelry and gold. I had never, of course, recovered my other baggage, with my plans, my designs, my hopes. All I had was a blood-stained diploma and a dirty passport. I should have to begin all over again. I did not relish being put off in Constantinople, but even that city would be safer for me now than Odessa. And I was no longer poor. Sooner or later I should have had to leave, anyway. In about two months the Bolsheviks would return. I should have become a victim of the Cheka.

In the large suitcase went my uniforms, including the one I had been wearing. I dressed in civilian clothes and put on an expensive fur coat. My pistols were still with me, in the pockets. Both coat and pistols could be sold if necessary. I had a file of forms, including marriage certificates. It was an easy matter to forge the appropriate information. I asked Madame Zoyea to come to me. I told the maid that the matter was urgent. Within half an hour, the proprietress was there. She was not surprised by the signs. I put on a good fur hat which matched the coat. I gave her fifty gold rubles. My passport and papers were, of course, in perfect order. I asked her to tell any callers I was engaged with one of her girls. I wondered if she could arrange a discreet cab for me, to take me to the docks at about five in the morning. She agreed and she kissed me. "I'll miss you," she said. "I think you were bringing us luck. What will happen when the Reds come back?"

I showed her my file of spare papers. "I'd advise you to make use of them for yourself and as many girls as you can. They're all pre-stamped, you'll notice. They merely need names and dates."

"You're very kind. But Reds are men . . ."

"They'll be trying to deny that fact," I said. "You should listen to me, Zoyea. Gypsies and Jews will not be the only ones to suffer under the Cheka. They're anxious to eradicate all signs of their own and therefore others' humanity." To be honest, I do not think I phrased my warning so elegantly. Time improves all conversations, particularly one's own. I was to see Zoyea again, I am glad to say, in Berlin. "You are only safe while men admit their vulnerability. When they pretend they are demigods, you should be afraid." We kissed once more. She asked if I would like to make love. I told her I needed nothing to distract me. We kissed shyly, then.

It was dark, of course, when I left for the Quarantine Harbor and the *Rio Cruz*. In a troika, we trotted through heavy snow, through an Odessa still excited, still alive. Some would call her sordid, but even in death she held a warmth and elegance denied more famous cities. Catherine had founded her. Catherine's spirit, at once cruel and intelligent, feminine and aggressive, remained in her. Catherine had courted Reason and been confused by Romance, but in her they had reached a kind of harmony that was Russian, though she was not. I saw Dietrich as *The Scarlet Empress* by von Sternberg. I loved it. It ruined him. The only Hollywood film of its day to lose money. We reached the harbor and to my relief the ship was active. People were going aboard. They were almost all rich Russians.

I do not think I was followed. Indeed, I have the idea my Commanding Officer might have given me the chance to escape. I have been shown considerable kindness. I do not deny it.

My papers were checked several times, first by Russians, then by grim-looking Englishmen. I walked up the gangplank. It vibrated under booted feet. I was on the deck of my first large ship. She flew English colors, but was probably a spoil of war, taken from some South American state which, in the heat of the moment, had decided to ally with Germany in the War. Many of the signs were still in Spanish. I climbed another gangway. There was no one to help me with my luggage. I reached a forward cabin on the upper deck. I opened the door. Mrs. Cornelius was not there. It was dark. I switched on the weak electrics. The cabin had been converted for two passengers. There were two bunks. There were washing facilities. I put down my bags and took out my cocaine. I had to keep certain thoughts at bay. The cocaine had its usual positive effect. I began to think of Constantinople. It would be warm there. I was very cold. The cabin had no proper heating system. I stretched out on the upper bunk, assuming that Mrs. Cornelius would require the lower. Her luggage, several trunks and cases, was stowed in one corner, near the forward porthole. I was still ready for trouble. It was possible I could be taken off before the ship upped anchor. The *Rio Cruz* rocked very slightly. The motion made me think we were leaving and that Mrs. Cornelius had missed the ship, but I knew enough to understand that the engines would have to begin turning before we would be able to head for open sea.

I got up from my bunk. I looked through the porthole. The sea was black, almost as if ice had formed on it. People came and went about the ship. I thought I heard shots, but from a good distance along the dock. I had left too easily and yet I accepted my good fortune. I had hardly questioned the fact that Mrs. Cornelius would again be the means of my salvation. Wrapped in my Russian fur, I fell asleep.

I was awakened by grey dawn and a song. It was Mrs. Cornelius. She was quite drunk. She had her hat on the back of her head. She was singing something from the British music hall. "We don't wanter fight, but by jingo if we do, we got ther ships, we got ther men, we got the money, too. We've fought the bear before, an' while we're Britons troo-oo, ther Russians shall not 'ave Constanti-no-pol. Oops, sorry Ivan. No offense."

She sat on her bunk. "I feel a bit queasy on boats, don't you? Orlways 'ave done. Oo-er." She was trying to remove her boots. I glanced at her wonderfully rounded calves. She sensed me behind her and looked up. She winked. She was delicious. Her perfume, her clothes, her confident womanhood. "Don't worry, chum," she said, to cover my embarrassment, "I'm not ashamed of 'em. I've reached me maturity, yer know. I'm used ter a bit o' admiration." She stood up in her stockinged feet and began to ease her back. "Cor! Wot a farewell party that was! Anyway, we're spliced, ain't we? They tol' me you was 'ere when them sailors 'elped me aboard."

"Do you mean married?" I asked her. I was not fully awake.

She shook her head. Evidently she had made her mind up on the moral score. "In name only, Ivan, old fruit. See, I give me word ter that Froggy. 'E ain't much, but 'e 'elped me get art o' that 'ell'ole. An' I like ter keep me word, if I can."

I accepted her decision. It would be many years before we were married in the carnal sense. The ship swayed. She was not of the latest design and had no sophisticated stabilizers, no Pratt and Whitneys, although, I was to learn, she had been built on the Clyde. I still felt cold. Snow was falling on the ship. It settled on rigging and rails. I thought it would sink us. But everything was purified against the blackness of that water. It was impossible to see the city through the blizzard. I searched for the outline of the Nicholas Church. Odessa was lost to me, as Esmé was lost, as Kolya was lost, almost casually.

I am not a Jew. I am not a racist. I remembered how the Jew in Arcadia had been kind to me; how I had loved him. The thought was not pleasant. I recollected the incident a day or so ago, now that I am old and selfish and unattractive. The selfish are only attractive when young. I have given much, but never as much as I have received.

Later, I would go out on deck and stand in the Russian snow, letting it cover me from head to toe, while the ship sailed steadily for the heat of that Holy City, our Czargrad, which, for the moment, the British had freed from Islam. We had fought for Byzantium more than once. We had been deceived by Patriarchs more than once. But we had known honor and we had taken that honor back with us to Kiev. From Kiev it had passed to Moscow. Bells rang from the shore. It was Christmas Eve. Moscow was lost. Christ was betrayed. Bells rang from St. Nicholas for the birth of the Saviour whose trust was mocked. The Reds swept in; the red tide rose and disgorged its walking dead, its ancient reapers of vengeance with their sickles: Carthage come from beyond the sea. Ghosts of Tartars and Turks laughed together beneath the windy banners of Islam, beneath the flapping banners of Bolshevism, beneath the banners of barbarism and cynicism and a passionless vengeance which dared to grace itself with the name of piety. Down from his hillsides came the Bandit Czar, the Steel Czar from the East, with four faces. Oh, my sister and my brother and my mother. You are fallen beneath the chariot of the Antichrist. Those whom I loved and who loved me; they are all fallen. They would not come to the city of sleeping goats, the city of the Jew. They would not come to Odessa and be saved by me. They thought Byzantium would save them, but Byzantium could not. The Greek could not come to Odessa. We fled before Carthage. The Greek could not come to Russia. Russia, knowing only pride, fell. They put a piece of metal in my womb. They poisoned me with their kindness. They confused me. Why did they not let me die? The Germans came, with their Ukrainian Cossacks, and they put a camp in the gorge where I had flown. And they put an old woman into the sea of ashes and they drowned her with their bullets and the blood of thousands. Jew and Russian mingled blood at last. Black goats bleat. What sacrifice is worth their death?

They rode through Russia with their flags and their machine guns and they took away our honor. We left it with them to die and had only our pride. They took away our language. They took away our Christ. But the Slavs know Carthage. The Slavs shall rediscover honor. They shall dig their weapons from the earth. Teach us your litany of revenge; speak to us in lies and feast yourselves on your caviar, your Georgian champagne, your game birds and your soups. You are ignoble. You have dishonored your land. You have dishonored virtue. Clap your heavy hands as your tanks roll past the Kremlin: then put your hands to your eyes, for the great guns shall turn on you and Russia shall have vengeance. Is that what you fear? Traitors! You are weak. Zion! Rome! Byzantium! All are stronger than Carthage. Odysseus returns. The Greek sleeps. The Greek wakes. Those cities are lost to me. Those virtues are lost to me. Everything is lost to me. But it will be found. The Greek's words were corrupted and his love was betrayed. Prometheus! Mercury! Odysseus!

Mrs. Cornelius came waltzing through the snow. She was still singing her song. I suppose it popped into her mind because she was looking forward to the Bosporus. She linked her arm in mine. Snow scattered. She began to drag me along the throbbing planks of the deck.

The Steel Czar longed for God. He won back our old Empire and made us strong again, and though it seemed that cruel Carthage had conquered, the Greek is waking. Byzantium endures. There is an Empire of the Soul and we are all its citizens.

Mrs. Cornelius said, "Yer get real snow in Russia, I'll say that!"

I asked her how she had managed to leave Kiev and the jealous Trotsky. "I come over dead bored. 'E come over worried, didn't 'e?" she said. "I woz 'angin' abart there, waitin' fer Leon till bloody May. Pregnant, an' all. 'E kep' sayin' 'e woz comin' an' then when 'e did it was on'y ter say good-by. So I got ther lads ter take me ter 'Dessa an' 'ere I am."

"The child? Was there a child?"

She turned her back on me as she brushed snow from her skirts. " 'E'll be orlright."

I became silent.

"It's not as if 'e'll know any different," she said.

I went below. The Chief Engineer was sorry for the Russians. He showed me his machinery. I told him of my plans for new kinds of ships, for aircraft and monorails. He was interested. He was glad, he said, to have a fellow engineer aboard. I asked him when we would be arriving. He told me it would be on 14 January 1920. My birthday. I was amused by this coincidence. Guns fired from the shore. They fired into mist.

I asked him about other craft he had served with. He said he had known many better ships than this, but that the *Rio Cruz* was seaworthy. He was from Aberdeen and had always been interested in mechanical things. We became friendly. There is a kind of brotherhood which exists among engineers.

I told him about the flying machine I had invented in Kiev, about my Violet Ray. He said he had certain ideas of his own: ships which would be jointed so that they would ride the waves naturally. He showed me some drawings he had made. They were rather crude. I began to sketch again, to illustrate the sort of notions I had conceived in St. Petersburg. I said that the future lay with us. It was our duty to lend our enthusiasm and knowledge in the cause of human comfort. We discussed such matters all the way to Constantinople.

MICHAEL MOORCOCK first made his reputation writing fantasy novels—with more than fifty titles published in England and America—and as the editor of the influential science-fiction magazine *New Worlds*. Of his more recent work, which includes *The Condition of Muzak* (awarded the Guardian Fiction Prize in 1977), Angus Wilson has written: "No one at the moment in England is doing more to break down the artificial divisions that have grown up in novel writing—realism, science fiction, social satire, the poetic novel—than Michael Moorcock."

His most imaginative and powerful book yet, *Byzantium Endures* offers further proof of Moorcock's versatility as a novelist and, again in Angus Wilson's words, "master of narrative."

Michael Moorcock lives in England.